# DEBBIE BOUCHER

*To Gilann,*

*Thank you for reading my book!,*

*Debbie Boucher*

# Millenial Fears

**Outskirts Press, Inc.**
**Denver, Colorado**

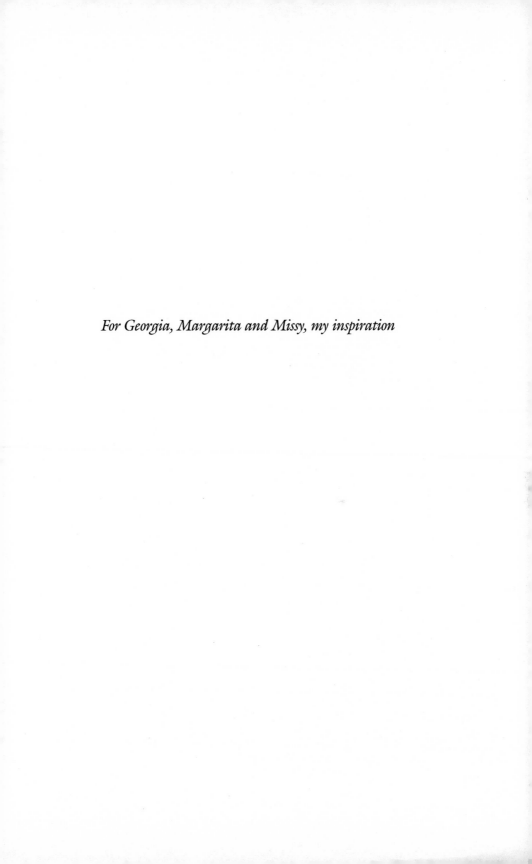

*For Georgia, Margarita and Missy, my inspiration*

# *Acknowledgments*

No book is ever written alone. I began this novel when I returned to Mammoth Lakes, CA, to resume teaching at Mammoth Elementary School after three years of working at the American Cooperative School in La Paz, Bolivia. I knew I wanted to write about the Latino families I worked with in my ski resort town. Over the years my former students have gone off to college and have enjoyed careers their hard-working parents could only dream about. You are my inspiration, along with three extraordinary people I have dedicated this book to. Georgia: MBA, astrologer extraordinaire, child of hardworking immigrant parents. Thank you for your friendship and guidance over the years, for the example of spiritual tolerance you set. Margarita: the heart and soul of bilingual education at Mammoth Elementary School. Thank you for your undying dedication to our community and for the difference you make. Your willingness to read an early draft ensures my portrayal of Latinos is accurate. Missy: it was your friendship with Margarita that sparked the idea in the first place. I bet you never knew that.

For critiquing early drafts of this novel I am grateful to Sands Hall, Waverly Fitzgerald, and Margaret DePalma. Without their encouragement this book would have stayed in a drawer. And finally, I want to thank my daughter, Jessica, who helped me with editing at the end of this long, drawn-out process, my husband Mike, and my daughter Nicole who have been very patient with how much time my writing takes.

# Rosa Rodriguez
## March 15, 1975

*Every mother thinks her child is the most beautiful in the world*
*--Latin American saying*

I'm no Europeña, none of this "life is suffering, and then you die" stuff for me. No, soy Mejicana, which means I believe life's a struggle, and then there's a fiesta. It's why after the priest celebrates Mass we celebrate with food and fun. Then the drinking gets out of hand, and it's hard to be married to a boracho like Roberto who smacks you around to have his fun. It's what brought on early labor and almost killed my precious Angelica. We're a happy people, we Mejicanos, except when it comes to love. That, we believe, is worth suffering for.

What helps is I'm Catholic, and I'm an astrologer. I see no conflict in this. Both honor God and utilize His divine guidance, and Dios mio, I could use some right now. It's how the Spanish won converts when they came to Mexico. The priests matched every Indian festival with a fiesta and Mass of their own. I'm sure they hoped their new beliefs would replace the old. What they had to settle for was the two coexisting, side by side.

I'm no heretic. I go to the hospital's chapel to pray. Then I go to the cafeteria with my *Ephemeris* and *House of Tables* to cast Angelica's chart, and what I see concerns me. It's why I have to find Angelica's astrological twin, that second soul born at exactly the same time and place as my daughter. Angelica's gemela del alma will have a life that mirrors hers, and that's the best kind of divine guidance I can imagine. The problem is the hospital staff thinks I'm nuts, running around, waking the new mothers who gave birth today, asking for the exact time of their child's birth. When Roberto discovers I'm not in my room, he comes after me, reeking of booze, accusing me of flirting with the women's husbands. I calm him down by taking him to the nursery to admire our nena in her crib, beyond the thick wall of glass.

Once he leaves to hang out with the men who wait for work on a corner near the hospital, I go to the pay phone and call my cousin Silvia. I tell her about the beating that brought on early labor, and she says that as soon as I'm released, I'm to take Angelica to LAX, that she'll pay our airfare to San Francisco. She's right. I should leave Roberto, but not until I find Angelica's astrological twin. Silvia promises that once I get to her apartment she'll help me widen my search. She knows someone in the police department. I agree only because Roberto is getting crazier by the minute. Then my cousin reminds me that while she believes in astrology, she thinks I'm overreacting. "So Angelica has a bad chart. So what? She was born a month early. That's the problem. It's not so much about fate, Rosa. It's about free will."

My laughter is bitter. "You mean you're not going to look at los naipes, that you're not going to cast an array of Tarot cards for Angelica as soon as we hang up?"

"If you want a happy ending," Silvia tells me, sounding annoyed, "you have to get away from Roberto, and you have to get Angelica away from him, too."

"All right. It may take me a couple of days, but I'm coming this time. I won't change my mind."

"Bueno. Call me when you know what you're doing, and I'll book a flight."

I find the hospital's social worker, the one who gave me the card with the women's shelter number on it. The social worker calls a counselor who insists I leave and go to their safe house immediately. I tell her okay, but first I must make a phone call.

# Jazmín Valdez
## June 17, 1993

*Las amistades no se han de romper, sino descoser*
*(Friendships don't break down so much as they unravel)*

The day before graduation, Jaz waited in her bedroom with her door shut until she was sure she was alone. There was no school. Finals were over for the seniors, though the underclassmen like her brothers Juan P. and Chuy still had tests to take today. Once her parents left for work, she tripped lightly down the stairs. In the kitchen she hummed as she filled a container with guacamole, something she rarely took on a picnic. Pedro would love this, the vegetables she cut and arranged in a Tupperware container: red peppers, white jicama, and green tomatillos, bold as the stripes on the Mexican flag. She filled a small vial with oil and imagined trout hitting their flies on the first cast, the sound of them sizzling in the pan.

Upstairs in her bedroom, she loaded the food along with a bathing suit and towel into her backpack. She slipped her fly rod case through the outer straps and cinched them tightly. Then she loosened them and inserted an Insulite pad, just in case. Her hands shook in anticipation of what she could no longer deny, that she and Pedro wanted each other, sexually.

A knock sent her downstairs. With her dog shut in the kitchen, she answered the door and kissed Pedro on the cheek.

"Where's Woofy?" Pedro asked.

"I thought you said it would be just the two of us today?"

He returned her sly smile. They loaded his truck. It sat in one of the spaces between their boxy condos. Fort Apache was what the locals called their complex, the units laid out in an oval that suggested the circling of wagons. Pedro flipped up the tailgate to his black pickup. YO was all that remained of the white lettering, the rest of TOYOTA having been detailed out.

He said nothing during the drive to the trailhead. Jaz had to admit it felt wrong not to have Steph along. It was Bert, Steph's dad, who had shown Jaz and Pedro the lake years ago, the small rock-bound treasure that teemed with native browns. It was there Bert had taught them how to fly fish. It had begun a series of summer outings the three friends enjoyed over the years.

It was also bad luck, mala suerte, as Mami would say, to vary a ritual. Jaz had no choice but to ignore this. Steph was busy with the "distant relatives" who were in town for graduation. Usually Steph invited Jaz and Pedro to her house the night before a fishing trip to tie "Hidden Lake Specials." They had all become so adept at tying these flies the owner of the local sporting goods store, Wally Brown, hired them to supply the tourists during the summer. Over the years Wally pressured them to reveal the location of their lake, but they held their secret close to their fly-fishing vests. Hidden Lake remained a speck on the topo map, rarely visited by anyone. Usually they made a day of it: hiking up, catching and releasing most of what they caught, keeping a few to cook. After lunch they'd take a dip in the lake's emerald waters before they hiked back down. Pedro parked at the trailhead. He unloaded their packs from the back of his truck, concerned that hers was so heavy. "Maybe I should take some of the food for you."

"I don't want you to see what I've brought. It's a surprise." Jaz felt nervous, eager to leave the dusty parking lot behind.

They strapped on their backpacks and hiked off into the shade of the forest. At the unmarked junction they paused to drink water. When he offered her a sip from his bottle, she kissed him instead, with a longing he seemed to return. As she pulled him toward a nearby meadow, he yanked back on her hand and guided her to the spur trail, faint as a deer track, that led to their secret lake. "Tranquilo, Jazmín. I'd like to get there in one piece."

"So we can talk? We tried that, remember?" Jaz's legs brushed the tiger lilies and shooting stars that overgrew the path. When would he acknowledge his desires, or hers? At the base of a rocky outcropping, Pedro removed his pack. He took off his T-shirt and used it to wipe his forehead. Then he stuffed the T-shirt into a side pocket, put his pack back on, and tightened the shoulder straps. Once he had secured his first foothold, he began the climb up the rocks to their secret lake. "Would you slow down?" Jaz panted. Her shoes rubbed her heels. It made each toe hold more excruciating than the last. Pedro stopped and nodded. His calves quivered as he edged sideways along a narrow shelf to the vertical chute that provided the easiest route to the top. Jaz's fingers clung to each grip. Every muscle in her body tensed as she heaved herself up. God was meting out His punishment. As if she didn't feel guilty enough already. How many times had she imagined herself losing her virginity with Pedro? How many times had she fantasized about where it would happen, and when? She climbed on, the pain in her arms and legs in direct proportion to the pleasure she expected to feel.

"You okay?" Pedro crept his hands and feet up the slick rock inside the chute.

"Sí," she told herself as much as him. A throbbing arose from within, like it had the night she and Pedro ducked out of prom early to drive up to the lakes. Once there, they spent hours lying on a sleeping bag in the back of his truck, exploring each other's bodies. Frustration set in when Pedro stopped short to wrestle with his faith's prohibition against premarital sex. But when he proposed marriage, it was Jaz who pushed him away. Now he grasped her arm and pulled her up over the rimmed opening of the chimney. His eyes shaded, he surveyed the lake, his deeply tanned back damp with sweat. When he said nothing, Jaz made her way down the glacially polished rock. "Guess we should have waited until after graduation, until Steph could come. I can tell you're thinking it's not the same without her."

"It was Steph who convinced me we should go by ourselves." He eased himself down beside Jaz and removed the Insulite pad from the bottom of her pack. "So why do I get the feeling you had something else in mind?"

"Oh, come on, Pedro. Don't pretend it didn't cross yours."

He smiled sadly. "You really don't get it, do you? Steph warned me this might happen."

"That what might happen?"

"Nothing." He held Jaz's gaze. Then he set her pad aside and removed his pack. From a side pocket he took out the cylinder that contained his fly rod and attached his reel.

Steph's suspicions came as no surprise. Her best female friend had been caught in the middle, Jaz and Pedro's go-between for months as they worked at Steph's parents' restaurant, Bert's Burgers. Whenever Jaz asked Steph to relay a message to Pedro, Steph would express her desire that they all remain friends. But sadly, that was proving to be impossible. At first, Jaz and Pedro's teasing degenerated into a war of petty words. Lately, it consisted of trading insults in rapid-fire Spanish. And while it should have been obvious to Steph that Jaz and Pedro's feelings for each other had changed, Steph failed to acknowledge it, which seemed odd to Jaz when she thought about it now.

With a fly attached to his hook, Pedro fed out his line. He whipped it back and forth above his head and released his thumb from the reel on his third try. "I told Steph it was a bad idea, us coming up here by ourselves."

"So let's talk." Jaz slipped her rod together, hooked a fly, and cast it out. "Because if we don't, Steph may be right, that things will never be the same for any of us again."

"Is that what you want? For things to be the same?" Before he could continue a trout hit his fly and pulled his line taut. He side-armed his rod and reeled the fish in. When it was close to shore, he flipped the brown up onto the rocks.

Jaz's line sang out. She knew enough to let the brown run until there was no fight left in it, and it would be easier to reel in. She cast a calculated glance at Pedro in an attempt to draw him closer as she brought her trout up onto the rocks beside his. In silence they watched their catch struggle. Ironic that fish suffocated out of water. Finally, there was nothing left to do but clean and gut them. Without a word Pedro set up the stove, and Jaz cooked. Pedro inhaled the guacamole and vegetables she brought, and while he engaged her in conversation about their families, he asked no questions about the college orientation she would attend in a couple of days. He still hadn't come to grips with her leaving. When he began to pack up, she placed a hand on his. "Before we go, let's climb up those cliffs and jump into the lake."

His gaze scaled the sheer rock beside the lake's cascading inlet. "I don't know, Chica. At this time of year, the lake's pretty cold."

"And the water's pretty deep. Come on. We always do it when Steph's here."

"Yeah, but not from way up there."

"Which is why I think we should do it, just this once."

Her words galvanized him. "Bueno." He turned his back, her signal to change.

Jaz touched his shoulder. He faced her. She removed her clothing slowly, happy he didn't look away, that he couldn't restrain his admiration of her body. She climbed to the base of the cliffs and scrambled to the top of the falls. From there she leapt into the water. She broke the surface and shrieked, "Oh God, Pedro, it's freezing, but it's worth it. Why don't you drop those Nike shorts of yours and come on in?" She whipped her long hair back.

At first he seemed to consider her suggestion. Then he appeared to think better of it. All he removed were his running shoes. He climbed up the rocks beside the falls. Without hesitation he lunged out and compacted his body into a cannonball that barely missed her when he landed. Exhilarated by his willingness to follow her lead, she splashed him and swam away, laughing as he pursued her out of the water and up the sun-baked rocks. On the promontory they lay beside each other, their eyes closed. Jaz took Pedro's hand. He squeezed back. When she turned toward him and caressed his chest, he turned away. She straddled him and pinned his hands to his sides, kissing him playfully until he threw her off. "Stop it, Jazmín. You know it's not right. That's what I told you up at the lakes, after prom. That's why--"

"You proposed? And when I said I wanted to wait, you took me home?" Jaz crept forward and cradled his face in her hands. "I'll marry you when I finish school." She kissed his eyelids, his flushed cheeks. "As far as I'm concerned, we're engaged, so it *is* all right."

"It's not." He pulled away. "If you love me--if you love God-- you'd marry me now instead of running off to San Francisco."

Knives flicked in her stomach. "How many times do we have to go through this? I'm sure I'll be getting some local scholarships which will help me get a good education."

"What matters is being a good Christian . . ." He never missed an opportunity to preach. He always tried to convert her to his ways. It was amazing, his faith in the Lord, but Jaz no longer listened to his arguments. It was hard to believe in a God that allowed Pedro to harangue her so. ". . . I know you're a spiritual person, Jazmín, but you lack faith." The silence that followed pierced her, sharp as the granite beneath her bare feet. Annoyed it seemed that she said nothing, his eyes sliced through hers, those blades of obsidian only he could wield.

"I'll come back every vacation, Pedro. I'll be yours forever once I graduate."

He laughed. His teeth gleamed in the sunlight. "All you and Steph ever talk about is how you can't wait to get out of this town. So I guess that's it then, that this really is good-bye."

"God said, 'Love one another.'"

Pedro got up and walked to the clothes she had shed. He slung them out to the ledge where she sat. "Stop tempting me. Stop thinking you'll change my mind."

Once dressed, she told him, "I can't believe in a God who won't let me go to college, who won't let me love you." She blinked back tears, only to have them stream down her face.

He came to her and held her. "Then stay, Chica. We can commute down to college in Madison, work at Bert's, and attend services at Evangelico. We both know it's God's plan for us to marry, so why not marry now?"

She memorized the feel of his arms around her, the rise and fall of his chest against hers before she shook her head and broke away.

"Bueno, Jazmín. I won't beg. Go to San Francisco." He gathered his pack and shouldered it. "I'll wait for you down below." He scampered up the outcropping to the top of the chimney. "But I won't wait forever."

Jaz breathed in the beauty around her: the dry scent of the granite cliffs, the fragrance of the columbine that grew in clumps from rocky fissures. She memorized the rings the fish made as they surfaced. She would never come here again, not with Pedro, not with Steph.

# Stephanie Bengochea
## June 18, 1993

*The best mirror is an old friend*
*--George Herbert*

The morning of graduation--the first day of summer vacation as far as Steph was concerned--the phone in her bedroom rang. And rang. It had to be Jaz. Who else could it be?

"¡Chica!" she said before Steph could even say hello. "Come on over. We're making tamales." Jaz sounded exuberant, considering it was only a few minutes past eight. Steph had looked forward to sleeping in, but her friend had other plans. "Steph? Are you there?"

"Yeah." She rolled away from the alarm clock on her nightstand, the phone pinned to her ear. "And you're crazy, Jaz. Certifiable."

"So get over here."

The thought of pork so early in the morning made Steph nauseous. "I thought your family only made tamales at Christmas."

"Or for special occasions. And I'd say this qualifies as one."

Steph stifled a yawn. "Could you give me an hour?"

"Andale pues." Jaz clicked off.

The phone set on her nightstand, Steph pulled her new quilt over her shoulders. *Pieces of heaven . . . Pieces of home . . . May you always rest in peace, Stephie . . . Love, Mom, Dad, Val and Char.* Steph ran her finger along the words sewn into the border, and while the last phrase struck her as unintentionally morbid, she loved the quilt Mom had made for her to take to her dorm room at UC San Diego. The rainbow pattern was a variation of Trips Around The World. The pastel patches blended into one another and shimmered with her every move. Remnants from the dresses Mom made for Steph when she was little had been used to make this quilt. It brought to mind the pride in Mom's eyes each time a hand-smocked creation was passed down to Valerie, then Charlotte, the sadness that crept in whenever a dress was finally put away. "For my granddaughters," Mom would say as she wrapped each one in tissue and tucked it into the cedar chest in her bedroom with a look that said she doubted she would ever have that pleasure.

Steph had received the quilt last night, after Baccalaureate, at a party for the "distant relatives." That was how Dad referred to Mom's family. Baba was what he called his mother-in-law. He gave Mary Margaret O'Riley a wink and a nod every time he said it to make sure she didn't mind, and strangely enough, Baba didn't. A prickly old lady, her wrinkled upper lip always smoothed into a smile whenever Dad called her that.

The nickname grated on Steph, like the needle of the stereo in the restaurant's kitchen that scratched away at Dad's favorite album, *Who's Next*. Steph wondered how her grandmother would feel if she knew Dad blasted "Baba O'Riley" through the kitchen's sound system to warn everyone his mother-in-law was in town. The ritual wasn't complete unless Dad sang along and wiggled his butt as he slapped the burgers on the grill. And if he twirled a separator sheet peeled from one of the patties above his head, well, that was his invitation to Beti Perez, the Chilean waitress, to grab one, too. Beti often did, shouting out tonelessly that white men should never, ever dance. To her what Dad performed before the leaping flames of his grill was a perversion of La Cueca, a Chilean dance that involved the waving of white handkerchiefs. Like a flag of surrender, Dad would lay his separator sheet at Beti's feet in a gesture that had the entire staff laughing, this scene having been played out often enough that whenever "Baba O'Riley" came across the airwaves of the local radio station, a smile crept across Steph's lips.

A crusty old biddy was what Mom called Baba behind her back, the two of them unable to occupy the same space without an argument. Mom's milky complexion and auburn hair was similar to Baba's own. Steph and her sisters bore little resemblance to these thin-skinned women. Must be the killer genes. Dad's darkness marked him as Mexican in Pleasant Valley, though he wasn't. His great grandparents were Basque. Generations of Bengocheas had marched legions of sheep up and down the eastern side of the Sierra Nevada Mountains. It made him a true local compared to the many transplanted residents that called this California ski resort home. His family still lived down in Madison, a ranching community in the desert valley thousands of feet below. The whole clan would be up in a few hours for graduation.

On the other side of the wall, Val and Char bickered, the paneling between Steph and her sisters' bedroom annoyingly thin. Dad teased Mom that only redheads had tempers, so how come his three dark-haired daughters took after her? Steph buried her head in her pillow when the phone jangled to life again. She pulled it to her ear, "All right, Jaz. I'm up, but I'm not--"

"Pedro just got here, Chica. And he says he needs your help."

A glimpse at the clock on the nightstand gave Steph the perfect excuse. "The Senior Brunch is in two hours. I'm not even dressed."

"We just wanted you to be part of it. Even Papi is here."

"Is Yessenia?" The thought of facing Pedro's mother was as bad as facing the smell of pork so early in the morning.

"No. She's covering for Mami at the condos. Por favor, Esteph." Jaz nailed her mother's accent, Juana Valdez's incessant nasal whine.

"All right." Steph cradled the receiver between her ear and shoulder as she tightened her drawstring pants. "Ya vengo."

Why the reluctance she wondered as she hung up. Wasn't this supposed to be the happiest day of their lives? At the brunch a number of local scholarships would be awarded. That afternoon they would deliver their speeches in Spanish and English at the graduation ceremony. Then everyone would gather at Bert's to eat a dinner that would now include tamales made by the Valdezes. Maybe she should get over there to make sure a few were left meatless.

Steph pulled a parka on over her camisole top and slid her feet into Ugg boots. The all-nighter would be fun, even if the objective was to keep the graduating seniors of Pleasant Valley High School sober. Bigger than prom, better than homecoming, it was sponsored by the entire community, and this year it was theirs to enjoy, so why this overwhelming feeling of sadness?

It coalesced in Steph's mind as a vision of Pedro. She could picture him at the ceremony, his mortarboard slightly crooked on his head, his robe a little short over neatly pressed slacks. He was her best friend, too, as close to her as he was to Jaz. Steph folded her new quilt, set it at the foot of her bed, and urged her feet to move. Her boots were lined with lead it seemed, not fleece. No matter what she and Jaz said in their speeches this afternoon, Pedro was right. Today marked the end of something, not the beginning.

It worried her that he had chosen to stay behind, to work at her dad's restaurant, unwilling to leave his mother and brothers to pursue a higher education elsewhere. Though he claimed he would commute down to Madison to take classes at their local community college, Steph doubted he would follow through.

Dust motes whirled in the sunlight that streamed through the dormer windows. The shiny particles stirred with each attempt she made to grasp them. Uncurling her fingers she studied the lines that threaded her palm. Why this fear of the future when she was about to extol its virtues? She ran over the opening lines of her valedictorian speech. The words rang hollow in her head.

Pedro was smart, but he had never loved school the way she and Jaz had. Mystified by her desire to study Spanish, and Jaz's desire to study English, he didn't see higher education as the key to a brighter future. If he commuted down to Madison, he would study something useful, like hotel and restaurant management, or computer technology. Their local community college offered all those classes and more, so what was the point of leaving the Eastern Sierra?

None, if Pedro's mother had her way. For such a petite woman Yessenia Garcia cast a gigantic shadow over the lives of her sons. There was a steely determination in her voice whenever she spoke, as if she were bearing witness before the Latino congregation at Evangelico. Her eyes grave, her Bible in hand, she looked as if she had just gotten up from reading scripture every time she came to the condo's door.

Steph remembered a younger, prettier Yessenia, sobbing on her parents' doorstep eight years ago, saying her husband, Raul, a cook at Bert's Burgers, had been robbed and killed while making a trip to visit his family in Mexico. It was still hard for Yessenia to accept that Raul was gone. And while there was no denying faith had helped her raise three sons in a country not her own, she used it to control them, demanding their undying devotion, their unquestioned loyalty, which they had given her--or at least Pedro had--until now. Steph would have dismissed this random thought if it hadn't felt like a revelation. She realized that with a little encouragement Pedro might pursue an AA degree. He could transfer to a UC in two years. But she could just as easily imagine Yessenia telling him his contribution to their household income would lessen if he attended college for anything other than career training. And if he worked more at the restaurant, when would he have time to study?

The door to her bedroom pulled shut, Steph trudged down the stairs. In the living room, she called out that she was headed over to the Valdez's condo, taking the Blazer, and wouldn't be long. Mom stuck her head out of the kitchen to nod rather than protest. On the couch sat Baba, her knitting needles clacking away, her brow wrinkled as if she feared dropping a stitch. She offered up a parchment cheek to Steph who kissed it before she went out the door. Too bad Baba's interest in knitting and Mom's interest in sewing had never rubbed off.

Her seat belt fastened, Steph turned the engine over and cranked the Blazer into gear, determined to shake off the sadness and fear she felt. They still had the summer. Their separate futures could wait. She parked in the guest spot between the Valdez and Garcia condos, relieved the drive over had soothed her. She knocked on Jaz's door. Her friend cracked it open. Her dog wriggled out. "Boyfriend!" Steph grabbed Woofy by his studded collar before he could escape and allowed him to lick her face.

"That's disgusting, Steph, knowing where that tongue has been." Jaz crossed her arms and shook her head at Woofy.

"It's okay. I'm back," Steph told the Jack Russell terrier. Her jokes about her single status never failed to elicit a laugh from Jaz. But it was more than that. Steph hated Mom's stubborn refusal to get a dog. Over the years, she had come up with one excuse after another. It was cruel to keep a big dog cooped up inside all day, worse to chain it to a zip line outdoors. And it was just plain stupid to own a small one. "Coyote bait" was what Mom called Woofy.

"Esteph." Juana Valdez rushed up and kissed Steph on both cheeks, as if they hadn't seen each other in weeks. "We all in here, mi hijita, stuffin' and wrappin'." Juana wore the purple velour sweat suit she favored for cleaning condos. Her hair seemed shorter, spikier than usual, its blue-black sheen the envy of the many Goths that populated the halls of Pleasant Valley High School. No amount of temporary hair color could achieve the same effect. She seemed too young to be the mother of three teenagers, but then she had been little more than a teenager herself by the time Jaz and her brothers were born.

Her husband, Antonio, made tamales in the kitchen. "It is nice of you to come and help, Stephanie." He smeared masa onto the cornhusks that covered the Formica table, the countertops as well. This was followed by pork filling he ladled from a kettle, careful not to splatter his dress shirt and pants. Woofy circled Antonio's shoes. The dog's nose twitched. Antonio filled a bowl with pork and set it down.

Jaz motioned toward the dining room. "We're in here, Chica, and don't worry. I made sure there are vegetarian ones for you. Pedro even put them in a separate casserole dish."

From a smaller pot in the center of the table, Pedro scooped out the masa. "Tuyas, Chica." He pointed at the tamales he had made. "They're picante, just the way you like them." His smile brightened the otherwise dreary dining room. Shadows plagued every corner of the Valdez condo. The wooden walls and green shag carpeting made it feel as dark as a forest, though there was a threadbare charm to the thrift shop finds that furnished it. Pedro's younger brothers, Luis and Gerardo, flanked him. On the other side of the table stood Jaz's brothers, Juan Pablo and Jesus Antonio, though no one ever called them that. Jesus Antonio went by Chuy. A soccer coach had misspelled his nickname on the back of his jersey years ago, and like the caramel on an apple, "Chewy" had stuck. Juan Pablo went by Juan P., which if you said it fast enough came out sounding like "wimpy."

"Wimpy, wimpy, wimpy," Steph chanted under her breath.

"Juan Pee, Juan Pee, JUAN PEE!" Juan Pablo shot back as he

stomped about, an imaginary Hefty garbage sack slung over his shoulder. It had been his favorite TV commercial when he first arrived from Mexico. Chuy laughed, as did Pedro, Gerardo and Luis, but they soon became quiet as they tucked the corn husks around the filling, the packets needing to be carefully sealed to prevent them from opening when the tamales were steamed.

"Las chicas locas." Pedro's grin made Steph self-conscious, aware she was staring at him. "Vámanos. Get to work."

"As soon as I take a picture." Jaz dashed out of the dining room and ran back in with a camera. "To capture this precious moment on film, los chicos fixing food when there's no paycheck involved. ¡Uno, dos, tres!" Jaz snapped the shutter.

"Basta, Jazmín. Unless you want it to be you and me and Yessenia makin' all the tamales for la Navidad." Juana stood in the doorway between the kitchen and the dining room. She cast an appreciative glance back toward her husband.

"You will come home, won't you?" Antonio joined Juana. He rubbed his forehead with the back of his hand.

"Ay, Papi," Jaz smiled sadly. "Of course I'll come home for Christmas. Did you think I'd go off to San Francisco and never come back?"

Antonio's dark eyes flashed at Juana as if that was exactly what he thought. "I should go to the restaurant, see if Bert needs my help."

"Don't worry, Mr. Valdez. I'm sure Dad has everything . . ."

A glance from Antonio stopped Steph from finishing her sentence. There was a hint of malice in his gaze, as if she had crossed some line. He cleared his throat and scuffed the olive shag carpeting beneath his polished shoes. "Your father may be my boss, Stephanie, but he is also my friend. And while he would never ask for my help on such a special day, I know he could use it." Antonio turned to Juana. "I will see you at the gymnasium."

"But Antonio, you already dressed, and we sittin' up front."

"I will wear an apron." His promise silenced Juana's protests. "Jazmín, hold the dog."

Jaz collared Woofy before he could chase her father through the kitchen and out to the garage. The boys wiped their hands on paper towels ripped from a roll that sat on the dining room table.

"¡Qué floja!" Pedro teased Steph as he carried his empty pot to the kitchen. "So much for calling us lazy. You didn't make a single one."

Steph snatched the pot from him. "I'll help by washing up."

"No, Esteph. You go home." Juana took the crusted pot from her. "You, too, chicos," she told Pedro and his brothers. "We see all of you at the brunch, ¿eh? Juan P. Chuy. Get dressed. Jazmín. You got Woofy?"

"Sí, Mami. When Steph tried to follow Pedro and his brothers out the front door, Jaz pulled back on her arm. "No te vayas. You just got here." In the dimly lit living room, Jaz looked a little desperate as she held onto Steph with one hand, her dog with the other.

It still amazed Steph how much they looked alike. The shadows accentuated Jaz's high cheekbones, her long narrow nose, and her large wide-set eyes. Their uncanny likeness had been remarked upon since they were five-year-olds in the same kindergarten class.

"Gemelas del alma," Jaz's mother sighed from where she stood in the doorway. "Or, how you say it, Hija? Astronomical twins?"

"Astrological." Jaz rolled her eyes, for according to Juana, she and Steph were soul sisters. And while they shared the same birthday--March 15, 1975--to Jaz this merely proved what Steph always said, that they were each other's "evil twin." Juana rattled off something else in Spanish. Jaz answered, her words mumbled, as if she were afraid Steph might understand. "Stay," Jaz pleaded when Steph turned to leave.

"Okay, if I can ask you something." Once Juana was gone, Jaz nodded. "So what do you speak when it's just you and your family, when I'm not around?" Steph asked. "Because when you speak like that, so fast I can't understand, it makes me feel . . ." *left out* was what Steph wanted to say, but didn't.

Aware it seemed of Steph's unvoiced fears, Jaz closed the front door and let Woofy go. "Mami and Papi usually speak to each other in Spanish, while the boys and I speak mostly English, but when we're together like this, it gets mixed up. I'm not sure I'd even call it Spanglish. It's as if we speak a language that is ours alone, that only a gabacha like you would understand, because it comes from the heart."

"No, Jazmín. De la alma." Juana was adamant as she came back in and stood beside her daughter. "Porque viene de un lugar que es más grande, Esteph. Más profundo."

There was no denying that the soul was bigger than the heart. That it encompassed more. Still, Steph wondered what the uninitiated observer would make of the tumultuous conversations she had witnessed at la casa Valdez over the years, at what she and Jaz had been unable to put into words until now. Funny, the fear she still felt, as if she were about to leave it all behind, this condo that had been her refuge. Another random thought, one of many that had run through her head, though she was unable to dismiss this one as she kissed Jaz and Juana good-bye.

# Rosa Rodriguez
## June 18, 1993

*Time is no longer succession and becomes what it originally was and is,*
*the present in which past and future are reconciled*
*--Octavio Paz*

"Calmaté, Rosa," my cousin says as she comes in. When I continue to sob, she asks, "Are the planets out of alignment to spite me?" Silvia looks weary. Her dyed-black hair is limp in spite of the floral scarf she's tied over it. Her coat is damp and wrinkled, as if she's been riding the Muni then searching on foot in the rain.

"I thought you didn't believe in parallel lives destined to meet at infinity." My voice is unintentionally shrill.

"I don't." She takes a pack of Chiclets from her coat pocket and pops one in her mouth. "But there's no other explanation for why you're in hysterics."

"My daughter--your niece--has run off with her high school boyfriend the day after graduation, and you expect me to be calm?" I put my hand over my mouth, before I ask, "Do you know where she is?"

"All I know is she's with Cruz." Silvia chains the front door.

I unchain it because our next customer will be here soon. "So she's not at his uncle's apartment?"

"No." My cousin removes her headscarf and begins to organize the kitchen. I help her set out the nail polishes and take the tub from beneath the sink. She drags the armchair in from the living room and positions it next to the hooded dryer in our makeshift salon.

"Did you ask him where Angelica and Cruz are?"

"Tío Tito was vague as to their whereabouts."

"Ay, Dios, Prima. It sounds like me and Roberto all over again."

Silvia arches a penciled brow. "And you know this because it's in Angie's chart?"

"I know this because of how I feel," I say, but the truth is while my cousin looked for Angelica I cast my daughter's progressed chart. I even drew up a synastry report with the birth data I wheedled from Cruz's uncle once I got Tío Tito to pick up the phone. Nothing fits, so why my daughter would run off with her gangbanger boyfriend is a mystery to me.

"You," Silvia intones in her deep voice. "You see everything in terms of your work." By this Silvia means the charts I do, not the beauty parlor we run in our Capp Street apartment.

"No, Prima. I don't see everything, just what matters." My cousin has never accepted my second sight, or my lack of control over it. "I thought you said los naipes told you Angelica should follow our advice and go to City College, take a loan from us instead of the bank." Silvia fingers the tattered pack of Tarot cards on the kitchen table before she slips them into her coat pocket. Worry etches her face. "You know something, don't you? Silvia, for the love of God, if you know where Angelica is, tell me."

My cousin shakes her head. "If I do she'll run, Rosa. She's desperately in love, desperate to make it on her own. Have you forgotten what that feels like?"

"No," I admit, because I still remember the good times with Roberto, before it got crazy.

"You want to know what else los naipes told me?" Silvia takes the Tarot deck from the pocket of the coat she shrugs off and turns up the first card. The magician holds a candle. A chalice and a mirror lay on a table before him. "This one told me we should hire a detective." I look up and narrow my eyes at my cousin. "For a fee they'll find anyone."

"Why would we pay for that when you know where Angelica is?"

"I don't mean Angie. I mean her gemela del alma, Estefanía." When I look puzzled, Silvia says, "It's time we learn about Stephanie Bengochea. We're both too close to this whole thing with Angie, but maybe if we learn about the life of her twin soul, we'll gain perspective."

My conversation with my cousin is interrupted when Señora Sandoval knocks. The tiny Colombiana is her usual gracious self. Her husband, Manuel, works for the police department. He's the one who helped me search for Angelica's gemela del alma when I first moved to San Francisco. He's the one who was able to access birth certificates in the state of California for females born on March 15, 1975. The name Stephanie Bengochea came up for a baby born in Madison, California at exactly the same time Angelica was born in L.A. Originally I dismissed Estefanía as a candidate because Madison is two hundred miles northeast of Los Angeles. But I now agree with Silvia that this may be as close as we'll ever get to finding Angelica's twin soul.

Silvia sets her cards aside as we prepare to do what we do best, which is treat our client Señora Sandoval like Cinderella since we now realize her husband is Prince Charming.

# Jazmín Valdez
## June 18, 1993

*No serás amado si de ti solo tienes cuidado*
*(You will not be loved if you only take care of yourself)*

With her final words ringing in the gym's rafters, Jaz returned to her seat. Her relatives were restrained in their applause, almost Anglo in their stiff reception of her salutatorian speech. At her request there was no whistling or foot stomping, no ay-yay-yay-ing or yip-yip-yipping. After their behavior at the Senior Brunch, it was a relief. Jaz had asked for Mami's help in this, and as always, Mami delivered. The extended family held back and remained bajo control.

Beneath the CLASS OF 1993 banner, Jaz met Steph and gave her a peck on the cheek, surprised when Steph seemed uncomfortable. A kiss in public had never bothered her friend before. A glance at Pedro helped. He gave Jaz the thumbs up from where he sat. Seated once again in the front row on the raised dais, Jaz felt as if she were up there on display.

A sharp intake of breath emanated from the audience. The gasp came from Mami. She flailed her hand, and it drew attention. Papi folded Mami's splayed fingers into his own, but this did little to ease Jaz's mind. The gesture, while incomprehensible to most of the audience, was the equivalent of hand wringing in the Anglo world, and Steph knew exactly what it meant. Jaz worried it would make her friend nervous. This seemed to be the case. Steph gripped the podium and looked positively green. She swayed as if she stood at the helm of a ship, unable to find her sea legs. "Bienvenidos a todos . . ." her voice wavered as the rafters shook and the bleachers rattled at the back of the gym.

To live in Pleasant Valley was to accept the fact the earth could shift beneath your feet at any time. All locals understood this. Small waves rippled through the wooden floor beneath a sea of folding chairs. Steph's grandmother, the infamous Baba O'Riley, blurted out, "What kind of a place do you people live in anyway?" She scowled at overhead lights that swung madly, her mouth stitched, the corners of her eyes seamed. "Between the snow and the fires and the earthquakes, there's always something. I'm here one day, and I'm a wreck!" The audience resettled themselves on chairs that no longer skittered and bleachers that no longer wobbled.

Steph smiled at her grandmother who sat in the front row beside her parents. "Gracias a Dios that's over. I guess God must know how I feel about public speaking. I'm just glad He didn't give me an easy way out." Applause greeted her remarks. "Let's hope the earth doesn't move again until after I'm finished."

Mami's version of hand wringing was not what had upset Steph, Jaz decided. What had seemed dramatic no longer did, thanks to the earthquake, even if drama had no place at a celebration according to her AP English teacher, Mr. Malone. The part of her speech about her family's struggle to come to the United States had been overwrought in his opinion. Slashing through it with a red pen, he had asked that it be shortened. In the end, Jaz left it out, deciding to keep that part of her past to herself. Was it genetic or cultural, her penchant for drama?

"Bien ama quien nunca olvida." Steph's statement in Spanish

elicited "¡Bravos!" from the Latinos in the audience. Jaz had suggested Steph use this dicho in her speech. They had been Abuelita's final words to Jaz last summer, her grandmother's way of saying, Be yourself. In retrospect the words felt prophetic. No one in Jaz's family had realized how close to death her grandmother was.

Steph's delivery of her speech in Spanish seemed effortless. It made Jaz feel jealous. Was it because English would always be her second language, never the language of her heart? She thought about what she and Steph had talked about that morning, before the Senior Brunch, before everything had changed. Jaz flicked the tassel of her mortarboard out of her eyes and tuned into Steph's words, in Spanish and then English. They had practiced together, had memorized each other's speeches. Jaz marveled at her friend's composure. She would lead the standing ovation Steph deserved.

The one for her at the Senior Brunch had been as unexpected as it was uncomfortable. After the awarding of the local scholarships, Father O'Malley had asked to approach the podium. The priest of St. John the Baptist looked self-satisfied, a bit smug as he told the audience the University of San Francisco had called him that very morning to say they would award a scholarship--a full one, mind you--to Jazmin Valdez to ensure her attendance in the fall. With that, Mami jumped to her feet, urging the rest of the family to join her in the whistling and stomping. Stunned, Jaz gazed out at row upon row of shocked faces. Instead of feeling happy, she felt drained. The award had been given for who she was, not for what she'd done. It made her feel like an intruder, the eternal outsider when all she had ever wanted was to belong.

The last-minute announcement of a free ride to USF had obviously upset the high school counselor. With a tight smile, Mrs. Martin stood and clapped with the rest of the high school staff, but her irritation was hardly disguised. Jaz knew from her college counseling sessions that Mrs. Martin took pride in knowing these things ahead. She felt it was the counselor's job to coordinate the financial awards, to make sure every deserving student was recognized, that each one received an equal amount of aid. When the applause died down, the hefty woman sank onto her folding chair and nearly collapsed it under her weight.

It was obvious what Mrs. Martin thought. As valedictorian, Steph deserved more. The local scholarships from the ski area and the geothermal plant paled in comparison to the money USF had lavished upon Jaz. And sadly, Jaz agreed with Mrs. Martin. The Rotary scholarship she received should have gone to Steph, but it was too late now.

Mr. Dexter, the principal, only made matters worse. He called Jaz up to the podium and praised her before a faculty that tugged at their collars and squirmed in their seats. "This is the first time someone from the Hispanic community has won a full academic ride," his baritone voice boomed through the PA system. "Oh, we've had our share of appointments to the armed service academies, and a number of athletic scholarships for skiing, but Jazmin Valdez's achievement is an honor for our school, for the entire community . . ."

Grateful for the tremor that struck, that rocked Mr. Dexter's world, Jaz watched the shock wave roll through the audience, one that had little to do with seismic activity. Once the earth was steady beneath her feet, she fled from the podium, eager to be off that raised dais, aware Steph's parents who sat beside Mami and Papi had remained seated during the ovation.

Bert and Jenny Bengochea's dazed expressions said it all. They were unable to comprehend why their daughter, the valedictorian of her class, was about to walk away from this awards ceremony with little more than pocket change toward her college expenses. Kind though they were, they obviously resented the preferential treatment Jaz received and Steph was denied because their daughter wasn't a "real" Latina. But mostly Jaz recalled being pierced by the realization that without adequate financial aid, Steph's higher education was on shaky ground.

After the awards ceremony, Steph gave Jaz a hug and whispered it was okay, that she was actually happy about what had happened. If nothing else, it would put an end to the vocal protests Jaz's father made to Father O'Malley after Mass every Sunday, that even with the help of local scholarships, he couldn't afford to send his daughter to a private Catholic college. Jaz kissed Steph's cheek and squeezed her hand, but when Steph let go, it felt as if they were being torn apart, that what had begun as a crack might widen into a chasm and separate them forever.

Jaz focused on Steph, on her long dark hair that trailed down the back of her forest green robe, on the gold National Honor Society stole she wore around her neck. Jaz concentrated on the inflections in Steph's speech, the words in Spanish and in English Jaz knew by heart, the ones she could have delivered as well if not better than her own. When the speech ended, she sprang up to lead the applause, saddened that Steph's smile was for Pedro alone.

Apart from the gritos Jaz's family sent up (their enthusiasm appropriate for mariachi music, not the "Pomp and Circumstance" the high school band struggled through), the rest of the ceremony went by in a blur. The remainder of the afternoon was spent at the condo with her relatives who mostly lived in Pleasant Valley or Madison. They had followed her family's lead of leaving Mexico to live and work in California. But what began as a trickle became a torrent when most of Jaz's relatives moved here. It was something Steph's parents complained about, the wave of illegal aliens that had washed over their state. It was simple, Jaz felt obligated to explain. The minimum wage service sector jobs here were better than what Mexico had to offer, which was nada. Besides, it was the American Dream, as her history teacher, Mr. Allen, pointed out, and Jaz's extended family were living proof, though what she longed to tell Steph's parents was the dream could turn on you and become a nightmare.

It was late afternoon by the time she retreated to her bedroom to read *Wuthering Heights*, a title not on her summer reading list for the literature seminar she was required to take as a freshman at USF. She waited for the phone call from Steph that never came. Her friend was busy, she told herself, bored, stuck entertaining her own relatives. And when at last it was six o'clock, Jaz raced out to her father's truck with the rest of her family, eager to get to Bert's.

"Who needs an all-nighter when we got this?" Mami hauled her ancient phonograph into the restaurant. After dinner, she planned to spin the 33 1/3 records of her youth and instruct the gabachos in the cumbia, quebradita, and norteño. The salsa lessons she would leave to Jaz.

"Let me take those." Jenny relieved Jaz of the casseroles filled with tamales. Piling one after another on her arm, Jenny rushed off toward the kitchen with Mami in tow.

Alone in the nearly empty restaurant it dawned on Jaz that Bert's Burgers should have been closed. The only reason it was still open was Steph's graduation. The Bengocheas usually shut down their restaurant after Memorial Day and didn't reopen until July, a standard practice in Pleasant Valley. June was too early to host the summer hordes, too late to welcome the ski crowd. It was when the Bengocheas and their staff took their well-deserved vacations, though it had raised many an eyebrow on the part of Jaz's teachers as she brought in the yearly note. Written in her father's best English, it explained she would visit the relatives in Mexico and would miss the rest of the school year.

"Why can't your family wait until school is over? It's only three more weeks," Ms. Smith had grilled her in front of the entire class one year.

"I don't know," was her uninspired response. What did second graders understand of their parents' plans? She was along for the yearly ride to see Abuelita in Paracas, the small town in Michoacán, Mexico her parents referred to as el ranchito. But as Jaz watched her parents with Bert and Jenny in the restaurant's kitchen, she realized it was one of many things that had bothered her over the years, that had made her feel caught--no, crushed--between two cultures.

"Why the school give you kids a week off here and a week off there when all us parents is workin', ¿eh? And then they complain when we take our vacation? I don't understand," Mami would say whenever Jaz presented the teacher's reprimand, written in poorly translated Spanish.

"You would think by now someone at that school would have figured out what our schedules are," Papi agreed. "It is not only Bert's that closes during the month of June--"

"That's why you should go with me, Antonio. To explain--"

"Basta, Juana. They would not listen, for they do not care . . ."

On and on it would go, year after year, the same conversation until Jaz insisted she be left behind so she wouldn't miss her high school exams. What she hated most was the school's refusal to make any exception to the rules that served the predominantly white culture.

So leave her behind her parents did, with Yessenia Garcia her freshman year, and the Bengocheas her sophomore and junior years, something Jaz regretted now. Gracias a Dios, she had convinced her parents to visit Abuelita last August. The old woman had died shortly thereafter. It had broken Jaz's heart and required two weeks off during her senior year to attend the funeral. The dress her grandmother had embroidered and given to her during that final visit was the only tangible memory left. It represented what life had been like before, her family's traditions coming alive during those rare visits "home." Now those ties were broken, surrendered to the inevitable passage of time and people.

"Hija ¿Que te pasa?" Mami stood beside her, guacamole and tortilla strips on the platter in her hand. "Why you not out there, talkin' with los chicos, ¿eh? I think it not on accident--"

"It's *by* accident, Mami. *By*."

"No te corrijo tu español, Hija. So why you correctin' my English?"

Ashamed, Jaz gathered Mami in her arms. "Lo siento."

Never one to hold a grudge, Mami hugged Jaz back. "What is it, Jazmín?" Her mother peered at her intently. "Why you not over there, havin' fun with Pedro and Esteph?"

Jaz regained control of her face, aware she had flinched at Mami's mispronunciation of her friend's name. "Ya me voy." She kissed her mother's cheek, though as she headed to the greenhouse section of the restaurant, she decided she had a right to be upset. After all the English lessons, after all the years her mother had lived in this country, why couldn't she pronounce Steph's name properly? Her friend always laughed it off, swearing up and down it didn't bother her, but Jaz wondered. It had bothered her terribly when people mispronounced her name, calling her *Jazz*-min instead of Haz-*meen*. It was why she had shortened it to Jaz, weary of explaining that the J in Spanish was pronounced like an H in English.

At the threshold to the greenhouse she stopped and winced at the slang her brothers used, their exchange no substitute for real Spanish. It seemed ironic she had been so insistent on not missing her classes, that she had excelled in English only to have her Spanish suffer (as had her brother's) due to its limited use. The writing sample she submitted to the Spanish Department at USF was so poor a letter had come saying she would need to enroll in a special course called "Spanish for Spanish Speakers" before the university would admit her to upper division courses. Behind closed doors, in the company of other Latinos, the letter assured her, her writing skills would be improved, this the legacy of a bilingual education that wasn't.

In the greenhouse a long table was set up. For the children, Steph explained several days ago in the strident tones Jenny used when she was stressed out. And while Steph despaired, her eyes raised to the beamed ceiling of her bedroom asking when--WHEN--would her mother consider her old enough to sit with the adults? Jaz had laughed, though she shuddered now.

It was an O'Riley family tradition, Steph said, to set up a separate table for the children at family gatherings. The segregation by age confirmed in Jaz's mind that in spite of Bert's Basque heritage, the Bengocheas were Anglo, Jenny firmly in control. Wasn't part of the family fun seating everyone together, the crying babies passed from cousin to niece to grandmother? A glance at Baba O'Riley, her lips pursed as she endured the noise that echoed through the restaurant, made it clear she would never tolerate crying babies. The "distant relatives," as Steph called them. They did seem distant even when they were near. Perhaps it was better to sit in the greenhouse away from the O'Rileys and the Bengocheas, away from Jaz's relatives as well.

A prick of conscience sent her to the kitchen to help. It made her wonder if she was more Anglo than she cared to admit. That was what Pedro said, the accusation thrown at her when she refused to follow his lead to live at home and commute to Madison for school. It was the Latino way, he insisted, along with Yessenia and Papi. Only Mami seemed to understand Jaz's desire to leave. And Jaz had to now, after her shameful behavior with Pedro. Had he told Steph? Was that why her best female friend seemed distant? No, he would never do that, anymore than she would. Some things were better off forgotten. In the doorway of the restaurant's kitchen, Jaz watched aunts and uncles trip over themselves in their effort to help. Her ties were here, to her adopted home of Pleasant Valley, the dusty highlands of Michoacán a distant memory, more a dreamscape than the yearly destination they'd once been. Her parent's vacant stares haunted her whenever they talked about it. The trips to Paracas had been a way to reconnect, the umbilical cord stretched, not severed. Now none of them would return. Her parents lived in California as exiles. With her departure, Jaz feared that she, too, would become an exile.

"I'm afraid we're closed tonight for a private party," Jenny called to several customers that tried to come in.

"Jenny . . ." Bert waved over the pick-up counter to the people, his signal that it was all right, that they could stay. All were locals, the families of Jaz's classmates, happy to find a restaurant open, to have a place to celebrate as well. They were hardy folk. Many held down two or three jobs to survive. There was no discrimination when it came to work in this town. Everyone labored relentlessly to make ends meet, your winter job followed by your summer job, your day job by your night job. And if you scrambled long and hard enough, you might just scrape by in an economy that thrived only when the tourists came.

"¡Chica!" Pedro kissed Jaz's cheek softly. "Let me take that for you."

"It's cold." Jaz pulled the zipper up on her fuchsia jacket and eased her spandex skirt down. "Besides, I should be in there. Helping."

"I think we both deserve a night off, don't you?" He pulled her by the hand toward the greenhouse, past Steph's sisters, Val and Char, who did look cold. Goose flesh covered their bare shoulders under the spaghetti straps of their pastel summer dresses. They giggled as they flirted with Jaz's brothers. But when Val and Char unleashed a string of Spanish expletives, Pedro blushed. He eyed Juan P. and Chuy who shrugged before they exploded into laughter at Val and Char's newly acquired vocabulary, picked up no doubt under their careful tutelage. But if this pyrotechnic display of gutter Spanish was an attempt on Val and Char's part to impress Juan P. and Chuy, it had failed. With their slight builds and mouths still full of braces, Steph's thirteen and fourteen-year-old sisters attracted little more than cursory attention from Jaz's sixteen and seventeen-year-old brothers.

"We're supposed to sit here." A chill ran up her spine when Pedro held out her chair. It was sandwiched between his and Juan P.'s. The place cards indicated Steph was seated on Juan P.'s left. They were being paired off again, like they had been at prom.

"I really should go to the kitchen." Jaz loosened her hand from Pedro's. "I'm sure Steph's in there, and that she could use my help."

"No te vayas." He hung on to Jaz. "You just got here, and you won't be missed, because you're right. Everyone and their second cousin is in there trying to help, which is why I'm staying out of the way, so Antonio and Bert can cook. Besides, Mamá is in there, and she'll be in there all night. You know how uncomfortable these things make her."

"How is she?" Jaz watched for the hurt in Pedro's eyes that told her he would never get over the loss of his father.

"It would be worse if I were leaving like you."

"Promise me you'll attend those classes you signed up for."

His shoulders sagged beneath the navy blazer he wore. "Bert has offered to move me up to prep cook. Antonio's willing to show me the ropes. It'll be a lot more hours."

"And a lot more money? Come on, Pedro. You promised you'd go to school."

"This is an opportunity I can't pass up. Maybe I'll take one class in the fall, and then--"

"Hey, you two." Steph looked demure in her little black dress, a design similar to what Jenny had sewn for Val and Char. "Let's get some food so we can get out of here." Steph led the way, past her sisters and Jaz's brothers who were still engaged in their X-rated conversation. Jaz followed Pedro to the main part of the restaurant, adjusting the hemline of her skirt as she went.

Good as Abuelita had been at embroidery, Mami hated sewing.

She loved the ready-made clothes available at the Kmart down in Madison. She bought whatever the family needed there, including the outfit Jaz currently wore. In spite of Jenny's offer to sew a gown for Jaz for prom, and a dress for graduation, Mami had refused. "No, gracias," she told Jenny. "If Kmart good enough for me, it good enough for Jazmín."

Jaz had worn the fuchsia-colored spandex suit with the spangled top to prom, the only short outfit amidst a swirl of longer ones. But this outfit seemed totally out of place tonight, even with the jacket zipped up, and the glitzy top safely under wraps. Pedro's navy blazer and khaki pants and Steph's little black dress with a string of pearls were in tasteful contrast to what Jaz wore. She longed to go home, to change into Abuelita's dress.

She recalled how she had balked at wearing the silver stiletto heels, relieved when Mami relented instead of being her usual stubborn self. "Bueno, Jazmín. Papi and me don't want you trippin' on your robe when you go up them stairs." Mami kissed her cheek as Jaz slipped into a pair of flats. "Just know there's nothin' wrong with bein' short, or wearin' a tight skirt and a pretty top like that one." Her mother yanked the zipper to her jacket down. With her cleavage exposed, Jaz felt naked. As she tugged up on her tube top, Mami laughed. "And there's nothin' wrong with looking like the woman you are, Hija."

The lips that brushed her cheek now were Pedro's. He cradled her in his arms from behind and whispered, "I can't wait 'til this is over so we can go up to the lakes to talk."

"There's nothing left to talk about. You're not changing my mind."

"Let me try."

When she faced him, his eyes frightened her with their dark intensity. But Steph's gaze troubled Jaz more. Her friend's laughter sounded canned, forced, as if Steph watched a sitcom that wasn't all that funny. "Hey, you two. What's going on?"

"Nothing." Jaz loosened Pedro's arms from around her waist. "Excuse me," she said as she retreated to the chaos of the restaurant's kitchen.

Jaz still wasn't packed for her orientation at USF. In spite of eliminating several items she deemed necessary, her suitcase wouldn't close. La vajila, the ancient valise. It was a last relic of their lives in Mexico. She pulled out the paperback she had pushed down the suitcase's peeling cardboard sides. Her dog-eared copy of *Wuthering Heights* looked more at home in the rickety crate that served as a bookcase in her bedroom. Her clothing rearranged, she knelt on the suitcase and clicked the rusted locks shut. When she stood up, the bag burst open and spewed clothes like a crazed jack-in-the-box. It was as if some mysterious force welled up.

Nervous at the thought of meeting the other full scholarship recipients that represented every minority imaginable, Jaz knew the explanation to her packing dilemma was simple. She took way too much. Was it because these items reminded her of people and places she feared she'd outgrow? Or was it a test to see if she could rid herself of these things so she could attain the future of her dreams? She purged this thought from her mind, the superstitions that ruled Mami's life. From the suitcase she dug out her bulky sweater and tossed it toward the closet. Once the rest of her clothes were back inside the valise, she leaned on the lid. Then she slid the belt from around her waist and looped it around. She fastened the buckle and exhaled. The locks hadn't chattered open in complaint. On the matted shag carpeting her cardigan sweater looked forlorn and forgotten. She loved its nubby texture, its raw woolen smell. Steph's grandmother, Baba, had knitted it for Jaz last Christmas. The letter from USF had warned that San Francisco was cold, even in summer. It seemed unwise to leave the sweater behind, yet if she didn't get packed, didn't leave immediately she feared she'd be stuck here, that she'd become a local for life. From her backpack she took out the embroidered dress Abuelita had made. She smoothed its wrinkles and tucked a loose thread behind a hand-sewn flower before she set it on her bed. She removed the mixed tape Pedro had made as a present. She extracted Esmokey, her stuffed bear. Now there was plenty of room, so like a pimento in an olive, she stuffed her red sweater into her green backpack and pulled the zippers up, relieved when they splayed in a metallic bow. Downstairs, Mami launched into a litany of last minute instructions. "Tell Papi there's cooked food in the refrigerator," she yelled at Jaz's brothers. "That he don't have to do nothin' but heat it up in the oven."

"Ah Ma," Juan Pablo's whine penetrated Jaz's bedroom door. "Why can't he just bring home burgers from the restaurant?"

"I don't like you eatin' nothin' but burgers and fries," Mami shot back. "And help Chuy with the dishes. Papi'll be tired. He don't need to be cleanin' up after the two of you."

"Who'll do the dishes when Jaz is at college?" Chuy asked.

"¡Ustedes!" A chorus of groans met Mami's response. "And no complainin'. You think you too good to wash dishes, ¿eh? What you think Papi do before he become head cook at Bert's? He wash dishes, he bus tables, and then he come home and help me."

The griping faded when the doorbell rang. Woofy barked furiously. Jaz cracked her bedroom door and peered down the stairs. Was it premonition or paranoia that stood the hair on her arms on end? Mami came into view. "Tranquilo." She shoved Woofy aside with her foot.

Jaz held her breath as Mami opened the door. Which of her friends would it be: Pedro to plead with her to stay, or Steph determined to pry from her what had happened with Pedro? "Esteph, mi hijita, come in. I sorry it take me so long. Jazmín ¡ven!" Mami shouted up the stairs as she struggled with Woofy.

It felt like an out of body experience to watch Steph. Her slight build and flawless morena complexion gave Jaz the sensation she gazed at herself in a cosmic mirror. Were they gemelas del alma, twin souls who inhabited different bodies? The summer before, Jaz had borrowed every book on astrology she could find at the public library in order to understand the significance of being an astrological twin, something Mami always made a big deal of though she never explained it to Jaz's satisfaction. That Jaz shared Steph's birth date right down to the minute (adjusted to Greenwich Mean Time) was an incredible coincidence in itself, but when Jaz studied the subject further, she realized Mami had underestimated the importance of proximity. The town of Paracas in Michoacán, Mexico where Jaz had been born was not exactly close to Steph's birthplace of Madison, California. Yet when Jaz called Mami's attention to this detail, she dismissed it. "Esteph's your sister, Hija. That why she found you, and you found her, ¿eh?" This was not enough to convince Jaz. She saw it as yet another example of the superstitious nonsense that poured from Mami's mouth, given the opportunity. Mami was forever tweaking scientific knowledge, fashioning it to accommodate her beliefs. She cooked in a similar manner, crushing dried herbs between her fingers, adding a dash of this, a dollop of that, sipping the broth in her big black cauldron of a pot, a sensual smile curving her lips as she declared, "¡Eso!" meaning this is what the dish should taste like, never mind what the recipe said, never mind the time-honored traditions of Abuelita's open-air kitchen.

Abuelita. Jaz returned to her bed and picked up the wrinkled dress her grandmother had sewn for her. Years of mystical pronouncements by Mami had left their mark, much like the pomegranate juice Jaz had splashed down the bib of this dress. Her carefree enjoyment of the messy fruit had stained her grandmother's gift, and no amount of bleaching on Mami's part could restore the embroidered bodice to its original condition. Jaz had worn it the day she left Paracas last year, convinced she would never see Abuelita again. Sadly, that fear had been founded. It caused her to curb her comments now. Seeing the future felt like a curse. The nagging urgency of her visions caused her to blurt them out at times. It upset everyone, especially when a prediction came true. Mami, of course, had a different take on it. "You and me, Jazmín. We got the gift," she'd say whenever Jaz complained. "And what good is a gift if you don't use it?"

During a recent fight, Mami had dragged Abuelita's dress out of Jaz's closet. At first Mami clutched it to her breast, the embroidered flowers no longer vivid, the stained bodice a faded pink. Then she waved the dress at Jaz and told her to remember who she was and where she came from. Yet today, when Mami brought out the dress, it had been different. No crying, no emoting, just Mami's quiet insistence that Jaz take it with her to San Francisco so she would never forget Abuelita. As if that were possible. Jaz buried her face in the dress. Then she tucked it into the outer pocket of her backpack.

Her bedroom door pushed open, Jaz hoped to catch her friend's eye, but Steph was enmeshed in a one-sided conversation. At the bottom of the stairs, her friend nodded politely as Mami went on and on, about how Jazmín would pick up her first scholarship payment tomorrow morning before orientation began, about how Jazmín had been awarded expense money during a special collection by the Latino congregation of St. John's. Jaz cringed, embarrassed by her mother's shameless bragging. She reached for the scrunchy in her jean pocket, ready to pull her hair out of her face, but as she watched Steph deal with her mother, Jaz stopped. Was it merely coincidence her best friend wore a white T-shirt tucked into tight jeans that were frayed at the knees? That her hair was pulled back in a ponytail, too? Jaz closed her door. Her heart raced. It had to be. How else could she explain it? If she and Steph were gemelas del alma, the threads of their friendship would never unravel over scholarships or money. She cracked the door and listened to Mami change subjects as abruptly as she did her tenses. "I miss her, Esteph, and then you go down to that university in San Diego . . ." Mami hugged and kissed Steph.

In spite of her status as Jaz's cosmic twin, Steph had never been comfortable with the smooching Mami unleashed on her. Steph crinkled her nose at what she described as all the slobbering that went on during arrivals and departures at la casa Valdez, though she didn't mind Woofy licking her face. Jaz could stand it no more. Her door flung open, she cried, "¡Chica!"

Steph's eyes shone with relief. Seizing the opportunity to escape, she jogged up the stairs, shut the door, and leaned against it. "God, I thought I'd never get away from your mom."

Jaz averted her eyes. She thrust her hair through the scrunchy and wound it tightly.

Steph's face crumpled. "I'm sorry. That was harsh."

"Not as harsh as what you said to me last night." Jaz fiddled with her olive drab backpack that sat rigid as a soldier on her cot-like bed.

"You shouldn't have snuck out of the all-nighter with Pedro. Juan P. and I were barely able to cover for you. And then, when you came back and told me nothing happened, well, what did you expect?" Steph had never been known to leave well enough alone. "So . . . ?"

"We talked. That was it. How many times do I have to say this?"

"Which means Pedro tried to change your mind again, about leaving."

That was only part of it, Jaz thought, too humiliated to explain the rest.

"Don't you want to get out of this friggin' town, and do something besides work at the restaurant, tie flies, and clean condos?"

"Of course I do, but it's not that easy."

"Easy? Chica, you'll be living on Easy Street as soon as you get to the University of San Francisco with all that scholarship money."

"It doesn't cover everything."

"Oh give me a break. So get a job then, or get on work-study, or become a real American like me, and take out huge loans."

"Steph . . . I'm sorry about Mami, about how she keeps rubbing it in."

"It's not that." Steph looked deflated. "It's that I don't know how to say good-bye."

"This isn't good-bye. It's orientation. I'll be back at the end of the week."

"I know, but I can't shake this feeling that nothing will ever be the same. And I know Pedro feels that way, too."

"I doubt that."

Steph sank down onto the bed and picked at a loose thread on the comforter. She pulled it, and the sun-bleached coverlet bunched up into buttery folds. "Then tell me what happened."

"It doesn't matter." Jaz took the thread from Steph's fingers and snapped it off.

"It does." When Jaz looked away, Steph said, "You know what scares me? It's all this fighting, all these secrets."

An involuntary shudder shook Jaz. "Trust me, if it were important, I'd tell you."

"Maybe that's why Pedro won't tell me, either."

Jaz felt relieved Steph was still clueless about the botched tryst with Pedro up at Hidden Lake the day before graduation. She took Steph's hand, happy Steph allowed her to hold it. "Jazmín ivámanos!" From the bottom of the stairs Mami yelled. "We better leave before Papi come home and change his mind about you and me goin'."

Jaz pushed the flimsy door to her room open. "Momentito."

"You're not taking Esmokey?" Steph lifted the tattered teddy bear from its place atop the sun-faded comforter. Her eyes scanned the room and lingered on the tapes that sat on the crate.

"I couldn't fit it all in. Besides, Esmokey might be safer here."

"Like you'd be, if you listened to your dad and Pedro?"

"I'm going, Steph, but the pressure is awful."

"What pressure?" Her friend's eyes glinted, more amber than brown.

"I'm worried about meeting the other scholarship students, about the placement tests. I'm afraid I'll let everyone down."

"Who would you let down besides yourself?"

"Here," Jaz took Esmokey from Steph along with the cassettes. From her backpack, she removed her yearbook. "This stays. My tapes and my bear go."

Steph smiled back. Then she walked to the door where the battered suitcase sat. Her attempt to lift it failed. "God, for such a small bag, it weighs a ton."

"Wait 'til you go to orientation. Bet you'll never get all your crud into one suitcase."

"Maybe not, but I think you should ask Juan P. or Chuy for help."

"Are you serious? My brothers were complaining about washing the dishes while I'm gone, not that they mind getting paid for it at Bert's."

"The slackers," laughed Steph.

Jaz shouldered her pack. With Esmokey stashed under one arm, she dragged her suitcase out of her room to the top of the staircase.

"You're sure you don't need any help?" Steph's forehead wrinkled.

"I'll be fine."

Jaz lined up the heavy bag and pushed it over the edge with one hand while she held onto the handle with the other. The suitcase lurched unexpectedly. She staggered down the first step and let go of the valise. The runaway suitcase picked up speed and tumbled end over end. It opened as it cartwheeled down the steps and spilled its contents. When it collided with the entryway table the suitcase shattered the table's spindly legs. The mirror that hung over the table crashed to the slate floor and sent a shower of glass shards over the wooden splinters. Woofy dashed out from the kitchen and barked ferociously at the mess.

"Earthquake!" shouted Chuy as he ran in.

"What the . . ?" Juan P. yanked the dog away from the glass. "Woofy iven!"

"¿Qué pasó?" Papi was in the entryway as well. He stared at the unnatural disaster at his feet. His gaze skipped up the stairs to where Jaz and Steph still stood. "You defy my wishes, Hija, and now you destroy my home?"

Jaz scampered down two steps at a time. "Perdóname, I was just trying to get my bag to the truck and it got away from me." She rushed past Mami who came in from the garage.

"Ay, Díos mio. What happen?"

Jaz scurried back with a dustpan and broom in hand. "Lo siento. Les pagaré por el espejo y la mesita tambíen." She whisked up the glass.

"Ay, Hija, it's not the money or the table I worry about. Es el espejo. Es mala suerte."

"Yeah, seven years bad luck." Juan P. studied the mirror that lay shattered on the floor.

Steph knelt beside Jaz and removed shards of glass from Jaz's clothing.

"You came here to say good-bye, Stephanie. Not to help Jazmín with the mess she has created in her hurry to leave."

Steph scrambled to her feet, tentative. "I'm so glad you changed your mind, Mr. Valdez, that you decided to take time off to drive Jaz and Juana over to San Francisco."

"Only because your father insisted I do so. He said he could not believe I would let my wife and daughter drive to that big city alone."

"So if Bert tell you to do it," Mami snapped her fingers at Papi, "you do it, but if I do," she threw up her hands and walked away. "But as for me, no complain."

Embarrassed, Jaz carried the broken mirror frame to the garage. With the house restored to a semblance of order, and her father's bag packed, she lugged her suitcase out to the truck. It was Steph who ran back into the condo and returned with Esmokey. "You're gonna miss this guy." Jaz took her bear and gave Steph a hug. "Call me as soon as you get back." Steph pulled out the chain around her neck. A silver Saint Christopher, a cross, and a Pisces medallion hung on the necklace. In the jump seat of her father's truck Jaz pulled out her necklace and waved her cross and medallions at Steph. It was the way they always said good-bye. The necklaces were the diaries that recorded their shared childhood. Jenny, Steph's mom, gave them the crosses for First Communion. Juana, Jaz's mother, gave them the Pisces medals for their quinceañera, or fifteenth birthday. Yessenia, Pedro's mamá, gave them the Saint Christophers as graduation gifts, to ensure their safe journeys as they left Pleasant Valley to go away to college.

Jaz tucked her necklace inside her T-shirt and nuzzled her bear. She inhaled his musty scent and remembered the bear that had visited her kindergarten class. "Only you can prevent forest fires!" had been her first memorable sentence in English. Esmokey was hardly recognizable now. As a child, Jaz dragged him everywhere. Her stubborn insistence that he sleep in her bed disturbed Mami who scoured the bear as scrupulously as she scoured her saucepans. It had left Esmokey looking like the carcass of a dead animal, his once-plush fur rubbed off, but to Jaz he was still precious. Esmokey had been the first present she received after moving to California, left on her doorstep Christmas Eve by an anonymous family she always suspected was Steph's. It was back when Jaz's family was poor, poor as the soil on Abuelita's farm. Every time they returned Jaz understood why they'd left. Abuelita farmed the rugged terrain of Michoacán with meager results. The old woman lived off the money they wired and for their yearly visits.

Pleasant Valley seemed quiet as they drove off, as if all the locals were taking a siesta. But the stillness was a mirage, like the water that crossed the highway out of town. It mirrored the White Mountains to the east and "evaporated" as her father's pickup approached. Papi turned north onto Highway 395. To the west the Sierra cut a jagged profile against the sky. A lone jet emitted a contrail, the vaporous wake fuzzy as a pipe cleaner before it blurred and faded from view. Jaz wished she were aboard that plane. Driving anywhere from her hometown took hours. The nearest big city was Reno, Nevada, though today they would head west across the Sierra, over a steep mountain pass that was followed by a treacherous descent.

The trip gave Jaz plenty of time to mull over where she stood with Pedro. His failure to see her off was no big deal. He was undoubtedly working at Bert's, covering for her in her absence. Still, there was no denying she left on bad terms with him. Steph was right about that even if she didn't understand why. Sorrow rose in Jaz's chest and lodged in her heart like a tiny fishing weight. She regretted her impulsive trip to Hidden Lake with Pedro the day before graduation. She had led him on and then pushed him away. She wished she could take it all back. Mami was quiet as well. During car rides she was usually animated, but today she sat mute as if she feared Papi's wrath. A man of few words, he was only too happy to let Mami carry the conversation. Jaz suspected her mother knew better than to make small talk about something Papi vehemently opposed. When they crested the Sierra, he said, "That gauge is going up, Juana. We are overheating."

"I take it in, Antonio, the day before graduation, just like you ask me to."

He allowed the truck to glide down the tight curves of the pass. His eyes darted from the road to the temperature gauge. The needle bobbed lower on the downhill, only to float up as soon as the truck hit the flats and he pressed the accelerator for power. Papi drove on in tense silence as he left the dusky mountains behind and threaded the truck through the golden foothills that cradled the Central Valley. When white wisps drifted back across the hood and obscured his vision, Papi pulled over. Slamming the cab door, he swore under his breath in Spanish.

Mami peeled her thighs from the vinyl of the truck's bucket seat and slid out to join Papi as he paced on the sun-softened asphalt. All pent up nervous energy, her flip-flops slapped as she trailed him. She had asked the attendant to check the oil and water, she told him, so she couldn't imagine what would be wrong with his nearly new truck. Papi walked back to the cargo space. From under the suitcases, he dug out a rag and a water bottle. He wrapped the oily cloth around his hand before he attempted to raise the hood. Clouds of steam billowed up like thunderheads. When the mists cleared, he told Mami the radiator was punctured.

Jaz fidgeted inside the cab as her parents engaged in yet another heated debate. It was already late and orientation began tomorrow, with or without her. As Pedro would say, she was zero for two in making good decisions: the one to seduce him, and the one to go away to college. Actually, she was zero for three. Her parents had no idea she'd turned down his proposal. She hadn't brought it up. It would produce a clash of wills much like the one she witnessed now. When Mami and Papi lapsed into an edgy standoff, Jaz leaned forward between the bucket seats, opened the glove compartment, and yanked out a road map. Unable to pinpoint their exact location, she climbed out of the cab and approached her newly squabbling parents with the only proposal that made sense. "If you can get me to Stockton, I can take the bus from there."

"Ay, Hija," Mami's liquid eyes watered. Her lips trembled. "This is not what I wanted."

"Caramba, Juana, this is exactly what you wanted," Papi said. "For Jazmín to leave, to go to a strange city and learn who knows what."

"It's a Catholic school, Antonio. She'll be fine."

"So you and everyone have told me, too many times." He studied the radiator and smeared oil stains down his faded jeans when he wiped his hands on his thighs. His white T-shirt, still pristine, blazed in the sunlight, in stark contrast to his mahogany skin. He dropped the hood of the truck with a loud *thwack*. "We should be able to get to a gas station, and from there, we can get you to the terminal, Hija, so that you can arrive by tonight--"

"But Antonio--"

"¿Qué quieres decir, Juana? We cannot make it to San Francisco. We might burn up the engine along the way. As it is, we may have to spend several nights in Stockton, which will leave Chuy and Juan Pablo staying with Yessenia for longer."

"She don't mind watchin' the boys. I call her from the garage." Mami's bright eyes muddied as she watched Papi take his wallet from his back pocket and rummage through it before he held the coin section upside down like a boy upending an empty piggy bank. "¿Tienes suficiente dinero para pagar el mecánico?" Mami asked.

"And as for the cost, pues . . ." Papi riffled through the twenties again, counting them carefully before he snapped his wallet shut.

"Por favor, tómalos," Jaz wrenched the crumpled bills from her own pocket.

"Hija, no, it's your money." Mami warded off the bills.

"Please. You need it right now more than I do. This would have never happened--"

"If you had listened to me." Her father's bitterness silenced Jaz.

They eyed each other through the shimmering heat. She handed the bills to Mami. Papi snatched them away and thrust them back. "I do not want your money, Jazmín. I want your respect, your obedience."

"Antonio, por favor--"

"Callaté, Juana." His anger was white hot, like the waves that wiggled up from the tarry asphalt. He wiped the sweat from his brow and stalked back to the truck's cab. "When we get to Stockton, I will leave you at the terminal. Then I will go and find a mechanic."

Jaz willed her tears away. She swiped at her cheeks as they limped into the city, stopping periodically to refill the leaking radiator. It clearly had a hole or two or three. Jaz wondered if the mechanic would be able to patch it or if the whole thing would have to be replaced. Her father's "new" truck was actually a "pre-owned vehicle," at least that was how the dealer in Madison had described it. The Chevy 4x4 had been purchased without a warranty. It had been a stretch to afford this much-needed vehicle and send her off to college at the same time. There was the scholarship money, but she needed to attend the financial aid presentation before USF would dole it out to her. And if she didn't get to orientation tomorrow, well, Jaz didn't even want to think about that. The money she had earned during her senior year was in a savings account in Pleasant Valley, but that was a problem, too, because all the banks were closed now, and she didn't have a debit card. The plan had been to open a new account in San Francisco and transfer the money accordingly. So even if her parents accepted the cash from the special collection at St. John's, Jaz had no idea if it would cover the cost of repairing the radiator, or the motel in which her parents would have to spend the night, or the bus ticket she would now have to purchase since this plan of getting her to orientation had failed.

At the Greyhound station, Papi hefted Jaz's suitcase to an unoccupied bench where she would sit with her mother and wait for the bus to depart. Then he went to the ticket window. When he returned his gaze never left the dirty concrete floor. The reek of urine reminded Jaz of Paracas, of how she had lined up with her mother and brothers in the terminal de transporte for positions in the camión, their suitcases providing seats for the truck ride out of the mountains of Michoacán. She recalled how Abuelita had stood as Papi did now, unable to look Jaz in the eye as she embraced her. It had been the sorrow of saying good-bye, and young as she was when she left Mexico, she understood there was a cost to a better life, that leaving changed everything.

Jaz loosened the ticket from her father's fingers. He closed his hand over hers and squeezed it, unable to meet her gaze. "Perdóname," she said as she kissed his leathery cheek. He held her in his arms a long time before he released her from his grip. Then he disappeared out the terminal door without looking back. Jaz sat beside Mami on the slatted bench. "He hates me."

"No, Hija. He loves you. He just bein' a burro."

"Why can't he be proud of me like you are?"

Mami's eyes searched the speckled acoustical tile of the station's ceiling, those dark stars in their grimy heaven. "Ay, Dios mio. I don't like you goin', neither, but you got to, so you don't end up like me. You deserve better, and college is important, so I'm told. Just do me a favor, ¿eh? Don't forget who you are, or where you come from."

Jaz unzipped the side pocket of her backpack and waved Abuelita's dress at Mami. They held each other. Jaz suggested she call USF to let them know what was going on. When she got through, she put Mami on the pay phone. The advisor assured her Jaz would be met in San Francisco, that other freshmen would attend orientation without their parents. Mami said little as Jaz prepared to board the Greyhound. Her eyes appraised every male as if he were a pervert who waited for the chance to paw her daughter during the long bus ride to the city. It upset Jaz that her mother's paranoia had become her own. She felt nervous about sitting next to a stranger in the dark for hours. "Ciao." She clung to the tiny woman who made her feel tall.

"Jazmín, preciosa." Mami's eyes were warm, sticky as caramelo. Her mother blew kisses as the bus rolled out of the station. When she was no longer in sight, Jaz turned away from the window. Her red sweater removed from her backpack and balled into a pillow, she closed her eyes, but sleep eluded her. She saw herself fighting with Pedro up at the lake. She saw the confusion in Steph's eyes as to why Jaz wouldn't confide in her. But the image Jaz couldn't shake was the one of her parents performing their dance of anger and fear. Her head throbbed as she imagined the tongue lashing Mami would endure because she had done the unthinkable. She had defied Papi and let their only daughter go.

# Stephanie Bengochea
## August 15, 1993

*It's only possible to live happily ever after on a day-to-day basis*
*--Margaret Bonano*

"Stephie?" A summer cold made Mom sound hoarse, as if she were plagued by the wintertime crud that had everyone sniffling from November to April. And this was August. "Stephie! Your order's up!" Mom seemed tired, too irritated to care she had startled a nearby customer. Her face taut, her skin opaque except where the freckles peppered it, she looked as if she couldn't muster the energy for her usual courteous manner. "Daddy's pounded on that bell twice, so you'd better--"

"Make it snappy." Steph picked up her order: two Bert's Burgers with everything on them; crinkle fries for Greg Morris; none for his date.

Dad scraped grease from the rungs of the grill, shaking his head in disgust as he wedged new plates beneath the heat lamps. Steph turned away quickly and smacked into Jaz.

"¡Ay, ca . . . ramba!" Jaz wiped Steph's order from her Bert's Burger's T-shirt and black shorts. She kicked it from the rubber mat in front of the counter to the floor of the kitchen, the grease staining her white tennis shoes. "Chuy? Juan P.? Could you please help us with this?"

Juan P. set down the tray of dirty dishes he carried to the dishwasher. A worried look crossed his face when Beti Perez, the veteran waitress, rushed in. He grabbed a long handled dustpan and broom to whisk up the spilt orders. Dumping the buns, hamburgers, lettuce and tomato into the trash, he then stepped between his brother and Beti.

"Who's checking these?" Beti slammed two glasses down on the stainless steel counter to the right of the sink. Her bleached blond bangs failed to hide the glistening lines on her forehead. "They're dirty, Chuy. It's the second time today someone's complained."

Chuy's face was shiny, too, bright as a copper saucepan. "Disculpe," he told the Chilena waitress, his expression contrite in an attempt to stake a claim on a share of Beti's tips.

"Carajo, Chuy--"

"Hey!" Dad cast a disparaging look their way. "You know I don't allow that kind of talk in my kitchen. Not in English. Not in Spanish."

"We'll trade," Juan P. suggested. He grabbed the nozzle, big as a showerhead, from Chuy's hand, and examined several glasses for lemonade pulp before loading them in the Hobart. Chuy hustled off to bus tables.

"Well, what are you staring at?" Beti demanded of Steph.

She lowered her eyes from hair that was burnt orange and frizzy, the results of a do-it-yourself dye job and a home perm gone wrong. Why Beti would try to transform herself into a curly headed blonde was beyond Steph, but it appeared that was exactly what the waitress had done on her day off. Shellacked into place, Beti's curls reeked of Aqua Net Extra Hold.

Her work attire drew Steph's attention as well. Instead of shorts and sneakers, Beti wore a tight skirt, seamed stockings, and toe-pinching pumps. Her T-shirt was deeply cut at the neck and slipped off her shoulder in a provocative manner that probably accounted for her being the most highly tipped waitress at Bert's. Her outfit would have looked ridiculous on just about anyone, and while there was no denying Beti had a pretty face, it grew ferocious now.

Jaz returned. "Steph dropped her order," she explained to Beti, which only upset Steph more. It sounded so lame, so totally pathetic.

"And that's why you're hanging around like you've got no place to go and nothing to do?" Beti's eyes never left Steph's. "Not that Daddy would ever dock your paycheck."

"Just tell me what you need, Stephie, so you don't keep the customers waiting." Dad gave Steph a look that conveyed disappointment in her, not Beti.

Her eyes downcast, Steph repeated the order. Jaz motioned for Steph to follow her to the drink station. "Where were you? I had to put my order back. It was cold, because there was no room for it under the heat lamps." Jaz dabbed at the stains on her T-shirt

"Pedro wanted to talk to me." Steph held two glasses up to the light before she filled them with lemonade and loaded them onto a clean tray.

"About?"

"About what happened up at the lake." When Jaz stared, Steph elaborated. "You know, the night of prom." Jaz looked relieved, but she also looked as if she was eager to leave. "It's okay, Chica. I'd freak out, too, if a guy asked me to marry him."

Jaz's gaze drifted to the kitchen. In the rear Pedro prepped by himself. He shucked corn and seemed surprised to look up and see Steph and Jaz watching him. With a grin, he returned to work, unaware this simple gesture of friendship relieved the tension. Jaz smiled apologetically at Steph and scooped up her order. She delivered it to a table near the entrance of the restaurant.

Still waiting, Steph continued to observe Pedro as he shuttled back and forth, corncobs in hand, to an aluminum pot that rattled on the stove. It was exactly what she'd been doing all summer long, sweating it out each time Pedro and Jaz's feelings for each other threatened to boil over. But now Pedro had confided in Steph, had told her what had happened, so it felt like it had been worth it. His smile, along with his disclosure, had dialed their three-way friendship back to its usual slow simmer.

Her order finally up, Steph delivered it to Greg Morris, his face stony, impossible to read. "What kept you, Bengochea?" His eyes were cold hard crystals.

"I'm sorry, Coach. I'll comp you the lemonade with unlimited refills."

With a smirk he asked, "Would Daddy approve of your offer?"

Steph ignored Greg as she unloaded his plate, though her former ski coach's sarcasm annoyed her. "Will there be anything else?"

When Greg's date shook her head, Steph nearly dropped the woman's order. Why hadn't she recognized this striking blonde before? But then she hadn't expected Greg to date someone who worked at ski school, who was only a year or two older than she was.

Diane Ross had garnered quite a reputation during her short tenure in town. A regular on the after-hours circuit that shifted from one ski employee's apartment to another, she was the reason the sheriff was ever on the lookout for under-aged girls partying with older guys.

Yet Steph understood Diane's attraction to Greg. The man definitely had an air of aloof glamour to him. And while there had been accusations of improper relationships with his high school racers, this only added to his allure in their eyes. His desirability increased every time he ignored their attempts to flirt with him. It was enhanced by every disdainful remark he made. To Steph it proved the man was perpetually pissed off, a trait she found incredibly irritating. But what intrigued her now was why he would date someone like Diane Ross.

What was he thinking? But as usual, Greg Morris wasn't. His

reputation nearly cost him his job Steph's senior year as she bashed her way through the slalom gates to bring home the state championship for the fourth time in as many years. And while nothing was ever substantiated, and no one could argue with his winning ways, Steph beheld the odd couple before her now and wondered if they should have.

"What are you gawking at?" Greg's gaze flicked from Steph to his date then back again. "You two know each other?"

"I'm sorry, Diane. I didn't recognize you at first. We were always so bundled up at ski school. Maybe I should take your order back to the kitchen and warm it up."

Diane's French manicured nails touched Steph's wrist lightly. "That won't be necessary." She flipped her long blond hair over tanned shoulders and adjusted the thin straps of her low-cut camisole top. "My order's fine. And so is Greg's." She popped one of his crinkle fries into her mouth. Her lips formed a sensuous pout as she chewed.

Greg smiled at Diane. "Then I guess you're dismissed, Bengochea."

Steph trudged off, upset he would belittle her now that she was no longer in high school, no longer part of his winning team. At the pick-up counter Juana pleaded with Jaz who shoved Steph's latest order out of the way to grab her own. "Por favor, take a break, Hija. Yessenia'll be here any minute. She want to eat with you, with Pedro and Chuy and Juan P. too. And Esteph, por supuesto." Juana gave Steph a hug. Her outpouring of affection was inconvenient. "Ask your mother," Juana told Steph. "Jenny won't mind now that it slowin' down."

"I think she will, Madrina." Steph picked up two plates of ribs.

"Por favor, Estefanía." Yessenia gave new voice to Juana's usual, whiny inability to take no for an answer. She stood beside her friend, her dark outfit in complete contrast to Juana's neon pink shorts and matching crop top, a look only Juana could pull off.

"Stephie's right." Mom braced herself against the kitchen door-way. "I hope you understand. Stephie will be covering for Jaz, the boys for Pedro."

"Of course." A look of sadness swept across Yessenia's face. Her lips straightened into that line that masqueraded for a smile. She shrank from Mom, no longer able to equal even Juana's inconsider-able height. And while Steph was touched by Yessenia's desire to include her, she welcomed Mom's businesslike manner as a way to escape the Latino sense of closeness that was cloying at times. Mom led Yessenia and Juana to a table in the greenhouse section of the restaurant, next to the one where Greg Morris and Diane Ross still sat. Always a model of prim reserve, Yessenia's black long-sleeved blouse and wool skirt had to be stifling. Steph suspected the mourn-ing clothes were worn to remind Juana that Jaz would leave while Pedro--the good and obedient son--would stay.

Joining her mother at the table, Jaz's lips stretched a bit too tightly over her perfect teeth, as if she were trying to convey that everything was all right, and there was no need to worry. But worry Steph did as she delivered her order of ribs to another table in the greenhouse. For while she was relieved she wouldn't have to grin and bear it through yet another drawn-out good-bye, especially with Greg Morris sitting nearby, there was something in the way Pedro looked at Jaz as he sat down that Steph hadn't seen since the night of graduation.

It was her belief that friends loved each other best when they were just that: friends. Once again she watched Pedro and Jaz flirt with crossing that line. Which was why she still felt miffed about them ducking out of prom early, and then again at the all-nighter. It had left her with plenty of time to speculate as to what they were up to. Their strained relationship afterwards only confirmed that something had happened in spite of Jaz's insistence nothing had. For months neither Jaz nor Pedro would tell Steph the truth. And while she was happy Pedro had finally seen fit to trust her with an explanation--if not the details--Steph wondered if it was only because it was safe to do so now that she was about to leave.

What bothered Steph most as she stood in the greenhouse watching her friends with their mothers was that she had been a little too happy to learn that Pedro's marriage proposal to Jaz had been turned down. Was it because she harbored unspeakable desires of her own? Or was it because her relationship with Jaz had healed, though like a festering sore, the scab was picked clean every time Mom or Dad brought up the issue of where the money would come from for college, as if what had happened at the Senior Brunch was Jaz's fault.

"You sure you can't join us, Esteph?" Juana's dark shiny eyes loomed large in her small heart-shaped face. She tucked a bra strap beneath her pink top and glanced at Jaz, which prompted an enthusiastic nod.

"I'm sure." Steph balanced her tray on her shoulder and hustled off.

# Rosa Rodriguez
## September 30, 1993

*Every day you play with the light of the universe*
*--Pablo Neruda*

"**M**anuel called back," I tell Silvia as she comes in. She sets the grocery bag on the kitchen table thoughtfully. "He checked the DMV data base, but the only address for Estefanía is a post office box." I cast off the doily I've been working on. The worn arms of the sofa need to be covered. The chairs and tables need help, too.

Silvia puts the produce away and the teakettle on. "Has Manuel checked the Pleasant Valley phone book? It might list the Bengochea's physical address. ¿Café?"

"No, gracias. Quisiera té." My cousin sets out two chipped teacups with mismatched saucers. She fills one with Néscafe and the other with a manzanilla tea bag. "Manuel hasn't done that, because it looks like Estefanía no longer lives with her parents." I pull my glasses to my nose, the magnifiers I wear around my neck along with my cross and Aquarius medal. I read my notes. "He traced a Stephanie Bengochea to the University of California in San Diego."

"It is an unusual name, so I'm guessing it's our Estefanía. What else did he find out? "

I squint at my notes. "The name of the dormitory where this young woman lives." I sigh. "Even if we had the money to fly down there, even it is our Estefanía, what would I say?"

Silvia laughs. "You'd quiz her about her life to see if there's any similarity to Angie's. And from what you've told me, Prima, there isn't. University of California," Silvia flails her hand and shakes her head. "Angie would've never gotten into a college like that."

"She could have if she'd never met Cruz, if she'd gone to a decent high school."

Silvia sips her coffee. "Bengochea . . . What kind of a name is that?"

"Basque."

"Estefanía is Spanish?"

"Her ancestors are. Manuel says he will try to find out more, provided we give his wife free hair styling as well as manicures and pedicures."

"Bueno." Silvia eyes my growing stack of astrology texts. Then her gaze travels to her collection of santos, those candles she buys at Mission Delores and lights faithfully, a prayer for Angelica constantly on her lips. When I go to the fridge, she becomes strangely nervous.

"¿Quisiera flan?" I open the door and search the shelves for the dessert I made last night, and I understand why Silvia behaves as she does. "Why didn't you tell me she came by?"

"I didn't tell you, because you won't let her be." It's my cousin's way of saying, *You're the reason she left, Rosa. If something happens, it's your fault.* "She looked hungry, like she's not getting enough to eat. I gave her the leftover pozole, too."

"And money?" When Silvia looks away I am so angry I leave the kitchen. How many times do I have to tell my cousin not to do this? The only time my daughter comes around is to take Silvia's hard-earned cash. In my room I calm myself with deep breathing.

Then I close my eyes and picture Angelica. Her hair is short now instead of long. Her shoulder is tattooed with a cross for Cruz. A tiny diamond pimples her nose. She smokes in an alley, and from the way she inhales it's not a cigarette. As to where she lives there are no numbers, no street signs, but I'm sure the alley is in San Francisco, even if I don't recognize the neighborhood. She is safe and looks happy "Which is enough for now," I whisper to myself, desperate to believe what I say.

# Stephanie Bengochea
## September 30, 1993

*If love is the answer, could you rephrase the question*
*--Lily Tomlin*

Xochitl was not the Latina roommate of Steph's dreams. To begin with, she was not Latina, something she was quick to point out. She was Chicana. There was a difference. Several days with Xochitl was long enough to make Jaz seem white by comparison. Steph had longed for a roommate who'd be willing to run across campus with her naked, someone who'd kiss a random guy in the dining commons just to make good on a bet. But that was Jaz, not Xochitl.

Steph's first night at UC San Diego, she tried to engage her roommate in Spanish conversation, something encouraged by the RAs at Muir College's Spanish Interest Hall meeting, only to have Xochitl answer every question Steph asked in English. For starters, her name was So-*cheel*, not Zo-chi-*tuhl*. Yes, she had been born here, raised in East L.A. No, she had never been to Mexico. Yes, she had brothers, all older, all in gangs. No, she didn't have a mom. Her mom had OD'd. And her dad? She was sketchy about him. She thought he might be in jail.

Dressed in baggy men's pants held up by suspenders over a wife beater, everything about Xochitl exuded attitude. "Anything else?"

she asked, and while Steph heard the rawness in her roommate's voice that convinced her much of what Xochitl said was true, Steph felt like saying, *Yeah. Are you a liar, a poseur, or what?* "Your turn," said Xochitl.

"I'll spare you," answered Steph.

A few days later, Xochitl came home from wherever it was she spent her time. Gesturing at the dress Steph had tacked to the wall above their bunk beds, Xochitl asked, "What's that?"

"Something I picked up in Tijuana." The dress reminded Steph of the one Abuelita had made for Jaz.

"You mean, you actually went on that stupid-ass trolley trip to TJ, with all the other gabachas who live in this fucking hall?"

"It was fun," Steph replied, daring to risk the wrath of Xochitl. "Like the potluck was after we got back. Or did you forget about the exchange last night with the Black Interest Hall?"

"Forget?" Xochitl's explosion of laughter was harsh. "You expect me to hang with the home girls, to eat their chitlins and collard greens and pretend I'm loving their shit for food? Jesus, Steph. Could you be any more of a wanna-be if you tried? Why don't you go to the beach and deepen your tan?" That Xochitl automatically assumed down-home cooking and Mexican food would never mix seemed xenophobic, completely racist. Once again Steph's expectations had been raised, only to have Xochitl tear them down.

"So tell me," Steph said. "Why are you here? Living on this hall?"

"Housing fucked up," Xochitl told her. "And as soon as those pendejos can find me a single room, I'm out of here." Xochitl's lips were full and unsmiling, wide as her forehead, broad as the flattened tip of her nose. The hoops she wore gleamed, as did her seal black eyes. Her skin was lustrous and dark, her hair curly, which made Steph wonder if the lady protested too much. Did Xochitl fear mingling with blacks because it would blow her cover as a Chicana?

Steph had had a hard time filling out the racial portion on the UC application as well. Should she check WHITE or HISPANIC or both? She was tempted to check OTHER, though she didn't. She sympathized with her roommate and would have liked to discuss the ridiculous notion of race with her, but she knew she never would. The topic would only anger Xochitl.

With the headphones to her Walkman plugged into her earring-studded ears, Xochitl seemed happy when Steph told her she was leaving, riding her mountain bike down the hill.

La Jolla quickly bored Steph with its aged population in prescription sunglasses and wide-brimmed hats ambling along a burnished shore. Back in the saddle, she rode to Pearl Street, for like most Pleasant Valley residents, she was a compulsive shopper, trained by Mom never to leave home without a list in hand due to the high cost of clothing in their ski resort town. Any excursion away from the Eastern Sierra required at least one stop at a mall to stock up on whatever could not be bought by mail order. But downtown La Jolla proved disappointing. The stores offered expensive ensembles that catered to the older crowd.

Tired of searching for non-existent sales items, Steph cruised through a residential area. The houses on the other side of La Jolla Cove spilled down sandstone bluffs to the sea, and it was there that she saw him. In neoprene long johns, he rode a short board, cutting left then right, racing up and down the faces of waves, in and out of the perfect curls that rolled over the rocks beyond shore. She knew little about surfing, yet as she sat on the bluffs, she was mesmerized, drawn to the graceful movement of this unknown surfer. He appeared fearless as he glided over reefs exposed whenever the tide was dragged out, riding waves that flung him toward the crescent shore. When he paddled in and headed her way, she rose. The powdery sandstone swiped from her baggy shorts, she heard him call out, "Do you need a ride back to Muir?" He scampered up the final rise, his board tucked under his arm.

"Thanks, but . . ." Steph cocked her head. "How did you know I was from Muir?"

"I've seen you in the hallways." He wriggled out of his wet suit. "I'm in your Spanish conversation class, in case you haven't noticed." She hadn't. She wondered what he looked like with clothes on and blond hair that wasn't plastered across his forehead. His board secured atop the rack on his Toyota 4Runner, he followed her line of sight to the mountain bike she had left in a heap. "I'll attach it to the back." Green eyes beckoned. The bungie cord he stretched across her bike formed an arc that rivaled his smile.

His name was Corey Carlsen. He charmed her into going to Torrey Pines. Parking just beyond the golf course, they strolled amidst the twisted trees. Parasailers jumped from cliffs and glided like hawks on thermals. He pointed out a nude beach below and suggested they go there on their next date. "Only if you'll teach me how to surf, and we keep our suits on," she told him.

"Well, all right," Corey laughed. "You've got yourself a deal."

They ended up in Del Mar, eating fish tacos at a surfer's hangout called Carl's, a place that reminded Steph of her family's restaurant. It turned out Corey had eaten at Bert's. His family vacationed in Pleasant Valley, summer and winter. At sunset he dropped her off at her room and extracted a kiss in exchange for a promise to take her surfing the following morning.

# Jazmín Valdez
## October 5, 1993

*Amores nuevos, olvidan viejos*
*(New loves help you forget old loves)*

"That guy, Marty? The one you went out with Saturday?" Rosemary was home from yet another shopping trip downtown, judging by the pink and white Victoria's Secret bag she plopped on her desk followed by her purse and keys. "He called again." Like a cat, Rosemary stretched. Then she arched her back, kicked off her shoes, and pulled her sweater over her head, tossing it to the floor. Her bed was a whirlpool of sheets and damp towels. She collapsed atop them and slung an arm over her eyes. She squinted at Jaz's tensor lamp. "Don't you ever do anything but study? You make me feel guilty, worse when I think about how envious I am that Marty is drooling all over you." Rosemary served up guilt southern style. It was a pleasure to hear that Marty had called, and that Rosemary thought Jaz had a powerful effect on him. But Marty's interest in her made Jaz uncomfortable at a certain level. "So how come you keep blowing him off?" Rosemary asked. Was it because Jaz didn't have to beg for his attention the way she did with Pedro, or was it because Marty's interest in her was so obviously sexual?

"It was the date from hell." Jaz flipped to a new page in her anthology. "I made the mistake of suggesting we go salsa dancing with my Spanish class, thinking it would be fun, a safe way to get to know each other, a cultural experience."

"And?"

Jaz tapped her highlighter on her thick text. "And I could tell Marty hated every minute of it, especially the dancing."

Rosemary sat up and reached for the pad on her desk. She ripped the top sheet off, folded it into a paper airplane, and took careful aim, pleased when it landed on Jaz's open book. "I swear, if you don't call him, I will, to tell him to quit mooning over you and go out with me. So get over yourself, Ms. Valdez, and the fact he can't dance, because that guy is so . . ."

"White?" Jaz felt embarrassed this had popped out.

"Hot," Rosemary replied. Her tone made it perfectly clear offense had been taken. Jaz removed the paper airplane from her anthology and smiled sheepishly at Rosemary. Marty's phone number was carefully written on the airplane's wing.

Rosemary's mouth formed a contrite little bow. "So call him, why don't you, or does affirmative action now apply to dating?"

"And what is that supposed to mean?" Jaz crumpled the paper airplane and threw it at her wastebasket, missing.

"I'm just saying that you might want to hang out with people who aren't Hispanic."

"I do that." Jaz was irritated she felt the need to defend herself to Miss Politically Incorrect. "I was thinking about inviting Marty to check out the murals in the Mission with me, to try some real Mexican food."

Rosemary's laughter sounded like a bad case of the hiccups. "My advice is to not do the salsa thing again, even if it's what you dip your chips into. Speaking of which, those nachos in Union Square were nasty." Jaz stared at her roommate who mixed her metaphors, split her infinitives, and dangled her participles, something that would never be tolerated from her. Yet Rosemary was the native speaker, in spite of her drawl, in spite of being far more interested in going out than studying. "Were you planning on changing before you head over to the library?" Rosemary shuddered and rubbed the sleeves of her long-sleeved white blouse. She pulled her sweater back on and smoothed her khaki pants. "It's cold as a witch's tit out there. Seems like it's always foggy here in Frisco. I thought California was supposed to be warm."

"That's L.A." Jaz sank onto her bed, her book clutched to her chest. She had forgotten she wore Abuelita's dress. Her text set aside she pulled the embroidered dress over her head.

"Well, don't change on my account. I just came back here to drop off a few things before I catch a movie with Gina." Rosemary's eyes were on Jaz's underwear, the bra that was dingy gray, the panties with the waistband stretched out from too much washing. "You should go downtown tomorrow, check out the sale at Victoria's Secret." Rosemary reached into the pink and white striped bag on her desk and pulled out a string bikini that was black and glossy, like Jaz's hair. "Y'all have the room to yourself if Marty comes over." Rosemary shot her panties at Jaz as if they were a rubber band, a naughty grin on her face. "Just don't forget to hang yours on the doorknob if you two decide to hook up." She put her panties away and checked herself in the mirror on the back of their dorm room door. Her purse and keys in hand, she feathered her blond hair. "Have I ever told you how much I love that nightie of yours? Where'd you get it? Mexico?"

"It's a dress, actually. A gift from my grandmother." Jaz took it to her closet and hung it up. "It's something she made for me. Too bad I ruined it, stained it with pomegranate juice."

"Well, I would have never known if you hadn't told me. And you do look kind of cute in it, like Selena, so maybe you should keep it on for Marty, but me? I'd ditch the underwear."

Out the door Rosemary went. Jaz felt thankful for the quiet in her tiny cell of a room, in utter contrast to what emanated from the hall. Laughter came through one wall. Music blasted through another. Could she really be the only freshman at USF who needed to study? She took off her bra and panties and threw them in her hamper. With Abuelita's dress slipped back on, she shoved her heavy book off her bed and reached for the phone on her desk. She wanted to call Steph, to talk rather than communicate by e-mail, but she hesitated. Her phone bill last month had been astronomical. The crumpled paper airplane retrieved from the floor, she punched in Marty's number, expecting to get his voice mail, surprised when his baritone sang out, "Hello?"

"Hi. It's me."

"Jazmin? You're actually returning my call instead of using that air-headed roommate of yours as your phone machine?"

"I'm sorry, it's just that I've been busy, and I figured I'd see you in class tomorrow, so if you're still interested in doing something this weekend, we could plan it out then."

"How about now? In fact, how about doing something tonight?"

"But . . . it's a week night."

"So? I'll see you in five."

With Marty's click, Jaz hit speed dial for Steph. "I did it, Chica. I just called him, and he's coming over. He'll be here any minute."

"Well, that's great, isn't it? So what will you do this time?"

"I don't know. Go out for coffee?"

"Corey took me surfing."

"That is so cool, Steph. How was it?"

"A whole lot harder than snowboarding."

Marty's knock surprised Jaz. "Oh my god. He's here already."

"Ciao, Chica, y que te vaya bien."

The receiver in the cradle, Jaz leaped off the bed to answer the door. When she opened it, Marty's smile widened. "Well, don't you look comfy. Were you in bed when you called?"

She crossed her arms over the stained bodice of her dress. "I didn't have time to change. I was on the phone with someone else just now."

"Your boyfriend?"

"My girlfriend." The breeze through the door lifted the hem of her dress. It reminded Jaz she had unconsciously followed Rosemary's advice, that she wore nothing underneath. "Maybe you should wait downstairs while I put on something warmer."

Marty shrugged. "We could stay here." His eyes took in the identical desks, beds, and closets that lined each wall. "Is Scarlet O'Hara gone?"

Jaz laughed. Then she pulled out Rosemary's chair for him and sat in her own. "I'm sorry about last weekend. Guess you don't like dancing."

"Not really."

She crossed her legs and pulled her dress down over her knees. "I only invited you because I thought it would be fun."

Marty ran a hand through his shoulder length blond hair. "Well, I've got my own ideas about fun. In fact, I'm heading to Santa Cruz to surf with some buddies from high school on Saturday. Want to come?"

"Oh, I'd just be in the way. Besides, I don't know the first thing about surfing."

"Tell you what." He stood. "Why don't you take me to that salsa club of yours Friday night, to give me a private lesson, and I'll teach you how to surf on Saturday, just you and me."

"I'd love that." As Marty headed for the door, she wondered if they would ever have anything in common besides shared physical attraction. When he turned, his sapphire eyes were startling. "How about lunch tomorrow? At Crossroads, instead of the commons?"

"Sounds good."

"So, I'll see you in class." He gave her a wry smile. "Can't wait to see what you have up your sleeve for Mr. Arndt this week during discussion."

Jaz grimaced. "I still feel terrible about that."

"The guy had it coming, taking you apart like that, in front of the whole class. I loved the fact you fought back, and so did everybody else. He'll never take you on again."

"Thanks, Marty."

He looked puzzled.

"For taking me on again."

"My pleasure," he said, before he closed the door to her dorm room.

# Stephanie Bengochea
## August 15, 1994

*If fate does not adjust itself to you, adjust yourself to fate*
*--Persian Proverb*

On her back, Steph studied the sky. It was bruised, black and blue, swollen with clouds. "Do you have to go back to San Francisco tomorrow?" She sounded whiny, even to herself. The wind ruffled the grass in the meadow as it carried her question off toward the Nevada border.

Beside her, Jaz yanked off her cap and freed her ponytail. She made a face because the elastic tugged the hairs at the back of her neck. "I still don't have all my classes yet. The ones I wanted were closed by the time I tried to enroll." A private despair enveloped her and billowed up like the clouds did. "God, Steph, where did this summer go?"

"I don't know."

"I wish we'd spent more time together. Just the two of us."

Instantly, the air temperature dropped ten degrees as a shadow passed over them. Steph's throat tightened at the thought of the year before, at how hard it had been to say good-bye. She sat up and picked a pale pink aster. She twirled it between her fingers.

"But as for me?" Jaz sat cross-legged, too. "No complain, even if we was always workin'." She mimicked her mom perfectly.

"At da restaurant. Or cleanin' condos. Or tyin' flies at Wally's," Steph piped in, guilty she mocked Juana Valdez, a woman she admired. "It was always somethin' . . . and now I'm thinking, what a waste." Steph tossed the aster into the churning water of the nearby creek.

"No." Sadness flickered across Jaz's face as she watched the aster bob away. "No, it wasn't a waste." She picked a dandelion and blew its angel hair across the stream. "But I do wish we'd done more, away from the restaurant, away from our families, away from . . ."

"Pedro?"

Jaz heaved a sigh. "What am I going to do about him?"

Unable to hold her friend's plaintive gaze, Steph pulled up clumps of grass. Why did she find herself looking forward to his hundred-watt smile, to the way his flinty eyes sparked whenever she teased him? No, the question was, what was she going to do about Pedro? Steph tossed the grass into the air. Bits suspended themselves like confetti. Now, if only the wind would carry her away, too.

Anything more than friendship with Pedro was out of the question. He was Jaz's ex-boyfriend, the born-again boy-next-door. He was off-limits, even if his overtures were less timid, harder to ignore. She would do nothing, for if she acted on her feelings, it would break Jaz's heart, and that was a fate worse than breaking her own. What she knew was this: when Pedro and Jaz hurt, Steph hurt, too. Ironic that her friends had continued to flirt and fight all summer long, ignoring their three-way friendship, that sacred trust Steph dared not break because once it was broken, she sensed there would be no choice but to look at the world differently. Maybe that was why Steph continued to keep an emotional distance from both Jaz and Pedro.

She wasn't the first or last person to suffer from unrequited love, to crave what was forbidden. Pedro was practically her brother, if not by blood then by a bond that ran so deep and went back so far it seemed as if he had always been there for her. And wasn't that the point, that their friendship survive? So why he and Jaz would cross that line and mess things up was beyond Steph. That she could forgive them stemmed from the fact she was in love with Pedro as well. It was why the Lord's Prayer was constantly on her lips: Forgive us our trespasses as we forgive those who trespass against us. The words moved Steph. She understood that once a mistake was made, all that was left was forgiveness. The sky lowered, woolen and soft, a harbinger of the fall yet to come. She pictured Mom, changing the bedding from cotton sheets to flannel, taking out the winter quilts, but this did little to comfort her. Nothing was black and white anymore, not even the clouds. "Do you remember," Jaz said, "how worried we were about Pedro last summer, because we knew he should leave, too? How we felt as if we could never come back, and if we did, nothing would ever be the same? Well, I think we were right."

"No, Jaz. We were wrong."

"About leaving or coming back?"

"About Pedro." Steph pulled the bill of her cap lower and zipped up her sweatshirt. She eyed the mountains to the east, those silver crests beneath a still turquoise sky. Why had Jaz picked today of all days to discuss her emotional meltdown with him? "I guess what I'm saying is I'm tired of all the drama, of waiting for the reconciliation that never comes."

"So you don't care anymore whether Pedro and I are happy?"

"I just think happiness shouldn't come at such a cost, that love--true love--is a lot less dramatic than people think." To Steph it was about keeping your mouth shut when you wanted to scream, about forgiving yourself and your friends for being who they were.

"You think I should leave, go back to USF, and forget about him? About us?"

"I'm just saying if you love each other, you'll remain close even when you're far away. I'm just saying you should let him . . . be."

"As if he'd ever let me be, or you for that matter. Dream on, Steph."

Which seemed all too true, that those who love us would ever let us be. *Don't forget your hat, Stephie. Don't wrinkle your forehead.* Mom had hurled this unsolicited beauty advice at her when she left, as if she were a child still living at home. With her fingertips she smoothed the lines in her brow in an effort to erase Mom's nagging from her head. "Maybe you're right, Jaz. Maybe everything has changed, and the summer's only proven that."

"Even so, I'm glad we came back. At the very least we made a ton of money." Jaz stroked the dried-out petals of a wild iris as if it were the face of an old friend.

"Yeah, but you didn't have to come back here to do that. You could have stayed in San Francisco, worked at Marty's father's firm."

"You're right. I could have. But I didn't, because I didn't want to."

"I know."

"Because you didn't want to, either?" Jaz tucked a loose strand of wind-whipped hair behind an ear. "It's why you didn't stay in San Diego with Corey and work."

Lightning cracked, and Steph felt that connection to Jaz as if she were feeling it for the first time. Whether sisters by blood or by birthday--or the bullshit Juana fed them about being *gemelas del alma,* cosmic twins, whatever that meant--they were restless spirits beneath a threatening sky, their memories tied to each other, their childhoods intricately laced. The truth was Steph felt closer to Jaz than she did to her own sisters. It was a love that wasn't demanded by default.

Their parallel lives this past year amazed her. They'd both been saddled with difficult roommates. They'd both lived away from home, away from the constraints of their Catholic parents, only to find themselves in relationships that remained unconsummated.

What was it that held them back? Was it love for Pedro, or fear they were about to betray him? The sky ripped open and unleashed a strobe light flash. Steph plucked another aster. She twirled it, more party favor parasol than umbrella, and tucked it behind her ear as drops the size of dimes splashed down.

She chased Jaz through the meadow in the rain and reflected on their day job. They had played true confessions as they cleaned the condos today. Their laughter swirled as they flushed away their sins with the Tidy Bowl Blue. Still, her friend's confession bothered Steph. Jaz had been subdued as they polished the chrome in the sink, the porcelain in the tub, and when Steph asked what was wrong, Jaz admitted she was scared to return to USF for her sophomore year, fearful that Marty would find someone new. Was Jaz psychic like her mom? And what about her? What was behind her own decision to leave Corey and return home, only to work her ass off all summer long? She dismissed these random thoughts when a bolt split the sky, the lightning close enough to make Jaz scream.

Her friend ran faster. "Oh my god, Steph. The hair on my arms is standing on end."

"Mine, too." But what struck her in that moment was that they *were* gemelas del alma. It wasn't money or fear of intimacy with their college boyfriends that had driven them home. It wasn't even their mutual obsession with Pedro. They had returned because like twins, separated by circumstance rather than birth, they had missed each other terribly. Steph's thoughts returned to Pedro as she and Jaz hurried through the side streets of Pleasant Valley. He was their northern star, the one true constant in their lives. He had always been there for them, and though they quarreled at times like brother and sisters, their affection for each other was real. Steph cared about him, and Jaz did, too, no matter how much she claimed to the contrary. *What am I going to do about him?* Like the thunder, Jaz's lament echoed in Steph's head.

Hail set them running faster. "Call me!" Jaz's words were swallowed in the hissing downpour. Her image blurred as she disappeared into the Valdez condo.

Steph jogged up the ribbon of road to her house half a mile beyond. Wispy tendrils rose from the steaming asphalt. The rain turned to hail and danced like popcorn on a cast iron skillet. In the mudroom, she stripped off her clothes. Upstairs in the bathroom, she toweled off. From her closet she took a Bert's Burger T-shirt and a pair of black shorts. Still cold, she pulled on a wool sweater to keep warm. Her sneakers laced and tied, her Gore Tex jacket zipped up, she walked to work wondering what to say to Pedro. Should she tell him about her confused feelings toward Corey, toward him, her childhood friend, now that they were no longer children? Jaz was off for the evening, so Steph had no one to talk to but him.

Her bare legs scissored through the sleet and the rain. The hailstones crunched beneath her feet. At the restaurant, she shed her jacket and peeled off her sweater. Her grandmother, Baba, had knitted the wool pullover for her and had given it to her the Christmas of her senior year. It brought to mind the herds of sheep that grazed in the meadows outside Madison, driven by the descendants of the original Basque immigrants, her dad's ancestors. Carved into the aspens that grew in the valleys of the Eastern Sierra was the Bengochea name, usually beneath a herder's crude rendition of a female nude. Sheep was what brought Dad's family to Madison, and him to Pleasant Valley where he could ski by day and flip hamburgers at night. His family still felt he'd rejected his heritage by calling the restaurant Bert's rather than Bengochea's. They still questioned his decision not to serve traditional Basque fare.

With her parents and the Valdez family off, she and Pedro did a bit of everything that night when unexpectedly large crowds inundated the restaurant. Her sister, Char, the hostess, turned people away because Steph and her other sister Val couldn't turn the tables over fast enough. Bedraggled campers lingered over slices of pie and steaming refills of coffee, reluctant to return to their rain-soaked tents. When at last all the customers were gone, Steph told her sisters and Pedro's brothers, Luis and Gerardo, to go home, that she and Pedro would close up.

They took their break on the back steps of the kitchen and sipped glasses of the fresh lemonade the patrons usually ordered by the pitcher. Not tonight. It had been too cold, too wet, though the clouds parted now and pinprick stars pulsed in an indigo sky. The scent of damp earth and pine was a welcome relief from the greasy odor that permeated the stuffy restaurant.

Steph downed the dregs of her lemonade and eyed Pedro. Her empty glass sweated in her hand. "Are you going to see Jaz after work?"

He shook his head. His Adam's apple rose with each thirsty gulp.

"It's her last night here. Are you fighting again?"

He nodded. The cords of his neck tensed as if he were gritting his teeth.

"You can't let her leave without telling Jaz what you've been telling me all summer, that you're still in love with her."

"And why should I do that?" The whites of his eyes flashed in the darkness. "I'm tired of begging Jazmín to marry me, to come back." He polished off his lemonade with a single jerk of his hand. "Besides, she can't wait to go back to San Francisco." He trained his sights on Steph. "Just like you can't wait to get back to San Diego, to . . ."

Steph pulled the elastic from her ponytail. "His name is Corey."

"Corey, huh?" Pedro rattled the ice in his glass. "Do you love him?"

She finger-combed her hair. "Let's not do this again."

"So you're in lust with him, just like Jazmín is, with that Martin

Donahue, *the third*." From his glass Pedro took the ice cubes in his mouth and spat them out. "What kind of pretentious name is that?"

"I still think you and Jaz should talk."

His mouth, set in a grimace, pulled down at its corners. "About what? Whether she should sleep with that guy the minute she gets back to USF?"

Steph sipped the water that had melted from the ice cubes in her glass, embarrassed he had heard her whispered conversation with Jaz at the beverage station the night before.

"Is that what you're going to do when you see that Corey guy again?"

She shrugged, not wanting to lie, but not wanting to encourage yet another rant on Pedro's part about the danger of venereal disease, not to mention the eternal damnation she would suffer at the hands of his unforgiving God.

"He'll break your heart, just like that Martin Donahue, *the third*, will break Jazmín's--"

"And what would you know about broken hearts?" Pedro's glass slid to the tips of his fingers. The depth of his sorrow surpassed her own. "That was harsh." When he still didn't respond, she said, "I'm sure you're tired of listening to us go on and on about our so-called boyfriends. I'm sure you're bored to tears by all our talk."

"No, Steph. What you don't understand is I'm glad it is all talk, or that it has been up 'til now." He gazed at the trees, at the tall shapes that rustled softly in the night's breeze. "What I'm bored with is my life, this job. I wish I'd left like you."

Grateful for this change of topic, she threaded her fingers through her hair and braided it. "It's not too late. In a year you could transfer."

"Which is what I'm planning to do, take more classes now that your dad is willing to give me a more flexible schedule."

"Well, that's great, isn't it? Because it really is cheaper to do your first two years while living at home." She wound the rubber band around the end of her French braid and snapped it tight. "Look, Pedro, I know how much your mom depends on you, for money, for help with your brothers, for moral support." Steph winced at this unintended pun, but it seemed lost on Pedro. His gaze was still on the trees that towered above them.

"It's why I had to stay, Steph. It's why I wanted you and Jaz to stay as well."

"I know." She took his hand and stroked it with her thumb. "It's what I love about you, that you always try to do the right thing. But it's time, Pedro. For your sake and your mom's." And though Steph stated the obvious, she couldn't quite picture it, for she understood that Pedro suffered not because Jaz had fallen in love with Marty, but because if he left, if he defied the tiny woman who had been both mother and father to him, it would break Yessenia's heart.

"Yeah, well . . ." Pedro stood and pulled Steph to her feet. "Break's over," he announced, his British accent a dead ringer for Sting's. Steph loved many things about Pedro, but his choice of music was not one of them. It bothered her he liked *Fields of Gold* almost as much as Dad did. Her taste ran more toward grunge rock, not that Dad would ever allow Pearl Jam or Nirvana to be piped through the sound system at the restaurant. Ranchera for Antonio and Mexican pop music for Jaz after the paying customers had left was about as exciting as it ever got around Bert's. Sting's hit "If I Ever Lose My Faith In You" played on the tape deck. Pedro's eyes told Steph he hadn't. They set to work and moved from task to task. Pedro made sure the dishwasher was switched off and the stove's gas canister was full. Steph mopped floors and scoured counters. Pedro was a younger, handsomer version of Dad, and for some reason that depressed her. He seemed old. If anything he was too responsible. When he looked up, she lowered her eyes to her reflection in the stainless steel she scrubbed. "Don't wear it out," he said.

"What?"

"That sponge. You're rubbing it ragged. And that counter? You've washed it twice." He flipped a dishtowel over his shoulder. "How about calling it a night?"

Steph tossed the sponge into the garbage sack and hauled it out to the bear-proof Dumpster. The moon rose over the restaurant as she returned.

"I can give you a ride," he said when she came in.

"Thanks." Steph headed to the storeroom to retrieve her sweater and jacket. At the back door she turned off the last bank of lights.

"How about going up to the lakes? I could use your advice about something."

"Or someone?" She set the alarm, locked up, and walked with Pedro to his truck. "Don't pretend you're not worried about Jaz."

He opened the passenger side door for Steph. "We used to tell each other everything," he rounded the LEER truck cap that now covered the back of his Toyota and finished his thought on the other side. "But now . . ."

"You think that she's changed, and you haven't?"

"She bites my head off about things that never bothered her before. And her mother? Por Dios, Juana is so superstitious. I don't know how Mamá puts up with it. It's why I'm worried. You see, I think Juana is having an effect on Jazmín that's . . ."

"Un-Christian?" Steph ventured delicately into this area.

"Well, at the very least, it's un-Catholic." He started his truck. "Have you ever noticed how candles go out when La Bruja walks into a room?"

Steph laughed. "Juana's no witch."

"It's true," Pedro insisted. "The next time Juana Valdez comes to your house, light some candles and see what happens."

"Now who's being superstitious?" The silence that accumulated in the truck's cab left no doubt as to what Pedro thought. Once again they were locked in a standoff. At the lakes, he pulled into a picnic spot. He stared at the moonlit water, at the small waves that lapped the silver shore. "Actually, it's you I'm worried about," she told Pedro. "And so is Jaz."

He shook his head. "Jazmín doesn't care about me."

"She does, and so do I." Pine boughs swayed and dotted the truck's windshield with droplets leftover from the storm. Steph took Pedro's hand. When he seemed to read too much into this, she let go and gazed out at the lake. "It's so beautiful up here."

"Maybe that's why I don't come anymore. The last time was the day before graduation."

"I thought you said you brought Jaz up here on grad night, and that's when you proposed, and she turned you down." Pedro looked so uncomfortable Steph steered the conversation in a different direction. "You know what else was beautiful? Prom. You and Juan Pablo looked so handsome in your tuxes."

Pedro relaxed. "So did you and Jazmín in your dresses. I'll never forget las chicas locas teaching Mr. Malone how to salsa. Juan P. and I thought his eyes would pop out of his head. Afterwards, he told us, 'Beware the Ides of March, gentlemen.'"

Steph's arm hair prickled at the reference to the birth date she shared with Jaz. "Seems like a long time ago, doesn't it?"

He nodded, though his eyes remained on the bolt of black satin water.

"Do you ever wonder what your life would have been like if your mom hadn't stayed here after your dad died, if she had taken you and your brothers back to Mexico?"

"What was it that Mr. Malone used to say?"

"That you can't go home again?"

"¡Eso!" Pedro looked startled, as if he'd forgotten where he was, whom he talked to. "Está bien, Pedro. Lo entendí."

His eyes glazed over, as if he wished it were Jaz who sat beside him. With a sigh he started the truck and drove Steph home.

The phone rang as she walked in the front door. She grabbed the portable in the kitchen.

"Chica," Jaz said, "I thought you were going to call me after work."

"I just got here." Steph took a packet of popcorn from a large carton in the pantry, evidence of Mom's latest shopping trip to Costco in Reno.

"So late? Where were you?"

"Up at the lake with Pedro." She cradled the portable between her ear and shoulder, put the popcorn in the microwave, and punched it on.

"So that's why he just got home."

Steph imagined Jaz watching Pedro go up the stairs to his condo, right across the driveway from hers. Their bedroom windows faced each other. Steph suspected they watched each other constantly, though neither of them would admit it.

"So what did you talk about?" Jaz sounded as if it were a strain to keep the tone casual.

"A lot of things. Like why he's so unhappy."

"Which is undoubtedly my fault."

"You know it's not." Steph took a mug out of a cupboard, filled it with hot chocolate, and mixed in the water. "Though I wish he'd left, like we did."

"Yessenia would never allow him to do that. She still tells Mami and Papi it was a huge mistake to let me go. I think she's secretly happy Pedro and I are no longer novios."

"She's heartbroken, Jaz. You rejected her son. You no longer want to live here."

"That's not true."

Steph removed the popcorn from the microwave. She held it gingerly by a corner to let the steam escape. "Why don't you come over, so we can do this face to face?"

"What about your parents?"

"They're down in Madison at a line dance." Steph filled another mug with chocolate and water and headed back to the pantry for another bag of popcorn. "They won't be home for hours. Come over, Jaz, so we can talk."

But they didn't. Instead, they watched *Pretty in Pink*, their favorite video from high school days. "Pedro's Ducky," Jaz said as the movie's credits rolled. "The sweet unappreciated friend. The would-be suitor." She stirred the kernels in her bag, spilled some on Steph's quilt.

"So who does that make me? Annie Potts?" Steph gathered the kernels as if she were still eight years old and playing jacks with Jaz. *Cherries in a basket! Six in a single swoop!*

"You're the girl at the prom. The one who bids Ducky come hither with her sultry eyes and dances away with him in the end." Jaz allowed her own eyes to smolder.

Steph tossed the kernels in her mouth. "If I didn't know better, I'd say you're jealous."

"So what did you talk about up at the lakes?"

"How beautiful you looked at prom."

Jaz glanced away.

"He's still in love with you, if that's what you're worried about."

"If that's true, Pedro sure has a funny way of showing it."

"Tell me what happened last year, the day before graduation, up at Hidden Lake."

Jaz looked shocked, which confirmed to Steph she had caught Pedro in a lie earlier that evening. Jaz closed her eyes and shook her head. "It doesn't matter--"

"But it does. It must, because Pedro won't tell me what happened either."

Jaz looked away and twisted a strand of hair around a finger. "What's important is that you and Pedro are still friends." The Tiffany lamp on the nightstand lit her face in a way that made her look haunted. "All you need to know is I did something stupid. Something that upset him." Her voice was high and tight. Tears were close to the surface. "And the strangest part is he says he forgives me, that he still wants to marry me." She got up from the sleigh bed and walked to the window seat. Parting the lace curtain, she gazed out as if Pedro lived across the street and she'd forgotten where they were. "The problem is even if he waits for me to finish school, I'm no longer sure I want to marry him. I mean, after what happened last year, and the way he treated me afterwards . . ." Jaz shivered. "Have you noticed he's getting a little . . ."

"Strange?"

Jaz let the lace panel drop. "Did he mention the candle thing to you?"

Steph laughed and dug out the last of the popcorn from her bag.

"I know it's ridiculous, but what scares me is Pedro believes it, that my mother's a witch, and I'm into heathen practices." Jaz stared at the TV, at the bright blue screen that's neon light eerily illuminated the room. "My favorite part of the movie is when Molly Ringwald makes her prom dress. I still wish Mami had let your mother make mine."

Relieved Jaz had moved on to a lighter subject, Steph said, "Well, you were pretty in pink." She clicked off the TV and set the VCR to rewind. "Do you remember the way your mom used to send you to kindergarten? Like you were going to the prom way back then?"

Jaz returned to the sleigh bed and dug through the kernels at the bottom of her bag. Her eyelashes fluttered, dark moths near the Tiffany lamp's flame. "I do," she replied quietly. "And what I'll never forget is Mrs. Simpson, the way she'd ask me, Are you going to a birthday party, Jazmin? And I had no clue what she meant." Jaz flicked at the corners of her eyes. Tears streaked her mocha skin. "It was the first time I realized I was different, Steph, but it wasn't the last." She tossed several unpopped kernels in her mouth and crunched the "old maids" with her molars. Then she crushed her bag and carried it down to the kitchen.

Steph followed, upset she had brought kindergarten up, that it stirred such painful memories. She saw herself in the horseshoe-shaped classroom, dressed in sweats and Sorels, the winter school uniform of the Anglos, while Jaz wore a frothy pink party dress with a sash that came undone and a crinoline petticoat that crinkled every time she sat. Steph recalled how Mrs. Simpson had told Jaz she couldn't go out to recess, afraid Jaz would slip on the ice in her leather-soled shoes. Jaz had sobbed afterwards, and Steph had been the only one to comfort her. "I was thinking," she began, "about what you told me today while we cleaned." She brought their mugs to the kitchen. "If Marty is with someone new, maybe you and Pedro should get back together."

Jaz tossed her bag in the garbage. Her eyes blazed. "That's ridiculous, Steph. That's like me telling you to get together with Pedro if Corey dumps you."

Taken aback, Steph wondered if Jaz was testing her. It forced her to lie. "Well, you don't have to worry about that, because Corey called me this afternoon, right before work." She turned to the sink to rinse the mugs, to escape her friend's suspicious eyes.

"I thought you said he was surfing in Mexico."

"He was, but now he's back." Steph dried the mugs with a dish-towel and put them away. "He's coming up here. Next week." Her little white lie was becoming a whopper.

"So how come you don't sound more excited?"

Steph tossed the dishtowel onto the Corian counter. "Because I'm scared, Jaz. Just like you. That Corey may no longer be . . . interested."

The accuser now stood accused. Jaz shifted uncomfortably. "Well, I hope Marty still is, because I know now that I am."

"Are you sure you're in love with him?"

"I wasn't at first. I'll admit I still had feelings for Pedro--"

"*Have* feelings," Steph corrected.

"Whatever." Jaz walked away from Steph, out of the kitchen and through the living room to the mudroom where she gathered her jacket and backpack. "Besides, it doesn't matter anymore, because it's over. After fighting with him all this summer--and last--I'm ready to go to the next level with Marty." She opened the door and turned to Steph. "So how about you?"

The question chilled Steph, as did the night air that seeped in through the open door. "Guess I'll decide when I see Corey, and I promise, Chica, that you'll be the first to know."

# Jazmín Valdez
## May 1, 1995

*Si te dieren el anillo, pon el dedillo*
*(If he gives you a ring, stick your finger out)*

"I feel predestined to do everything badly," Jaz told Marty when he stroked her neck.

"Sounds like Ms. Dyjkstra and 'British Literature' are getting to you."

Jaz loved his touch, craved it like she craved coffee, after sex and before classes.

"What's up?" He yawned and scratched the downy hairs on his chest.

"It's not school-related." But that was a lie. Martin Donahue, the third, was definitely school-related. Jaz would have never met him if they hadn't been in the same freshman seminar, if he hadn't rescued her from an unrelenting string of dates that led to nothing but a few wrestling matches. He had been her best friend at USF her freshman year, unlike Rosemary, her southern belle roommate, who ignored Jaz most of the time and was hostile the rest. She had fallen into his bed upon return from Pleasant Valley, grateful to lose her virginity after a long summer apart.

He propped himself up. "Are you going to tell me, or do we play twenty questions?"

Acid pooled in her stomach. His grin indicated he expected an entertaining story. It still astonished her she commanded the attention of a guy who looked like he'd stepped from the pages of a J. Crew catalog. At first, she worried Marty would abandon her for an Anglo girlfriend, but he hadn't. And though he warmed her bed, or she his, every night in their single dorm rooms, she rarely introduced him as her boyfriend. Smart move. With the news she was about to dump on him, he'd dump her fast.

"Don't wrinkle your forehead," he said. "It makes me nervous."

"Why?"

"It means you're worried, and when Ms. Disaster worries . . ." he emitted a low whistle.

She was about to live up to her nickname again, only this disaster had nothing to do with a missed deadline for a paper. She closed her eyes in an attempt to banish the feelings of failure associated with the many things she had done badly since arriving at USF.

There was no excuse for the tirade she unleashed upon the TA of her freshman seminar last year when he accused her of plagiarism. He was only trying to please the course's demanding professor who didn't have the time (or the cajones) to confront her himself. Of course, she would have never met Marty if she hadn't hurled multilingual insults at the idiot, much to the delight of the other students in the seminar. Shortly after her outburst Marty arranged their not-so-blind date. The rest, as people liked to say, was history, for her magical romance with Martin Donahue, the third, was about to end like everything else in her life: badly.

"Jaz?" Marty looked paler if that was possible. "You look scared," he said.

"I am, because I think I screwed up on a test."

"So what did you do this time?" A ghost of a smile flitted across his lips. "Turn in an essay 'riddled with grammar and spelling errors'?" The last part was said in a parody of Professor Deidre Dyjkstra, Jaz's current nemesis in the USF English department. It was the tone she took with her woefully inadequate students. "I can't believe you misspelled her name on that last assignment. I think you've got a mental block when it comes to Ms. Dyjkstra."

Mental block. That was putting it mildly. The woman was a bitch. Ms. Dyjkstra had made it clear she liked nothing about Jazmin Valdez. Her outfits were too sexy. Her dialect (what dialect?) was too pronounced, especially in her writing. Ms. Dyjkstra categorized Jaz's style as nonstandard English. Her propensity for turning in late assignments with typos proved she was lazy. Ms. Dyjkstra (or was it Dijkstra?) used all this to make her point: Jaz was not a serious student, not worthy of her scholarship, and not representative of the minority admissions made by the university. Didn't she understand she was a role model for other young Latina women? All this after Ms. Dyjkstra reamed Jaz's paper during their first one-on-one meeting.

Jaz left Ms. Dyjkstra's office wondering why she ever decided to major in English and Spanish. Not that this woman cared if Jaz dropped her class. In Ms. Dykstra's book, Jaz was relegated to the ranks of the unprepared undergraduate, a young woman seeking a MRS, not a BA. Marty thought Jaz's travails at the hands of Ms. Dyjkstra were entertaining and pure BS.

Jaz looked at Marty and wondered what he saw in her, apart from the obvious. "It wasn't that kind of test," she explained.

He rose from the bed and started to dress. "Was it a Spanish lit paper? A calculus assignment?" Marty grimaced. "Oh man, don't tell me you flunked another physiology lab."

"Not exactly."

"Then what?" He slid into his blue shirt and khaki pants.

"I flunked a home pregnancy test."

He stopped buttoning.

"Actually, I'm late."

"But you're on the pill." His voice cracked. "You said it was safe to stop the condoms."

"I just wanted to make sure, so I took this . . . test."

"And?" He wrinkled his forehead, ignoring his own advice.

"I tried to follow the directions but I must have done something wrong because nothing happened. There was no pink line, no blue line. There was no line, Marty. No line."

He shied away, her words like a gale-force wind funneled through the Golden Gate. "Look," he sat down beside her. "Go to student health services at St. Mary's and ask them to make a test. There's no way they'll screw it up." He retrieved his sweater from her desk chair and took his time pulling it over his head. Her tiny room gave them no privacy.

Jaz hadn't felt this riled up since that day in freshman seminar last year when Marty flirted with her after she bawled out the TA, and the man beat a hasty retreat. She remembered Marty telling her he loved her spirit. Was that what kept him coming back? Was that why he'd hung in there long after she heard Rosemary advise him to get over the "ethnic thing" and get on with it? One look at Marty's face, at eyes as soft as his chambray shirt, told Jaz what had initially attracted him might repel him now.

"So what if I am?" she said.

"You're not, but I'll go with you to St. Mary's if you want." The tenderness in his face melted her fears. Still, she felt fragile as she admitted to herself (not for the first time) that Marty knew her, and yet he didn't. It was the basis of their attraction, past and present. They kept each other guessing, but this time there could be no guessing.

"How about we do it this afternoon, when classes are over?"

She strapped on her watch. All hope of coffee was gone. The outfit she wanted to wear was on the floor of his room.

"Sounds good," Marty kissed her forehead, "because you're on the pill, right?"

"Right." She opened the drawer of her nightstand, horrified the disc wasn't there, that she had left it at his place, again.

"So there's no way you could be pregnant, but if it'll make you feel better, we'll have another test made. Just to be sure. I'll see you at St. Mary's at one."

Marty went out the door. Her temples pounded in sync with his footsteps down the hall. What she had failed to mention was she'd changed prescriptions, and the progesterone-only pills were supposed to be taken in a consistent manner, something she was incapable of doing.

At student health services, Marty kept her company in the exam room while the nurse tested the urine sample. He told her there was nothing to worry about, but when the nurse returned with the results, Marty looked as numb as Jaz felt. *Beware the Ides of March.* The phrase repeated in Jaz's head as she dressed.

"I don't believe this," Marty said once they were in the elevator. Was this the prelude to good-bye? "I don't believe you would change prescriptions and not tell me."

"I didn't think it would matter. I thought birth control was birth control."

"Yeah, so we thought." Outside of Saint Mary's, he turned up the collar of his jacket.

"I guess I should've taken the pills at the same time every day." Not erratically as she had since she never knew where they would be, in her room or his. It had to have been the night of her birthday, when they hadn't used a condom, and she hadn't taken a pill on time in days.

"Well, it's too late now," he said, as they crossed the street and walked past St. Ignatius Chapel. His eyes were a dismal shade of grey, gloomy like the sky. She imagined what he was thinking: Ms. Disaster, pregnant while using birth control?

"I'm sorry. If you want, we could talk about getting an . . ."

"Abortion?" He stopped, his eyes incredulous. What little color that was left in his face drained. "I would never ask you to do that, unless you wanted to. So do you?"

She felt light-headed, as if she might evaporate with the mists. "I think we should."

"It doesn't sound like you want to."

"I don't, Marty, but what choice do we have?"

The wind whipped the flags in front of the library into a rabid frenzy. He took her by the hand and led her to a bench. "We could get married."

She wondered if she'd heard him correctly. She'd been worrying about losing her scholarship, that in a few weeks she wouldn't be allowed to take finals, and that if the test results were disclosed by student health services to the dean, USF would kick her out and cite a lack of morals. She had been worrying about the mortal sin upon her eternal soul, the lie she would carry to her grave if she went through with an abortion, and about whether her family would allow her to come home to raise the baby if she kept it. A marriage proposal had never been factored in.

"Jaz?" He removed a strand of hair stuck to her face. He took her clammy hands in his. "I love you. Even before we got the results, I decided that if you were pregnant, I'd propose."

It seemed safe now to assume he was her boyfriend. "I love you, too." She buried her head in the pillow of his shoulder and dug her teeth into her lower lip. A vein, visible beneath the skin in his neck reminded her he was a blue blood, or at least his ancestors were. She imagined them as the characters she and Marty read about in

Ms. Dyjkstra's class. It explained why his essays were brilliant while hers were lackluster. She didn't belong to that world, or with him.

"Say yes." Marty looked vulnerable. He looked gorgeous. When she nodded, he kissed her, and his lips expressed his relief that she had accepted and wouldn't abort their child. "There's just one thing," he said when they came up for air, his mouth in a serious line that alarmed her. Marty was usually all smiles. "Mother. You'll have to pass muster."

"What does that mean?"

"She's very old-fashioned. Strait-laced. British."

"I thought you were Irish Catholic."

"That's my father. Mother converted. She was brought up Anglican. High church, which is close to being brought up Catholic. In fact, my oldest sister was born almost nine months to the day of their wedding."

"But your mother wasn't already pregnant, was she?"

"No. Mother definitely saved it for marriage, but as Grandmother would say, she had a bun in the oven by the end of the honeymoon."

Jaz laughed at the description of the Donahues, at the unfamiliar idioms. None of these had emerged from the pages of the novels she and Marty read for their British literature class. And none emerged the following evening when Jaz met her future in-laws.

Martin and Carolyn Donahue lived in an exquisite house at the end of a tortuous road, high above the Orinda Country Club. Everything about the drive there intimidated her. Until now Jaz had only ventured out of San Francisco by bus to travel back and forth to Pleasant Valley. The city provided an urban haven with plenty to do, so there was no need to explore the suburbs. Crossing the Bay Bridge revealed a world unknown to her.

Marty gave her a running commentary as he drove. He pointed out Treasure Island, Berkeley and its university, the Caldicott

Tunnel, and finally the Orinda exit on the other side of the hills. They left the freeway. The Jetta chugged up the road. The houses, which ranged from rambling ranches to mini estates, impressed her at every turn. A few skirted a gash in the valley below, the golf course gauzy through fog that thickened in the dwindling light. By the time Marty parked in the hanging driveway of his parent's home, Jaz felt dizzy.

His parent's house was custom-built, angular on the outside, light and airy within. It floated out from the hillside, walled by wood paneling that faced floor-to-ceiling windows. Beyond the glass were decks that jutted out. The design was intended to maximize the view, which would have been spectacular on a clear day. With the fog, there was nothing but a white void. Low clouds acted like sheers on the windows and veiled the country club below. The furnishings were sleek rather than modern. Most of the cabinetry was built-in. The gas flames in the fireplace gave off little heat. Form was clearly favored over function, the fireplace an elaborate centerpiece that made Marty's childhood home seem all the more chilly.

His parents' reception of her was icy. Martin Donahue, Senior looked jaundiced. His teeth, hair, and what should have been the whites of his eyes were yellow. He proffered a hand that felt so cold it was slippery. His muttered words were hard to grasp. Carolyn Donahue's greeting was equally cool. Her eyes were as pale as the flames in the fireplace. She never smiled, this woman who would become Jaz's suegra, or mother-in-law, if she passed muster.

Jaz spent the evening searching for facial expressions, gestures, anything on Carolyn and Martin, Senior's part to discern their true feelings about the proposed marriage. The British and their stiff upper lip, she thought, reminded of *Middlemarch*, a novel she and Marty had analyzed for Ms. Dyjkstra's class. Maybe this was familiar behavior to him, but it was foreign to her. Mami and Papi touched and talked until they were sure their guests felt at home. Jaz wondered if she would ever feel at home with Martin, Senior and the glacial Carolyn, her blond hair coifed in a crown of lacquered curls.

After drinks and hors d'oeuvres, the senior Donahues suggested they adjourn to a dining room that belonged in a San Francisco designer's showroom, not a house in Orinda. The silver candelabras emitted a wavering light. The lace tablecloth beneath the bone china had been stiffly starched. The stargazer lilies in the cut glass vase were so perfect Jaz assumed they were silk imitations until she caught a whiff of their pungent scent. She sat, terribly self-conscious, ill at ease as she tugged down on her skirt and buttoned up her sweater.

Dinner looked delicious but proved unsatisfying. It reminded her of eating out with Marty and his high school friends. She remembered how his ex-girlfriend Tara raved about the California cuisine, the chef whose small portions left Jaz hungry. It was similar to what Carolyn served now, the food attractive to the eye at the expense of the stomach. Jaz took tiny bites as she conversed with Martin, Senior. Toward the end of the meal there was a gnawing in her gut, as if she were a car running on empty. The conversation sputtered along and failed to ignite, so in the end she allowed it to spark out, the only sound the clink of silver against china.

As the evening wore on, she felt as if she were invisible. With a little encouragement from Marty, she would have tried to charm the Donahues, a technique that had worked well at USF. True, she had met her match in Ms. Dyjkstra, and she wasn't exactly taking USF's English Department by storm. Still, Jaz prided herself on being likable, on being able to fit in, though judging by the frosty parting at the door after an evening spent with Carolyn and Martin, Senior, she knew she never would. It was obvious they hated her, and that her marriage to their son would take place over their collective dead bodies.

"Mother said she thought we should have the reception at Casa Moraga," Marty said once they were back on Highway 24.

"She did?" Perhaps Jaz had missed that while trying to figure out which fork to use.

"We discussed it yesterday, during the phone call."

Jaz imagined the silence at Carolyn's end when Marty announced his intention to marry a pregnant Mexican immigrant. "Does your mother think I trapped you?"

Marty gave Jaz a pained look and ground the Jetta's gears. "Mother thinks I should change my major from English to business, or perhaps to computer science." And while that might have been true, Jaz envisioned his mother, a frown fastened between her eyebrows as she discussed "the phone call" with her phlegmatic husband. "You'll be happy to know you're the first date I've brought home since I took Tara to the prom."

"I'm honored," Jaz said, wondering if she was. "But I have to admit I'm surprised your mother didn't offer to pay me off if I'd promise to have no further contact with you."

"Mother liked you. So did Father. Couldn't you tell?" Marty dimmed his headlights as they entered the Caldicott Tunnel. Jaz would have to take his word for it. "You're wrinkling your forehead again."

She turned to her fiancé, still not used to the idea of Marty as her boyfriend. "I'm concerned about how Mami and Papi will react."

"You haven't told them?"

"I decided to wait until I passed muster with your parents before I'd go and upset mine." She rubbed her eye sockets. "Ay carajo."

"I love it when you talk dirty." Marty downshifted. The backup on the Bay Bridge was heavy.

She studied her husband-to-be's profile, the strong nose and jutting chin. "You seem confident we're doing the right thing."

"I'll admit I was nervous, afraid Mother or Father might try to talk us out of it, but they were calm, I thought, under the circumstances." Marty inched the Jetta toward the toll plaza. "Don't worry. Once they get to know you, they'll love you like I do. You'll be family."

There was no chance of that, though what Jaz worried about was if Mami and Papi would ever treat her like family again.

# Stephanie Bengochea
## May 3, 1995

*He who foresees calamities suffers them twice over*
*--Beilby Porteus*

Corey's phone rang and jarred both of them awake. "Yeah?" He looked irritated as he snapped the light on, half asleep as he squinted at his watch. "Yeah, she's here but she's not--"

"I'll take it." Steph interrupted his rehearsed speech on a hunch. He handed the phone to her and padded off to the bathroom. "¿Chica?"

"Oh thank God you're there." Jaz sounded shrill.

"What's wrong?"

"It's your mother. She was in an accident."

Steph reminded herself to breathe. She checked Corey's watch.

"Your father called me when he couldn't get you at the apartment. I didn't think you'd want him to know you're practically living with Corey, so I told him I'd track you down, that you'd call him at the hospital."

"Mom's all right, isn't she?"

"She will be. Eventually."

"Which means?"

"She has a broken pelvis, a broken leg. She'll be laid up for a while."

"Oh God." Steph rubbed her forehead. "I'd better call Dad and book a flight to Reno."

"I could take the first bus out of the city this morning and meet you there. We could ride home together from Reno."

"Are you sure? What about your classes."

"Screw my classes. Where will you be tonight?"

"Here," Steph said as Corey returned from the bathroom. "Are you all right?"

"No," Steph said. "But I will be, thanks to you."

They met at the Reno bus terminal later that day and walked to a nearby Basque restaurant where Steph's family ate after shopping trips. Picnic tables topped with red-checkered tablecloths lined an immense dining room. Wine bottles with candles stuck in them provided the only light. The floor was covered in sawdust. They sat at one of the few smaller tables and ordered the prix fixe meal. After the waitress brought their salads, Jaz asked, "Did you talk to your father?"

Steph nodded and set her fork down. How could she eat, let alone talk about what weighed upon her so heavily? It was as if she was trapped in a cabin with snow on the roof, and the snow was about to shed. But if she had the courage to unburden herself, to tell Jaz what was really going on, she feared all that snow would crash down and crush them both.

"You don't have to talk about it if you don't want to," said Jaz.

"It's just hard." The wax on the candle in the wine bottle rolled down. Steph blinked back tears and scuffed at the sawdust on the floor. It stirred up a blizzard that irritated her nose, rubbed raw from being swiped at too many times.

"Did your father explain what happened?" Jaz handed Steph a tissue.

"She hit a deer." Steph closed her eyes, unable to clear away the awful image, the terror Mom must have felt. "Val and Char were with her."

"Oh my god, were your sisters hurt, too?"

"No, just shaken up," Steph said, feeling shaken herself.

"And this happened yesterday?"

Steph nodded. "They were coming back from the orthodontist in Madison. It was twilight so Mom didn't see the herd crossing 395. She swerved to avoid a doe and a fawn, but she couldn't miss the buck. It came up over the hood and smashed the windshield. She lost control and rolled the Blazer. Thank God for seat belts."

Jaz closed her eyes and crossed herself.

"You were right about Mom being laid up for a while."

"How long?"

"Months. She'll need physical therapy to walk again."

When Steph didn't go on, Jaz's forehead wrinkled. "Why do I get the feeling there's more to it, that there's something you're not telling me?"

"Because there is." Steph chose her words carefully. "I've decided not to take finals."

Now Jaz put her fork down. "Did your father ask you to do that?"

"No, but I don't see how he can manage by himself." Steph sipped her water. "It's not just my sisters and the housework. It's the restaurant. Dad depends on Mom to help run it."

"Yes, but I can't imagine him letting you drop out of school."

"Well, he'll have to." When she saw Jaz's startled face, Steph said, "I was planning on dropping out anyway, even before I got the news about Mom." She took another sip of water and swallowed hard. "Do you remember how Mr. Malone used to tease Juan P. and Pedro, how he used to tell them 'Beware the Ides of March'?"

Jaz rubbed her arms. "We're not talking about your mother's accident anymore, are we?"

"No." Steph waited for the waitress to remove their barely touched salads and replace them with bowls of lamb stew served from a tureen on a cart. "I'm pregnant, or at least I was until yesterday. We'd been using condoms, but the night of my birthday, we were drunk, so . . ."

Jaz's mouth opened. Her hands drifted down to her stomach.

"I'd just come back from the clinic. I was staying with Corey to avoid my roommates at the apartment. It's not the way I'd planned to do it, though I have to admit Mom's accident bailed me out of an awkward situation. You see, I was about to break up with Corey."

"But . . . why? I thought you loved him."

"I thought so, too, until he was such a jerk about my pregnancy. Can you believe he expected me to marry him?"

The muscles at the corners of Jaz's mouth twitched, as if she were working hard to remain expressionless.

"And then, when I said no, he got all high and mighty about the abortion, said he should have a say in the decision. So I told him to take a friggin' leap off the cliffs at La Jolla Cove, that it was my body, and I'd decide."

"But why wouldn't you marry him, Steph, or at least keep the baby?"

She slumped down in her chair and pretended she wasn't the coward she knew herself to be. In spite of the brave face she wore she felt as if Jaz could see the lack of courage that had been exposed. Her eyes burned and tears trickled out no matter how hard she blinked. "That's the hell of it," she finally said. "I didn't think it through, even with the mandatory waiting period, even with the counseling. Corey and I fought about it for days, and now, I realize that if I'd had any idea I was headed home anyway . . ."

Jaz was up, her eyes gemlike in their clarity. "Don't." She hugged Steph and rocked her. "Who else knows about this?"

"No one besides you and Corey."

"Maybe you should give him another chance."

"With me up here and him down there? And all the awful things I said?" Steph wiped her cheeks with the back of her hands. "I killed our baby, Jaz. I rejected him. Why on earth would he want me now?"

"Because he loves you. He was with you last night. He obviously cares." Jaz handed her a paper napkin from the plastic holder on the table.

"Or feels guilty," Steph blew her nose, "and he's not even Catholic." She shook her head. "I couldn't let him marry me out of pity or duty or . . . whatever. I'd only want him to stay if he loved me. But after fighting for nearly a week, I thought it would be better to abort so there'd be nothing between us. I didn't want him to drop out of school to support me and a baby when I wasn't completely sure how I felt about him."

The napkin in Jaz's hands had shred from all her twisting of it. Bits still fluttered to the floor and landed in the baby pink curls of sawdust that covered it.

"What's wrong?"

"Nothing." Jaz collected the bill from the waitress. She waved Steph off and paid for them both. On their way to the Greyhound Bus station, it seemed to Steph that it was Jaz who walled herself off, as if she were the one steeling herself for the long ride home.

# Rosa Rodriguez
## May 4, 1995

*God is where you let him in*
*--Latin American oral tradition*

"Is she pregnant?" I bar my cousin from the kitchen, unwilling to let her come in without telling me the truth. Silvia nods. "I knew it," I mutter. "Is she all right?"

"We don't have time for this, Prima. Señora Sandoval will be here any minute."

"Señora Sandoval can wait." Silvia snaps her gum until I drop my hand from the doorjamb and let her pass. The floral housedress she wears under her wool coat is even more faded than mine. It makes her look old. "You have to tell me where she is."

"If God wanted you to know He'd let you see Angie's address. It's His way of saying, Leave it alone." My cousin lifts my cross from under my Aquarius medal to remind me which set of beliefs is more important. "All you need to know is that she's been to the doctor, and he says everything is fine."

What we don't discuss is that I tried to follow Silvia this morning. She gave me the slip at the BART station when she boarded an outbound train instead of the inbound one, just before the doors closed. She pretended not to see me, but I could tell by her fleeting smile that she had.

My latest progressed chart for Angelica indicates a problem pregnancy, as well as a troubled partnership. I was so worried I asked Silvia to track down Cruz's uncle to find out where he and Angelica currently live. In my mind's eye I see them working at a restaurant, but I can't make out its name. I see them fighting in a tiny apartment with too many people, which tells me Cruz has yet to give up his gang-banger ways. I see them smoking, cigarettes now, though I pray for the sake of the nene that they quit. And then I see Lake Tahoe, which makes me wonder if they went to Nevada for a quickie wedding. I call Manuel, Señora Sandoval's husband, and he assures me there is no marriage license on file in the Golden State or the Silver. Lately, when I ask him to help me find Angelica, he comes up with an excuse. Neither she nor Cruz has a record, he tells me, and her driver's license still has the Capp Street address on it. And as for Angelica's gemela del alma, Estefanía Bengochea, all he knows is that she's a student at UCSD who gets good grades, so I doubt Estefanía is married or expecting a baby.

I go back to the kitchen and suggest to Silvia that we fly down to San Diego and contact Angelica's gemela del alma. "And do what, Rosa? Frighten that poor girl?"

My cousin is right. It's time to let the "astrological twin" concept go. But what I can't shake is the idea that I should shift gears with my forecasting. It was in the progressed chart I cast for myself while I waited for Silvia. But mostly it's just based on reading the *San Francisco Chronicle*. Business is booming for many of the small firms that call this city home. It's why I want to begin casting natal charts for these "computer-based companies." Of course it means I'll have to buy a different kind of astrology book and study hard, and that I'll have to buy a computer and learn how to use it. But that's okay. I'm ready for a change, for a challenge.

For now, I help Silvia set up the kitchen for Señora Sandoval. I think the Colombiana feels guilty about the trade we made with her husband, Manuel. It's why she refers so many new hair and nail clients our way. She says her son Francisco still talks about Angelica, about how he had a crush on her when they were in high school. Señora Sandoval thinks they are made for each other, though I see nothing in their charts to indicate this. Still, if Cruz leaves Angelica after the nene is born, I might try to get Angelica and Francisco together, because ¿quíen sabe? It might bring my daughter and grandchild home.

# Stephanie Bengochea
## June 1, 1995

*Therefore, spare your jealousy, or turn it all into kindness*
*--Dorothy Osborne*

S teph opened her eyes, disappointed to find herself tucked in her
sleigh bed beneath rafters that were dusty and full of cobwebs,
confirming that yes, she really was home. The telephone in her
room rang. She quickly picked up. "I told you not to call again."

"¿Chica? It's me."

Steph sat up and pulled her quilt around her. "I thought it was
Corey. Where are you?"

"At my parents' house."

"Which means you're home for the summer?"

"Not exactly. I need to talk to you. Could you come over?"

"Boyfriend!" Woofy wagged his tail and snorted with delight.
Steph enjoyed the feel of his tongue on her hand. "So where is everyone?" she asked Jaz, who led her from the tiled entryway to the
kitchen.

"Workin'." Jaz poured soymilk into a mug and handed it to
Steph.

The Valdez kitchen usually smelled of coffee in the morning, not the spicy odor that curled up under Steph's nose. She eyed the milky tea that steamed in her mug. "What is this?"

"It's chai, part of my new diet."

Steph set her mug down, harder than she intended. "And that's what couldn't wait?"

"No. I need to talk to you about the summer. But first, how's your mother?"

"Don't change the subject. Don't invite me over here at the crack of dawn on my day off and tell me you've decided to stay in San Francisco and work at Marty's father's firm this year."

"Actually, I'll be taking a full load of classes at USF."

"And that's supposed to make me feel better?" Steph brought the mug to her lips. When the tea scalded the roof of her mouth, she spat it into the sink.

"Sorry. I didn't realize it was so hot." Jaz took the mug from Steph and topped it off with cold tap water. "Here. Try it now."

Steph blew on the milky mixture and took a second, cautious sip, surprised the tea tasted peppery yet sweet. "It's good. Is it herbal?"

"No, it's a black tea, though this one is decaffeinated."

"Since when did you give up caffeine?" Steph stepped back and landed on Woofy's tail. He yelped. Then he forgave her with his doleful eyes. "I'm sorry," she told the Jack Russell terrier. Was it her imagination or had Woofy understood? His tail wagged him. He deposited Ratty, his well-chewed squeeze toy at her feet and pouted eloquently, then he barked, which was his suggestion that a game of fetch might be more fun than whatever Steph had in mind.

Steph sat at the kitchen table and played with Woofy as she waited for her friend to join them. "I am sorry," she told Jaz. "I know I'm overreacting. It's just that I was looking forward to you being home, to us working together. It'll be lonely here without you. But if you need to take classes, I understand. Just promise you'll visit so I'll have that to look forward to."

Jaz nodded. Then she looked away. Her chin quivered.

"What is it? What's wrong?"

"Papi." Jaz wiped her eyes with the back of her hand. "He was asleep last night when I got home, when I told Mami. He still doesn't know. I'm afraid he'll be upset."

"Why would your attending summer school upset him? I would think he'd be happy since it'll help you graduate sooner and move back here, unless of course you stay in San Francisco and marry Marty." A sense of dread came over Steph. "Oh God, that's it, isn't it?"

"The ceremony is in three weeks."

"Three weeks? But . . . why?"

"Because I love him?"

Steph narrowed her eyes. "Are Marty's parents pressuring you? Because if they are--"

"No. It's not that."

"Then why now, because no one--other than Pedro--cares about premarital sex anymore."

"I'm pregnant."

It was all Steph could do to maintain a stunned stare, the truth so unbelievable it had to be true. She felt as if she were trapped inside a fish bowl, her world watery, parabolic.

"It's why I didn't tell you until now. I wanted to do it in person. I knew you'd be upset, too." Jaz took the retractable leash from the coat rack and called Woofy. The leash snapped onto his collar, she pulled on a sweatshirt over her tank top and jeans. "We could all use some air." Woofy's toenails clicked as Jaz walked him out of the kitchen to the front door.

Steph followed. "But . . . how?" The words popped from her mouth like bubbles.

"Oh, the usual way. We were drunk, careless." Jaz sounded jittery, like the jays that screeched in the white firs outside the Valdez condo.

Steph regretted she wore only a thin cotton top and leggings. "How far along are you?"

"Ten weeks."

"Ten weeks?" Steph stopped in her tracks. The calendar pages flipped backwards in her head. "Then that night in Reno, when I told you about my abortion, you were--"

"Pregnant. Just like you. Or you were. And you have to believe me when I say I didn't tell you because your mother was hurt, and you were about to break up with Corey and drop out of school. It just seemed like your problems were far greater than mine."

Steph didn't buy this, though she said nothing. She walked quickly to catch up with Jaz who was trying to jerk her dog away from the Jeffrey pine near the Garcia condo. "Does he know?" Steph's gaze flicked from Pedro's house back to Jaz.

"Not yet, though Mami is probably telling Yessenia as we speak. I'm sure she'll be eager to share the news with him. It will prove her right, that I never should have left." Jaz grabbed Woofy by the collar in an effort to yank him away from the tree, but he wouldn't budge. Instead he turned his attention to the manzanita bush, in search of Tigre, Yessenia's cat. "Besides, Pedro and I have no claims on each other."

"Your family still thinks you're coming back here, that you'll marry him some day, not to mention the fact Pedro carries a torch for you the size of the Statue of Liberty's."

Jaz sighed. She wrapped her arms around herself as Woofy lifted his paw in a pointer's pose. From the opposite side of the manzanita bush Tigre crept out. Woofy dove through the bush and charged after the cat. Jaz jabbed the retract button on the plastic handle to no avail. The leash sang out as if a large fish was hooked on the line. "Steph, help me!" Jaz cried from where she lay, impaled on the thorny bush.

# Jazmín Valdez
## June 1, 1995

*Quien bien te quiere, te hará llorar*
*(The one who loves you best will make you cry)*

"Jazmín?" Pedro stood in the doorway of his condo, dressed in green and gold Pleasant Valley High School sweats. "You're home for the summer?"

"Not exactly. Could you please help?"

On the other side of the manzanita bush, Woofy jumped, nonstop. Tigre taunted him from the lowest branch of the Jeffery pine, the tiger-striped cat hissing and whipping his tail.

"Ven, Amigo." Pedro took the leash and reeled Woofy in as the dog leaped like a marlin.

"Thanks," Jaz told Pedro when he helped her out of the bush. "You wouldn't think Woofy would still be interested in Tigre after all these years."

"You know what they say about old dogs and new tricks." Pedro's eyes held hers a second too long. Then he crouched down to pet Woofy.

"I swear, Pedro, that's the last, absolutely last time I'm taking that dog for a walk."

"Tranquila, Chica. He's just showing Tigre who's the boss,

even if we both know it's pointless." Pedro rubbed Woofy's ears. "Remember how your mother tried to give him away?"

"How could I ever forget? Oh, Woofy, what am I going to do with you?"

The dog shivered, as he had the day she originally spotted him, barking in the snow outside the condo's window. She recalled how Mami brought him in, fussed over him, how she fed and played with the Jack Russell terrier until Papi got home. Papi agreed with Mami that the dog was lost rather than abandoned, but after weeks of advertising in the paper and on the radio, Jaz got her wish. Woofy was hers.

Never an easy pet, the dog's barking disturbed the neighbors. Then he bit the UPS man. This brought out the animal control people to make sure Woofy had tags and up-to-date shots. As a last resort, Mami offered him to a passing stranger. It had been an act of desperation, Jaz realized, her mother doing this only after a series of costly lock-ups. To this day, Woofy persisted in running out the front door to chase anything that moved, be it a cat or a car. What would he do if he caught one, she wondered. Still, there was no denying his escapades had caused her parents to spend what little money they had ransoming him, so while Jaz adored Woofy, she understood that for Mami and Papi he had been nothing but a nuisance.

"What a lovely little dog!" The unknown lady cooed to Jaz and Mami as they walked him one day. When the well-dressed woman bent to pet Woofy's head, Jaz winced, unsure if the dog would wag his tail or bite the hand that stroked him. Surprised, Jaz watched Woofy allow the woman to scratch his tummy, wriggling in delight at the touch of this total stranger.

A conspiratorial gleam shone in Mami's eyes. "He's good with children," she told the woman, a small mentira. Woofy was affectionate with Jaz and her brothers.

"How is he with other animals? Horses, for example?" The lady continued to stroke Woofy. The dog, usually high-strung, seemed to like it.

"Oh he's good, but . . ." Mami's pause seemed calculated to pique the lady's interest.

"But what?" she asked.

"We got to get rid of him. The landlord." Mami swiped at her cheeks for dramatic effect. "You know anyone who'd like a cute little doggy?"

"Mami . . ."

Jaz's mother gave her the evil eye.

"I would," the lady replied, "as long as he's okay with horses."

Woofy departed immediately. Jaz was banished to her room and threatened with punishment if her whimpering could be heard. Mami promised to get her a new dog, happy to be rid of Cujo, as she referred to Woofy. But Mami's plan failed. The woman reappeared on the Valdez's doorstep the following day, much to Jaz's joy and Mami's consternation.

"Why you return such a cute little doggy?" Mami asked.

"He attacked my horse! So viciously I had to get the vet up here from Madison." The woman thrust Woofy's leash toward Mami. "You lied to me, Mrs. Valdez." The woman turned on the heel of her riding boot. Annoyed, Mami gave Woofy the evil eye.

Woofy's fur was soft now, warm beneath Jaz's palm. She glanced at Pedro who had remained by her side, petting him. "Just because you're difficult doesn't mean I don't love you."

"Igualmente," Pedro smiled.

"I'll leave you two to stroll down memory lane."

Jaz shifted her eyes from the loving gaze of one friend to the hateful glare of another. "Oh God, Steph. I'm so sorry. I didn't mean to--"

"Ignore me?"

"Why don't we take Woofy for a walk?"

"I don't think so." Steph strolled over to Jaz. "'Bye Boyfriend," she told the dog, though her eyes were on Pedro. "Did Jaz mention she's only here for a day, because she's busy with finals and planning a wedding? Oops." Steph's hand went to her mouth, though it did little to hide her smile. "I guess she forgot to tell you about that since we're not invited."

"Of course you're invited," Jaz replied, her shoulder nearly dislocated when Woofy lit out after Tigre again. "Maybe I should take him home, since he's acting like such a psycho."

"No," Steph insisted. "Let's take Woofy for that walk, for old time's sake. He does seem a little stir crazy, like me, and as for Woofy acting like a psycho? Well, you know what they say about dogs, how they tend to take on the personalities of their owners."

Pedro fidgeted, obviously uncomfortable, but it was Steph's unapologetic stance that frightened Jaz more. Steph wouldn't forgive Jaz this time. Her decision to withhold the truth when Steph had faced the identical predicament a few weeks ago had changed their relationship. What Jaz feared had finally happened, even as their lives paralleled each other's in weird ways.

Gemelas del alma, cosmic twins, as Steph liked to joke. But this was no joke, Jaz thought as she watched her friend walk away. Were they condemned to share the same destiny, or had fate merely played another trick on them? It was spooky, Jaz's sense that they had both become pregnant the night of their twentieth birthdays. But while Steph had shared her despair over a terminated pregnancy and relationship, Jaz had decided to withhold her decision and go for the fairy-tale ending by marrying the rich boy from Orinda. And while she hadn't exactly lied that night in Reno, she knew she had been less than truthful. It explained Steph's cruel intentions toward her now, why her friend had gone to such lengths to expose her secret to Pedro, the only other person whose opinion mattered to Jaz as much as Steph's did.

Pedro's anguished gaze followed Steph down the driveway.

"Go after her," Jaz told him. "Here, give me Woofy's leash."

"No, I'll take him, because it's you who should go after her. It's been rough on Steph, being home again. It's you she needs to talk to."

"We tried that." Jaz felt disheartened, then distracted when Woofy began to jump again.

"Maybe we should take him on that walk," Pedro suggested. When Jaz nodded, they made their way through the condominium complex, past the pool and Jacuzzi, past the bulbs blooming in the flowerbeds until at last Pedro spoke. "You were going to tell me, weren't you?"

"Por supuesto," Jaz said, though her words felt like a lie.

When they reached the other side of the complex, Woofy darted out. Pedro yanked him back, saving the dog from coming under the wheels of a truck. The driver swerved then yelled, which only caused Woofy's agitation to grow. The dog yapped at the man until he drove off. The tires of his truck squealed as he laid a patch of rubber in the middle of the road.

"I swear, Pedro, I give up. Maybe we should take Woofy back to my house and have a civilized conversation there."

"I think it's better if we talk out here." They continued to circle the condos. Woofy's paws skittered back and forth across the asphalt. "How did your mother take it?" Pedro asked.

"Not well." Jaz dug her hands into her sweatshirt's pouch. It was chilly even in the sunlight. Early June was still early spring in Pleasant Valley.

"And your father?"

"He still doesn't know." She stopped walking to stifle a sob. "I'm so scared, Pedro."

"Of what?"

"That he'll never speak to me again. That he'll disown me."

"You're his little girl, Jazmín. He'll be thrilled to walk you down the aisle."

"Not when he realizes I'm getting married because I'm pregnant."

Pedro's silent astonishment became fuming anger, which was exactly how Papi would react. Jaz took Woofy's leash from Pedro. As she hurried away the dog strained against his collar, his breathing agonized, like Pedro's. She walked on, praying she wouldn't have to give either one of them CPR. "Martin Donahue, *the third*?" Pedro matched his stride to hers. She nodded and willed the tears to stop. "¡Qué pendejo!" That Pedro swore shocked her. Unlike Jaz, Pedro never swore. "Do you love him? Or are you marrying him because you have to?"

She shut her eyes and shook her head. What could she say? Did she love Marty? Did Marty love her? He had only said it once, the day he proposed. After that, their talks had been about parenthood and finishing school. Love had never entered into any of those conversations. "It's why I didn't want you to leave, Jazmín. I was afraid something like this might happen. And now that it has, I want you to know I still love you. I never stopped."

"Pedro. Please. It's too late."

"It's not."

Jaz wiped her eyes. "So what are you saying?"

"I'll take care of you. I'll love the baby as if it were my own."

"I'm not asking you to do that. What I'm asking for is your understanding."

And that she would never have. It was in his eyes. Love, yes. But understanding? He took Woofy's leash from her and stalked off, stopping when her dog sniffed the daffodils and snowdrops that grew in his mother's garden. "What I'll never understand," he told her when she reluctantly joined him, "is how you could leave your family, how you could leave me."

"Pedro--"

"But I forgive you, just like He forgives you. I told you that last summer, and I'll say it again." He faced her and took her in his arms. "Stay, Chica. Marry me, at my church."

She broke away. "This is exactly why I left. God, I'm barely a Catholic anymore, and you expect me to become a born-again Christian?"

"If you'd just accept Jesus Christ as Lord and Savior--"

"I have, Pedro. Catholics--even imperfect ones like me--have."

"Unless you are reborn of the spirit--"

"Carajo, I've been baptized. I've been to confession. I'm having the baby when I could have aborted--"

"You were going to abort? And now you won't because the rico decided to marry you?"

Was that the truth? Would she have come home and announced her pregnancy if Marty hadn't proposed? Jaz shut her eyes and pondered Steph's alternative reality, one that could have easily been her own.

"Tell him you've changed your mind, that you're in love with me, and that you're staying."

"But this isn't my home anymore."

"You think you're ever going to fit into that white man's world?"

"I have, Pedro."

"Yeah, right. Like when you changed your name, like when you became a cheerleader. As if we'll ever fit in, Jazmín. In your dreams."

"Look at you, still wearing your football sweats, playing stilo Americano because soccer wasn't cool. Don't tell me you didn't want to fit in. You did, Pedro. Just like me. And now I've done it again, at USF, and with Marty, and thanks to my scholarship, I'll be able to fit in classes, after the baby is born."

At first Pedro said nothing. Then he shook his head. "Funny. I thought you'd be a better mother than that."

"Because all good mothers stay home? Even your mother couldn't live up to that one."

"I'm just saying . . . come home."

"I'm going home. Tomorrow." She took the dog's leash from Pedro.

He stooped down and picked a bunch of snowdrops from his mother's garden. He caressed each tiny budding head, as if he understood he would have to content himself with what he could never hold. "I thought you loved me." He handed her the bouquet.

"I do love you, Pedro. I never stopped. But Marty loves me, too, and we're having a baby." She buried her face in the flowers. "What I need right now is a friend, because Steph . . ."

With a sigh of resignation he said, "Okay, I'll talk to her. Just know that my offer stands, in case the rico changes his mind." Pedro kissed her cheek and climbed the stairs to his condo. Jaz climbed the stairs to hers, knowing the rift with Steph would not be so easily mended.

The Stone Canyon Bar and Grill was nearly empty when she and Pedro entered it that evening in a last ditch effort to locate Steph. The bartender loaded up tapes as customers dribbled in. All were locals, recognizable from high school days. Some had stayed in town (like Pedro) while others had returned when things didn't work out (like Steph). It wasn't long before their friend came in on the arm of a stranger. Catching sight of Jaz and Pedro, Steph pretended not to see them and ensconced herself in the corner booth. "I'm going to the bathroom," Pedro announced, his not so subtle hint that if Jaz was going to beg Steph's forgiveness, she should do so now. But Jaz didn't. Instead she gazed longingly at her friend who had refused her phone calls all afternoon. Was this the end? Their families would be heartbroken. Every excuse Jenny made as to why Steph couldn't take Jaz's calls hurt. Why did Jaz cling so? Was it because she had never bothered to keep a journal, her friendship with Steph the only record she thought she'd ever need? There was Pedro, but their relationship was different. She understood this now, sad it had taken everything falling apart. Steph really was her sister, her gemela del alma.

Steph waved to several Anglo friends and invited them to join her. With that Jaz lost her nerve. She thought of Bert, Steph's father, who had always looked out for Jaz's family. It was Bert who had informed them about the amnesty program that allowed them to become legal residents, then citizens. But in spite of Bert's kindness and support, he had no idea what it was like to be an illegal alien, treated as if you were an invader from Mars. Perhaps that was why after living in this country for nearly twenty years, Papi had never really assimilated. His thoughts were still those of someone who lived in eternal exile and wished for nothing more than the opportunity to return home. It meant that if her friendship with Steph ended, Papi would take Steph's side. Such was his loyalty to Bert, the gabacho who had given him work. Jaz watched Steph laugh with her white friends and was pierced by another realization: no American could ever imagine the labyrinth of paperwork or the contemptuous treatment endured by people of color and foreign birth at the hands of U.S. Immigration--INS--in Fresno, California. The summons to appear would arrive in their post office box with only a day or two to spare. Always understanding, Bert gave Papi the time off whenever he requested it. But Dewey Mitchell, Mami's boss in those days, who counted on her and Yessenia to clean his condos before the next group of tourists arrived, would not. "I'm sorry, but what can I do?" Mami told Dewey at his office, Jaz and her brothers dragged along because they didn't have a phone.

"Last time you were gone a full week, Juana. During ski season."

"Yessenia will cover for me."

"That's no good," Dewey replied. "I've got fifty units that need to be cleaned. Yessenia can't handle it by herself. I'll have to hire someone else, someone who wants the work."

"No, Mr. Mitchell, please. You don't understand. They make us line up for hours. We can't even go to the bathroom, because if we do and they call us, we go to the end of the line."

"What I don't understand is why you'd risk a job that pays you eighty a day to go to Fresno again." With that Dewey Mitchell slammed the door to his office in Mami's face.

"¿Qué te pasa?" Jaz felt frightened when her mother just stood there.

At first Mami stared a hole through the door. Then she grabbed Jaz's hand, her knuckles white beneath her café con leche skin. "No te preocupes, mi vida. Juan P. Chuy. Vámonos."

A week later they returned from Fresno, to a morning routine that had altered. Mami was no longer the first one dressed. Instead, she remained in her bathrobe as she cooked and got Jaz and her brothers ready for school.

"Aren't you going to work today?" Jaz asked, reluctant to leave.

"No, mi amor. From now on, I work for me, not Dewey Mitchell. Jamás," she hissed, her defiant promise to herself, as she kissed Jaz good-bye and gently pushed her out the door.

*Jamás. Never again.* It whispered in Jaz's ear as Steph sat in the corner booth, surrounded by her Anglo friends. "You want a Coke?" Pedro was back from the bathroom. He motioned to the waitress who took their order. He held his hands up to the candle on their table, wide-eyed, as if he were a Boy Scout before a campfire. "Who's that guy over there with Steph?" To Jaz Steph's body language clearly communicated that whoever he was he was no stranger. "Is that beer she's drinking?" Pedro sounded ticked. "The bottle she's holding is brown."

"You mean you don't have a fake ID like every other local in town?"

"¿Los locos?" He jutted his chin at Steph's friends. "¡Ay, Dios! They're kissing! Tell me you recognize him, because Steph would never kiss a stranger, would she?"

"¿Quién sabe?" Jaz took a sip of the Coke the waitress brought.

"You two, you're sinvergüenzas. Steph was here last weekend, with a different crowd, kissing someone else I didn't know."

"So now you're checking up on her?"

Pedro hung his head. "Only because she's been partying hard lately." He downed his Coke. Did Pedro's attraction to Steph have something to do with saving her, or . . . ?

"Are you in love with her?"

Pedro's dark eyes bored into Jaz. "You just don't get it, do you?"

"That you're jealous?"

"No!"

"That you're morally superior to us? ¿Las chicas locas?"

"¡Tampoco!"

"Then if you're not in love with Steph, and you're not jealous, why can't you relax?" *And pay attention to me*, Jaz wanted to say, amazed by her own jealousy. "You realize this may be my last night in this stupid town."

"It's the blond hair, isn't it?"

"What?" She set her glass down with a *clack*.

"Martin Donahue, *the third*. Tu novio. He's blond, isn't he?"

"So what if he is?" Jaz twirled her glass.

"You and Steph. You've got this thing about blondes. I remember in high school, all the guy had to do was have blond hair, blue eyes, and play football, and you two were enamorada."

"You think I'm marrying Marty because he's a blonde?"

"No. You're marrying him because he got you pregnant." Pedro ordered a second Coke. Then he heaved a great sigh. "Look. I'm sorry. That was harsh, as Steph would say. But you should remember who you are, Jazmín, and where you come from."

"As if you'd ever let me forget."

"So are you two going to fight all night or what?" Steph sauntered over with her fair-haired stranger. "But then I guess that's Jaz's way of saying good-bye because it's safer, isn't it?" Steph's companion shored her up. His hand crept perilously close to a breast barely covered by her halter-top. "It's much safer than telling the truth, not that Jaz would know the truth if it came up and bit her in the butt."

Pedro glared at Steph. "You're as bad as she is." He grabbed his green and gold letterman's jacket off the back of his chair. "I'm out of here."

"Me, too," said Steph's mystery man, planting one on her, giving her plenty of tongue.

"My bus leaves early, and it's obvious you don't want to talk, so . . ."

Steph's hand was on Jaz's arm. "So talk."

"Only if you'll be my Maid of Honor."

Steph sat down. "All right. I'll come to your wedding. I'll even ride over with your mom and dad, because I have a feeling Pedro won't be bringing me."

"It might just be Mami. I'm not sure Papi will go, either." Jaz didn't want to cry in front of Steph, but when her friend hugged her, the tears flowed. "As long as you can forgive me, even if Papi and Pedro can't, I'll be all right." She studied her friend's eyes. "You have to believe me. I wanted to tell you that night in Reno, but I couldn't, not after what you'd been through."

"It's okay, Chica," Steph said quietly. "I'll be there."

"Thanks, because if none of my family shows up, Carolyn Donahue will be thrilled."

"Do candles blow out when your mother-in-law walks into a room?"

Jaz laughed and cried simultaneously.

"So why not stay here and marry Pedro? That's what you talked about today while you walked Woofy, isn't it?"

Jaz's mouth opened then shut. That Steph would know this should come as no surprise."You're still in love with him, aren't you?"

Jaz nodded.

"Then why deny it? Or him?"

"We'd fight all the time. We'd make each other miserable."

"What about Marty? Are you sure you love him, that you want to become Mrs. Martin Donahue, the third?"

Jaz flicked at her eyes. "As sure as I am about anything right now." She kissed Steph's cheek and whispered, "Ciao, Chica."

"No, Jaz. Hasta pronto. Y que te vaya bien."

# Stephanie Bengochea
## December 14, 1995

*In a small town, past and present stand side by side, almost too close to
tell the difference*
*--Terry Teachout*

The blizzard blew Juana in as it blew out every candle in the
living room. *La Bruja*, Pedro's voice whispered in Steph's ear.
As she leaned against the front door to close it, Steph wondered if
the candles in her bedroom still burned. "Esteph," Juana kissed her
cheek. "A little something for you." From her tote bag Juana pulled
out a damp gift. "¡Feliz Navidad!" The package in Steph's hand was
small and compact. It had the solid heft of a book.

"Any word?" Mom asked from where she sat on the couch, crocheting a pastel afghan.

"I just talkin' to Jazmín, and she tellin' me she hope to finish her
finals before the nene come." Juana brushed snow from her short,
spiky hair. She hung her coat in the mudroom.

"Wishful thinking," Steph murmured. Magical, in fact, that Jaz
thought she could fit a baby into the schedule she juggled.

Juana straightened from taking her boots off, her tote bag slung
over an arm. "You tellin' me somethin' I don't already know, like
you and Jazmín, you talkin' again?" She looked hopeful.

"Sí, Madrina." The happiness that flooded Juana's face was the best gift Steph could ask for, but the silence that followed was awkward. It was as if Juana expected Steph to share the details, something she had no intention of doing. Steph twirled a loose thread from the hem of her sweater around a finger. "Val and Char made Christmas cookies. Would you like one?"

"No, gracias. I just droppin' off gifts in case I gotta go to San Francisco in a big hurry. But with all this snow . . ." Juana shook her head and padded off in her stocking feet to the living room. She plopped her tote bag in front of the couch. The bag bulged as she scavenged through it. At last she came up with the gift she was looking for. She thrust it at Mom.

"You shouldn't have," Mom said, though her hazel eyes glowed.

"Of course I should, when you been so good to me. Now it my turn." The box Juana held dripped on the floor, on the wood Steph should have spent the morning waxing. Juana pressed her gift on Mom. "Open it. Please." Mom removed the limp ribbon and tore off the soggy paper. Dye stained her fingertips. When she lifted the lid and saw nothing but an envelope on wafer-thin cotton, she looked up. "Por favor." Juana winked at Steph. Mom slid the card out and read it, only to drop the card on the water-colored afghan that pooled in her lap.

"What is it?" Steph set down her unopened present from Juana.

"My way of helpin' out," Juana said.

"With what?" The skin on the back of Steph's neck prickled.

"Have you discussed this with Antonio? Or Bert?" Mom's fingers tapped Juana's card.

"No, because it my present to you."

"Would somebody please tell me what's going on?" Steph demanded.

Mom handed the card to her. "Juana's offered to work for you at the restaurant."

"What about your business?" Steph asked Juana.

"Por favor, Esteph, let me--"

"No." Steph backed away. She pleaded with her eyes for Mom's help.

"Stephie's right, Juana. You don't have time to do this."

"Sure I do. I still clean. I just cut back so I can work at Bert's, too. And as for me, no complain." Juana seemed undaunted by the anxious look Steph cast in Mom's direction. "We don't need so much money now. Jazmín, she got that scholarship, and a husband, too. And Juan P., he workin' at the condos. And Chuy, he livin' at home, drivin' down to Madison, takin' classes, just like Pedro and Esteph do."

Steph widened her eyes at Mom, but Mom remained quiet, her expression pensive, that of a porcelain doll. Steph handed the card back to Juana. "It was my decision to come back, Madrina. Don't you think it should be my decision to leave?"

"And now you can, mi hijita, 'cause I take your place."

"Did it ever occur to you I might not want to leave?" Juana fanned herself with her card. Mom set aside the afghan and reached for her cane. "Here." Steph sprang to Mom's aid.

"I've got it." Mom struggled up off the couch. "Come on, Stephie. Let's put that cider on and get those cookies, and then we'll discuss this. Calmly." Mom limped away.

"Are you serious?" Steph blasted through the kitchen's swinging door, not caring if Juana heard what she and Mom said. "I thought you needed me here. I thought you wanted my help."

"I do, but what about your education, your boyfriend?"

"Pedro?" Juana interrupted from the doorway.

"No, Corey. The boy in San Diego," Mom told Juana over Steph's shoulder.

Relieved when Mom escorted Juana out of the kitchen, Steph

punched down the dill rye dough that had been rising in a bowl on the sideboard. Its yeasty smell permeated the dishtowel she had used to cover it. From the pantry she took a bottle of cider and poured it into a pot, its *glug, glug, glug* strangely comforting. From the spice rack she gathered cloves, nutmeg, and cinnamon sticks, which she tossed into the cider. She tried to ignore Mom and Juana as they discussed her on the other side of the door. Snippets of their conversation, with words like "depressed" and "lonely," seeped through the cracks and set Steph on a slow boil with the cider.

The cookies arranged on a platter, she continued to eavesdrop, marveling at how easily Juana worked her magic on Mom. But it wasn't long before La Bruja cast her spell over Steph as well. She had to admit it was tempting to take Juana up on her offer. Still, Steph knew that to do this she would have to act fast. The university officials would be gone in a matter of days.

"I think it could work," Mom told Steph as she carried the platter of cookies to the living room. "Juana wouldn't do it for long."

"Mom . . . it could be months. You're still . . ." *on a cane*, Steph almost blurted out.

"Don't worry," Juana said. "I work as long as Jenny need me."

"Have you talked to Antonio about this?" Steph asked Juana.

"Daddy will talk to him," Mom said.

"So Antonio can't say no?" Steph plonked the platter of cookies on the coffee table. Mom followed Steph into the kitchen, her face taut. "Antonio didn't want Jaz to go to college," Steph told her, "so why on earth would he allow Juana to work for me?"

"Because it's time." Mom hobbled toward Steph. "You deserve a life of your own. You've already missed two quarters."

"What difference will two more make? I'll go back."

"Will you?" There was fear in Mom's eyes. Or was it regret? She had married Dad after a single season of working at the ski area by day and in his fledgling burger joint by night. She had never returned to college.

"I'll go back, Mom. I promise. But not until you're better."

"I won't be better until you go back." Mom's expression fragmented into a mosaic of love and guilt, each tile grouted into its separate place. She leaned on her cane and tugged on the loose thread in Steph's sweater. "If you put that in my room, I'll fix it."

"Like you want to fix my life?"

"For crying out loud, Stephie, let me help." The skin beneath Mom's freckles reddened, a sign that like a burner, Mom was just warming up. "I'm worried about you," she said, unable to keep her voice low. "You're unhappy here, yet you don't want to go back to San Diego. Why?" Steph shrugged and turned away. "It's Corey, isn't it?" Steph nodded as she gathered teacups from the sideboard for the mulled cider that bubbled on the stove. "He called again." Steph ladled the cider into the porcelain teacups. "I'm running out of excuses."

"I know, Mom, and I'm sorry," Steph set the cups on a tray, "but you can't fix us, and neither can Juana. Besides, why should I get my hopes up only to have Antonio Valdez crush them? He'll never go along with Juana's crazy scheme."

"He might if Daddy were to insist."

"Which Dad won't, because I would never ask him to do that."

"Well, if it'll help you to get on with your life, then I will."

Steph carried the tray. The cider spilled when she pushed the swinging door open with her shoulder. "What if I told you that I don't want to leave, that I'm happy here?"

"Take Juana's offer." Mom held the door with her free hand. "I'll talk to Daddy."

"¡Hola chicas!" Juana greeted Steph's sisters as they came into the mudroom. Val and Char shed their race team jackets and ski pants they had worn home over their restaurant uniforms. "I got gifts for you," Juana sang out as she searched through her tote bag.

DEBBIE BOUCHER

She brought out two small boxes with a flourish.

Val and Char bounded in to open their presents. "Scrunchies! Gracias," they cried, kissing Juana's cheek before they pulled off their ski hats and gathered their hair into ponytails. "I make 'em just like I do when Jazmín and Esteph is your age."

With their slight builds and their long dark hair, Val and Char reminded Steph of how she and Jaz must have looked when they were still bussing tables at Bert's.

Juana turned to Steph. "So where's your gift from me?" Steph looked around, embarrassed her present had been kicked under the coffee table and had left a water stain on the wood floor. "No lo abres frente de los demás." Juana motioned to the staircase.

Steph led the way, wondering why Juana wanted her to open her gift away from her mom and sisters. In her attic bedroom, the candles still burned, forgotten when she dashed downstairs to answer the door. Shocked, she was about to extinguish them when they appeared to snuff themselves out. *A draft*, she told herself.

Juana had already breezed into the room. She sat on the sleigh bed, her eyes on the package Steph held in her hands. "Open it. Please." Steph sank down beside Juana and picked at the tape. "Just like Jazmín," Juana sighed. "She never rip the paper."

Steph digested yet another similarity she had failed to notice over the years. She slipped the book from its wrapping and read its title. "*Spiritual Astrology?*" She cocked her head at Juana. "You know I don't believe in this . . . stuff."

"Of course you do. Es tu destino."

"My destiny is to believe in astrology? That's just . . . silly."

"Why you sayin' this to me, mi hijita." Juana looked hurt.

"Because . . . it makes no sense. So let's just leave it at that. That we agree to disagree, because it's obvious we don't believe in the same things."

"So now you sayin' you don't believe in me? What about Pedro?

128

Do you believe in what he and Yessenia believe?"

"I guess I do," Steph said, though she realized how unconvincing this would sound, having voiced her fears and doubts to Juana too many times.

"Well, then I just makin' sure you get both sides, ¿eh?" Juana rose, ethereal as always. She glided to the nightstand. Her fingers grazed Steph's new Bible. "From Yessenia?"

"From Pedro."

"You goin' to church with him? I don't see you at Mass no more."

"We've been going to the Valley Church."

"And Yessenia's lettin' him do that? Skip services at Evangelico?"

"We like the singing."

"Then come back to St. John's. Mariachi Mass is six o'clock on Saturday."

"I like the Valley Church."

Juana sat beside Steph on the sleigh bed. "You like Pedro."

Steph started up. "I should go. See if Mom needs anything."

Juana pulled her back down. "You go see Corey, and Jazmín, after the nene come."

"Why are you doing this?" Tears welled up faster than Steph could banish them.

"'Cause it's always somethin'." Juana kissed Steph's cheek. "One excuse after another. We talk more about it when you know what you doin'," Juana said, and then she left.

Out in the driveway Pedro pulled up in his truck, but instead of coming to the door as he usually did, he honked the horn long and hard. Steph raced downstairs past Mom who sat in the living room on the couch, crocheting. In the mudroom, Steph put on her jacket and squatted down to lace her boots. "Did you call?" Mom's crochet hook slowed.

"I'm reinstated."

"Housing?" Mom set the afghan aside.

"Handled."

"Corey?" Mom was up, shuffling toward her without the cane.

"No answer when I tried."

"And just how hard did you try?" A second, longer beep warned her Pedro was about to leave. "You tell him to drive slowly, Stephie, to drive carefully. Promise?"

"I promise." Steph popped up and kissed Mom's cheek. Then she ran out the door, only to slip and nearly fall. When she opened the passenger side door, Pedro launched into a sermon she had given him ample time to prepare.

"We're going to be late--thanks to you--and it's finals."

"Tranquilo." She slammed her door and buckled her seat belt. He backed down the steep icy driveway. "Mom was quizzing me."

"¿El subjuntivo?"

"About returning to UCSD."

He gripped the steering wheel. "When?"

"Winter Quarter."

"Which means you'll be leaving in two weeks."

"I knew you'd be upset."

"I'm not upset."

"Then go ahead, Pedro. Quiz me. On the subjunctive."

"Maybe I should, since you always butcher that one."

"Gee, do I? And here I thought I was finally getting the hang of it. So be honest with me. How often do you and your mom use it?"

He looked at her oddly. "About as often as you and your mother use it in English." Her question suddenly seemed petty. They drove through Pleasant Valley in silence, the streets white except where

Cal Trans had peppered the snow with cinders to provide traction. Once they were on 395, Pedro said, "I'm surprised you'd leave while your mother's still on a cane."

"There's someone who's willing to cover for me at Bert's."

"Your fairy godmother?" She appreciated his deceit, the façade he didn't care about her leaving. Still, it bothered her that he would only let her get so close. She had hoped there would be more to their relationship with Jaz out of the picture. A squall set in. Pedro followed a snowplow. Orange stakes kept him from running off the road. With the loss of elevation, the visibility improved. The asphalt reappeared and spread before them like an inkblot. "Another week and we'll see nothing but headlights coming up the highway," he said. "You wouldn't leave before New Year's, would you?"

"No, but classes begin January eighth, so . . ."

"So who's your fairy godmother?"

"Juana."

"¿La Bruja?" Pedro's lips curled. "Juana knows nothing about being a waitress."

"Well, she seems to think she does. Or that she can learn. Mom and Dad don't seem to care, which makes me wonder if Juana offered to do it for free."

Pedro gave her a sidelong glance. "Mr. Malone used to say there's no such thing as a free lunch. Other than what your parents have to offer us at Bert's."

"I thought you liked my parents."

"I do."

"Then what is it about Juana that you don't like?"

"She's not a Christian."

"She goes to Mass."

"Catholics worship idols."

Once again silence fell, like the mantle of snow that blanketed the mountains, their peaks crimson in the diminishing light. Steph longed for the peace that passeth all understanding, but she couldn't let Pedro's comments go. His certainty about everything made her feel uncertain. "There was a time, not long ago, when Catholics thought they were the one true church, and that if you believed differently, you were going to hell. I'd like to think that time has come and gone."

"Juana's into the occult," he said, his final verdict on the subject.

Steph thought about her Christmas gifts, *Spiritual Astrology* and the Bible. Like strange bedfellows they lay side by side on her nightstand, untouched. She had refused to crack either one of them because they came from people who vied not only for her heart, but also for her soul. "And just what exactly is the occult to you? The Halloween carnival we enjoyed as kids?"

"It glorifies witches."

"It's a harmless tradition."

"You see? Juana's poisoned you, just like Jazmín, with all that gemela del alma crap."

"Is it swearing if you don't take the Lord's name in vain?"

Pedro was not amused. "Maybe we should practice el subjuntivo."

"Maybe we should talk about tomorrow night."

"You said you'd go."

"I've changed my mind."

"Mamá was looking forward to having you there with your new Bible. Catholics know nothing of the word of God."

"There's a Bible study at St. John's. I think I'll go there--with Mom."

Pedro shot her a frazzled look. "Why are you trying to pick a fight with me?"

"Because it might make it easier to leave you in a couple of weeks."

"It's that Corey guy, isn't it?"

"*No*, it isn't."

"He called you again, didn't he?"

"Yes, but I haven't taken his calls."

"But once you're back in San Diego, you'll see him."

"With twenty thousand students?" Steph laughed. "I doubt that."

"He'll find you. I know I would. Is that what you want?"

"What I want is to get out of here, Pedro. To go back to school." His hands tightened on the steering wheel. "There's nothing left for me here."

"Nothing, or no one?"

Steph studied his profile. "Come with me." He eyed her skeptically. "We could live together." Aware her suggestion made him uncomfortable, she added, "As roommates," working hard not to sound sarcastic. She wanted him to take her seriously. "We might have to share a bathroom. Think you could handle that?"

"If you're as slow in the bathroom as you are at leaving the house, I'd never get to class on time. You and Jazmín, you really are alike in that way. Talk about a tortuga." His smile faded. "Still is, I guess. Mamá says Juana told her Jazmín is overdue. Is something wrong?"

"No." Steph felt irked the conversation had turned as it often did to Jaz and the baby. "The doctor screwed up on her due date. It's not like her pregnancy was planned."

"So you've talked to her?"

"We've exchanged a few e-mails. You'll be happy to know that I took your advice and made the first move." Jaz's latest missive had spoken of suffering through exams with back pain, of sleepless nights with false labor. Steph closed her eyes. What if she had accepted Corey's offer to marry her? What if she hadn't married him but had kept his child? Would Pedro have proposed to her as he had to Jaz? But that wasn't what obsessed Steph. What kept her awake nights was the terrible knowledge that she should be pregnant, too. If only she had talked to Jaz before making her decision. Steph felt sure their daughters--yes, daughters--who had been conceived on the same night would have been born on the same day, the next generation of twin souls. The legacy would have continued as inevitable and incredible as were their parallel lives. Pedro's truck fishtailed on a patch of ice. He eased off the brakes and downshifted to slow their descent. With her eyes wide open, Steph's dream of raising a child dissolved. And while it convinced her there was free will, she felt damned to her self-imposed limbo. Ironic that even though she and Jaz were speaking again, Steph was aware that at least for now, their fates were separate and irrevocable.

"I'm glad you're in touch with Jazmín again," Pedro said.

"What about you? Do you and Jaz still talk?"

"Not really."

"Why?"

"She's married. It's over." The sadness with which he said this only added to Steph's sense of loss, to the gloom that deepened with the darkness. If she had learned anything in her months of attending church with Pedro, it was that she should forgive Jaz and forget their differences. Maybe then she could forgive herself. She removed her jacket, warm now, as she waited for some further observation on Pedro's part. She had grown accustomed to his protracted silence, but tonight it made her squirm. If he knew she had aborted Corey's child, would he still want her to stay? "So what about us, Steph?" he asked. "Are we over?"

*No*, she admitted to herself, even though she knew they had no future. Steph recalled what Jaz had said, the summer before their sophomore years. That Jaz couldn't be with Pedro because they'd fight all the time. Perhaps it had been love at first slight for Steph as well, though what she told him was this. "We're friends, Pedro. Just like you will be again with--"

"Jazmín?" He gave her a look that said he doubted that.

Steph reached for his hand. "You know how much you mean to me." She wondered if he had any idea. He'd rescued her from a deep depression. He'd been the reason she stopped drinking and sleeping around. He'd inspired her to consider becoming a Christian. Steph had yet to share this with anyone. She knew her parents suspected something. She rarely attended Mass with them anymore. "It's why going back to school is difficult," she told Pedro. "It's why I want you to come with me. We both need to leave. It's one thing to live here like my parents do, by choice, with a family and a thriving business. It's another to be stuck here like we are, with little hope of better education or opportunity."

"Mamá has had nothing but opportunity here. She loves running the cleaning business with Juana. She doesn't feel stuck."

"Maybe not, but don't you? Don't you want something more?"

"What I want is to marry a good Christian woman." His eyes penetrated hers, as if he could read her soul. "What I want is someone to love, someone who will love me back, someone to share my life with, my beliefs. Someone who will pass those values on to our children."

"Who will home school them and control their every thought?"

"Who will protect them from evil."

Steph felt the words well up, molten as the lava trapped beneath the ground they drove over, the lava that rattled doors and windows at times to remind everyone that it, too, might explode. "There's a great big world out there, and you seem to have no interest in it." Pedro's jaw tightened as he drove across volcanic tablelands lightly dusted with snow, the tuff cliffs ashen in the twilight. At the Madison city limits, she asked, "Aren't you the least bit curious?

Don't you want to open your mind to new ideas and new places?" Her question reverberated in the cab as he pulled into the parking lot before the single row of squat portables that was Madison's sorry excuse for a community college.

"I love Pleasant Valley, Steph, the whole East Side. I thought you loved it, too."

"I think I appreciate it more from a distance." She wrenched her door open. "I'm leaving in January, Pedro, whether you come with me or not."

# Jazmín Valdez Donahue
## December 15, 1995

*Amor con amor se paga*
*(Love can only be repaid with love)*

Maria Stephanie Donahue was born December 15, 1995, at UCSF's Children's Hospital in San Francisco. Jaz went into labor as she wrote her last final late that afternoon. Her essay jotted into a blue book, she turned in the exam and called Marty by cell phone (an early Christmas gift), saying she was on her way to the hospital. Her water broke in the lobby. By six, Marty was coaching her, timing her contractions. By seven, they were parents. Excited and exhausted, they celebrated their daughter's perfection and called their families. Carolyn and Martin, Senior came over from Orinda that night, eager to meet their granddaughter, though it wasn't until the sixteenth, the day Jaz was released from the hospital, that Mami arrived by bus.

"Ay, mi amor. ¡Qué preciosa!" Mami peeked inside the tiny bundle Jaz cuddled in her arms. "Maria. ¡Qué bella! Como la mamá de Papi, Abuelita."

"Could you take the diaper bag for me?" Jaz asked Mami as they stood in front of the hospital with Marty and his mother waiting for Martin, Senior to bring the car from the garage.

"I'll get it," said Marty.

"No, I'll get it," said Carolyn.

*No, I'll get it,* Jaz wanted to scream, tired of the circus-like atmosphere. The drive to the apartment on Golden Gate Avenue was brief, and once the senior Donahues had departed, Jaz and Marty settled in, with Mami there to play nursemaid to Maria.

Papi didn't come. According to Mami, he couldn't leave the restaurant during the busy holidays. But that was a lie. Steph had complained to Jaz in a recent e-mail that the restaurant was slow. Papi hadn't come because he hadn't forgiven her for marrying Marty instead of Pedro. The last time she and Papi had spoken was the day he walked her down the aisle. After that, he all but ignored her, treating her as he did Abuelita, as if Jaz were a dead relative. She wondered if Mami lit votives in her bedroom on el día de los muertos, if she decorated that dusty shrine to mourn the loss of her only daughter.

Jaz's first week as a mother passed softly, like wind over water. She felt as if she were playing house, Mami present at the tea party they packed away at the end of each day. Maria's baptism took place on Friday, the twenty-second. The priest, an elderly Irishman, made the sign of the cross on Maria's forehead as if he marked her with indelible ink and claimed her as his own. His gaze fastened to Maria's foggy eyes, he presented her proudly to those gathered at Saint Ignatius. Mami was proud to be the grandmother and comadre. Her blouse drooped under the weight of all the religious medals she wore, the sign of the water bearer beneath The Fisherman's cross. There would be no dereliction of duty on her part. She would see to it that the ways of the church and the stars were honored. She saw no conflict in this. There was no need to abandon one set of beliefs for another, Mami told the senior Donahues as they walked back to the Golden Gate Avenue apartment. Martin, Senior and Carolyn looked at each other askance. Once they left, Mami insisted Marty go out and buy a tree. She decorated the potted pine with booties, a cap, matching mittens, and a sweater, all knitted by Jenny, her afghan draped around the base. On the twenty-third Mami departed by bus to Pleasant Valley, a route Jaz feared she would no longer travel.

# Rosa Rodriguez
## *December 23, 1995*

*I was born to be born, to remember the steps of all who approach, of*
*what pounds at my chest like a trembling new heart*
*--Pablo Neruda*

"She had the baby, didn't she?" I slide my cross and my Aquarius medal back and forth along their chain. Silvia nods. My cousin loads books into bags while I go through my clothes. "I should buy some new dresses. Mine are all frayed at the hem, unraveling, like I am." Silvia nods again and heaves a sigh. "I'm sorry, Prima, but I have to do this. I have to move, even though you don't want me to." Silvia says nothing. "Is the baby a girl or a boy?"

"A girl," Silvia answers. "As usual you were wrong."

"It's an imperfect art. Like law or medicine, it improves with practice."

"It's a pseudo science, Rosa."

This from my cousin who puts her faith in Tarot cards, though what I say is this. "My clients don't seem to think so. They say my timing is impeccable, that my intuition is accurate, accompanied by a knowing that is the gift of second sight."

"Not when it comes to Angie," Silvia replies, her patience wearing thin. She stoops to roll her stockings, which prompts me to do the same. Then she walks to my desk and fingers my typewriter. "When are you going to buy a computer?"

"When I find someone who has the time and patience to show me how to use it. Are you going to give me the birth data," I ask Silvia, "or do I have to impose on Manuel again?" Señora Sandoval's husband is due any minute. He has a truck in which he will move my half of the furniture to an apartment on Golden Gate Avenue. Normally I wouldn't be able to live in such an expensive part of town, but one of my clients just bought a run-down Victorian divided into two units when his stock options doubled the day after his company's initial IPO, something I helped him plan. He was so pleased with my forecast he offered to let me live in the ground floor apartment for free. Well, not exactly free. Like Manuel, I will offer Eduardo advice "in perpetuity." I think those were the words he used. That Eduardo, he's so guapo, so nice. If only I could introduce him to Angelica. Maybe then she'd see the light and leave Cruz, even though it will be harder to do now with the nena. "What's the baby's name?" I ask Silvia.

"Maria. Maria Rosario Cardoza de Rodriguez."

"Como Abuelita." I bring a fist to my mouth to stop my lips from quivering.

"Como tú, Rosa." Silvia takes a box of gum from her dress pocket. She offers me a piece. When I shake my head, Silvia pops a Chiclet in her mouth. "Although Angie reversed the order to Maria Rosario instead of Rosario Maria. It proves that Angie still loves you."

"Then why won't she come home?" I grab a doily from the sofa to wipe my eyes. "It's Christmas. We should be celebrating, not avoiding each other."

"For the same reason you have decided to leave." Silvia waits for me to level my gaze to hers. "We all need our space." She helps me pack up my Smith-Corona. "You really think you can make a living in the new year by doing business forecasts and no longer doing hair?"

I shrug. "Just promise me one thing, that when you take Maria Rosario's chart to Angelica, you tell my daughter how sorry I am. You tell her how much I love her, how much I miss her, how much I want to be a part of her life."

"Te prometo," Silvia says, though I wonder if my cousin will even deliver my Christmas gift. It doesn't matter. I will cast Maria Rosario's natal chart anyway. I need to know how to help my granddaughter even if it must be from afar. When I pull on my coat and walk to the front door, Silvia asks, "Where are you going? Manuel will be here any minute."

"To Mission Delores, one last time." It's the perfect name for that sad old church where I will light my candles and pray: for Angelica, for her nena, for Silvia, and for me.

# Stephanie Bengochea
## January 2, 1996

*To see what is right and not do it is cowardly--Confucius*

The day after New Year's, Yessenia came into the restaurant. Steph watched to see if Pedro or his younger brothers would come in with her, but Yessenia stood alone. She smiled at Steph and walked toward her. "Table for one, please."

"Take your pick, Yessenia. It's a slow night."

She pointed to the greenhouse, "Perhaps you could sit with me. I don't like eating alone."

Steph eyed the Bible Yessenia had brought. "I'll see what I can do," Steph said. In the kitchen Dad worked alone. He chopped onions on a cutting board he kept surgically clean, a task he usually delegated, but there was no need for a prep cook tonight. Bad weather had kept the tourists away over the holidays. Business was off, way off. It explained why Dad waged his knife strokes with a vehemence that made Steph fear for the ends of his fingers. The kitchen was empty. Every surface from the stainless steel counters to the polished concrete floor was too bright and shiny "Dad?" Steph held her hand up to ward off the glare. "Could I take a break?"

"You just got here," he replied, without looking up.

"I know, but Yessenia's out there, and she wants to talk. And I don't want to appear rude. I leave the day after tomorrow."

"Hey, Beti. Front and center," Dad called to the only other employee at work that night.

On the back steps of the kitchen Beti sat, smoking. "Yeah, yeah, yeah." She crushed her cigarette and flicked it away. Then she slung a clean apron around her thick waist.

Dad leveled a withering gaze at Steph. "Make it snappy."

*Yeah, yeah, yeah.* The words rang in Steph's head as she left the kitchen to sit with Yessenia and wait for Beti to take their order.

"So, what'll it be, ladies?" Beti whipped out her order pad a little too fast.

"A Bert's burger," said Yessenia, "and a lemonade, please."

"A grilled vegetable sandwich for me," said Steph.

Beti snatched the menus from Steph and Yessenia's hands and hustled off.

"I hope I haven't caused you any trouble," Yessenia said.

"She was on her break. Dad suggested I--"

"Make it snappy? Then I'll get right to the point. Pedro doesn't want you to leave."

"Only because Pedro knows he should be going with me."

"My son knows his place, and his place is here."

"Just like my place is here?" Steph studied Yessenia.

"Your mother isn't well. Juana has a family, a business to run."

"It's Mom and Juana who want me to go. They understand I'll come back when I finish my education. They trust me, Yessenia. Why can't you?"

"Ay Dios, Estefanía, it is not a matter of trust."

"Then what?" Steph could suffer Yessenia's hangdog expression no longer.

"It's a matter of respect. But since you don't seem to understand that, then I guess there is nothing left to say." Yessenia opened her Bible and began to read it.

"I'm sorry if I seem disrespectful, but knowing where you belong is not the same as knowing who you are. And I think the only way to find out is by leaving what is good and safe behind. Because once you return you appreciate it so much more. You understand there is a difference, that you've made a choice, and you're no longer willing to accept life as a matter of luck or fate or, as you would say, God's will."

When Steph got up to leave, Yessenia said, "I'm surprised Antonio would go along with Juana's plan to take your place. But then I guess La Bruja has worked her magic on him as well."

"Stop calling her that. She's your friend, your partner. It's insulting."

"It's a nickname, Estefanía. Nothing more. Juana calls me Gorda, and I don't take offense. It's a term of endearment. I would have thought your Spanish classes would have covered that part of our culture by now."

Steph believed otherwise, but she kept her mouth shut.

Beti returned, only to slap Steph's order down on the table. "So, now you've decided to work and waste good food? Give me a break." Steph sat down and bit into her grilled vegetable sandwich. "Will there be anything else?" Beti asked Yessenia.

"No, gracias. Es mi culpa que trabajas sin reposo." Yessenia's words failed to appease Beti. The Chilena left in a huff. Yessenia sighed. "Pedro tells me you refuse to see him."

"He knows I hate good-byes."

"Which is why I came, to invite you to Bible study tomorrow night."

"It's my last night here. I should be with my family."

"Por favor, Estefanía," Yessenia said between bites. "He already misses you."

"And I already miss him. He's been a wonderful friend."

"It seems to me you have become more than friends."

Steph put her sandwich down. "Is that what bothers you?"

Yessenia sipped her lemonade.

"It is, isn't it?" Steph stood. "It's why you're here. You're happy I'm leaving, because I'm a threat now, just like Jaz was." Steph gathered their dishes. "Let him go, Yessenia."

"Pedro doesn't want to go."

"But he does, though he won't go without your blessing."

Yessenia returned her attention to her Bible.

Steph carried their dishes to the kitchen. She dumped them in the sink with such a clatter Dad looked up from where he stood at the grill. A wet cloth in hand, she returned to Yessenia's table. "What's that saying everyone's so fond of at Evangelico and the Valley Church? Let go and let God?" Steph picked up Yessenia's Bible. She took large swipes with the cloth before she set the Bible down on the damp table. Back in the kitchen, Steph announced, "Break's over."

Dad gave her a weary look and shoved the *Fields of Gold* cassette into the sound system. Beti removed her apron and fished a cigarette from the pack that bulged in her skirt's back pocket. With a wry smile, the Chilena headed to the back steps for a smoke.

Steph bumped into Corey at the Price Center her first day of classes. They chatted, but she begged off seeing him until the weekend, promising to go to Windansea to watch him surf.

Saturday morning he picked her up early and took her to where they first met. That golden afternoon was a far cry from this silver dawn. Steph gathered her knees to her chest as she sat atop dun colored cliffs that undulated down to the water, La Jolla's petrified sand dunes. A salt breeze blew in from the ocean. It stung her face and bare legs. Covered in white caps the water flashed as if it were a gigantic writhing fish. By nine, Corey gave up and paddled to shore. "Are you cold?" he asked as he scampered up the cliffs.

"A little. How about you?"

"Just bummed. It's completely blown out." He peeled off his wet suit and strapped his board to his truck's rack. "How about some coffee?" At the Starbucks downtown, she ordered a latte while he ordered a mocha. They sat outside at a small metal table in wire mesh chairs. Their beverages warmed their hands. "So, is it good to be back?" He looked as tentative as he sounded.

"I guess." She sipped her latte, the smell of rotting seaweed strong, incongruous in that concrete canyon of upscale stucco storefronts. What had once been shiny seemed dull and tarnished. Even the sky was no longer platinum but the color of the dirty pockmarked sidewalk beneath Steph's flip-flopped feet. What was she doing here? What was she doing with him? There was no going back. Surely Corey understood that. He sat beside her, expectant, though she said nothing more. Then he downed his mocha and tossed his cup into a nearby trashcan.

"Maybe I should take you back to the dorm."

"Maybe you should."

"Come on, Steph. Are we ever going to talk?" He scraped his chair closer to hers.

"About what?"

"Oh, I don't know. How about the abortion, or your mom, or how you act like everything that happened was my fault."

Steph stood and gathered her trash.

"Look. I think that if we could just--"

"What, Corey? What? You think that if we talk it will make it better? Or that maybe we should make another baby and keep it this time?"

"Don't you want us to get back together?"

"What I want is to finish my education."

"And that's it?" Corey blurred before her, everything now the color of her tears. "Steph . . ." He called her back gently, his eyes opaque, like the sea glass he had gathered at the cove, that he had taken to the jeweler's to be made into a necklace. He had given it to her for Christmas their sophomore year. She wore his gift alongside the one with the Saint Christopher, the cross, and the Pisces medallion beneath her T-shirt.

"It's hard," she told him. "Being back here, being reminded of what we had, and what we lost." She fingered the slender chain around her neck, the delicate clasp at the back.

"It was your choice."

"I know, which only makes it worse, because you were right. You told me I'd regret it, and I do. So very much."

He pulled her down to her chair, around to face him. He took her hands in his. His knees touched hers. She felt cold, underdressed in her shorts and sweatshirt. She had forgotten that while the winter was mild in La Jolla, it wasn't exactly warm. Corey tried to get her to look him in the eye. "Talk to me, please." But she couldn't. All she could do was shake her head and sniff. "If you can't talk to me, then how about calling your friend?"

"You mean Jaz?" Steph feared he meant Pedro. When Corey nodded, Steph relaxed, right down to the soles of her feet that were numb, her rubber thongs insubstantial against the cold pavement. She thought about the two necklaces she wore and wondered if Jaz still wore the one that was identical to hers. "You know, Jaz is married now. She just had a baby."

"No way!"

"Yeah, and it gets even stranger. You see, her husband is a surfer, just like you, and he still rides on the weekends, at Mavericks and Steamers."

"Oh man, I've always wanted to surf up north in the winter."

"While Jaz sits home, breast-feeding, trying to figure out how she can keep her scholarship and take care of a baby, all at the same time."

"So, what's wrong with that? Shit, that could have been us."

"Exactly." Steph dropped his hands and leaned back.

Chastened, Corey's forehead scrunched up, as if he was trying

to take it all in. At last he sighed. "I'm sorry. About everything."
He pulled her up to her feet and gave her a hug. He walked her
back to his truck. "Would you believe I still wonder sometimes if it
would've been a girl or a boy? So what did your friend Jaz have?"
Corey unlocked the truck's doors.

"A girl." Steph chewed her bottom lip.

"Wow." His eyes clouded, no longer the color of sea glass, more
the color of the overcast sky. "You know, I still don't understand
why you said no to all that."

She looked away. "Mom was hurt."

"We both know you decided long before that." She nodded
and climbed into his truck. He held the door open. His sandy hair
curled around his ears, dry at last. "So, no regrets. That's what you
said, remember?" She nodded once more, but when she tried to
close the door, he held it open. "I still love you, Steph, and I don't
want to lose you again."

She pulled out his necklace. "You never did."

# Jazmín Valdez Donahue
## January 26, 1996

*Buen principio, la mitad está hecha*
*(A good beginning is half the battle)*

Christmas had been spent in Orinda with Marty's family, while New Year's was celebrated quietly at home. The break between semesters in January allowed Jaz and Marty to enjoy being new parents. Reality, however, set in the first day of classes.

"You can't bring her to lecture with you," Marty said as Jaz bundled Maria into the jogger stroller. "What if she cries?"

"I'll leave and ask to borrow someone's notes." Jaz tucked Jenny's afghan around Maria.

"Why don't you take the semester off? Mother thinks it would be best."

Jaz stood up to Marty, disappointed she came only to his shoulder. "I'm sure your mother thinks I'm crazy for wanting to keep my scholarship, for not allowing your father to subsidize me." Jaz looked through her backpack to see if she had remembered everything.

"As a matter of fact, she thinks you're incredible, and so do I." Marty kissed her forehead and unknotted her tension as only he could, with his gentle smile and subtle touch. He stooped down to stroke Maria's cheek. "You, too," he told his daughter who slouched in her stroller, a Christmas gift from the senior Donahues. When Maria began to whimper, Marty moved the stroller back and forth. "When will you look into day care?"

"I'll do it today, after classes." Jaz lifted her backpack to her shoulder. Would she have room for the textbooks she needed to buy with all the baby stuff she carried? She already felt tired, and it was still early. It didn't help that Marty looked like Mr. GQ in his crew neck sweater and khakis. He planned to meet his father after class at the Commonwealth Club where they would eat lunch and discuss his future.

"Mother mentioned--"

"Would you leave it alone and leave it to me?" Jaz blew bangs out of her eyes.

"All right." Marty helped Jaz carry the stroller out of the apartment. "By the way, what's for dinner?" Like the fine San Francisco mist, the answer settled upon Jaz and sank in slowly. There was nothing for dinner. She hadn't been to the store. She wasn't even sure she had enough Pampers for Maria, let alone formula if she didn't have the time (or the milk) to nurse. Marty moved the stroller back and forth again when Maria started to cry. Then he kissed Jaz, rather passionately for being out on the street. Smoothing her wrinkled brow with his thumb, he said, "Don't worry. I'll get take-out."

The walk to USF soothed Maria. She slept through Jaz's first lecture, only to scream with a vengeance during the second. Jaz left without collecting the syllabus. By noon, she felt as cranky as her daughter, ready to give up as she walked home through a light rain. At the steps to the apartment, she sensed she was being watched. Twisting around, she spotted the woman who had just moved in across the street, the one who always smiled, always waved. It wasn't the first time Jaz had been observed by this busybody. Marty had dubbed her "the neighborhood watch." There was something strange about the Latina whose eyes followed Jaz in and out of the apartment day and night. It was as if she lay in waiting for an opening Jaz had so far refused to give. *That ends today*. Jaz motioned for the woman to cross over.

"Here." The stranger grabbed the bulky stroller. "Take your baby in out of the rain."

"We can carry it together." Jaz felt guilty the unknown woman was taking the brunt of the load and getting soaked in the process. "How about you take this, and I'll get the stroller?" Jaz slipped her backpack from her shoulder, only to have the zipper separate, which splayed her notes and books across the damp sidewalk. When the wind gusted, a syllabus flew out into Golden Gate Avenue. Several pages of it floated up against the grill of a passing car. The rest lay crumpled, embossed by the car's tires.

"¡Carajo! ¡Qué día!" Jaz wailed as more pages blew down the road.

"¡No me digas!"

Jaz stared at the woman, surprised to hear the accent of her mother, the Michoacán phrase Mami so often used. "I'm sorry. I shouldn't have sworn like that."

The woman bent down to pick up a book stuck to the sidewalk, drenched from the water the car had splashed over it. "What's this?" The woman pulled a pair of dangling half glasses to her pudgy nose and examined the one book that had nothing to do with Jaz's studies.

"Oh, that? It's just something a friend sent me."

"*Spiritual Astrology?*" The woman peered at Jaz over the rims of her half glasses.

"I'm not reading it for school."

"Are you an astrologer?"

"Oh my God, no," Jaz laughed.

The woman dropped her scolding-mother stance and took up her previous posture as Jaz's new best friend. "You look like you're hungry, mi hijita. Like you never have time to eat. Would you like to join me for lunch? I've got arroz con pollo on the stove."

It was stupid to say yes, to trust this woman because she was Latina and wore the scent of cilantro, which reminded Jaz of Mami's kitchen. But Jaz was exhausted, and there was no food at home, so she nodded and followed the lady across the street. Up a steep set of cement steps Jaz and the woman hauled the jogger stroller to the door of a Victorian false front in dire need of paint. The once great house had been divided into apartments, and thankfully, the woman's was on the first floor. As soon as they were inside, the woman excused herself to the kitchen and told Jaz to make herself at home.

Piles of astrology books lined the hallway. Jaz lifted Maria from the stroller, grateful her daughter still slept, that her head rested on Jaz's shoulder. The living room was light and airy with a bay window covered by sheers. Beneath it sat a sofa, its fabric sun-faded and well worn at the arms. Mismatched chairs faced the window, the cushion of one indented and warm to the touch. Jaz wandered into the kitchen, across a black and white hexagonally tiled floor. She sat at a table covered by a red-and-white checkered oilcloth that felt damp, as if it had just been wiped down.

"Please, tell me about yourself, especially about your interest in the stars," the woman said as she arranged chicken and rice on two plates. "Because I'm an astrologer, too, so when you finish reading *Spiritual Astrology*, maybe you could lend it to me."

"I told you, it's not my book."

"Tranquila. I realize you attend a Catholic university, that you're reluctant to admit it."

"But I'm not an astrologer. You have to believe me."

"Then I do," the woman said, "though I think you are, and you just don't know it yet." She hesitated before she added, "It's why I've been anxious to meet you."

Jaz stared at this woman, dumbfounded. Was it her imagination or did the woman emit a rosy glow? "Your bathroom?" Jaz asked.

"It's down the hall."

"If you'll excuse me." Jaz carried Maria back to her stroller. From the kitchen she walked past two bedrooms to a bathroom that confirmed her suspicion. Every room in the apartment was painted pink. Relieved she wasn't seeing auras, Jaz still felt shaken by this lady who acted as if she were the Grand Inquisitor herself. Upon her return Jaz collected Maria from the stroller and seated herself at the kitchen table. "I'll admit I've read some books about astrology," she said, "but it's only because my mother is interested in the stars."

"¡No me digas!" The woman brought a bowl of salad to the table, followed by plates piled high with chicken and rice. She settled into her chair and turned her attention to Maria who still slept peacefully in Jaz's arms. "¡Qué linda nena! ¿Cómo se llama?"

"Maria."

The woman startled. Recovering quickly, she asked, "¿Y tu nombre es?"

"Jaz."

"Jazz?" the woman huffed in English. "What kind of Mexican mother would name her daughter after that crazy gringo music?"

"It's short for Jazmin, or Jazmín. Jazmín Maria Valdez de Osorio. I shortened all of that years ago, so forgive me . . ." she waited for the woman to supply her name.

"Rosa. Rosario Maria Rodriguez de Avila, but like you, I shortened it." Rosa wore a knowing smile. "In my line of work, a name so Catholic becomes a liability. Here. Let me hold Maria while you eat."

Jaz couldn't believe she would willingly hand over her child to a total stranger, but that was exactly what she did. For the first time since she had come to San Francisco, Jaz felt inexplicably at home. Perhaps it was the warmth radiated by the Pepto Bismol walls, a sharp contrast to the fog outside, the mists that made Jaz's hair behave as if it had a life of its own. "So you're an astrologer?" Jaz ate with one hand and smoothed her frizzy hair with the other.

"Claro. Como tú--"

"I told you, I'm not an astrologer."

"Is your friend?" Jaz was confused until Rosa said, "The one who gave you the book."

"Steph?" Jaz snorted. "No, though according to Mami, we're gemelas del alma."

Rosa's lips parted. When she finally spoke, she said, "Then believe me when I tell you it's no accident your friend sent you that book." Rosa looked as if she was about to say more, but instead she pursed her lips. It occurred to Jaz that like Mami, Rosa was about to offer a piece of her mind rather than chicken. "Where you always running off to? For two weeks I'm out there, waving at you, at that handsome gabacho husband of yours, and you ignore me." Jaz tried to defend herself, only to have Rosa say, "So now that we've met, it's time to cast your chart."

"My what?" Jaz almost choked on a chicken bone.

"The baby's, too. As a gift," Rosa added quickly. She rearranged Maria in her arms. "And one for your husband. I assume you know when and where he was born. I'll need that information for the synastry portion of the reading." When Jaz's mouth opened, Rosa explained, "A synastry chart examines you and your husband's compatibility, as well as areas for concern. It's a useful tool for predicting what lies ahead."

"But . . . I'm not sure I want to know all that."

Jaz's protest was met with hearty laughter. "Everyone wants to know the future." Rosa brought Jaz a pad of paper and a pencil and insisted she write down all the data. "I'll have the charts together for you in a couple of days. And as a part of my service, I'll explain everything."

"That's very kind of you, Rosa. But I can't afford all that." Jaz's nose began to twitch. Dust clung to every surface, even if there was a coziness to the clutter. "Would you mind if I opened this?" Jaz asked, as she tugged at a window that must have been painted shut.

"I'm sorry it's so stuffy in here." Rosa brought the stroller into the kitchen and gently deposited Maria into in. Then she proceeded to grill Jaz about her family, her marriage, and her studies as they cleaned up. When Rosa began asking questions about Steph, Jaz became uncomfortable. Her own chores silently nagged at her. Using that as an excuse to leave, she was halfway out the door when Rosa remembered the broken backpack and ran in for it. From the pack Rosa removed *Spiritual Astrology*, its paperback cover still wet, curling at the edges. "Perhaps we could work out a trade. If you lend me Esteph's book, I'll do your charts for free."

"You can keep the book," Jaz told her. "Steph won't mind." And while Jaz felt guilty to give the book away without reading it, her mind drifted to her more immediate problem of buying groceries and getting to the Laundromat before it closed. With Jenny's afghan tucked snuggly around Maria, she headed across the street to her apartment.

"Gracias, mi amor." Rosa trailed Jaz. "I'll consider it payment-in-full for services rendered. Why don't you let me watch your nena tomorrow while you go to class?"

"Oh Rosa, that's too kind. And it's too much. How could you possibly watch Maria and draw up charts at the same time?"

Rosa's laughter was contagious. "Like I said, I'm a professional. I raised my own daughter while working from home."

"Okay, then. How much would you charge?"

"How much can you afford?" When Jaz hesitated, Rosa said, "Don't worry. We'll work the money part out later. Pues, hasta mañana."

"Ciao, Madrina," Jaz told Rosa, happy at last to have found one.

That night, Jaz was relieved to report to Marty she had solved their day care problem. Meeting Rosa had been a nightmare, what with the loss of Jaz's syllabus and her daughter's temperamental behavior, but the following day, as she dashed home along Golden Gate Avenue, Jaz found herself looking forward to seeing Rosa almost as much as to seeing Maria.

Late as usual, Jaz tripped on the uneven sidewalk in front of Rosa's Victorian apartment house. It was after two and her breasts hung heavily with milk. Up the cracked concrete stairs she ran, happy Rosa stood at the bay window. She waved Maria's tiny fist at Jaz and buzzed her in. On the couch Jaz collapsed. Maria squirmed in her arms and mouthed the air as Jaz prepared to feed her. "Por Dios, Rosa, even with your help, I'm so stressed." Jaz lifted her sweater and unhooked her bra. "How in the world did you do it? Raise a daughter and work?"

Rosa laughed. "Why are you so hard on yourself? My cousin would say "stressed" is simply "desserts" spelled backwards." Rosa went to the kitchen and returned with plates of molded custard that shook in her hands as she walked. "Here. Have some flan."

"Maybe later. I need to feed Maria first. My breasts are killing me."

"I had hoped you'd be hungry, too. You're too thin, Jazmín."

"No te preocupes."

"En serio. ¿Estás comiendo? ¿Estás durmiendo?"

"There's no time, Rosa. And then when I do fall asleep, I have the strangest dreams."

"Díme, mi hijita. I interpret dreams, too."

Jaz returned Rosa's sly grin. "Is there anything you don't do?"

"Los naipes. It's my cousin who reads Tarot cards. ¿Pero a mí? I put my faith in the stars, God's map of our lives in the heavens that guides us while we're here on Earth." Rosa walked back to her kitchen and returned with a roll of paper towels and Windex. "So, I don't do Tarot cards, and I don't do windows, though I should. As if it isn't gray enough outside already." She stood on the sofa in her stocking feet, rubbing madly at smudges on the bay window. "Mejor, ¿eh? Bueno, díme tu sueño. Because you're not going home until your nena has had her fill, and I'm not showing you your chart until you tell me your dream."

"My chart is done? Already?"

"Claro."

"Oh please, Rosa. Will you show it to me? And explain it?"

"Un sueño, primero."

Jaz recounted the dream that had woken her this morning, just before Maria screamed to be fed. It still troubled her because she had dreamed about Pedro, her father's choice for yerno, not Martin Donahue, the third. It had felt so real, she told Rosa, especially when Pedro held her and kissed her, when he told her he forgave her and wanted her back.

"Astral projection," Rosa said. "It felt real because you were there." Before Rosa could continue, a client came to the door to pick up a chart, surprised that Jaz sat nursing Maria.

"Are you Rosa's daughter?" the tall, bearded man asked.

"Not exactly," Jaz told him, embarrassed that Maria sucked noisily at her breast.

Rosa looked as if the question had upset her, too, but by the time she returned from the bedroom that functioned as her office, she was smiling once again. "Here's your chart, Eduardo." Rosa opened it. Her hand hovered over each page as if she read it by Braille. Much of the discussion centered on the timing of a stock split for a recent IPO, whatever that was, though the more Rosa talked, the more Jaz tuned in. When Eduardo grew restless, Rosa closed the report. "Are you sure you don't have time for me to explain it to you?"

"Sorry, Rosa. Gotta run. But I'll be in touch."

Rosa handed the report to Eduardo along with a tape and accompanied him to the door.

"That was fast," Jaz said. "How come I can't get out of here in under an hour?"

"Because you're not some hot-shot software engineer who runs his own start-up."

"And he hired you to do his chart?"

"It was a progressed chart for his company, mi amor."

"You're kidding."

"I'm not." Rosa went to her kitchen and returned with forks. She balanced a plate of flan on the doily that covered the arm of the couch so Jaz could reach it and breast feed at the same time. "You'd be surprised who uses astrologers these days. Smart people. Respectable people." Jaz brought Maria to her shoulder and burped her before she set her daughter down in her bassinet. She ate her custard in silence and savored the dulce de leche topping that reminded her of Mami's and Abuelita's. "What are your plans when you finish your studies next year?" Rosa asked. "Will you stay home and be a good mamá to Maria? Or will you work?"

"To be perfectly honest, I'm not sure what I'll do."

"Not sure? Then why don't you quit school and study astrology with me? Eduardo keeps referring business associates my way. It won't be long before I'll have more clients than I know what to do with. The best part is you could work from your apartment, like I do."

Too weary to take on the issue of working outside the home, Jaz decided Rosa was no different than Mami in this respect. It seemed strange she would bring up the idea of Jaz working with her, though the more Jaz thought about it, the more she was intrigued. "I used to study Spanish and English. I just switched to business and computer science, like Marty."

"¡No me digas! Could you help me buy a computer?"

"You don't have one?"

"You seem surprised, mi amor."

"I am. How do you cast your charts?"

"By hand."

"But there's software. It's open source. You can download it for free from the Internet."

"The inter what?" Confusion flooded Rosa's moon face, only to be swept away by a sunny smile. "We have so much to learn from each other, and it's going to be fun."

And it was. It also saved Jaz a fortune in daycare as she traded services with Rosa. Jaz helped Rosa purchase a computer. She signed her up with an Internet provider and taught her to navigate the World Wide Web. Jaz sat with her friend every afternoon when she returned from classes and showed Rosa how to use astrological software as well as a word processing program. And as Rosa typed up the interpretations of her clients' charts on the computer instead of tediously pecking them out on her ancient Smith-Corona, Jaz studied astrology.

# Rosa Rodriguez
## February 13, 1996

*Only because I err do I find what I am not looking for*
*—Orides Fontela*

"Happy Birthday, Mom."

I blink, unsure of what I see. My daughter, my precious Angelica, sits at my cousin's kitchen table with Maria Rosario in her arms. Speechless, I wipe away my tears before I walk to them both. "Permiso." Angelica nods and hands me my nieta. Maria Rosario is asleep, and while she is larger than her mother was at two months, she looks exactly the same. "Preciosa." I smile down at Angelica. "Como tú."

"Sit down," Silvia says. "Dinner is almost ready."

I ease myself into the chair my daughter pulls out for me so I don't wake my nieta. "This is the best birthday surprise you could ever give me," I tell my daughter.

"Good," she replies, though a funny smile plays at her lips. "Because there's more."

"Why don't you take off your jacket, Hija, make yourself comfortable."

"I can't stay." When Angelica sees the pain and confusion in my face, she says, "All you need to know is that I'm clean and sober,

∞ 161 ∞

Mom, and that I have been for almost a year. As soon as I found out I was pregnant, I stopped drinking and smoking."

"And Cruz?"

"Unfortunately, no." Angie helps Silvia bring plates full of enchiladas to the table, a salad in a wooden bowl. "But that's not our biggest problem at the moment."

"Angie has become a born-again Christian," Silvia tells me when she sits down.

"¡No me digas!" I say, unable to ignore my cousin's grim expression.

"It's why I'm here. I'm returning this." Angie pulls crumpled sheets from a pocket of her coat. It's the natal chart I cast for Maria Rosario. "Here, let me have her," Angelica suggests, "so you can eat."

"Are you sure you won't join us?" Silvia asks.

"I'm sure." Angelica rearranges Maria Rosario in her arms.

I force myself to take a bite although I feel as sick as Silvia looks.

"Before I leave, I need you to explain something." Angelica goes to the living room of the Capp Street apartment. She returns, and with her free hand she slaps *Spiritual Astrology* and the deck of Tarot cards between Silvia's plate and mine. "Why do you have these?"

"Hija, there is so much we should talk about--"

"You're both Catholic, both Christians, and these are of the Devil."

"If that is what you believe, then I respect that, and so does Silvia. We'll never speak of it again. We just want you and Maria Rosario to come home."

"Even if it means giving up your livelihood?" When I hesitate, Angelica gives me a self-satisfied smile. "No, I didn't think so." She walks to the door.

"If you don't plan on staying with Cruz, then where will you go?"

Angelica turns to me. She lifts Maria Rosario to her shoulder when my nieta begins to cry. "Why don't you cast one of your charts, Mom, or have Silvia cast an array of cards, or light candles at Mission Delores and pray to idols? And if God is silent, well, then you have your answer, don't you? Because it's supposed to be about trust and faith, and clearly, you have neither. You never have." And with that, my daughter and my nieta leave.

# Jazmín Valdez Donahue
## January 6, 1997

*Las buenas palabras quebrantan las penas y ablandan los corazones*
*(Kind words relieve worries and soften the heart)*

For her senior project, Jaz wrote the following proposal: She would set up Rosa's company on a more professional high-profile basis. She would create a web site that would include a chat room, with e-marketing links to business cycle reports and discussions of future trends. Jaz hoped this proposal would impress Professor Caldwell, her senior thesis advisor so he would count the hours she spent training Rosa as an internship. Jaz had it all worked out, the solution that would allow her time with Maria and Rosa. A year into the friendship, Rosa was not only Jaz's madrina but her mentor as well, for as Jaz installed software and organized Rosa's business she had learned enough about astrology to become a believer.

Marty, however, was skeptical. Delighted that Jaz had switched from English and Spanish to business and computer science as he had, he seemed upset by what he read that night as he and Jaz sat huddled over Chinese take-out. "What you forget is USF is a Catholic school." Marty shoved her proposal back across the table. "Professor Caldwell will never go for an astrological consulting firm."

"But that's the beauty of it, Marty. Professor Caldwell will never know." Jaz whipped out the business card she had designed.

"Rosa Rodriguez: Business Consultant and Futurist?" Marty's tone was snide. "So your plan is to make it look as if she's part of some think tank when she's just an astrologer?"

"Rosa is far more than just an astrologer." Jaz snatched the mock-up of the business card from Marty's hand. "I'm trying to protect her."

"What about protecting me? Professor Caldwell is my advisor, too. We'll need his help to find internships this semester, and his recommendation later on to find jobs."

"What I don't understand is why you've never liked Rosa when she's been nothing but nice to you and me and Maria."

"What I don't like is her influence over you."

"And what exactly does that mean?" Jaz stood. She cleared away the empty white cartons from the table and stuffed them into the overflowing trash.

"It means you spend as much time over there as you do here. It means you know as much about T-squares as you know about T-charts. It means that when we both graduate in May, you'll need to get a real job in the real world, because I'm not sure I'll be able to find something that will support us right away. It means your days of discussing tea leaves and grand trines with Rosa will be over."

Jaz began to shake she was so angry. She grabbed the edge of the counter. "We'll still need child care, and I can't imagine a better person to watch Maria than Rosa. She adores her."

Marty stood and put his arms around Jaz. "She adores you. And so do I. I understand why you love her. She treats you like a daughter, Maria like a nieta, but . . ."

Jaz felt herself drown in the depths of Marty's sapphire eyes. "But what?"

He dropped his embrace and walked to the sink. The water on, he rinsed the utensils they'd used. "Mother says she'll help us with child care once we're in the East Bay."

"When I just put a deposit down on that house in the Inner Sunset?"

Marty allowed the water in the sink to run. "I thought we were going to discuss that. I thought you agreed with my idea that we should move out of the city and commute if necessary."

"I had to give the agent an answer, or we would've lost it. You said you liked it, so when Ann called last night, saying she needed a decision, I said yes. I'm sorry. I know I should have waited, but I'm glad I didn't since you got home so late from the Warriors' game."

"I only took Father because you wouldn't go with me."

Jaz sighed. "Maria would have been climbing up and down those steep stairs, scaring us to death. What fun would that have been?" She turned off the water. "Look. I'm sorry I made the decision about renting the house without you, but if you think about it, it makes sense. I have a feeling we'll find work here in the city. Living in the Inner Sunset will make our commute shorter, and it will allow Rosa to continue watching Maria."

"Rosa, Rosa, Rosa." Marty caught Jaz from behind when she turned away. He nibbled on her neck and her ear, which he knew she liked, turned her toward him, and kissed her. "All right," he said. "We'll rent that great old house, but I want you to keep in mind that we have other options, of where we live, and of who provides our child care."

Jaz's vision she presented to Marty convinced her that like Mami she was clairvoyant. She and Marty did find work in San Francisco. Jaz landed her job after she graduated. As a minority female who was bilingual, her technical background and business skills led to an offer from InfoSys, a company that installed software for small firms and trained their staffs. Under the watchful eye of her boss, Judith Tindall, Jaz worked in technical support, and a year later, in May of 1998, Judith promoted Jaz and put her in charge of information technology, or IT, which meant Jaz had a salary and stock options.

Marty's career path proved rockier. It made his fears about supporting a family seem prescient as well. His internships at PG&E led to a job offer upon graduation, but within a few months he quit to work at Bank of America. His short-lived career as a systems analyst came to an end on an evening in June, 1998, when a classmate called and offered him a position as a software developer.

"I'd like to do it, if it's okay with you," Marty told Jaz over dinner. "Stewart says he can't pay me much to begin with, but in a year, who knows?"

"I'm making plenty of money," Jaz replied, "so if it doesn't work out--"

"You just love to rub it in, don't you?" Marty's gaze seared her. "The fact you earn more than I do, that you've succeeded while I've struggled." He pushed back roughly from the kitchen table and strode to the highchair where Maria fussed, demanding to be released. "I'm not a woman or a minority, Jaz. It's not the same out there for me. Not to mention I've had it up to here with the corporate world. The way I see it, I might as well join Stewart in this venture, because as you just pointed out, I've got nothing to lose."

Jaz sat in stunned silence as Marty carried their whiny daughter to her crib. She sensed that if she were to lose his love, she might lose Maria as well. It was something Rosa had warned about two years ago when she explained their synastry (or lack of it) while comparing Jaz's chart to Marty's. Up until now, Jaz had refused to believe what Rosa said, that if she didn't do things Marty's way, he might leave and take Maria with him. But now she felt unsure.

Once Maria was asleep, Jaz sought Marty out, surprised to find him seated on the living room couch, flipping through the channels. "If this start-up goes well," he said, "we'd be able to move out to Orinda, and you wouldn't have to work."

She sat down beside him and cleared a spot for herself by shoving aside the unfolded laundry. She took his free hand in hers. "I like the city. I like working with Judith." She studied her husband's profile, as he worked hard to ignore her. "What is it, Marty?" He shook his head. His eyes never left the muted TV. "Something's wrong." She loosened his tie and helped him out of his jacket. "You seem angry with me, and I'm not even sure what I've done."

He nuzzled her neck and unbuttoned her blouse. "Don't you want to have a house of your own? To play tennis and not work?"

"No," she kissed his ear. That was Carolyn Donahue, not her. "I'm happy with things the way they are. But you're not, and that worries me." Marty pulled away and listlessly flicked through the channels again. She slipped her hand inside his shirt and caressed his chest. "You just need the right job. Judith suggested that you talk to Mark."

"I'm not calling your boss's boyfriend. I can find something on my own. As a matter of fact, I think I have. All I'm saying is it hasn't been easy out there for me."

And though he kissed her now as if he wanted sex, right there on the unfolded laundry, Jaz heard herself say, "And you think it's been easy for me?"

"Actually," he positioned her on the couch, "Yeah."

She stiffened beneath him, like a twig beneath his foot. It bothered her that Marty took a certain pleasure in breaking her. Sensing her lack of interest, her hostility, or both, he rose and punched off the TV, abandoning her to the unfolded laundry she lay on. Jaz pulled the afghan Jenny had knitted for Maria from the arm of the couch and wrapped herself in it. Tears streamed down her face as she wondered why Marty refused to be proud of her, why when

it came to her work, he withheld his praise and approval. He had
made too many unkind remarks about it, too many times. There
were the jokes he told his parents, over drinks then dinner, the conversations that ended as soon as she walked into the room. Her
success and Marty's lack of it had been attributed solely to her sex
and ethnicity, rather than her training and talent with clients. At
first, Jaz had been sympathetic, but now she felt resentful. Marty
wallowed in his self-pity. He wore it like a badge of honor with his
family in order to elicit their sympathy. But what irked Jaz even
more than his disparaging remarks about her career at InfoSys were
his endless pot shots about her astrological consulting with Rosa.

"I told you this would be a problem, so why are you acting so
surprised?" Rosa responded the following afternoon when Jaz recounted her latest tale of marital woe at the hands of her husband.
"It's his Mars conjunct his midheaven in the tenth house, oppos-
ing Uranus in the fourth. He's ambitious, more macho than any
Mejicano you could have married. He wants you barefoot, pregnant, and in the kitchen."

"That's just your way of saying, I told you so, Rosa. It's what
Mami does any time I complain. She still thinks I should have married Pedro."

Rosa looked troubled. "Then you misunderstand me, Jazmín.
That's not what I'm saying at all." Rosa tugged her knee high ny-
lons up under the hem of her drab housedress. "I'm just saying I
thought you believed what I told you about Marty, what I've told
you many times. Astrology is to be used as a guide, not accepted as
some dark fate." Sighing loudly, Rosa returned to work, leaving Jaz
alone with her thoughts. When Rosa left the bedroom that served
as her office to call a client, Jaz slipped in and ran a chart for Pedro.
Feeling anxious, she ripped the sheets from the printer, only to have
her madrina enter the room and act like a madrastra. "Who's that
for?" Rosa demanded, sounding every inch the evil stepmother.

"No one," Jaz lied, clutching the report she hid behind her back.

"¡No me digas!" Rosa snatched the papers from Jaz's hands. Her half glasses lifted to her nose, her eyebrows shot up. "Pedro?" She removed her glasses. "You dream yourself beside him, and now you cast his chart?" Rosa shook her head. "This is no good, Jazmín. Let me run a progressed chart on you and Marty, so you'll know when things will get better, because they will. You believe that, don't you? What's the dicho in English? 'This too shall pass'?"

"Sí, Madrina. No te preocupes."

"But I do worry. I want you to be happy." When Jaz began to cry, Rosa walked with her to the couch under the bay window in the living room. "Do you really believe you've made a mistake?" she asked as they sat down. "That you'd be happier with Pedro?"

"I don't know, and I guess now I never will." Jaz flicked away a tear.

"Pedro's all right, isn't he?" Rosa took Jaz's hand.

"I suppose so. He's getting married." Rosa dropped Jaz's hand and raised her own to her mouth. "You know my friend Steph? The one who sent me that book? She called to tell me about Pedro's wedding last night, right after Marty and I fought. I didn't get the details, other than it's this weekend, and Steph thinks I should come. So what do you think, Madrina? Should I go?" Rosa closed her eyes, as if she were hearing more than Jaz's words. "We've drifted so far apart. I can't believe Pedro didn't tell me, that he didn't even send me an invitation." Jaz began to cry, "My whole family--all my old friends--they treat me as if I were--"

"Go home, mi hijita."

"But this is my home, Rosa, with Marty and Maria and you."

"Trust me, Jazmín. It's time you went home."

# Rosa Rodriguez
## *June 18, 1998*

*Our destiny is no better than the next, so everyone should accept theirs*
*--Jorge Luis Borges*

"Astrological triplets?" Silvia stares at me in disbelief. She unchains the door to the Capp Street apartment we once shared. Behind her I see a Tarot deck arrayed on the coffee table, a pack of Chiclets, and a teddy bear. My nieta, however, is gone. I close my eyes and see Angelica clutching Maria Rosario to her breast as she rides the Muni, but as to where they go, I have no idea. "Why didn't you tell me Jazmín and Angie have the same birthday?" Silvia demands, but as soon as she does I can tell she understands. "So you meddle in Jazmín's life now because Angie refuses to let you meddle in hers?" My cousin's accusation hurts.

"I never imagined a scenario like this, or that there would be two Marias, born the exact same day. It's why I'm here, Prima, to beg you to tell me where Angelica is."

"So you can do what? Stop her from marrying Cruz? I bet you'd stop Stephanie Bengochea from marrying Pedro Garcia if you could. I bet you ran a chart on Estefanía, and on her novio, too." Silvia's attack is calculated to keep me on the defensive, to avoid answering my question.

"Actually, it was Jazmín who ran the natal chart on Pedro."

"Then I'm guessing when you compared Estefanía's and Pedro's charts it wasn't good."

"Their synastry is worse than Jazmín's is with her husband."

Silvia slits her eyes at me. "Did you tell Jazmín that?"

"No, of course not, because like you," I gaze at the Tarot cards scattered across my cousin's dinged-up coffee table, "I believe in free will."

"Then why are you here?"

"I told you. I have to talk to Angelica."

"And tell her what?"

*Don't marry Cruz!* I want to scream.

"Angie's mind is made up."

"Then what do you suggest, ¿eh?"

"I suggest you go to Mission Delores, and that you light three candles: one for Jazmín's marriage, one for Estefanía's, and one for Angie's." When I don't budge, Silvia says, "The truth is I have no idea where Angie is going, or where she's getting married because she didn't invite me to the wedding, either."

My guess is South Shore. It's why I see Lake Tahoe every time I try to locate Angelica in my mind's eye. "Did you give her money?"

"Of course I gave her money, as a wedding gift."

I set a crisp one hundred dollar bill next to the teddy bear. "The next time you see Angelica, you tell her this is not about control." Silvia returns the bill. I stuff it back in the pocket of her floral house-dress and gaze at my cousin's proud, stoic face. We could be sisters, gemelas del alma as well. "This is about love," I say before I leave.

# Jazmín Valdez Donahue
## June 19, 1998

*Donde no hay amor, no hay dolor*
*(Where there is no love, there is no pain)*

Jaz gazed at the mountains, those yawning gates that guarded the west. She imagined Conestoga wagons following this historic trail, their white canopies stiffened by the sun, those bleached tunnels that sheltered the pioneers driven over the Sierra Nevada by fever dreams of gold. Was she any different than those early settlers other than she made this trip in reverse? She resettled herself and turned up the air conditioning. Even a modern asphalt highway couldn't unkink this torturous road. The Jetta whined as she downshifted, leaving the smoggy sprawl of the Central Valley behind. The cool dapple of the forest drifted over the Jetta as she angled it through one curve only to accelerate through another. Behind a scrim of leaves she saw the lime green growth that tipped the trees, the emerald pools of streams that glinted in the sunlight. Her car climbed, its gears straining, her stomach lurching each time she whipped it around a bend.

She felt guilty it was Pedro's wedding that lured her back. Was she jealous? She had no right to be. The last time she'd come home was to announce her own marriage. Still, it bothered her that it was

Steph who'd called to invite Jaz to a ceremony Pedro hadn't seen fit to invite her to himself. She crested the summit and negotiated a series of hairpin turns that twisted down the eastern side, grateful Maria slept in her car seat. Jaz stretched. Her back unknotted along with the road. Foliage rushed by, wild as a mountain stream. Aspen, birch, and pine trees laced a canopy overhead, and in spite of all that green Jaz felt blue.

It wasn't just her marriage to Marty that had kept her away. It was everything: a father who ignored her; a mother who nagged with every phone call; her strained relationship with Steph. Perhaps that's why she rarely left San Francisco anymore. Golden Gate Park wasn't the Sierras, though it did provide a refuge. She jogged Maria there in her stroller along the park's winding paths, the cool hand of the fog never far away. Like so many of the city's transplanted residents, Jaz remained enthralled by the bottle green water of the bay, the oak-studded hills that rose on every side, but now it was the mountains that called her name. *Home! Go home!* the Jetta's tires sang each time the car strayed onto the highway's grooved shoulder.

"¡Mi vida!" Mami cried as she greeted Jaz at the door. "¡Preciosa!" She took Maria in her arms, bringing her nieta to her shoulder. Then she asked, "How come you wearin' glasses?"

Jaz removed her lenses. "I flunked the eye chart the last time I renewed my license." She walked past her mother into the entryway and rummaged through her purse for her glasses case.

"Where's Marty?"

"He couldn't come. He couldn't take the time off."

"I ride the bus over to see you and Marty all the time. And he can't take the time off to come see me, and you can't, neither?"

Embarrassed, Jaz clicked her glasses case shut. "Is Papi home?"

"Not 'til dinner." Jaz sucked in her breath at the thought of seeing him. Whenever she inquired about her father in her phone calls, Mami's response never varied. "He workin'," she would say, and the conversation flowed on from there. Still, it galled Jaz that Mami allowed him this excuse, even if the issue at the moment was whether he would acknowledge Jaz as a married woman and the mother of his only grandchild. "Are you gonna help me fix food?" Mami asked.

"Por supuesto." Jaz followed her mother into a kitchen that smelled of burnt sugar.

In a patch of sunlight, Mami set Maria down. She laughed when Woofy scurried over to lick Maria's face. "I so happy you comin', I make flan."

Jaz hugged Mami. The kitchen was still the heart of the Valdez home. Love emanated from it, just as it had from Abuelita's whenever Jaz and her family visited. Her grandmother always baked flan whenever they came. During their final visit, Jaz recalled how Abuelita murmured endearments to Mami in a language that sounded strange to Jaz's ear. Nahuatl, Mami explained. It made Jaz wonder now if Abuelita had reverted to her native tongue before she died because only those words could express how she truly felt. During that visit Abuelita's chickens had circled her feet, much as Woofy circled Mami's now. Her mother stumbled over him as she paddled a tortilla between the palms of her hands.

"Bueno ¿Qué quieres comer? ¿Quesadillas? ¿Enchilladas?"

"I'm not all that hungry at the moment. But a glass of water--"

"I cookin' all morning, and you tellin' me you don't want my food?"

"Of course I want your food, Mami. It's just . . . How about one of those tortillas? They look like they're still hot. And no one makes tortillas like you." Mami beamed. In one floured hand she brought Jaz a glass of water, in the other a tortilla. Jaz pictured her mother hovering above the tortilladora. Once the masa had been pressed flat, the disc was placed on the hot surface of the skillet where it would puff up as it sizzled. When she was little, Mami would remove the first tortilla and roll it up. Then she would pop an end into Jaz's mouth and tug the other end with her teeth, as if they were dogs fighting over a bone. When it dropped to the floor, they'd laugh and feed it to Woofy. Now Mami worked alone, no daughter to share the ritual with. How abandoned Mami must feel Jaz thought as she watched Maria play with Woofy. She made a silent promise that she and her daughter would never become so estranged. When Maria pulled Woofy's tail Jaz said, "¡No, Maria, no!" concerned when Woofy limped away to his spot under the table to lick his back legs. "Mami, is he okay?"

"He just gettin' old, Hija. His legs don't work like they used to." Lately all of Mami's news about Woofy was heart wrenching. "He don't want to go out no more," Mami continued. "It so sad. I open the door yesterday to go to Yessenia's, and he just stand there."

Jaz seized the opening she had been waiting for. "Is Pedro getting married at Evangelico?"

A troubled look crossed Mami's face before she turned away, circumspect as she adjusted the flame beneath a pot on the stove. "At the Valley Church, I sorry to say."

"And how does Yessenia feel about that?"

Mami shrugged. "She upset about a lot of things these days." The renewed silence held until the dam her mother had erected could no longer hold. "Ay Hija, I tell Esteph to call you, 'cause you should be here. You two's friends, and nothin's gonna change that." Mami lifted the lid on a pot and gave its contents a stir. "So how long you stayin' after the wedding?"

"I drive back Monday. I wish I could spend more time--"

"Don't tell me you busy." Mami slashed the air with her spoon. "We all busy, ¿eh?"

Jaz felt shaken by the anger that seeped from Mami every time this subject came up. As far as Jaz was concerned, her reluctance to visit should have been as clear as the Eastern Sierra sky. "Do you really want to know why I never come back here? Do you?"

*No*, Mami's eyes blazed. "Set the table, Hija. Papi will be here soon." Was it loyalty that made her mother so blind? For three years Papi had neither called nor visited. His abandonment had created a hole in Jaz's heart that neither time nor distance could fill. Before Jaz could pursue this, the front door clicked open, and Woofy trotted over to greet him. "Look who's here?" Mami lifted Maria from where she played on the floor, banging a set of metal measuring cups together. She offered her nieta to him as if Maria were a fine wine that awaited his approval. "Preciosa, te presento a tu abuelito."

Papi stiffened at the Spanish word for grandfather. He was just past forty. Not a trace of silver streaked his thick black hair. He held Maria at arm's length and examined the teeth she flashed at him, like the tiny pearls that graced her pierced ears. At last his face softened, as if he saw some remnant of the daughter he had lost, though Maria hardly resembled Jaz. Her eyes were more hazel than brown. Her curls were the color of honey. Papi eyed the Baby Gap jeans. "I thought you said she was a girl," he told Mami. "Without the earrings I would have never known."

"Ay, Antonio. Of course she's a girl with that beautiful face." Mami gooed at Maria.

"But those pants."

"She wearin' a dress to the weddin'."

Jaz approached her father, heartbroken when he locked her out by pulling Maria to him.

Mami's nose twitched. "I think I smell something, Hija. Go change her, and I go call your brothers." Mami walked to the kitchen door. "Chi-cos. Ce-na," she yodeled up the stairs.

The meal would have been a silent, somber affair without Mami's running commentary about the extended family's affairs. "And then they arrest Rafael for drunk drivin'. So Marcos was drinkin' in the car. So what? He wasn't drivin'. But they take away his license, too."

"Do Rafael and Marcos have an attorney?" Jaz asked between bites.

"Public defender. Buena gente. Speaks Spanish, but the judge?" Mami shrugged.

"It's against the law, Mami."

"You think you tellin' me somethin' I don't already know? They just got here, Hija, and in Paracas, everyone go on picnics all the time, and the men, they always drinkin' in the car--"

"They're in California now." Jaz wiped her lips with a napkin before she went on. "And surely, after everything Jenny's been through--"

"That happen down on 395 when a deer jump out. Rafael was drivin' real slow. He was almost home, but the police? They pull him over anyway."

"Which is the point." Juan P. stared at Jaz. His sullen face mirrored her father's. "They pick on us, or have you been gone so long you've forgotten?" Her brother jabbed his fork into his enchilada and stuffed a large piece into his mouth. "If the truck has a gun rack and it's driven by a gabacho, they let him go, but if it's rusted and driven by a Mejicano, then it's out of the car with your legs spread and your hands up."

Her family's defense of her cousins' drinking and driving escaped her, especially in light of the chaos a car accident had created for Jenny Bengochea. "How is Jenny?" Jaz asked Mami, eager now to change the subject.

"She back at work, and I back to cleanin' condos, gracias a Dios." Mami crossed herself. "I don't know what she'd done if Esteph hadn't come home."

Jaz shoveled her food faster.

"You're taking the news about Pedro pretty calmly," Chuy said.

Jaz studied her youngest brother. He looked so much like Juan P., so much like Papi. He was no longer a gangly teenager. "I have to admit it feels weird, like I was invited as an afterthought. If Steph hadn't called, I would've never known Pedro was getting married."

Chuy gaped at Jaz as if she were an alien from another planet.

"So who is Pedro marrying?" she asked.

"Steph," Chuy answered. He glanced at Juan P. "We thought you knew."

Shaking his head, Juan P. pushed back from the table and cleared his dishes, something he had never done while Jaz lived at home.

"Where you goin'?" Mami asked Juan P.

"There's a Bachelor Party, or some such shit."

"You watch your mouth, Hijo," Mami scolded. She turned to Jaz, her eyes grave. "I thinkin' Esteph tell you."

Jaz lifted Maria out of the high chair. "Well, she didn't." Up the stairs Jaz climbed, Mami's footsteps behind her, slapping out a rhythm to match the ache in Jaz's head. Claustrophobia set in at the threshold of her room. It felt cramped. Everything appeared untouched, as if Mami still held out the hope Jaz would see the error of her ways and return.

"You're upset, Hija." Jaz chafed under Mami's gaze. "I know Esteph want to tell you."

To avoid facing the pity that oozed from Mami, Jaz lay Maria on her cot-like bed and squished her daughter into her pajamas. "Why did you ask Steph to invite me when it's obvious she doesn't want me here?" Jaz stopped fastening the closures on Maria's pajamas, struck by what seemed so obvious now she wondered how she could have missed it. "So what else have you and Steph been talking about behind my back? What else haven't you told me?"

"Esteph tell me you unhappy with Marty."

"Well, I don't know where she got that idea." Jaz snapped the final closure shut on her daughter's pajamas and lifted Maria to her shoulder, cuddling her and whispering in her ear.

"¿Tu le hablas español a Maria? Me soprendes."

"Why would my speaking Spanish surprise you?" Jaz carried Maria to her portable crib and tucked Esmokey next to her, remembering how Steph had run back for him the day Jaz left for orientation at USF. Now he belonged to Maria, and the bear was never far from her side.

"Marty don't speak no Spanish," Mami's hushed voice followed Jaz out of the bedroom. "So I thinkin' you don't speak it no more, neither."

"I speak Spanish every day, with Maria, with Rosa, on the job at InfoSys." Jaz closed her bedroom door. "Did you think I would forget?"

"There are many things you forget. Like where your home is."

"You know why I don't come home, Mami. It's Papi. How can you ignore the way he treats me? How can you let him behave in ways you'd never allow from me?" Despite her attempt to modulate her voice, Jaz was unable to contain her anger.

"Don't you say that when Papi work so hard for this family. Don't you use him as your excuse for why you never come home, 'cause I know it not the reason."

"Then tell me, Mami. What is?"

"I think you afraid."

"Of what?"

"That you make a mistake when you turn down Pedro."

"That's ridiculous."

"And now you upset he marryin' Esteph, 'cause you know it should be you."

"¡Basta!" Jaz flung the word at her mother, unconcerned she might upset her daughter who babbled on the other side of the bedroom door. "All those phone calls . . . Why didn't you tell me?

Could it be that it's you who's forgotten who you are?"

"¿Qué?"

"You're my mother. Mi mamá." Jaz fled down the stairs.

"Jazmín." Mami pursued her.

"And I'm your daughter. Tu hija. Not Stephanie Bengochea."

Jaz grabbed her car keys and slammed out of the condo. Her chest heaved as she studied the parking area that held the Jetta and the space for Pedro's truck. All afternoon she had wondered where he was. Now she knew. He was out with Steph on some last minute errand. Down the steps Jaz ran, only to climb the mirror image ones that led to Pedro's condo next door. She rang the buzzer. Yessenia greeted her with a sharp intake of breath. "You're here?"

"No thanks to you or Mami."

"Did Pedro invite you?"

"No, but he should have. So where is he?"

Yessenia's fragile features imploded. "At Stone Canyon, though I'm not sure you should go there, Jazmín. I'm not sure you'd be . . . welcome."

"Well, I'm kind of getting used to that. Not being welcome in my own home. Or at my friends' wedding. So tell me. Do you approve of Estefanía? Or is she too white, too Catholic?"

"You know how much I wanted you to accept Pedro's proposal."

"¡Mentirosa! You were happy when I left, thrilled I'd turned Pedro down. After all, I was pregnant with another man's child."

"If Pedro could forgive you, then so could I."

"Oh, please. What you could never forgive was that I might take him away, but then I guess you never imagined him falling in love with Steph."

Yessenia's gaze shifted to the hallway. "Why don't we take Woofy for a walk?" Pedro's younger brothers, Luis and Gerardo, stood there.

"No. I'll leave," Jaz said, "because it's Pedro I need to talk to. Not you."

"If only you had obeyed your father. If only you had stayed."

"Then I'd be marrying Pedro instead of Steph? Is that what you think? You don't know that, Yessenia. No one can predict the future."

"But Juana did. She told me you and Pedro would fall in love. It was years ago, when we first cleaned together. After Raul . . ." The tears were disconcerting. Jaz was uncertain as to whether Yessenia wept over the loss of her beloved husband or the impending loss of her son. Yessenia motioned to Pedro's brothers that it was okay, that they could leave. Then she sat on the orange couch, the only bright spot in a living room that consisted of avocado shag carpeting and darkly paneled walls.

Jaz sat beside Yessenia. "Pedro and I did fall in love. We still love each other. We always will. But that doesn't mean we should marry. In some ways, we're close, but in other ways, we're different." When Yessenia continued to cry, Jaz scanned the coffee table for *La Biblia*, but Yessenia's Spanish Bible was nowhere to be seen. "Steph will be a much better wife to Pedro than I could ever be," was the only consolation Jaz offered. "Cuídate," she told Yessenia before she left. Hurrying down the steps of the Garcia's condominium, Jaz decided to leave her purse behind in order to avoid another confrontation with Mami. She backed the Jetta out and began to drive through the side streets in a haphazard fashion. In the lot behind Stone Canyon Bar and Grill, she left her car straddling two parking spots. Juan P. saw her before Pedro did. His smile vanished as soon as she walked in. He grabbed her by the arm and pulled her around a corner. His fingers dug into her flesh. "You're hurting me." Jaz shook her brother off.

"Déjalo en paz." Juan P. glanced over his shoulder. "He doesn't know you're here, so why don't we keep it that way?"

"And give him a heart attack when I show up at the wedding? I need to talk to him."

"And say what?" Juan P.'s face darkened. "That you've changed your mind?"

Jaz lowered her eyes. Her lips trembled.

"You've broken his heart, Chica, over and over again. Let it be. Besides, it's Steph you should talk to, not Pedro."

Jaz chastised herself silently for not being strong enough. As if she could control the tears that welled in her eyes, allowing them to shine but not fall. At last she glanced up at her brother. "Do you know where she is?"

"At home. Jenny is putting on a last-minute shower."

"For all the 'distant relatives'?"

"Jaz. Don't."

"Don't tell me what to do, Juan Pablo."

"And waste my breath?" Her brother sighed. Then he pulled her to him and kissed the top of her head. "I'm sorry. This must hurt like hell."

She held him, amazed he had grown so tall, that he was hand-some the way her father must have been at this age. "You have no idea." She wiped her eyes. "And you have no idea how much I've missed you."

"I've missed you, too." He kissed her cheek. "Actually, I'm glad Steph invited you, even if she wasn't completely honest. You should be here. Steph knows that."

Jaz pulled out her necklace with the silver Saint Christopher, cross, and Pisces medallion on it. She knew now why she had worn it. "I guess there's only one way to find out."

Juan P. nodded and let Jaz go.

Jenny's smile contorted into a frown once she realized it was

Jaz who knocked at the door. Steph came into the mudroom. Her mouth quivered at the corners. After giving Jaz a long hug, Steph ushered Jaz into the living room and introduced her to the "distant relatives" as if Jaz was merely late. The shower dragged on. Jaz motioned Steph to the kitchen, but it was impossible to talk. After everyone left, Jaz and Steph dried the dishes Jenny washed and put them away. "How about we drive up to the lakes?" Steph suggested.

"Are you sure you want to do that, Stephie?" Jenny stood before the kitchen's swinging door, her arms crossed. A solemn look hollowed her freckled cheeks.

"I'm sure." Steph yanked Jaz past Jenny.

At the lakes, they wandered in silence. Jaz was grateful for the quiet of the stars after an evening full of family myths and forced laughter. "Your grandmother, Baba," she began.

Steph nodded. "Yeah, she's something else. Drives Dad nuts. Mom, too."

"I've always sensed some tension there."

"Those two can't be in the same room without the fur flying. I hope they get through Saturday in one piece."

"I hope I do, too."

Steph took Jaz's hand and squeezed it. Then she straddled a log as if it were a horse and ran her hand over the rugged bark. "I'm sorry." Her voice broke. "I know I should have told you. I tried. I really did. But I just couldn't find the right words."

"How about I'm in love with Pedro, and I want to marry him?" When Steph looked morose, Jaz sat beside her. "Are you still mad at me about that night up in Reno? When I couldn't find the right words, either?"

Steph sighed. "I was, for a long time, but that's not why it was so hard to tell you about Pedro. It's just that everyone has always assumed the two of you would marry."

"Well, I guess Mami found her surrogate in you."

"You're the one who left, Jaz. You're the one who never comes home."

Jaz gave her friend a sidelong glance, "Does it ever annoy everyone how perfect you are?"

"Sounds like you're the one who's annoyed."

"Actually, I'm jealous, of all the time you get to spend with Pedro, and with Mami, too. It's obvious they like you better than me." Jaz's shoulders slumped. She picked apart the bark on the fallen tree, then she tried to piece it back together, as if it were a puzzle she needed to solve. "I'm sorry," she finally said. "That was harsh, as you would say, so you may find this hard to believe, but all I want right now is for you and Pedro to be happy."

Steph swung a leg over the log and dismounted. "Because you're so happy with Marty?"

"And that's another thing. Why did you tell Mami I wasn't?"

"Remember that night when I called, and you'd just had that fight with Marty?"

"Ay, Chica, I just needed to vent. Marty loves me, although he was a little freaked out the other night when I left my Palm Pilot and cell phone on the nightstand before we made love, just in case an important client of Judith's called."

Steph dug her shoe into the pumice and stood. "Then why isn't he here?"

Jaz's throat tightened. "I didn't want him to come."

"Because of Pedro?"

"Because of Papi."

"Oh." Steph sank down onto the log again. "How's that going?"

"He hardly speaks to me."

"That's . . . awful, Jaz. I'm sorry."

"Not half as sorry as I am. So believe me when I say I wish you and Pedro all the happiness in the world, because I always had a feeling that someday you'd . . ."

"Be together?"

Jaz nodded. "Remember that summer after high school when we all worked at Bert's?"

"And you and Pedro did nothing but fight?"

"And you shared all those deep thoughts with him?" When Steph hung her head, Jaz said, "We don't have to talk about it if you don't want to."

"You really want all the gory details?"

"Yeah, Chica, like, whatever happened to Corey?"

"When he graduated last year, we broke up," Steph replied flat-ly, as if Corey had been a mere blip on her radar. "And then, when Pedro showed up at my new apartment . . ."

"In San Diego?"

Steph nodded. "Said he decided to transfer when Dad told him I wouldn't be coming home for the summer."

"To UCSD?"

"To San Diego State. After a few months of living separately, we found a place with some Christians."

Jaz cocked her head. "You're a . . ?"

"Christian? I know. Another thing I should have told you. It's just hard to explain to people who don't . . ."

"Believe?"

Steph ignored Jaz's sarcasm and went on. "Pedro got me in-volved with his church in Mission Beach. We ended up renting a house there, with his friends, and . . ."

"You decided to get married," Jaz finished the story, surprised Steph had ended her relationship with Corey, lived with Pedro for almost a year, and become an Evangelical Christian. But mostly, Jaz was amazed Steph had failed to mention any of this. It made her friend's weekly e-mails seem as vacuous as Mami's phone calls. "Why didn't you tell me?"

"You never asked," Steph replied, though what she implied was, *You never wrote.* "But you're right, Jaz. I did fall in love with Pedro that summer when we were home from college. It took me a long time to admit it to myself, to sort out my feelings for him and for Corey."

"Who will be your Maid of Honor?"

"My sisters."

"But I'm your sister, too. Your gemela del alma, remember?"

"I couldn't do that. Have you up there as I marry your novio."

"Mi amigo, Steph. My neighbor. My first crush."

"Why do you always try to make it out that it was Pedro who cared, and you didn't?" Steph sounded annoyed. "You did care, Jaz. You still do."

Jaz ran her hand back and forth over the fallen pine's bark until her palm hurt. Then she brushed it over her hair, aware Steph watched her every move.

"Don't be scared," her friend said. "Be brave. You remember, don't you?"

Jaz did. Her hand tingled, as if rubbing it over the bark had conjured up this vision from the past. They had sat like this before, on a fallen log, on a sunny afternoon, the Bengocheas and the Valdezes enjoying a fall picnic with their young families. Jaz recalled the crispness of the aspen leaves, how they crackled underfoot, how everyone leaped from rock to slippery rock as they crisscrossed a stream full of red-bellied trout, the fish gaudy as they spawned. After lunch, Jaz and Steph scaled a huge, lightning-scarred Jeffery pine tree, its broken branches the stubby rungs of their ladder. Out on a limb they sat, balanced precariously, until Mami's voice became raw with emotion when she discovered their perch. "¿Jazmín? ¿Esteph? ¡Ay, Dios!"

"Careful," was all Jenny could manage. Lines carved crevices in her forehead.

"Don't worry, Mommy. We're fairy princesses," Steph called to Jenny. Then she rubbed her palms across the tree's puzzle bark and stroked her hair. "We're magic."

"¡Chicas! Climb down. ¡Ahora!" Mami sounded hoarse, her voice ragged with fright.

"Careful," Jenny repeated, as if she were in a trance, unable to take her eyes off her rock-a-bye babies in the gigantic treetop.

Steph managed to shimmy back toward the massive trunk. Jaz slipped when she tried. She could still hear Jenny's horrified gasp, Mami's frantic calls to Bert and Papi. But what was remarkable was how Steph remained calm as she climbed down the tree, how she stopped every now and then to rub the bark and stroke her hair. "Don't be scared," she told Jaz. "Remember. We're magic," she said as she lowered herself, the rounded rubber toes of her tennis shoes seeking out each peg-like branch. "Be brave," she smiled, encouraging Jaz to follow, assuring her she wouldn't tumble from the Jeffery pine like some flightless newborn bird.

Jaz recalled how she had stroked her own waist-length hair desperate to believe in Steph's magic, how her focus became the tree's bark that was thick and red. Its sweet smell calmed her as she made her way down, filling her lungs with the scent of vanilla, then pineapple, then butterscotch, until Mami and Papi were able to help her to the ground.

Jaz rubbed her hand across the bark on the fallen Jeffery pine where she and Steph sat now. She inhaled deeply as she stroked her hair. "How will you wear it on Saturday?"

"Half up and half down, with a veil attached under the flowers."

"Just like I did," Jaz murmured. Was this merely a coincidence?

"God," Steph said, "I'd forgotten. Or maybe I didn't. Do you mind?"

"Pedro didn't come to my wedding. He'll never know." Jaz

stood and motioned for Steph to follow. Then she took out her necklace. "And be sure to wear this."

Gemelas del alma, Jaz thought, as her two friends married, Jaz the Matron of Honor at Steph's request, Val and Char relegated to the rank of bridesmaids. It pleased Jaz when Steph insisted on doing this, though it upset everyone else, especially Pedro. He shifted uncomfortably throughout the rehearsal, turning from Jaz every time she tried to catch his eye. During the dinner that followed, she tried to engage him in conversation, but Juan P. took his role as Best Man seriously and never left Pedro's side.

What Jaz enjoyed most about the wedding was the music. The catchy Christian tunes played by the resident rock band at the Valley Church were inspirational, even if Steph's "distant relatives" looked scandalized by the closed-eyed swaying and uplifted palms that accompanied the congregation's vocal adoration of the Lord. What followed was a moving ceremony that ended in a chaste kiss. Pedro and Steph cast shy glances Jaz's way before they plunged down the aisle to greet their guests. Jaz trailed them, wondering if they had held back on her account.

The music at the reception (held at Bert's) was a curious mix of grunge (what Steph loved) and soft rock (what Pedro preferred). It made for an uneven effect. Nobody danced. Jaz overheard Steph's grandmother, Baba, ask about the honeymoon. A brief backpack in the local mountains, Steph replied, aware Jaz listened. Disclosing nothing further, Steph excused herself to cut the cake. After the bouquet was thrown (to Val who was thrilled to catch it) and the garter was tossed (to Chuy who snatched it triumphantly out of the air), the newlyweds departed, JUST MARRIED scrawled in pink paint all over Pedro's black truck. As her friends drove away, Jaz realized he had successfully avoided her. Was it guilt? She longed to tell him she was happy. If only he had given her the chance. With that, Jaz knew what she would do.

The next morning, she skipped Mass and drove to the trailhead instead. She set off up the path, wondering if she would encounter Steph and Pedro on their way down to attend the Valley Church's service. At the unmarked junction, she waded through tall grass that covered the path and feared she had hiked to Hidden Lake in vain. Pedro would only bring Steph to this place if it held a special meaning for them. Jaz's heart banged hard. Her head throbbed even harder. How could he forget their final time up here? She considered turning back, unsettled by the memory of that day, how they discovered they harbored desperately different desires.

The sight of Pedro's tent pitched on the rocky outcropping near the inlet stream, where she and Pedro had fought so bitterly, confirmed that everything had changed. The smoky scent of fried trout and wild onion reminded her of the lunch they shared that day. Granite gravel crunched beneath her boots. Pedro looked surprised when she emerged from the trees.

"Is there enough for me?" she asked.

Pedro turned to Steph who crouched beside him, cooking on the stove. "Did you--"

"No." Steph kissed Pedro before he could protest and wandered off into the forest.

"Why are you doing this, Jazmín?"

The fish sizzled in the pan as she composed her reply. "I needed to say good-bye, and as you know, I've never been good at that." He looked out over the lake, as if he were remembering it, too. "I'm sorry, but I've been trying to talk to you all weekend, and I knew if I didn't come up here, I'd be kicking myself all the way back to San Francisco, for not letting you know . . ."

His eyes cut to hers. "For not letting me know what?"

"That I'm happy for you. And for Steph."

"Are you?" He sounded unconvinced.

"Of course. What did you expect? You're still my two best friends." He turned off the gas stove and walked to the edge of the outcropping, where it sank into the lake. He picked up a shard of granite and skipped it across the water's surface. Jaz followed and stood beside him. For a while they said nothing, until at last she broke the silence. "Why didn't you tell me?"

"Because I didn't want to hurt you."

"But I'm married, Pedro. I have Maria now, and Marty."

"Steph says you don't love him, that Marty won't allow you to be who you really are."

"Will you allow Steph to be who she is?"

"She's a Christian. Like me."

"But what if she wasn't?"

"She is. And you could be, too, if you'd just stop messing around with astrology."

"Steph told you about my consulting?"

"I was the one who suggested she send you that book." Pedro chucked another rock toward the water. It sank with a *thunk*. "I told her Juana meant to give it to you."

"Steph told me she read *Spiritual Astrology*, that she liked it."

Pedro glared at her. "She reads the Bible now."

"Hey, you two." Steph carried the pan of fried trout over. "How about some lunch?"

"Jazmín was just about to leave," Pedro told Steph.

"After you walk me back to the meadow," Jaz replied. When Steph nodded at Pedro, Jaz kissed Steph's cheek. "Ciao, Chica. Be brave, and remember, I'm a phone call or an e-mail away." That said, Pedro had no choice but to accompany her back to the spur trail. Jaz wondered if she was the only one with unfinished business as they climbed down the rocks that surrounded Hidden Lake. The simple wedding band he wore caught the sunlight from time to time, a reminder that he now belonged to Steph.

"What are those?" Pedro jutted his chin toward the tall yellow flowers in the meadow.

"I'm not sure." She had never been good at identifying the yellow ones. There were too many of them, though she recognized the buttercups, their petals like liquid sunshine.

"I'm sorry. I know I should have told you, but I couldn't." He told her this in Spanish, as if he were trying to soothe her, the way he had so often when they were children. "I think it was because I was still angry, still jealous of Martin Donahue, *the third*."

"No, Pedro. I'm the one who should be sorry, because I'm jealous of you and Steph."

"Don't be," he said, his eyes on something only he could see. "I used to be so sure of everything, that the Lord had a plan for my life, and now?" He brushed his hand over the tall yellow flowers they waded through. "The only thing I'm sure of is I'm supposed to be with Steph." As if reading Jaz's mind, he added, "And it's not because I'm going to save her."

"No, it's because she's going to save you."

"Maybe." He smiled sadly. "Maybe it's why God became man for such a short time."

"Because it's hard?" When he nodded, she asked, "So we're still friends?"

"Para siempre."

At the intersection to the main trail they kissed each other's cheeks. If they had learned anything it was this: you only get a few friends in life, so you should treat them with care.

A sorrow of a different kind awaited her at home. There was no denying Woofy had grown old. Despite the arthritis in his rear legs, he escaped out the front door when she opened it. He wouldn't wander far. His days of chasing cats and cars were over. No one tried to bar his exit from the condo any longer. Jaz fetched his leash and took him for a walk past the Jeffrey pine near Pedro's condo.

The next day she awoke at four and tossed until five. Deciding to get up and off to an early start, she ran into Woofy at the bottom of the stairs. The dog wagged his tail and clawed his well-worn spot on the front door until she let him out. She went to the kitchen and switched on the coffee maker, startled when her father appeared. "You are leaving, Hija?" His face was stern. It made Jaz feel like the sneaky teenager she had once been. "Without so much as a good-bye to your mother or brothers or me?"

"No, of course not. Did I wake you?"

"No. Jenny's family is still in town. I have been opening the restaurant for Bert."

"I see," Jaz said, realizing that until now, she hadn't. Papi had been pulling double shifts, not avoiding her. "Would you like break-fast?" she asked him.

"I will get something to eat at the restaurant."

"Please, Papi. Marty loves my huevos rancheros. They're not as good as Mami's, but I'd love to make them for you."

"Bueno, Hija." He sat down at the table. "Andele pues."

Jaz longed for him to ask her about her life, but he didn't, so she fed him and waited for Papi to reveal some small part of himself. In the end what she settled for was the silent warmth of his company. As she cleaned up, she opened the cabinet under the sink. The garbage needed to be emptied. She took the sack out to the pail in the garage, but it was also full. To save Mami a trip to the Dumpster, Jaz pushed up the garage door and slung the sack over her shoulder.

Shadows scattered at her approach. Before the enormous metal bin lay a creature. An overpowering stench warned her it had fallen prey to attack. Jaz gasped and staggered back at the sight of the bloody mess that had once been Woofy, his gutted carcass almost unrecognizable in the dawn's coming light. Her cries in the garage brought her father running.

"Ay, Dios mio, Hija." Papi held her as she dissolved in his arms.

"It's my fault. . . . I let him out. . . . I should have known better."

"The coyotes. . . . They got Tigre this year, too."

Jaz looked up at her father, and burst into tears again.

"Go inside."

"But I should bury him." She headed to the garage to hunt for a shovel.

"Let me help you." Her tears gushed anew at the sight of Papi's stoic face. He found a shovel and returned to the kitchen for a garbage sack. A grimace thinned his lips. "Are you sure you want to do this?" She nodded and followed him, unable to watch her father scrape her beloved dog off the asphalt and bag his remains. "Where should we lay him to rest?" he asked.

"In the forest. It was his favorite place."

"De acuerdo. Ven."

They walked, leaving the road behind to follow the trail. At a clearing near a clump of lodgepole pines, with the blue jays screeching and the chickadees darting in the pewter sky, she said, "Aquí, no más, Papi. This is where Woofy would want to be."

"He always stopped here with me, too." When Jaz looked surprised, he said, "After you left, I walked him. We came up here often."

Jaz teared up at this revelation. "You'll miss him, won't you?"

Papi set down Woofy's bagged remains and held her. "Not as much as I will miss you."

Monday night, as Jaz drove home from work, she heard the single blast of a siren. In the rearview mirror a barrage of lights flashed. One of SFPD's finest was urging her to the side of Seventh Avenue. She lowered her window and asked, "Is there a problem, Officer?" trying to imitate Marty's authoritative manner the day he was stopped on the Bayshore for speeding. The motorcycle cop shined a flashlight in her eyes, blinding her. "Step out of the car, please, and have your license ready."

She leaned over and fumbled through the contents of her purse that lay strewn across the passenger seat. Her glasses case located, she took it in hand along with her license and shoveled everything back in. "Are you going to make me walk a white line or touch my nose? Because I'm so nervous I'm not sure I can." She shivered in the evening gloom, aware people had gathered on the sidewalk beneath the street lamp.

The cop took her license. "You're supposed to wear corrective lenses?"

"That's correct." He shot her a glance that said she was being a smartass. She waved the case. "I forgot to put them on. That's what I was doing when you pulled me over, going through my purse to find them."

"Do you have any objections to a breathalyzer test?" Jaz buttoned her jacket, chilled by what the cop implied. She peered over his shoulder, relieved the crowd had begun to disperse. "Do you have any idea how much you were swerving around on Lincoln?" he demanded, annoyed her attention had wandered.

A truck roared by, belching black smoke. The diesel fumes made Jaz's eyes tear and her nose run. "If you'd just let me explain," she pleaded when the solemn-faced cop turned to walk back to his motorcycle. "All right! I'll take the test. I was just trying to find my glasses, and I've got so much crud in my purse that even when I dumped it out--"

He held up a hand and returned. "I get the picture." He shone his flashlight on her license. "I suggest, Ms. Donahue, that next time you pull over and put your glasses on."

"Oh thank you, Officer. You have no idea how much I . . ." her smile dissolved when the cop jotted furiously on his pad. "You're writing me up?"

"Reckless driving."

"Mommy!" Maria's plaintive cry reminded Jaz her daughter sat strapped in the Jetta.

Jaz raced to Maria's side. "Mommy's here. It's okay."

"Distracted mothers are dangerous." The cop tapped his pen on his pad before he tore the ticket off. "Let this be a warning to you."

She watched his leather clad figure kick start his motorcycle and hammer away.

At the door to her home Marty removed the ticket from between her teeth. "Reckless driving?"

"I can explain."

"Explain?" He stripped Maria from her arms. "There's nothing to explain. When you run late, you're a disaster waiting to happen." He hustled off. "Where's the diaper bag?"

Jaz juggled her briefcase, purse, and exercise duffle as she trailed Marty down the hallway. "I'll have to go back out. I left it in the car."

Marty plopped Maria into her crib and turned to the changing table. "I don't believe it." He ran a hand over his closely cropped blond hair. "We're out of Pampers again." He faced his wife wearily. "If you'd just told me, I could have picked some up on the way home."

"There's plenty in the diaper bag. If you'd just let me go out there--"

"That's not the point. The point is it's always like this." His nostrils flared, perhaps because urine fumes filled the air. "When are you going to take the time to train her? Mother says she should be out of diapers by now, that she should be in a real bed."

"Don't start in on me, okay?" He looked exasperated rather than angry. Jaz set her bags down. "Look, I'm sorry. I know you're right. I'll have some more days coming with all the overtime I'm going to have to put in. In about a month or so I should have time to train Maria and buy her a real bed. But for now, I'd better get out there before the car seat is stolen--again." Jaz searched her purse for her cell phone. It was not in its case. She rushed out to the Jetta for the car seat, concerned the diaper bag wasn't there, either. She remembered putting it in the car, talking to Marty on the cell phone, then seeing the flashing lights in the rear view mirror.

"Where's the diaper bag?" Marty lingered forlornly in the doorway as Jaz came in.

"It's not in the car. And I can't find my phone, either."

"Jesus, Jaz. Did you leave them at Rosa's?"

"No, I called you, remember? To say I'd be late. I know I had the phone and the diaper bag with me when I was pulled over."

"What does the diaper bag have to do with the cell phone, unless . . . Did you throw it in there?" Marty followed Jaz to Maria's room.

"I must have," she wailed as she tried to piece it together. "The cop said I was driving erratically while I was looking for my glasses. My purse was dumped out all over the front seat, so I may have dropped the phone in the diaper bag when I pulled over." She sank into the rocking chair in which she had nursed Maria. "A crowd gathered." Jaz recalled her daughter's cry, alarmed now. "Do you think someone could've robbed me while I talked to that cop?" She bolted from the rocking chair and dug through her purse, "Carajo, Marty, my wallet's gone!"

"But your purse is here. Why would a thief take a diaper bag?"

"He must have seen the phone inside it." In her crib, Maria stood on tiptoe, naked. She had taken off her clothes and soggy diaper and was waving them at Jaz.

Marty headed for the door. "I'll go pick up some Pampers before Maria catches cold."

"No, wait." Jaz kissed her daughter and took her out of a crib that no longer contained her. In the living room she picked up the phone and punched in her cell number.

"You're calling the police?" Marty took his keys from a hook by the front door.

Jaz shook her head. She put Maria down and listened to her cell phone ring.

"You're calling the thief?" A grin spread across his face. "He'd be crazy to answer."

"Well, that guy was crazy to mess with me." Her phone purred and went silent, again and again. Marty turned away just as someone picked up. "Now you listen to me, you son of a bitch," Jaz hissed, "I've had a rotten day, and my little girl is standing here, wet and naked. You can keep the fucking phone, but you toss that diaper bag in front of 1370 7th Avenue, before I sic that motorcycle cop on you, ¿comprende?" She slammed down the receiver.

Marty laughed. "I don't believe you." He kissed her. Then in his best Arnold Schwarzenegger voice, he said, "I'll be back."

A few minutes later, he burst through the door. "Look!" He held a package of Pampers in one hand, the diaper bag in the other.

Jaz snatched the diaper bag and rummaged through it. "The phone's here! And my wallet!" But her happiness was short-lived when she went through the billfold. "And I thought we had a thief with a conscience ¡Qué cabrón! He cleaned me out."

Marty's eyes were tender. Jaz turned from him, but he refused to be put off. "You were great," he said, "the way you called him, the way you shamed him into bringing it back."

"He took all the credit cards, over a hundred dollars in cash. What kind of a crazy world do we live in where someone goes into your car during a traffic stop to steal a diaper bag?"

A purple vein in Marty's forehead began to pulse. "That's not all he could have stolen."

*Mommy!* The memory of Maria's cry forced Jaz to steady herself on the arm of the couch. She sank down and unleashed an anguished sob.

Marty sat beside her. "Shhh, it's okay." He turned her face toward his.

"No, it's not, but gracias a Dios, Maria's fine." She wiped her eyes. "I'll go bathe her."

For dinner, Jaz defrosted leftovers. Marty seemed grateful to be eating a meal that didn't come in a white bag with plastic forks. And while he doled out details to Jaz's inquires about his conversation with his father, regarding a loan to start Donahue and Associates, Marty's idea to create a website that matched highly skilled computer programmers to contracts with Bay Area firms, she couldn't recall the last time they'd had a real conversation. It worried her. Speaking in complete sentences to your spouse seemed like a minimum requirement for marriage. After calling the credit card companies, Jaz vacuumed, the noise a welcome distraction, even if the upright zooming back and forth across the living room carpet scared Maria. Once her daughter was in bed, Jaz folded laundry until Marty cornered her. "We should talk."

"I said I was sorry."

"Would you stop and listen?" He pushed the laundry aside and pulled her down onto the couch. "I've had it with raising a kid in this city. I think we should move."

"You're overreacting."

"I'm not. Tonight was a close call. Thank God nothing happened to you or Maria." Then Marty got up and paced. When he stopped his walking to nowhere, he said, "Father believes Donahue and Associates will do well, and that the demand for computer contractors will only grow. In a year we might be able to qualify for a home loan on my salary alone. Think of it, Jaz. You could quit working. We could move to Orinda and have another baby."

"I'm not sure I want to do that." When he stared at her, she said, "I'm sorry. It's just this new account I'm working on for Judith. It couldn't have come at a worse time."

"For you, or for Rosa?" A muscle in Marty's jaw twitched. "So why were you late? What was it that Rosa needed to talk to you about?"

"Her consulting business is really taking off. She can't handle it all by herself."

"And that's why you don't want to move, because of Rosa?"

"She's my friend, Marty, and Maria's baby-sitter, and she asked me to become her business partner." There, it was out, not like it would ruin an evening already ruined.

"Business partner?" The words exploded from Marty's pale, thin lips. "And what kind of business would that be? 'Madam Rosa's Fortune Telling Service'?"

"So you get to do Donahue and Associates, but I can't consult?"

He looked confused. "Working with Rosa has served its purpose. You don't need that any more. You have a great job at InfoSys. If you want to keep it, I'd support that, but--"

"But what? You think consulting with Rosa won't be lucrative? Well, I've got news for you. It is. People subscribe to our business forecasts because we give them advice as to what to expect: how long start-up will last; how much capital they'll need--"

"By casting horoscopes? Come on."

"Come on, yourself. You want to see our client list?"

"You mean Rosa's client list. You still work for InfoSys."

"You'd be surprised who's on that list, who's into this."

"I don't care, as long as you're not." He walked away. Then he turned back, looking as thrashed as she felt. "Why can't you be happy being a wife to me and a mother to Maria?"

Jaz's mouth opened but nothing came out.

Marty's scalp turned pink beneath his blond crew cut. At last he sighed. "I'm going to bed. And you should, too. Five-thirty will be here before we know it."

In the morning he didn't bring up having another child or moving to the East Bay. Relieved, Jaz made sure she got home from work early. She cooked pozole and handed Marty a Corona with a slice of lime in it as he walked in. "I know you're tired, and that the last thing you want is to discuss work, but I need your advice before I make a decision regarding Rosa's offer."

"Oh, man, here we go." Marty's eyes bulged beneath their closed lids.

"Please. Don't be that way. I value your opinion. I wouldn't bring it up if I didn't." This seemed to pacify him. He sank onto one of the red vinyl upholstered chairs at the retro kitchen table and sucked down half of his Corona before he said, "Okay, shoot."

Jaz joined him at the table. "Remember what Professor Caldwell told us our senior year? That most successful start-ups are collaborative, that going it alone can be a recipe for disaster?"

"And that's why I have to help you help Rosa?"

"Your skills compliment ours."

"Up to now you said all you needed was a PowerBook and a broadband connection."

"And a great idea. That's why I want to do this, Marty. It will allow me to work closer to home, to be a better wife to you, and a better mother to Maria. Remember how Professor Caldwell asked us what do you wish exists and doesn't?" She got up and served Marty a bowl of pozole. Then she put some through the blender for Maria. As Marty ate in silence, she said, "I know what you're thinking, that the timing's all wrong, which is ironic since what Rosa and I do is publish business forecasts that are based on astrological cycles. And according to the charts I ran today, the time is right for both of us to launch."

"When so many dotcoms are melting down like pats of butter?"

"Ours won't. If you remember, Professor Caldwell enthusiastically endorsed our ideas because there's never been an easier or cheaper time to start a new company."

Just then Maria ran in. "Daddy!" She could always bring a smile to Marty's face. He picked up his daughter, put her in her high chair, and brought her a sippy cup of milk. "What I remember is his concept regarding LILOs, ventures that require little in but put lots out."

"He approved our projects because he believed with so many people newly connected to the Internet, web-based businesses would have the potential of becoming real moneymakers."

"As long as we're willing to work hard and be patient."

"And we have a great product for the twenty-first century, which we do."

Marty brought Maria a plastic bowl of stew. "There's just one catch. Our companies have to make other people money."

"Or help them save it, and our websites will do both." She brought her bowl of pozole to the table. "Think of it, Marty. If we launch now, we'll learn how to survive on fumes. Imagine what could happen if our ideas take off? And the best part is you're a software developer who knows programming languages. That alone will save us tremendous amounts of money."

Marty took a thoughtful sip of his Corona. "I could start building the digital scaffolding this weekend."

Jaz kissed her husband's cheek. "It'll seem like we have staffs of twenty, not two."

"Three, if you count Rosa. So how will she pay me?"

"With equity in our company."

"What about marketing and advertising?" He got up and served himself a second helping of pozole. "According to Professor Caldwell, the reason so many start-ups fail is distribution. How will people find our sites?"

"We'll start by contacting people who are already clients, mine with Rosa, and yours with Stewart. That way we'll find out what works, and what doesn't. And with your skills, we can make changes to our websites quickly."

"You can't swing the bat much lower than that." Marty wolfed down his pozole.

"Our satisfied customers will tell their friends," Jaz told him between bites.

"And the rest will find us through search engines?" Marty went to the fridge and took out two more Coronas. Jaz loved this, the sense of partnership without pretense. "It'll keep our overhead low. I don't plan to fail, and I know you don't, either, because I take to heart what Professor Caldwell told us, that without risk there is no innovation. If we're smart about distribution and marketing, then what I envision is slow, steady growth."

Jaz lifted Maria out of her highchair. Once her daughter was in the living room playing with her toys Jaz returned. "It wouldn't surprise me if by the end of the year our websites log 10,000 visits per week."

"What about revenue?" Marty took a thoughtful sip of his second beer.

"Along with our services, we'll sell display ads to the businesses that use us, which should cover the server fee. By the way, how'd that meeting with your father go?"

"He suggested Stewart and I approach a venture capital firm. He gave us the names of several that prefer start-ups because if they catch on, they grow exponentially."

Jaz shook her head. "I don't think we need to borrow money, anymore than we need someone to write up a business plan, or sell it to investors. The display ads alone could make our companies self-sustaining in a year."

Marty clinked his second beer to hers. "The reason so many dotcoms fail is their business plans don't work because the cost of mapping everything out is higher than the actual cost of trying it."

Chilled suddenly, Jaz said, "If the dotcom bust continues, our websites will do well."

"Yeah," Marty agreed. "Maybe that's why Stewart is so scared."

"He is? Well, then, maybe he'll finally look at Rosa's website and take our advice."

Marty took a long pull on his Corona. "So, what will you call your new company?"

"I have no idea." Jaz set her bottle aside. "All I care about is that I can run it from Rosa's apartment while being a wife to you, a mother to Maria, and an IT director for Judith."

# Stephanie Bengochea Garcia
## December 14, 1998

*Youth is a religion from which one always ends up being converted*
*--Andre Malraux*

S teph seated herself in front of Dad's laptop and wrote:

CHICA, THANKS FOR THE TEA. I'LL LET YOU KNOW WHAT I THINK. TAKE NOTE OF MY NEW E-MAIL ADDRESS, A HOTMAIL ACCOUNT BECAUSE WE'RE BACK IN PLEASANT VALLEY, AND YES, IT'S WEIRD. WE'RE STAYING WITH MY PARENTS UNTIL WE FIND A PLACE OF OUR OWN. THANKS TO THEM, WE PICKED UP A COUPLE OF SHIFTS AT BERT'S THIS PAST WEEK, BUT I DON'T THINK THEY'LL BE ABLE TO THROW MUCH OUR WAY. YOU KNOW HOW IT IS, THE LOOKS, THE WHISPERS, BUT WITH SO MANY PEOPLE OUT OF WORK, I UNDERSTAND, ALTHOUGH IT'S HARD SOMETIMES TO BE THE BOSS'S DAUGHTER. I LOOK AT BETI, AND I WONDER HOW SHE DOES IT. TWENTY YEARS OF SERVING BURGERS, OF SMILING AT FLATLANDERS WHO DEMAND THE MOON, THEN LEAVE YOU NO TIP. IT'S BEEN SLOW, BUT DAD IS KEEPING EVERYONE ON. I TELL YOU, THERE'LL BE A PARTY THE DAY THE HOLIDAY HORDES ARRIVE. I ALMOST FORGOT. I'LL BE WORKING FOR SKI PATROL. EMT CLASSES BEGIN NEXT WEEK. GREG MORRIS CLAIMS HE ONLY HIRED ME BECAUSE OF MY SPANISH. AS FOR PEDRO,

HE'S HELPING JUAN P. AT THE CONDOS, DOING REPAIRS, SO WE'LL SURVIVE. I'M SORRY I HAVEN'T WRITTEN MUCH SINCE THE WEDDING, BUT THOSE DAYS ARE OVER. I MISS YOU. ABRAZOS TO MARIA AND MARTY.

Steph connected to her family's dial-up server, a hassle compared to the DSL she had enjoyed at UCSD, and sent her message hurtling through cyberspace, thankful for this electronic miracle that allowed her to stay in touch with Jaz for less than the cost of a phone call. E-mail was more fun than letter writing. The countless thank-you notes Steph had written after the wedding had dampened her interest in that. She shut down Dad's PowerBook.

In the kitchen Mom offered Steph a cup of coffee. "Thanks, but I'm having tea today." Steph filled a mug at the sink and relished yet another taken-for-granted luxury of living in the mountains. No more bad-tasting tap water. She placed a tea bag in her mug, her mug in the microwave, and punched the beverage button on.

"You sure you don't want coffee?" Mom poured herself a cup.

"Jaz sent me this as a Christmas present. She wants my opinion of it."

"So Jaz is a tea drinker now?" Mom stirred half-and-half into her mug. "Which means you must become a tea drinker, too?" Mom still hadn't forgiven Jaz for receiving the Rotary Scholarship, or Dad for awarding it to her. Steph wondered if Mom's bitterness stemmed from the fact all she consumed in the morning was coffee. "Is Jaz pregnant? Again?"

"No," Steph told Mom, though the question made her wonder. What she knew for sure was Mom seemed brittle, like her hair that had lost its coppery sheen. Her recovery had been slow. She no longer used a cane, and the physical therapy sessions were becoming less painful, but she had lost a lot of weight and still had little appetite. When she did eat, her diet was atrocious. Steph made a point of curbing her comments about the deep-fried onion rings and greasy burgers that were Mom's staple fare at home and at the restaurant. After the accident, Steph suggested Mom include vegetarian entrees on the menu, an idea that was met with eye rolling. Steph felt certain Mom had gone along with it at the time to absolve her guilt, yet the restaurant's menu now included soy burgers and a grilled vegetable sandwich, proof these items were popular enough to be listed as more than whiteboard specials. She was about to suggest she and Mom experiment with more meatless fare when Mom asked, "So what's on tap for today?"

"Dewey Mitchell is showing us a studio. Then I'm up at the mountain." Steph removed the tea bag from her mug and joined Mom at the table. "I'll be able to relieve you at five."

"So late?" Mom rose, a look of tired resignation on her face.

"Mom. . . . If you ever need me to . . . I don't know, to do anything--"

"I don't." Mom slung the dregs of her coffee into the sink and limped out of the kitchen. The door swung madly in her wake. Everyone in town admired her. *She never complains* was all Steph heard. But then Mom didn't have to. Her martyr's pose said it all. It made Steph feel as if she had screwed up by dropping out of school and coming home to help after the accident, then returning to UCSD to complete her degree, only to come home again now.

Steph neglected to tell her mother that between looking for housing and ski patrol training she had also scheduled an appointment at the clinic. She brooded about her wedding night six months ago up at Hidden Lake. Pedro had slipped the condom out of the side pocket of his pack, surprised when she took it from him, his eyes tender once he understood what she opened herself to. The problem was nothing had happened. Steph felt certain it was God's punishment for aborting Corey's child. It was why she might allow Juana to practice Reiki on her, whatever that was. Into the kitchen Pedro trotted still panting from his run. The look he gave Steph reminded her of the way he used to look at Jaz. But instead of feeling reassured, Steph felt scared. A love so great brought with it expectations that might be impossible to fulfill. She gave him a tepid smile over her tepid mug of tea. He kissed her forehead and went to take a shower.

After a quick bite Steph left her parents' house with Pedro to meet Dewey Mitchell who showed them yet another in a long line of dismal studio apartments. Her childhood home was no palace, but it seemed like a mansion compared to the places Dewey schlepped them through. Steph worried about what she would say regarding this one. It was obvious Dewey thought he was doing them a favor. And perhaps he was, which meant if this run-down, all-electric unit with a northern exposure and no wood burner was as good as it got, she was in trouble.

"We could share Carlos and Ana Claudia's place," Pedro whispered in her ear.

Annoyed by what he took to be a disparaging remark, Dewey said, "I should warn you if you want this one, you'll need to fill out the application and the credit check form immediately." He locked up. "Another couple is interested. It'll be gone by the end of the day."

Steph glanced at Pedro, "Thanks, Mr. Mitchell, but I think we'll pass."

Dewey's thumbs found the belt loops of his jeans. "This is a good deal, Stephanie. I actually held off renting it because your mom and dad are two of my favorite people in town. They told me you kids were having a heck of a time finding anything you could afford." Dewey rocked back on the heels of his cowboy boots. "I'm not sure what you had in mind, but on your salary," he cast a derisive look Pedro's way, "you may need some help qualifying."

"She said no thanks." Pedro strode away, his contempt for Dewey Mitchell undisguised. His mother had worked for him years ago until he fired Yessenia and Jaz's mother Juana as well.

"Have it your way, son. Just make sure you explain to Bert and Jenny that this was your decision, not mine." The buttons on Dewey's flannel shirt looked like they would burst with every aggravated breath he took. "Now Jenny, she's a trooper. She never complains," he told Steph. "The way she's back at work, as if that accident never happened."

Steph lowered her eyes and followed Pedro back to the truck. At the end of the driveway, a couch sat upended, its stuffing torn loose. Black plastic sacks surrounded it, their contents ravaged by coyotes. Steph thought of Tigre and Woofy as she studied the grapefruit rinds, tan eggshells, and coffee grounds that were scattered across the snow. No bloody tracks ringed the mess, but it depressed her nonetheless, much as the cheaply constructed units Dewey had offered them. What really irked her was his insinuation he would be doing them a favor by ignoring their credit rating, or lack thereof. The last thing she wanted was to share an apartment with Ana Claudia and Carlos, friends from church, but that was their only option now.

What had possessed her to return to Pleasant Valley during ski season? The seasonal workforce that ebbed and flowed in and out of town had already snapped up every decent rental. She and Pedro could have stayed in Mission Beach, worked until spring when they would have had their pick of places at rock-bottom prices compared to the dumps being shown to them now. Why on earth had she agreed to come back? She'd done it for him. He missed the mountains and had never adapted to the Southern California beach scene. The day San Diego State signed off on his graduation checklist, she found him outside their shingled cottage loading the truck. After a phone call to her parents, who seemed less than enthusiastic about their imminent return, she and Pedro told their house mates goodbye, something that seemed incredibly impulsive to her now.

Pedro drummed his fingers on the wheel. They were sitting in the clinic's parking lot. "Why are we here?" she asked.

"You have a ten-thirty appointment."

"Oh God." She popped the truck's door open. "I totally forgot."

"Should I go in with you?" Pedro seemed reluctant to leave.

"No." She climbed out of the truck and waved him off, hoping Juan P. would have something for Pedro to do today. Once inside the clinic she was called back immediately. She checked her watch. She would have to catch the shuttle up to the lodge by eleven to be out on the snow by twelve. Her appointment was with the nurse practitioner, Nancy Adams, not Dr. Jameson, who was a family friend. Nancy had attended to Steph's needs, physical and emotional, when Steph returned home the first time. The nurse was the only person in town who knew about Steph's terminated pregnancy, so Nancy could be trusted to handle fertility testing discretely. "When will you have the results?" Steph asked as she slipped on her clothes.

"In a couple of days," Nancy told her. "I'll call you--"

"I'll come by. I don't want to upset Mom. She's been through enough already."

"What about Pedro?" Nancy asked. "Have you told him about any of this?"

"No." Steph turned away to zip her jacket.

"Why don't you both come in Friday afternoon? I should know something by then."

"The problem is our schedules." Steph glanced at her watch and shouldered her backpack. It was five past eleven. Nancy removed her glasses and rubbed her eye sockets. The white coat made her look drawn in the fluorescent light. "Neither of us have set hours yet," Steph told the nurse, "and if I don't leave right now, Greg Morris will fire me before I even finish training."

Nancy frowned. "You're sure I can't call you about this at home?"

"I'm sure." Steph took her chart to reception. Then she scooted out the door. Down the street she ran, picking her way over the icy patches. The ski area shuttle waited for her at the bus stop. The driver, Kevin, was another friend who attended the Valley Church. He shared his good news with Steph. He and his wife Melinda were expecting a baby. Steph congratulated him, though this depressed her even more. When the bus pulled up to the lodge, she leaped out and bounded up the stairs to her locker. The last one out to line up, she dreaded what Greg would say this time. "Late again, Garcia," his eyes were iridescent in his deeply tanned face. "I thought you wanted this job."

"I do." Steph was breathless, still adjusting to the altitude after a week home. She was no longer a local, no longer a teenager with unlimited energy. The overload of training, working, looking for housing, and probing her body's mysteries, was getting her down.

*She never complains,* Dewey Martin's voice whispered in Steph's ear.

"Did you hear what I said, Garcia?"

"I'm sorry, Greg. I heard the part about the gondola, but then--"

"You zoned out, and that's dangerous. So grow up and prove me wrong. That you're not that giddy high-school girl I used to coach. That I didn't make a mistake by hiring you."

She nodded and swallowed hard. He seemed to take pleasure in criticizing her in front of the other trainees. Her first day, he told her to quit skiing like an instructor and get down the mountain fast. He laughed the next day when she crashed in the terrain park due to not gaining enough air to clear a jump. Steph's wrist still hurt from that one. He called her "Garcia" to let everyone know the only reason he'd hired her was the mountain's requirement that they have a Spanish-speaking patroller on the slopes at all times. But she would handle it. She would prove herself by taking whatever he dished out. If he extended her hours, she and Pedro wouldn't have to depend on her parents for a place to live or for work.

Her training group headed straight for the top of the mountain in the gondola. The plan was to follow Greg down to mid-chalet, the lodge halfway down, and stop there for further instructions. As she skied in tight formation with her fellow trainees, a boarder crashed through the trees just above her. She ducked and fell, popping out of her skis, to avoid a collision with the idiot who was not in the area where aerial stunts were allowed. It was a common problem with tourists who didn't always confine their tricks to the terrain parks. But what alarmed her was in jumping over the snowcat-created berm, the boarder had narrowly missed her head. Shaken, she brushed herself off as Greg laid into the guy. They were always young males, these hot-dogging types, but when the boarder defended himself, Steph blanched.

"Hey man, I'm sorry. I'll take a lesson. Just don't pull my ticket."

"Corey?" Steph pushed up her goggles.

"Steph?" He allowed his to drop around his neck and smiled when he recognized her.

"You know this moron?" Greg asked.

"Unfortunately."

"Take him down, Garcia. Write him up in the office."

"But--"

"No buts." Greg's forehead creased. "Christ, he nearly took you out."

Steph nodded and clicked back into her bindings.

Greg reached for his radio and called base one, saying she was headed in with someone who would lose his ticket for the day. "After that take a break. Make sure you're at the gondola by two." With that Greg was off. The rest of the trainees followed. It left her alone with Corey.

"We'd better get down there," she said.

"You're really going to bust me?" Corey's golden curls fell from his beanie as he shook it out. His wind-burned face convinced her the previous day had been spent on the slopes.

"What did you think?" she asked. "That I'd let you go once Greg was gone, because you used to mean something to me?"

"Well . . . yeah."

She felt undone by his boyish charm, angered she was still susceptible to it. God, he had nearly killed her. She wondered if he had any idea. "They're expecting us at main lodge." She poled over to him. "If we don't go now, they'll send law enforcement after you and fire me."

"Steph, I'm sorry. I really am."

"I know you didn't do it on purpose, but frankly--"

"I won't catch any more air outside the park. I promise."

"So how many times have you been out riding this year?"

"Would you believe it's my second day?"

"Well . . . yeah."

He laughed. She told him to go ahead, that she would follow. During the descent she enjoyed watching her ex-boyfriend carve and shred until the responsibility of working ski patrol hit her. If this was what the season had to offer, more surfer dudes like Corey who thought they could ride the mountain the way they rode the waves, it would be a long season.

Steph had grown up on skis and had only taken up snowboarding in high school. She recalled how Dad disapproved when the mountain decided to let the renegades in. With their baggy pants and beanie caps, they engendered a good deal of discussion over the burgers and lemonade Dad served to the locals who loved to debate Pleasant Mountain's policy of shared slopes. It was the future of the industry many argued, pointing to the declining number of skier visits. It will ruin the ambiance for the loyalists others insisted, equally vehement the hormonal males and ditzy blondes with their punk rock blasting in the terrain parks would scare away the older, moneyed crowd. Steph rarely engaged in these discussions. She witnessed no schism. And while it amused her that this newly come group made up of surfers and skaters saw the mountain as another wave or skateboard park to conquer, she only knew she loved riding as much as she loved skiing. With a boot in both worlds, she still remained undecided as to which fit.

Steph took Corey to the office where his ticket was voided. She put in a good word, saying it was due to inexperience, not irresponsibility. She made sure he would be allowed to purchase a lift ticket the next morning provided he enrolled in a lesson.

"I don't suppose I could get you as my instructor," he said as they left the office.

"I don't teach anymore." She checked her watch.

"Let me treat you to a hot chocolate."

"I'm not sure that's a good idea."

"Why?"

"This is a small town, Corey, and I'm a married woman now."

"And I'm a friend who's trying to apologize."

His smile was his act of contrition. It destroyed her resolve and reminded her that her fingers were numb. Wrapping them around a mug of Nestlé's might not be a bad idea. They passed through the beverage line and found a secluded spot in the cafeteria where they could talk. "Are you up here with your parents?" she asked.

"With a friend."

"Anyone I know?"

"Ashley."

"That ditz? She always did have the hots for you." Steph recalled how Ashley would show up at Corey's dorm room, asking lame questions, scowling if Steph offered a solution to Ashley's problem of the day. Steph downed the last of her hot chocolate. "I should go."

"I'm sorry." His hand covered Steph's.

"I know." Beyond Corey there was an immense wall of glass. Through it Steph watched the skiers and boarders who whooshed down, only to slingshot back up the hill on the chairlift.

"Have you told Pedro?" Corey asked.

"No." She longed for that unbound feeling, to be anywhere but here.

"Do you still work at Bert's?" Corey finished his cocoa and wiped his chocolate mustache away. She nodded. "Then Ashley and I will grab some dinner there."

"I'm not sure that's a good idea."

"Don't worry. I won't say anything. I just want to see you again, one last time."

It was a cue for a hug, but she dared not. "Where's Ashley?"

"Outside, probably getting ready for her afternoon lesson. Why?"

"I could arrange for you to join her."

"How?"

"I know people at ski school. If you have a credit card, you could take that lesson today, instead of wasting half a day tomorrow."

"Thanks." His smile was more than that of a grateful friend.

Once everything was set Steph told Corey, "I'll see you and Ashley tonight." Corey nodded. As he wandered off to retrieve his board and surprise his girlfriend, Steph felt a pit form in her stomach. It was how she always felt whenever she sent Corey Carlsen away.

As promised, he brought Ashley to Bert's. As expected, he flirted with Steph, which made her all the more relieved Pedro was off for the evening. But what Steph hadn't counted on was running into Juana Valdez--literally--as she turned away from the pick-up counter. "Ay, Madrina. What are you doing here?" Steph had nearly spilled Corey and Ashley's burgers down Juana's red jumpsuit. As it was the glasses of lemonade on the tray had tipped over. "I thought you were going to Madison to see Monster Trucks at the fairgrounds with Antonio."

"I tell him to take Pedro y los chicos, that they enjoy it more than me. I just here, pickin' up my order to go, unless you need me to stay and help." Juana grabbed a towel to mop up the lemonade that still dripped onto the floor.

Steph set her tray down. "I wonder at times how you did it, how you cleaned condos and waited tables. I'm exhausted after a week of this and ski patrol."

Juana shrugged. "It go okay, until Dewey Mitchell complain to your father that I talk too much, that I not quick enough with the food. It remind me why I not workin' for him no more."

"I don't know how you and Yessenia were able to stand it all those years." Steph filled clean glasses with lemonade.

Juana's gaze wandered to the crowd that milled in the lobby. "You turn those tables over. That's what your father always tellin' me. What station you workin' tonight?"

"Numbers three and four." Steph nodded in the direction of the greenhouse, to where Ashley and Corey sat, waiting for their order.

"Bueno. Then after work, you come over, ¿eh?"

"I promised Pedro I'd look at this week's *Gazette* to see if there are any new listings."

"I hear you gonna live with Ana Claudia and Carlos."

"Says who?" Steph adjusted her grip on the tray.

"Yessenia."

The bell at the pick-up counter rang out. "Dad gets upset if I talk too much."

"You tellin' me something I don't already know?"

Steph couldn't help but smile. "I don't know how to thank you for taking my place."

"You thank me by comin' over tonight and lettin' me practice Reiki on you."

"I don't get off until nine."

"Then make it snappy, 'cause Antonio, Pedro y los chicos, they home at eleven."

Steph nodded and hustled off with Corey and Ashley's order that was growing cold.

At nine she left Bert's and drove to the Valdez condo, unprepared for what lay on the other side of the front door. Candles illuminated the living room. Entranced, Steph dropped her pack on the entryway's tile and slid out of her jacket and shoes. "Es bonito, ¿eh?" Juana said.

"The light. It transforms this place. And none of the candles are blowing out."

Juana made a face at Steph. "We be in the dark if they do."

"It's absolutely magical, Madrina."

"It's Reiki. It change your life, like it change mine."

"Where did you learn how to do this?" Steph freed her ponytail from its elastic and allowed her hair to glide over her shoulders.

"In San Francisco."

"From Rosa?"

"From one of her clients." Juana seemed childlike as she liberated cushions from the couch, but instead of building a fort with them, she lined them up on the floor.

"I can't begin to imagine the trouble the two of you could make together."

"She's buena gente. I feel better knowin' she watchin' over Jazmín. Maria, too."

"Do I need to take my clothes off?"

"Ay, Dios mio, no. What you think I run here? A massage parlor?"

"Should I be quiet? Or can I ask questions?"

"What you want to know?"

"Well," Steph snuggled face down onto the cushions, "for starters, I thought Rosa was an astrologer not a masseuse."

"She is." Juana warmed her hands over a nearby candle.

"Then what does Reiki have to do with astrology?"

"Nothin'." Juana's answer hung in the air, suspended. The touch of her hands made Steph stiffen. Her madrina merely closed her eyes and waited patiently for the placement to be accepted. She appeared to concentrate, as if she were delving deeply into the tissue of Steph's body. "One of Rosa's clients, he do Reiki. I meet him when I go over there, and he talk me into takin' his class the next time I visit Jazmín. So I did. And I like it. The problem is I need to practice before I go back and take the next level. That's why I ask you to let me do this, because my family, they won't let me near them." Juana increased the pressure of her hands. Her lips moved as if she were reciting a prayer.

Turning her head from side to side, Steph asked, "What exactly are you doing?"

"I talkin' to los angelitos. I listen. I do what they tell me." Juana's lips moved again. "Do you believe in los angelitos?"

"I've always thought of you as my guardian angel. Did you know that?"

Juana nodded. She shifted her hands down Steph's back. Warmth radiated with each new placement. Juana continued to listen and wait. "Los angelitos. They tell me . . . everything."

With that, Steph tensed. "What you afraid of?" Juana asked as she repositioned her hands.

A wave of nausea rolled through Steph. Her stomach began to churn. The contractions felt vaguely familiar. "It's just that there's a lot . . ."

"That I don't already know?" When Juana lifted her hands suddenly, Steph realized her skin was as hot as a griddle. A moment later Steph's back began to spasm, only to relax when Juana kneaded the muscles as if they were a ropey, glutinous dough.

Steph lifted her head. "What happened just then?"

"Lo siento, mi hijita. I was just thinkin' about somethin' in my own life, in my own body. It got nothin' to do with you. I be more careful next time, ¿eh?" Juana went on to explain that Reiki involved touch more than massage, and that it came from Japan. It was a way of allowing the body to tell the practitioner what troubled each client. But that only happened if the client wanted the practitioner's help. Juana insisted she was merely an instrument, a conduit that channeled divine intervention. "It los angelitos," she said as she palpated Steph's back.

"So is my body telling you something you don't already know?"

Steph's attempt at humor seemed lost on Juana. Her brow wrinkled. "Seeing that boy today. That Corey? It nearly . . . kill you?"

"My God," Steph scrambled up from the cushions. She glanced fitfully at the flickering candles. "How on earth did you know that?"

"Ya pues, it don't take no angelitos for me to see how you lookin' at him tonight, or how he lookin' at you--"

"No, I mean," Steph studied Juana, spooked, "it's true. Corey almost killed me today."

"¿Qué?" Juana reared back on her knees. Steph told her about their near fatal collision. Juana looked ashen in the wavering light. She urged Steph to lie down again. When she did, Juana placed the palms of her hands on the small of Steph's back. "No, there's somethin' else, somethin' deeper with that Corey."

"I don't love him anymore, if that's what you're worried about."

Juana moved her hands up Steph's back. "There's a hueco, a hole in your energy field."

"In my what?"

"Roll over." Juana's hands were under Steph's body.

"Why?" Steph resisted Juana's efforts.

"Because that hole I'm feelin', I think it near your tummy button."

"It's belly button, Madrina. And that's it." Steph knelt then stood. "That's enough hocus-pocus for one night."

"Hey? Where you goin'?"

"Home." Steph walked to the entryway. "I've got ski patrol in the morning."

"Chuy tell me he see you leavin' the clinic today, that you run in and out of there so fast you don't even see him, don't even say hi. Why?"

Steph shifted, uncomfortable. "I didn't want to be late to training."

"That not what I mean. I askin' why you at the clinic?"

"I had to have some tests made." Steph rubbed her forehead.

"You dizzy?" Steph nodded at Juana. "That because you stand up too fast. Lie down. We not finished." Steph complied with Juana's request, unsure as to why. She closed her eyes, relaxed by Juana's steady, loving touch, only to be overcome by the sensation of wings brushing her face. It was as if her breath were being sucked away. She had felt this sensation before, the day they sucked the baby from her womb. "You pregnant?" Juana asked.

"No," Steph said, aware suddenly that every candle in the living room flickered.

"That hueco, it comin' from your womb. Los angelitos, they say you wish it were full." When a tear ran down Steph's cheek, Juana asked, "You happy with Pedro?" Steph nodded. "It just make me sad knowin' you want a baby, and it not happenin'." Several candles blew out. Steph sat up and hugged her knees. "Por favor, Esteph. Let los angelitos tell you why." Steph searched Juana's eyes and decided she would. "Bueno. On your back." Juana moved her hands above Steph's abdomen, only to unexpectedly double over, her lips stretched over bared teeth.

"What is it?"

"That hueco. It because you had a child and you . . . lose it?" Juana gasped, as if she were resisting the urge to be sick.

"That's right." Steph's voice was little more than a whisper.

"With that boy? With that Corey?" Steph nodded. She sat up and wiped her eyes with the hem of her T-shirt. "Why you not tell me?" Juana asked.

"I told no one except Jaz. And now I've told you, which I shouldn't have."

"But you didn't, Esteph. Los angelitos tell me."

"Please, Juana. Pedro doesn't know. No one knows. I feel so guilty, like I'm being punished by God."

"Because you . . ?"

Steph nodded. "And now that I want children . . ." Juana took Steph's hand and looked as if she were close to tears herself. "It's why I was at the clinic today, to find out what's wrong. So what about the future, Madrina? Do you see any . . . ?" Juana closed her eyes, as if she were waiting for los angelitos to speak. Cool air brushed Steph's face and extinguished every candle in the room. She felt drained, like her energy was being sucked away, steel to a magnet. She rose and switched on a lamp. She watched Juana, expectant. "Do you see any children?"

Eyes still closed, Juana shook her head sadly. "Not with Pedro."

Work usually began at six, but the following morning it began at four with a phone call. "We've got eight inches, and it's still coming down," was Greg's terse report. "Pass it on and get up here." Steph took her phone tree from the nightstand drawer and called Casper. His machine picked up. She wondered how many of the other rookies would get the message. There had been a party last night. It was obvious Casper never made it home.

Morning meeting was sparsely attended. Scott Hansen, the director of ski patrol, began by saying he had never left the day before, and neither had Greg. They had spent the night in the first aid room on cots. "There's a pineapple express going on," Scott said, explaining that orographic lift was warming the clouds as they moved up over the mountains, and that when the moist Pacific air collided with cold continental air it created snowstorms. "It's what makes the Sierras the ultimate snowmaking machine. The range funnels cyclonic winds and loads the pack with snow ten times faster than it can fall." Scott currently commuted to University of Nevada, Reno, to complete a master's in snow science. He planned to work as a Forest Service avalanche forecaster for the central Sierra once he got his degree. Years ago his father had worked as a hydrologist, traveling the entire length of the Sierra crest, charting the depth of the snow pack and collecting samples for analysis. Scott still dug snow pits on Pleasant Mountain.

He took the rookies out to show them his latest one, what the various layers looked like in this particular weather sequence. "Snow goes through a metamorphosis under pressure that can transform it from a thing of beauty to something treacherous in a matter of hours." Scott went on to describe the interaction between terrain, weather, and the snow pack. He used all three to calculate hazard. Once they were back inside the patrol room at main lodge, or base one as Scott called it, he announced, "I'm looking for someone to transcribe years of hand-written records to a spreadsheet. If anyone's interested, please let me know." Steph was. While the other trainees took a break, she talked to Scott. "Come in tomorrow, and I'll get you started."

Scott's charts were incredibly detailed. They recorded date, time, temperature, precipitation, barometric pressure, wind speed and direction. There were anecdotal notes about the core samples he took, that he melted to gauge the snow's water content. The day after she set up the spreadsheets for Scott, Steph arrived for training, concerned now because snow was still falling. As assistant director of ski patrol, it was Greg's turn to train the rookies. He began by going over the avalanche control plan, reviewing the hazard forecast Scott had meticulously made. Greg explained that pairs were normally assigned to the routes, though only the primary slopes would be dealt with today. The secondary slopes would have to wait until the storm eased. There was little danger of skiers getting caught in an avalanche since those slopes were accessed by chairlifts that couldn't operate in the wind. To release those slopes the patrollers would have to trek up the ridge and belay each other down from one spot to another. Holes would be drilled and charges would be strung together with a detonation cord so they could be set off all at once. Hand charges would be used on the primary slopes. It was a safer, more reliable way to release slides. The howitzer, an artillery piece, was even better, but without visibility it was out of the question. It was also loud. Its concussion could shatter windshields in the main lodge's parking lot. "Go back to your lockers for your mountaineering skis," Greg told the rookies.

When everyone returned, Scott took over and directed the explosives training. The hand charges would need to be filled with gelatin dynamite. The charges came in fifty-pound boxes. At two pounds each there were twenty-five shots per box. Fat and waxy, the reddish color of the charges made them look like salamis. To arm each charge with a cap and fuse assembly Scott showed the rookies how to cut eighteen-inch lengths of fuse from thousand-foot rolls, each fuse a thin orange cord housed in a plastic textile sheath. Then Scott directed the trainees to set out the caps that came one hundred to a box. Each cap had to be crimped to its fuse. On the side of the box Scott pointed to the burn time. It said forty seconds, but at altitude, he explained, it was twice that. He divided the rookies in half and assigned Steph's group the task of testing each new box ordered and recording on the flap what the actual burn time was. Greg helped with this. Steph marked the first box she tested 70 SECONDS. Once all the boxes were labeled, Greg showed her group how to use a non-sparking punch to poke holes in the side of each charge pack. Then he showed them how to attach the blasting caps and fuses to each bomb with duct tape. Finally they set out. The primary slopes were cleared first. The secondary slopes were dealt with after lunch. It was almost dark by the time Greg and Scott sent the rookies home.

The following day, the storm eased, so the trainees prepared for round two of avalanche control. In the back room of the ski patrol office the equipment was cached. Beacons, probe poles, snow anchors, karabiners, rope, and explosive materials were stacked in separate lockers, ready to be ransacked by the often-harried patrollers. Backpacks for hauling the charges were lined up against the opposite wall and were used to carry the sticks of dynamite, fuses, and blasting caps Steph's group had been taught to lash together with duct tape the day before. Personal backpacks were used to carry first aid kits, extra gauze, bandages, and tongue depressors that could be used as bite sticks. "Man versus nature. That's what avalanche control is," Greg told them once they were ready to head up the hill. "We play war games out there to keep people safe." Steph envied his confidence. No matter what personal demons Greg fought, storms made him come alive. She admired that. He was a seasoned veteran, someone who had worked his way up in a job that required him to be part cop, part paramedic, and part explosives expert. "Never forget that wind is the architect of avalanches." He drew the rookies' attention to the plate glass window behind him, a window that was quickly becoming buried. "The way it sweeps across those ridges and whips down those slopes sets up stress if the existing pack hasn't adjusted to the new load."

"As if this mountain can be tamed," Steph murmured to Casper who stood beside her.

"A control is not a social event, Garcia," Greg barked. "You must weigh speed with thoroughness, your goal always to be quick yet complete. The charges are predictable, even if the snow is not. Just make sure the fuses are actually lit today before you toss them. We don't want tourists coming across unexploded ones. Now, let's get to it."

The next day, because the weather was bad again and most of the slopes were closed, Greg invited the trainees to sit in folding chairs. Then he walked to an overhead projector and flipped it on. Photos from Steph's Forest Service textbook lit up the screen. Greg concentrated on the ones of the resort. Red lines delineated past slides, which were considerable. One of the oldest ski areas in the west Pleasant Mountain had operated since the end of World War II. The lesson complete, Greg snapped off the overhead projector. "Before we break for lunch, I'd like to tell you about my first day of training for avalanche control. My instructor told me always to turn on my beacon and put it in a zipped-up pocket of a zipped-up jacket before I went out. He told me the point of the lesson he was about to conduct was not the hazard of overly huge snow packs, but the hazard of overly huge confidence. Then he took me up to the ridge where we cut snow with our skis until a six-inch hump formed above us. For the briefest moment, I watched the snow unzip, tear loose, and fall as a slab. It knocked me off my feet and ripped my poles from my hands, my skis from my boots, and my goggles and gloves off. It didn't bury me, but it took quite a while for my instructor to dig me out. Needless to say," Greg concluded, "it was a lesson I'll never forget."

*No kidding.* To Steph it sounded like a fraternity hazing gone wrong.

Greg must have seen the look on the other rookies' faces, because he added, "What it taught me was respect for newly fallen snow, the most unstable natural substance on earth." He studied the latest storm out the almost completely buried window. "Time to go home," he said.

Overnight the snow stopped, but that just led to grueling work the next day. Much of it entailed hauling rookies playing injured skiers down the mountain, and then hauling hundreds of pounds of line and stakes back up to rope off the dangerous areas. "It's a bit like being in the military," Steph told Dad that night when she arrived late at the restaurant.

"I know." He seemed irritated by her exhaustion rather than her tardiness.

"You worked for ski patrol?" Dad had never told her this. It was a hunch.

He nodded. "My last year was Greg and Scott's first." He went on to explain that Steph's bosses had been hard-core climbers in Yosemite who'd come to Pleasant Mountain in response to an ad that read *Wanted: Mountaineers for winter work with explosives.* But instead of discouraging Steph, Dad's story perked her up. It made Greg and Scott seem like real-life action heroes, men who spent summers scaling walls and winters seeking that same intense high by blowing up snow. Annoyed, Dad said, "I take it Greg told you what the pay is."

"Less than waiting tables, more than minimum wage."

"I take it he told you you're the only married employee and one of a handful of women." Steph nodded. "So why take the job?" he asked. But before Steph could formulate an answer, he snapped, "And don't tell me it's for the fun and adventure. That just means you're the type that needs to be needed, that you seek the adrenaline rush you think comes with saving lives."

What Steph recalled was the adrenaline rush she had felt when Greg hired her. "So why did you do it then?" she asked her father.

His gaze became soft, diffuse, as if he looked inward, backward, something he hadn't done in a long time. "In the beginning I did it to get first tracks in powder that came up to my nose." Dad gave her a knowing smile. "I guess like me you're a ski bum at heart. There's still nothing I'd rather do on a sunny winter day." He became businesslike once again as he tended the burgers on his grill. "The reason I quit was after ten years I had hearing loss from all the explosions and recurring headaches from all the nitroglycerine I handled." When Steph stared at him, he added, "I still do. It's in my bloodstream, Stephie. It'll be there for life."

"And that's why you didn't become a lifer like Greg?"

"I'm just saying I don't know why you'd want to do such dirty, dangerous work."

"Okay, then I'll smoke jump this summer instead of working here." Dad had regaled Steph and her sisters with tales of parachuting into the backcountry to fight forest fires. "And don't tell me it was okay for you to do it because you're a man."

Dad looked annoyed. "Rumor has it both Greg and Scott are about to bail." Steph felt her jaw drop. "That's right, and they're college graduates, just like you, though from what I hear Greg's had to take up massage to get out." Dad fell silent, his eyes still on her. "There's one more thing. Jobs like smoke jumping and ski patrol cultivate a certain mentality. The upside is the friendship and trust that develops. Everyone has each other's back out there."

"So that's why Greg is constantly on my case," Steph quipped.

"He sees it as his responsibility."

Steph wasn't so sure. "And that's why he's such a sexist? His comments have already caused one female rookie to quit."

"I doubt that," Dad replied, "because if there's one thing I know about Greg Morris, it's that he doesn't suffer fools lightly."

# Jazmín Valdez Donahue
## March 15, 1999

*La tristeza que más duele es la que trás placer viene*
*(The sadness that hurts most is the one that follows pleasure)*

By January Rosa's workload had doubled. Marty insisted Jaz give notice to Judith. What he hadn't counted on was Judith's suggestion that Jaz stay on at InfoSys as a consultant, placed there by Marty's new company, Donahue and Associates. It allowed her to work as much or as little as she pleased. It was the perfect solution, especially since Donahue and Associates was now the leading service for placing computer contractors in San Francisco. After several false starts, Marty's career had finally taken off. His brainchild of matching highly skilled professionals to temporary assignments could not have come at a better time, for even he could not have predicted the demand that would be created by Y2K, the programming glitch from Hell.

"What is this Y2K I keep reading about?" Rosa asked, an appropriate question Jaz thought, considering it was the Ides of March. "At first it sounded like some new forecasting software that would put us out of business, but now the *Chronicle* says our computers will all crash next year because of it." Rosa folded the paper. "Does it have to do with hardware?"

"No, Madrina. It has to do with software, and it's going to take a lot of code to fix it, or the forecast for businesses and government could be grim come January first." Jaz sipped her tea. Then she nibbled at a piece of the birthday cake Rosa had baked.

Rosa set the *Chronicle* aside. "Is this Y2K some sort of bug?"

Jaz appreciated Rosa's ongoing attempt to become tech savvy. "It is, and it's created all kinds of millennial fears, which is good news because Donahue and Associates will make a fortune off it."

"¡No me digas!" Rosa's vacant smile told Jaz her madrina had merely skimmed the article, that Rosa hadn't a clue what Jaz was talking about. "So things are better between you and Marty?" Rosa asked, changing the subject.

"It's funny." Jaz studied the tea leaves in the bottom of her cup. "Remember how he used to always check up on me? How he almost seemed jealous of you?" She took her dishes to Rosa's rust-stained sink in the kitchen. "Well, that's no longer the case. If anything our relationship suffers from benign neglect." She ran the water and washed the cups, saucers, and plates. "Marty does nothing but work, and then, when he is home, he seems . . . preoccupied."

"Did he forget your birthday, mi hijita?" Rosa dried the dishes Jaz handed her.

"No, of course not." She flashed her new watch at Rosa. She felt sure they'd continue the celebration after a dinner at his parents' house that night, if Marty didn't cancel to work late again with his new administrative assistant, Dominique Reynolds. He wouldn't dare, not on Jaz's birthday, not when he hadn't seen his parents in months. Still, it bothered her, the way Marty's voice had caught the night before when she called to ask him for help organizing her home office, and he told her he was too busy. She had made time to help him set up his new office last November, so why couldn't he help set up hers? She walked out to the hallway where her boxes of files sat stacked. They resembled leaning towers of Pisa and looked as if they would topple any minute. They reminded her of the boxes she carried the day she helped Marty move.

"Here, Mrs. Donahue," Dominique said, coming to the rescue.

"Please, call me Jaz," she told her husband's newly hired assistant.

"If you'll call me Dom." The attractive young woman set the boxes on Marty's desk. "Would you like me to make coffee, Mr. Donahue? I just found the pot."

"That would be excellent, Dom," Marty smiled.

It was strange, Jaz thought, as she turned away from the boxes in Rosa's hallway. She fingered her platinum watch, thrilled by her husband's gift, yet she couldn't shake the memory of that day. It had been annoying the way the willowy blonde brought Marty his coffee, as if she were a puppy presenting her master with a bone. Jaz remembered berating herself for feeling jealous every time Dom sashayed in with a new box of files to be organized.

"So this Y2K is what's bugging Marty?" Rosa seemed amused by her own joke. "You think that's why he's so preoccupied?"

*No*, Jaz decided, though what she said was, "You know how that new program by Astrologic keeps freezing, and I explained it wasn't your fault because the program was full of bugs, or mistakes? Well, Y2K is a mistake that has to do with dates. When we roll over to the year 2000, most of the mainframes around the country won't be able to handle it."

Rosa regarded Jaz silently, as if she didn't completely understand.

"Those computers were programmed back in the '70s to recognize '00 as 1900, not 2000. The programmers used the last two digits instead of all four to save time and money. But now that the millennium is almost here, it's a problem, and unless the code is fixed, there will be no business as usual after January 1, 2000."

"So Marty has come up with the software to do this?"

"It's even better than that. His company supplies the programmers who know how to fix the code. It's why everyone we know is cashing in."

"Then we should, too, by telling companies what to expect in the year 2000 and beyond."

"With a 'Millennial Fears Forecast'?" Jaz kissed Rosa and dragged her to the kitchen table. "Why, that's absolutely brilliant, Rosa!" From her purse she took her Palm Pilot and jotted notes with the stylus. "We'll market it as an adjunct to our basic service. Advertise it on the web site." She looked up. Rosa had her half glasses on, delighted it seemed by Jaz's enthusiasm. "Listen to this." Jaz read from the screen. "Y2K got you down? No worries! For $19.99 our Millennial Fears Forecast will tell you what to expect through the year 2000 and beyond." Rosa's smile looked as if it had been plastered on. "It's cheesy, isn't it?"

"Cheesy?" Rosa obviously thought this was a culinary remark.

"I know, I know. The copy needs work, but--"

"It's why you should read today's paper." Rosa went to the living room to retrieve the *Chronicle*. When she returned, she said, "It's already happening, those millennial fears you're talking about. It says here there's a group that thinks the world is coming to an end--today."

Jaz couldn't help but laugh. "Have you ever heard of 'The Ides of March' or read Shakespeare's *Julius Caesar*?" When Rosa shook her head, Jaz explained, adding, "The only fear I have is that if Marty and I don't get our act together and decide where we want to bring in the new millennium, we won't get a reservation. Of course, the new millennium doesn't start until 2001, not that anyone cares." Jaz cupped her chin and leaned an elbow on the table. "All this hype," she sighed, "and it's still months away."

"That could work to our advantage," Rosa said. She rolled the

*Chronicle* and slapped her palm with it. "You know what I think? That you computer people made the whole thing up."

"No, Rosa. It's no hoax. Banking, social security checks, even air travel could be affected if people don't take Y2K seriously."

"You know what else I think?" Rosa's glow matched the pink walls of her kitchen, of the entire apartment. "That Millennial Fears is a much better name for our website than Astrocast."

"I'll run it by Marty." When Jaz got up and headed to the living room, Rosa trailed her. "Right now, I'm more concerned about dragging Maria away from *Barney and Friends*. I don't want us to be late for a birthday dinner given in my honor by Carolyn and Martin, Senior."

Rosa offered to keep Maria overnight. That way Jaz could salvage an evening spent in Orinda by having a romantic tryst with Marty afterwards. It was such a thoughtful gesture Jaz was surprised by Marty's lukewarm reception of it. As they drove across the Bay Bridge, Jaz checked her platinum watch, encouraged she would walk through the senior Donahue's door on time. That would rattle Carolyn. Jaz decided to give dinner two hours, max. Then she'd feign a headache and suggest to Marty that they drive home through Tilden Park where they could make love in the car with a view of the city's lights glittering in the distance. Anything to spice up their sex life, to prevent Marty from begging off by saying he was too tired. And while it was true that running a new business was exhausting, especially since finding good programmers to stave off Y2K was becoming more difficult, Jaz needed Marty to do this, if only to reassure her that she hadn't lost her touch.

Marty rallied as they ate their meal. He conversed affably with his parents. His confidence and self-esteem had been restored by his success. Always pleasant, he was a born schmoozer, better suited to his role as the head of a personnel company than he had ever been to the lonely life of a software designer. His youthful vigor had matured. It gave him a can-do spirit that was attractive. He had taken his place beside the young technocrats and nerds who currently ruled San Francisco. Like them he believed he'd inherit the earth and make fists full of money doing it. At least that's what he told his parents. No, he reassured them, the sky was not falling due to Y2K. In fact, for Donahue and Associates, the sky now had no limit.

After dinner, Carolyn produced a small gift. "Happy birthday, dear Jazmin." Carolyn passed the box across the table.

Jaz loosened the handmade paper and raffia ribbon. Earrings, she guessed as she slipped the box out. With the lid lifted and the cotton batting removed, she looked up and smiled. "They're gorgeous, Carolyn. Thank you so very much. And thank you, Martin."

"Carolyn's the shopper," Martin, Senior chuckled.

"Why don't you put them on," Marty suggested.

Jaz excused herself to the bathroom, aware her mother-in-law's eyes followed her from the room. It made the back of Jaz's neck prickle. There was something vaguely familiar about the silver discs in the box. She couldn't imagine why which bothered her since it would be rude not to wear this gift of jewelry at a dinner given for her. Once inside the bathroom, Jaz examined the earrings more closely. There was no denying Carolyn Donahue had exquisite taste. Always impeccably dressed, her sense of style was something Jaz had come to admire. But as soon as she clipped the earrings on, the pain reminded Jaz of where and when she had worn them.

The earrings had been a present, given to her by Carolyn right after Maria was born. Jaz recalled how nervous she was that first Christmas, afraid Marty's parents wouldn't like her carefully selected gifts. And while her presents had been graciously received, there had been little enthusiasm regarding them. Carolyn had given Jaz the silver earrings, and then as now, Marty had insisted she try them on. All through dinner Jaz had sat, miserable because the elegant earrings pinched her ears. Once she was safely in the car, she removed them and slipped them between the layers of cotton batting. At home, she slung the box into her underwear drawer, the place where gifts languished when she wasn't sure what to do with them.

The following day, she took the earrings to a fancy jeweler near Union Square and asked him to remove the clips and mount posts since her ears were pierced. When he explained it wouldn't work because the earrings were too heavy, she asked him to adjust the clips. It was no use. Jaz wore them once more in the presence of her mother-in-law, then she tucked them between the layers of batting and put the box into her underwear drawer, resigned to giving them to someone who could wear them without pain.

The earrings languished beneath her bras and panties for over a year until Jaz grabbed them one night as she dressed. It had been Carolyn's birthday, and as always, she and Marty were running late. Rather than admit to her husband she had forgotten to buy his mother a gift, Jaz grabbed the first box she fingered in her underwear drawer. She wrapped the small box in the car, tying it in such a way that Carolyn wouldn't notice the paper wasn't fastened with Scotch tape. By the time they pulled into the hanging driveway of the senior Donahue's home, Jaz had averted a family disaster. She came armed with a birthday gift for her suegra, even if she had no clue as to whether she gave her mother-in-law a recycled necklace or bracelet.

Carolyn oohed and aahed at the gift only to wince in pain as soon as she clipped the silver earrings on. Jaz nearly choked on the asparagus tip she chewed, appalled by what she had done. Marty got up, ready to perform the Heimlich Maneuver, only to have Jaz cough the culprit into cupped hands. Embarrassed beyond words, she excused herself to hide in the bathroom where she wondered how she would get through the rest of the evening. Had she really recycled this gift to its original giver? To her mother-in-law who disliked her and would hate her forever once she realized what Jaz had done? She returned to the table, aware Carolyn had removed the earrings. With a placid smile on her face, Carolyn inquired as to whether Jazmin was all right, satisfied when Jaz nodded sheepishly. Thankfully, there was no further mention of the earrings.

The smile Carolyn now wore was the same one she had worn that night. Clearly, she knew, and she relished her revenge. "More roast beef or Yorkshire pudding, Jazmin?"

"No, thank you."

"Now, don't tell me that you're on a diet? With your svelte figure?"

"Mother." Even Marty seemed uncomfortable with Carolyn's solicitous manner. Usually he was as oblivious to it as was Martin, Senior.

"So who is going to tell her, Marty?" Carolyn asked. "You or me?"

"If you'll excuse me." Martin, Senior wiped his mouth and stood.

"I'm sorry, Carolyn," Jaz apologized out of habit. "I--"

"I'm sure you don't want to make it a late evening," her mother-in-law interrupted, "what with work the next morning and Maria at the home of your . . . business partner." Carolyn rose, which prompted Jaz and Marty to do so. She escorted her son and daughter-in-law to the door. It was odd, Jaz thought, to have a birthday party without a cake. Perhaps while she was in the bathroom, Marty had promised his mother he'd take Jaz to task about the earrings on their way home. But to her surprise Marty said nothing as they drove away. When she suggested they drive through Tilden Park, he agreed. At their favorite overlook he pulled over. Jaz kissed him, and even though he didn't kiss her back, she said, "Thank you for getting me out of there, and for my watch. It's the most beautiful, thoughtful gift." When he didn't respond she sank into her bucket seat. "Okay. Say what you have to say, Marty, so we can get this over with."

"I guess I shouldn't be surprised that you figured it out, that you know it's over."

"I'm sorry about the earrings. I thought I'd grabbed the box with the cross from Yessenia, or the bracelet Mami gave me for Christmas."

Marty looked perplexed. "What does jewelry have to do with this?"

Her arm hairs stood on end. "What did you mean when you said it's over?"

He studied the yellow and white grid of lights in the distance, the storm clouds that had rolled in off the Pacific and splashed the windshield with rain.

"I told you, Marty. If Donahue and Associates doesn't work out--"

"I'm talking about us, Jaz."

The lights beyond the Jetta's windshield turned into a blurry haze as the rain hammered down. She fingered her watch in disbelief. "I don't believe you."

"Well, you have to." He looked so hurt, so utterly crestfallen. It crushed her.

"It's Dom, isn't it?" When he looked away, she said, "How could you?"

"You're never home. All you care about is Maria and Rosa and your work."

Tears spilled onto her cheeks. "Then I'll quit my job. I'll stay home. I'll even move to Orinda. Anything you want, Marty, just as long as you'll stay." He sat, indifferent to her hand on his arm, his eyes unblinking, as if he were mesmerized by the grid of lights that dissolved before them in the rain. "It wasn't that long ago you told me you wanted another baby." He removed her hand from his arm. "So don't you dare tell me you've fallen in love with Dom."

"But I have. It's why I can't go on like this. It's not fair to any of us."

A necklace of headlights inched along the Bay Bridge. Jaz tried to clear the images that shimmered in her head: the diamond solitaire earrings Dom always wore, the ruby heart that graced her throat. Jaz unfastened the clasp of her platinum watch. "I should have said something the minute you hired her." Jaz smacked the watch into Marty's hand. "So why don't you give this to her for her birthday, because I can't go on like this, either."

"What are you saying?"

"That I'm leaving, and I'm taking Maria with me."

"What? You can't. It's not fair."

"Fair?" She stared at him, incredulous. "There's nothing fair about this."

"Then let me leave while you and Maria stay put. Until we figure things out."

Jaz snatched the watch from his hand and dangled it. "Was this supposed to buy me off?" That's what his gifts of jewelry had done for Dom. Jaz stuffed the watch into Marty's coat pocket. "Well, I've figured things out, Marty, and I want a divorce."

He didn't beg her forgiveness as she had hoped he would. If this was a test of love and commitment, Jaz discovered there was none. He cranked the car into gear and drove home. Once his bags were packed, he took a taxi to Dom's and left Jaz crying in their half-empty bed.

# Rosa Rodriguez
## *March 15, 1999*

*When light winks at me, I respond by winking at it with my shadow*
*--Roberto Juarroz*

I buzz Silvia into my apartment. "You're upset," I say as I let her in. Out of habit Silvia glances left and right. Then she goes back to check the shingles on my Victorian house for the telltale holes that pockmark her brick building. "Cruz is back."

"¿Y Angelica y la nena?"

"No." I usher Silvia in. Her floral headscarf and black wool coat are damp. To my surprise it is raining, hard. "Angie called to warn me that we should both be careful."

"They're no longer together?" I picture Silvia's apartment, the one we used to share on Capp Street. Every santo candle she owns is lit and burns low. In the flickering light I see her scrape Tarot cards off the table and deposit them into their well-worn box when the phone rings. I see the fear in her eyes as she talks to Angelica. I open mine and ask, "Are they divorced?"

"They've separated. Angie sounded heartbroken when I talked to her."

I turn away and try to conjure up a vision of my daughter, but for some reason it's Jazmín I see, alone in her bed, crying. I check my watch. It's eight forty-five, so unless this is a scene of the future, it makes no sense.

"Angie said things should be easier now that she's no longer supporting Cruz."

"Silvia, you should stay here and avoid the old neighborhood. It isn't safe."

"I have to go back, Rosa. What if Angie decides to return?"

"Like she did after la nena was born?" The memory of what happened just over three years ago still haunts me. There she was, my daughter, sitting at Silvia's kitchen table, the night of my birthday, telling me she was clean and sober and a born-again Christian. I was so happy, so convinced it was the miracle I'd prayed for I didn't anticipate what would happen next. What I remember now is the judgment that increasingly distorted Angelica's features. I can still hear the words she flung at me regarding *Spiritual Astrology*. I wanted to explain the book was a gift from her gemelas del alma, Jazmín and Estefanía, but I knew Angelica wouldn't listen as soon as she inferred I'd burn in hell unless I renounced my satanic ways. Then she left and took my nieta away, even though I promised to change. Silvia uses money to maintain a tie, something I disapprove of, but at least she knows that Angelica returned to Cruz to try to make a go of her marriage, something that sadly has failed. "The next time she calls," I say, "tell her to come here. Cruz doesn't know where I live."

"Yet." Silvia ties on her floral headscarf and shrugs into her coat. "Buy a chain for your door," she says. Then she pauses before she leaves. "Rosa? What, if anything, do you see?"

I close my eyes, a prayer on my lips. The vision in my mind's eye is muddled. I see snow, a chairlift, two skiers traversing a steep slope in a storm. But that can't be right. It's Estefanía who lives in Pleasant Valley, not Angelica, unless she and Cruz live in Lake Tahoe, and they didn't just get married there. What I tell my cousin is this. "She's in the mountains."

"Well," Silvia bends over to roll up her stockings, "that's good, isn't it?"

I'm not sure. I feel cold, scared, short of breath, though I nod to Silvia. I kiss my cousin's cheek and watch her disappear in the pouring rain.

# Stephanie Bengochea Garcia
## March 16, 1999

*Every moment of one's existence, one is growing into more or retreating
into less. One is always living a little more or dying a little bit*
*--Norman Mailer*

Steph's cheekbones ached as the alarm exploded beside her head. She dragged herself out of bed and sashed her robe tightly around her waist. It was freezing. By closing their door, she and Pedro had enjoyed a modicum of privacy, not that they had needed it, but it had shut out the warmth of the wood burner. Her job with ski patrol required that she be up and out of the apartment by five-thirty. It gave her first dibs on the bathroom, a dubious privilege. Icy cold water spewed from the tap. She waited for the temperature to rise, to entice her to drop her robe and plunge beneath the prickly needles that spurted from the energy efficient showerhead. Ana Claudia complained she had to run in circles to get wet. Steph's preferred method was to twist and turn. A glance at the clock confirmed her lethargy would prevent her from ingesting anything solid before work. She pulled on thermals and socks as she debated whether to ask Pedro to take their laundry to the Laundromat. This chore was neglected the day before not because of her birthday as much as a hectic schedule that had kept her away from the apartment until late, only to have Jaz's phone call keep her up hours longer, sleepless with worry.

Pedro brought Steph tea. "So are you going to tell me about it?" A minty aroma wafted from the mug in his outstretched hand.

She squeezed past him to the bathroom. "Tell you about what?"

"Your phone call with Jazmín."

"I told you last night that she and Marty are having problems."

"Then maybe she should come back here for a while."

Steph exhaled as she hunted for the blow dryer in the jumble beneath the sink. "Admit it, Pedro. You're still in love with her, aren't you?"

"Let's not have that same tired argument again."

Steph took the mug of tea from him sheepishly and inhaled. A sinus infection would almost be a relief. Then she could go to the clinic, get an antibiotic, and stop slugging down cold medicine that masked her symptoms but never completely rid her of the pain. She kept her back to her husband, her face out of range of the mirror, afraid he might see her accusation had been calculated to put him on the defensive, that his persistent guilt-ridden interest in Jaz was what would prevent him from asking the question Steph dreaded most: Where were you last night?

She switched on the blow dryer, thankful when Pedro left her alone. The door closed, she set the shrieking device on the back of the toilet and breathed deeply. It lessened the pain in her chest, the pressure in her sinuses, but the metallic whine of the dryer made her headache worse. She uncapped the cold medication, shook out two tablets, and tossed them in her mouth. She washed them down with the tea. Steam from the shower misted the mirror. She reached for the dryer and aimed it at a moisture-laden spot. The droplets dissolved, and her face came into focus, as if she peeled back layers of gauze. Starved for air suddenly, Steph felt certain if Pedro knew how she'd spent the night of her birthday, her marriage to him might dissolve as well.

It had been after ten when she tiptoed into the apartment the night before, afraid she would wake Ana Claudia. She had washed her hair and scrubbed her body until it felt raw, intent on rinsing away the aromatic oils Greg had used. The scents were so tantalizing, so unlike anything she ever wore, but their residue remained and penetrated her pores. She toweled off and wrapped herself in her robe, secure its wood smoke smell would mask any fragrance that lingered. She was drying her hair when Pedro surprised her in the bathroom. He asked why she was still up, why she'd gotten home from class so late. Jaz's phone call brought his questions to a halt. Afterwards, Steph pointed out it was midnight, and that they both needed to get to bed. Once there, Pedro kissed her, but Steph used her sinus headache as an excuse to roll away.

Jaz's phone call had been a shock, but mostly Steph was grateful it hadn't been Greg. *The body never lies, Garcia,* his parting words after a kiss that sent her flying out his door.

"Let's make the bed." Pedro's suggestion brought her back, as did the sound of a snowplow coming down the street. Steph moved to the window to watch it, drawn by the sound of metal scraping over asphalt. Sparks flew up from the snowplow's blade as it passed. "Are you going to help?" She nodded, though she continued to study the road's newly glazed surface. It reminded her that the apartment's freezer still needed to be defrosted. She helped Pedro make hospital corners. "Why do I get the feeling you don't want to talk about Jazmín's phone call?"

"Because I don't. It's bad news, Pedro. Marty left her."

Pedro straightened.

"I didn't tell you last night because I wanted you to get some sleep."

"Did you get any?" He pulled the comforter up over the pillows.

"Not much."

"I knew it would end like this." He sat on their neatly made bed. The despair in his eyes confirmed Steph's accusation that his feelings for Jaz had been on the mark.

"I tried to talk her into coming back," Steph said, "but you know Jaz."

"Why would she stay in San Francisco? All the people she loves are here."

"And who love her."

Pedro gave Steph a tortured look. "I love her like a sister."

"Is that how you feel about me?"

"You were the one with the headache last night."

"Well, whenever I want to, you always give me some lame excuse."

"Because you're crazy, Steph. Because you're only in the mood when Ana Claudia and Carlos are here, and the walls are paper thin."

"We listen to them all the time. Why can't they listen to us?"

"Keep your voice down." Pedro eyed the door to Ana Claudia and Carlos's bedroom. "So how come you got home so late last night?"

"I told you. Class ran late, and I'm going to be late now if--"

"Then we'll talk about it at lunch. Up at the lodge."

She turned in the doorway. "The parking is terrible, and the shuttle takes forever. Are you sure this can't wait until tonight?"

Pedro shrugged. "Juan P. doesn't have anything for me to do today." He walked over and took Steph in his arms. "I wish it was your day off, so we could . . ." he kissed her lips, her forehead, rubbing madly at the smudge of ChapStick he left there. "You smell . . . different."

She broke away. "I'll see you at eleven. And don't worry about Jaz."

He searched her eyes. "It's not Jaz I'm worried about."

In the ski patrol office, Greg sat hunched over the duty roster he filled out at his desk. He barely gave Steph a glance when she came in. "We're headed to the top, Garcia." He clicked his pen shut. "Those sticks won't cut it in these conditions. Go back and get your planks."

"Yes sir," she muttered.

"I'll meet you at the gondola. Bring your pack and the transceiver. You may want to wear face protection."

Steph watched Greg's immobile face. When he said nothing about the night before, she left. Ten minutes later, she found him putting sticks of dynamite in a ski patrol backpack outside the gondola hut. She dropped to her knees and chided herself for feeling skittish about handling explosives. Avalanche control should have been a routine part of her job by now. She had performed it with Greg all winter long. Once the charges were loaded, they climbed into a car. It exited the building and was immediately broadsided by a gust. The cable buzzed each time the wind swung the car out over the trees. "It's blowing a gale up top," she said, her voice rising.

Greg scowled at the swirling snow. "Maybe I should radio for Scott."

"No, no." She waited for his response. When there was none, she added, "I'll be fine."

"Will you?" His eyes gave her no quarter.

"Greg, about last night--"

"Save it." He studied the clouds that veiled the peak.

She took no offense. On the mountain he was as dedicated to her as she was to him, their bond cemented by the stressful work they engaged in. It instilled in her the ability to anticipate his needs before he did. Greg recognized this and had begun to trust her, to confide, and now that he did, Steph felt as though she were addicted to him and to her job. At the end of each day she found it harder and harder to walk away. What worried her most was the end of the season, something she dreaded. It would take an act of defiance for her to no longer see him.

Their car clunked into mid-chalet and slowed to a crawl in the chute. Scott Hansen was there. He shoved the door to the car open and jumped in. "I'm glad I caught up with you." As head of ski patrol, Scott outranked Greg in the hierarchy that took responsibility for safety at the Pleasant Mountain Ski Area, and because of that Scott constantly straddled a line. Half his time was spent convincing his superiors he was getting the resort open as quickly as possible. The other half was spent convincing Greg and the veteran patrollers he wasn't compromising safety. Rather than getting easier over time, Scott admitted to Steph one day as she transcribed snow survey data that it was getting harder. Corporate types were concerned about the bottom line. They expected Scott to make decisions based on this new economic reality, which meant he could never get it wrong. "Are you sure you can handle the conditions up there?" he asked her.

"How bad is it?" A look at his face and confidence deserted her.

"It's a complete whiteout at times," Scott admitted. "There's a bald spot in the saddle with flying debris--ice, grit, rocks, you name it--not to mention the cornice, which is a monster." And while Scott's appraisal of the situation was logical, she couldn't help but wonder if Greg had said something. Or did Scott merely suspect? He was more than Greg's boss. He was a friend. Scott even resembled Greg in that they were both darkly blond, deeply tanned, and their eyes were glacially blue. Both had worked their way up to positions of responsibility at the ski area. But Scott had chosen to remain single while Greg had blundered through two marriages and two divorces, both with pretty young female ski patrollers. It meant Scott would recognize the signs, and from the way he looked at Steph, he thought he did.

"Then it's your call," she told Greg, wondering whom he would choose: Scott, the veteran and old friend; or her, the novice and new temptation.

"Garcia can handle it," Greg told Scott. The car was coming to the end of the chute. Like a rocket, it was about to blast off. "This is your stop," Greg reminded his boss.

"Stay in contact," Scott replied.

Greg held the door to the car open so that Scott could leap out. The door shut, the car careened from the building, only to sway when it was buffeted by the wind. "Thanks for sticking up for me," Steph told Greg. His eyes remained on the ridge top, on the plumes of ice that poured over a cornice poised to release. She read the concern she had come to know so well. "Why don't we shoot it down with the howitzer?"

"Too risky. Wouldn't want to miss and send a shell into the cross country ski area."

"Can't this wait until the weather lifts?"

"Spring Break starts today. All those crazy college kids will be up here, like that ex-boyfriend of yours. I wouldn't put it past a few to sneak up to the top whether it's open or not." Greg rubbed his shadowed eye sockets, indicative of the sleep he hadn't got.

"You're sure you want me up there with you?" When he didn't answer, she said, "I won't be offended if you think I'm not--"

"You're up to it. We need to do this," he added, to shut down her nervous chatter, "to prove we can still work together."

"Last night," she raised the subject again aware they were almost out of time to explore any doubts on either of their parts. "I crossed a line. I want you to know . . ." They were at the top. The car door opened. He clambered out. Steph stumbled out behind him, disappointed he had dismissed her need to discuss it, terrified by the chance he gave her now to prove she was the professional she claimed to be, not just an employee who suffered from a school-girl's crush.

Greg checked the explosives again. "I'll go first and plant the sticks, while you make the cuts. You come when I give the signal. Cut in between my marks to test the ridge. I'll wait until we're both clear of the area before I detonate. The visibility's so poor you'll have to listen to the radio, and listen carefully. I want us well out of range when the ridge blows." He looked up at her. "Chunks could break off unexpectedly from the concussion of the shock waves."

"Not much chance of that happening with all this wind."

"On the contrary, it makes it a whole lot more likely." Greg suddenly looked his age, like the world-weary veteran of the mountain he was. He dug through his pack again. "I know I've been on your case all winter, but I have to warn you--"

"I want to go."

"You've got nothing to prove, to me or to Scott."

"But I do. It's why I want to do this."

Greg slung his pack on, pulled his goggles down, and zipped up. She did the same. They walked to the exit of the building, switched on their transceivers, and went over the plan a second time before they headed out. It was worse than expected. She regretted not wearing a facemask, which was pure vanity on her part. She looked ridiculous as it was, bundled up against the elements, her hair tucked into her ski cap, her goggles covering much of her face, though they offered little protection against the blowing particles that made her cheeks feel as if they were being sandblasted. March roared in. It howled. Almost spring by the calendar, this was the worst weather of the winter.

As she and Greg clicked into their skis, Steph's mind wandered. Her patrol job would end soon, as would her EMT training. It meant they'd have no reason to see each other unless she pursued the bodywork course he taught in the spring, the one he'd pitched so personally to her the night before. Absentmindedly, she followed too closely in Greg's tracks. His radio off his belt, he barked, "Wait up, Garcia." She felt chastised until she saw his grin.

*Wait up, Garcia.* He had used the same line on her the night before, the night of her twenty-fourth birthday, when the delicate balance of their relationship had been upset. Her heart beat fast as she shuffled along behind him. Her role had shifted from that of the pupil who admired the teacher to that of the protégé taken under the master's wing. The night before had felt like an initiation, a rite of passage. Greg had already decided to elevate her to confidante. Would she now become the consort? Scott had insinuated that that might be the case, and it probably explained why Greg had turned down Scott's offer to be his partner today.

"I should get home," Steph had told Greg as the other students in the EMT class streamed out the doors of the fire station.

"Not yet." His eyes drew her away from those who donned jackets and prepared to face a late winter storm ushered in on Arctic winds. "I'd like to show you something first, something you said you were interested in as a career."

"Bodywork?" She could barely contain herself. After Dad revealed Greg's secret source of income, Steph asked him about it, but he refused to discuss it with her.

"Consider it my birthday present to you." Greg lowered his voice. "My table and oils are at home. Why don't you follow me over there?"

"How long?" she checked her wristwatch. It was just past nine.

"An hour, tops."

"You know I won't pass up this invitation."

"Good, because you won't get another."

"One hour, Morris. And it'd better be good."

"Oh, I'm good, Garcia," his eyes penetrated hers. "I'm good."

As she followed him to his apartment in the truck, Steph analyzed her rash decision. At home, Ana Claudia would go to bed early. A sound sleeper, she would have no clue what time Steph got in. Pedro was at Bible Study with Carlos, and if they grabbed a cup of coffee at a café, which was their usual habit, they wouldn't be home until ten-thirty. In theory Steph was safe as long as she kept track of the time.

But that proved difficult. Shy and nervous, she undressed and slipped under the sheet, while Greg played the part of the cool professional. He talked her through the massage, careful to keep any part of her he wasn't working on covered. What registered was the tone of his voice more than his words. It conveyed that he was a true believer, the body his god. He explained the rationale behind everything he did. It was as though he'd allowed her into his inner sanctum and exposed his true self. She doubted he did this with anyone but Scott, so why her, and why now?

Her favorite part was the aromatherapy. Greg wafted scented vials under her nose with each transition. He explained that by appealing to the olfactory sense, memories and toxins were released that could be drained from the body by massage. His touch was firm but gentle, entirely different than Steph's electrifying experience of Reiki with Juana. Greg's therapy was earthbound, not something that came from heaven above. She felt secure he wouldn't uncover the secret buried in her gut. On the contrary, his stroking soothed her. She felt safe in his experienced hands, and to her discomfort, aroused for the first time in months.

When he asked her to turn over from her stomach to her back, she hesitated. How could she continue to lie naked beneath a flimsy sheet with a man she'd have to face at work the next day? Ever the professional, he kept his back to her until she indicated she was ready. Then he took her right foot and kneaded it as he explained reflexology. A few spots were tender but mostly it was pure pleasure. No one had ever caressed her feet before. Steph feared that if she didn't keep her wits about her, she might moan in delight. Greg worked up her leg, which made her feel vulnerable and embarrassingly moist. He must have sensed her mounting discomfort because he went no higher than her knee. He left her on the table to change the tape of soft, spacey music that played, and with the absence of his calming touch, anxiety washed over Steph. She had no idea how long she had been there, yet she didn't want to leave. He anointed her hair with fragrant oil and massaged it into her scalp. She felt as if she'd died and gone to heaven, right there on Greg's massage table. She must have smiled because he stroked her neck and said, "It feels good, doesn't it?"

"It's so sensual." Embarrassed by her inappropriate choice of words, she opened her eyes, startled to discover how close his face was to hers. Drawing herself up, she struggled to keep the sheet from slipping until she gave up and let it drop to her lap. Greg's eyes widened. His mouth opened, but no sound ushered forth. She guided his hands to her chest and held his gaze. She didn't flinch when he cupped her breasts. He massaged them in a gentle circular motion, and when he kissed her, she allowed his hands to run up and down her slickened torso.

It was Steph who broke away, who fled to his bathroom to throw on her clothes. They stuck to her body as if she were soaked in sweat, not oil. She rested her head against the door before she opened it to face him. He sat quietly in his living room, his table broken down, the music turned off. "Steph . . . I'm sorry." On the verge of tears, she felt humiliated by her loss of control, and profoundly moved by this man. He came to her, and she enjoyed his touch as her clothes glided silkily over her body. "When I invited you here, I knew this might happen, but you're a married woman, and I had no right to--"

"Greg," she interrupted, "I knew this might happen, too, and I'm not sorry it did."

He looked shaken. "I thought you were happily married."

"I thought so, too."

He broke away. "Don't let this ruin your marriage or our working relationship."

"Are you saying tonight was a mistake?" She refused to let him back away from it.

"You know what I mean."

"Do I?" She held his eyes. "All those months. All that talk." She shook her head. "I was just trying to find out if there was any truth--"

"It's past ten, Garcia. You should get home."

"Don't put me off like this."

"Well, what else am I supposed to do?"

She stared at him until she knew. "You could teach me what you showed me tonight."

"Ah, Steph, you'd just be using those classes as an excuse for us to be together."

"You're a healer, Greg, and I want to become a healer, too."

He rubbed his neck. "You think we could keep it professional?"

"We have, for months. You would've never kissed me, never touched me, if I hadn't let you." She faced him so he would have to look at her. "All that aside, I'm interested, really interested in the bodywork. Tonight was incredible. You're incredible," she held his gaze. "I can't remember the last time I felt so good."

He opened the door of his condo. "You should go."

"Let me take the course. Please don't shut me out because I screwed up."

"We'd have to be careful, because you're right," he scuffed the worn carpeting near the entry with his shoe. "People are talking."

"I've managed to stay away from you this long."

He glanced at her. "I'm not sure." When she brushed past him to leave, he said, "I'm not talking about your interest or your ability, Steph. I'm talking about me."

She was amazed he thought she should do this, not because he was attracted to her, as she was to him, but for herself. Her self. She choked back tears, saddened now by her reckless behavior. "Greg . . . It'll never happen again. I promise. I'm so sorry . . ."

"Don't be." He held her until she broke away. Then he followed her out into the blowing snow. "I'll call you."

"No, don't." She took the scraper out of Pedro's truck.

"But we should talk."

"How about tomorrow at lunch?" She hacked at the ice crystals on the windshield.

"Too risky."

She got in the truck. The dashboard clock read ten after ten. She turned over the engine and cracked the crystal-studded driver's side window. "Don't worry. I'll figure something out."

"You do that. After you talk to that husband of yours, because I think you two have some . . . issues." He smiled sadly. "The body never lies, Garcia."

The preferred method to produce slides was to blast away at the ridge with the howitzer, but with visibility barely beyond their ski tips, it was not an option. Ski cutting, applying direct pressure to the snow, and hand charges were what she and Greg would have to use. Occasionally, when the wind shifted, she caught a glimpse of the top of Pleasant Mountain, of the gondola building, and the dark hulking shapes of the buckets. Moving from anchor point to anchor point, Greg removed the hand charges from his pack. Usually they were placed at predetermined points along the route, but today he tossed them into a white void. The wind prevented Steph from hearing the telltale hiss or smelling the sulfur. Greg held each charge to the snow to make sure the plastic sleeve of the fuse had melted before he threw one of Steph's handcrafted bombs. He swore every time a blast failed to trigger a slide.

"Oh great," she radioed when Greg paused to rub his shoulder. "An injured pitcher, just in time for softball season." She watched to make sure no chunks cut loose before she signaled for him to move on. Horrified, she gasped into the radio slung across her chest when she thought she saw the slab above their heads heave as if it were about to dislodge from the buckling cornice wall. "Hangfire!" she shouted as snow fractured and tumbled down, barely missing them.

"That was close," Greg radioed back. Steph watched him inch ahead, using his skis as if they were antennae. She tuned into the snow as well, intent on feeling its tension. Greg picked up a handful and studied it beneath a hand lens. When that became impossible due to the wind, he tossed it away. "I estimate water content to be six percent," he radioed.

"When yesterday it was ten?" Steph knew what that meant. They needed to get out of there fast. The snow they skied across could shift any minute.

"Call me when you're clear," was his last instruction as they slowly traversed the steep slope, one at a time in each other's tracks. Steph hoped this safety measure would ease the weight on the pack and prevent them from getting caught in a slide. She knew it was too late when she heard what sounded like the thunder of a coming train.

"Greg!" she radioed. "I'm going for a ride!"

"Try to get to the flank," he yelled before he called Scott for back up.

The wall of white blindsided her. She was carried by snow that sucked her down until her head went under. She wrenched her hands up and shoved them across her chest until she could cup them over her nose and mouth to create an air space, an action she had practiced many times during training to prepare her for just such an event. When she came to rest, she could only manage shallow breathing, trapped as she was beneath the crushing weight of the collapsed cornice that had her pinned somewhere on the side of Pleasant Mountain. It was dark. She panicked when she realized she couldn't move anything except her hands, that her limbs were already numb. The transceiver activated on her jacket, she prayed Greg would pick up the signal. She had no idea how many minutes had passed when she heard the scratching above. A pole struck her in the chest near her hands. She latched onto it and tugged back.

"Atta girl. Hold on." It was Scott's voice, not Greg's. Two shovels dug at her from forty-five degree angles. Greg and Scott stopped just short of her face to clear a space with their gloved hands. "She's conscious, breathing on her own." Scott peeled away the ice that had built up around her nose and mouth, evidence she had come close to suffocating. Her lungs labored as if a boulder sat on her chest. She had to consciously pull air in and push it out, but it was better than panting in the dark, worried she was about to smother in the snow that hardened around her. "No signs of hypothermia, hypoxia or hypercapnia." The three H's as Greg called them, the final two the lack of oxygen or the excess of carbon dioxide that came from breathing in a confined space. "She's in shock."

"Steph," Scott clapped gloved hands near her face, "wake up." Less than four minutes. That's how long it had taken to find her. Avalanche victims lose consciousness after that. "Where the hell is that basket?" Scott shouted into his radio. Steph couldn't make out the static-filled reply. She felt as if she were fading in and out. Greg continued to dig her out, as if he were a dog in a frenzy over a forgotten bone. From his pack Scott whipped out a space blanket and snapped it in the wind. Like a silvery parachute it came to rest on her. It brought to mind the gossamer weight of the sheet that had covered her the night before, when Greg's touch and voice had made her feel safe and secure. Now he appeared anxious as he tried to free her from her frozen straitjacket, reluctant to touch her, as if he feared broken bones.

"How many fingers?" Scott thrust the middle three before her face. She opened her mouth but nothing came out. "Just blink when I get to the right number. One . . . two . . . three? Atta girl." Scott looked relieved. His tense crouch relaxed. The next part went by in slow motion. Scott checked her vital signs. Greg splinted her ankle and arm and wrapped her in coarse blankets. The laborious descent in the basket hurt, as did the bits of conversation that floated back to Steph on bitter winds. "You should have thought with your head instead of your dick."

"Let it go, Scott. It was an accident. Could've just as easily been you or me."

"Bullshit," was Scott's reply. "Garcia screwed up because she's a rookie. She couldn't handle it, but she's got a nicer ass than mine, so you chose her."

"Are you questioning my judgment?" Greg's voice was raw with wounded pride. It made Steph ache. Would he be fired because of her?

"There'll be an investigation." Scott's tone indicated he took no pleasure in what he said. "There'll be questions. Accusations."

"Garcia was up to it. Don't second-guess me now. Accidents happen. She's been doing avalanche control with me all season."

"Yeah, I know." Scott's edgy acknowledgment of this ended the exchange. She must have blacked out, because the next time Steph came to, she was on a stretcher, being jostled through the parking lot. Greg hopped in the ambulance with her. "Write the report first," Scott pleaded. "Then you can go to the hospital, after she's seen her family, her husband."

Greg slammed the ambulance door in Scott's face. There was a haunted look to him as he hovered over her. It told Steph just how lucky she had been. An urgent thumping rattled the ambulance's door. "Open up!" Greg jerked the latch loose and came face to face with Pedro. "Where is she?" Greg gave Steph's husband a hand up. "What happened?" Pedro asked.

"Avalanche," Greg muttered.

"Pedro?" Steph croaked. Her mouth wasn't working right. He buried his head in her shoulder. It was the first time she had ever seen him cry.

The next time she awoke, it was because someone had taken her hand. "Stephie? Can you hear me?" There was naked fear in Mom's face. Her hazel eyes glistened. She looked insubstantial, colorless in the weak light of the hospital room. *She never complains. And she never cries.* Steph felt alarmed by Mom's behavior. "You don't have to say anything."

"But I do." Steph's voice sounded gravelly, hoarse. "To think it takes something like this for me to realize how stupid I've been." She closed her eyes. Fear welled up. She had come so close to missing this opportunity. Mom hugged her. "Where's Dad?" Steph asked.

"Outside." Mom wiped her nose and pushed her auburn bangs out of her eyes. "They'll only let one of us in here at a time. I'll get him."

"No. Don't." The words tumbled out from Steph's stiff lips.

Mom took Steph's hand. "What is it?"

"Where's Pedro?"

"He went . . . home."

"Something happened, didn't it?" Steph waited patiently for the pieces to click into place. "In the ambulance. With Greg."

"I'm surprised you remember. There was . . . an exchange of words."

"Oh God." Steph's mind reeled. Had it continued at the hospital, in front of Steph's family and the medical staff? "I guess everybody thinks Greg and I are . . ." Steph shut her eyes.

"He's in love with you, Stephie, and so is Pedro. So what are you going to do?"

"I . . . I don't know. Everything's so screwed up. My marriage. My job."

"The important thing is you're all right. That's all I care about."

A nurse cracked the door. "The rest of your family would like to see you, Stephanie."

"We'll be finished here in a minute, Helen." When the nurse shut the door, Mom took Steph's hand. "You're right. We do need to talk, because I found something under your bed, in your room the other day, something I sucked up with the vacuum cleaner, that frightened me almost as much as you being caught in an avalanche."

"What was it?"

"A pamphlet about infertility." Steph closed her eyes. "I spoke to Juana about it, and--"

"Mom, I can't. I just can't right now."

"Which is fine. I just want you to know that I'm here for you, just like you were there for me, after the accident." When Pedro opened the door, Mom turned to him and said, "Her medication is kicking in. I think we should let her rest."

Steph squeezed Mom's hand before she allowed it to slip away.

# Jazmín Valdez Donahue
## *March 16, 1999*

*Con quien vives, quien eres*
*(Tell me whom you live with and I'll tell you who you are)*

R osa carried the portable phone, her moonlike face no longer serene. She passed the receiver to Jaz who grabbed it and launched into a response she had planned to what she feared would be Marty's latest assault. "If you're going to start in on me again about the custody--"

"Jazmín?"

"Pedro? How . . . How did you know I was here?"

"I found Rosa's number in Steph's address book."

The hairs on the back of Jaz's neck lifted. "What's wrong?"

"There's been an accident, but don't worry. Steph will be all right."

"Like Jenny was all right after her accident?"

"Es un milagro, Jazmín, y gracias a nuestro Señor, a Jesus Cristo--"

"Would you cut the Christian miracle crap and tell me how she is?"

"There are broken bones, but no head injury, no hypothermia."

"Hypothermia? Pedro, what happened?"

"She was caught in an avalanche. . . ." The incredible story poured out as the phrase *Beware the Ides of March* ran through Jaz's head. It was a miracle indeed Steph had survived, but when Pedro filled in the details, Jaz suspected a new crisis snowballed, one that could bring Steph's marriage to an end. ". . . So her boss, that Greg guy? He won't let me near my own wife. Says he's in charge until we get to the hospital. So I told him to fuck off."

Jaz couldn't help but smile. "Where's your Christian charity, Pedro? Your manners?"

"You're lecturing me on buenas modales? If I didn't love you so much, I would have never put up with your filthy mouth all these years."

"What?" She wasn't sure she'd heard him correctly, or that she wanted to.

He sighed into the receiver, his first real pause during a breathless recounting of the terrifying events that had taken place. "I said . . . I love you."

Clearly, Pedro was in shock, but Jaz couldn't let his comment pass. "Steph--your wife, my friend--is in the hospital, and you love me?"

"Caramba, Jazmín, I love you both. You know that." He tried to brush the whole thing off, but he sounded shaken, as if the truth surprised him as well. "Let's not do this, Chica," he said so tenderly Jaz found herself wishing they were still neighbors who had never grown up, never fallen in love, that their lives weren't as complicated as they were.

"You'd better give me Steph's room number," Jaz told him. "I'll have to call her. With this storm I'm not sure when I'll be able to get there."

"The doctor has her on some heavy duty stuff. Maybe you should wait 'til you come."

"Which may not be for another couple of days."

"Why? You know how to drive in the snow."

"I have to talk to Marty first."

"You tell that pinche güero not to come near you."

"Steph told you about me and Marty?"

"Claro. It just proves that I was right, that he's a jerk--"

"Pedro . . . I appreciate what you're trying to do, but it only makes me feel worse. In fact, this whole conversation reminds me of that summer at Bert's when all we did was fight."

"Then why talk to Marty? Or do you need a reminder that the Devil is alive and well and living with his administrative assistant?"

"I'll need his permission to take Maria out of the city. Besides, what difference does it make? When I talk to Marty, I get angst. When I talk to you, I get attitude. You said it yourself, that we shouldn't be doing this when Steph's so badly hurt."

"She'll be fine. All she needs is you and me, not her job, or boss, or EMT training."

"You wouldn't make her give that up just because Greg's the instructor, would you?"

"I might, if I thought it would help us have a baby."

Jaz knew she'd have to be careful not to betray Steph's confidence of the previous night. "Is it a good idea to have a baby when you don't even have a place of your own yet?"

"We'll find one as soon as ski season is over."

"But a child, Pedro. It's such a huge responsibility."

"And a joy. It's why you married Marty instead of me. Because of Maria."

"I married Marty because I loved him, and God help me, Pedro, I still do. I adore Maria, but if Rosa hadn't come along when she did, I don't know what I would've done."

"You'd be here with your family and friends, and we'd be helping you."

"San Francisco is my home now."

"Why are you so stubborn? Is that güero paying you alimony to stay?"

"If Marty gets his way, I won't even get child support."

"What? Why not? He left you."

"He's suing me for full custody."

"That guy is such a pendejo! I never did understand what you saw in him, other than he was rich and blond and you had a child together. And now he wants to take Maria away?"

"He insists Maria will be better off living with him. Hang on a minute. I've got another call." Jaz put Pedro on hold, upset by what occurred to her, that perhaps her strongest bond to Marty had always been Maria. It would explain why custody had become such a bone of contention. At a hideous meeting that morning, with all the aggrieved parties present, (including Martin, Senior, acting as counsel to Marty, and to Jaz's surprise, Dominique Reynolds), an unbelievable discussion ensued. Martin, Senior proposed an arrangement in which Maria would live with Marty full-time while Dom stayed home to play mother. The implication was clear, that as a divorcée forced to work with a three-year-old in childcare, Jaz would make the inferior mother compared to the inexperienced but enthusiastic Ms. Reynolds. Never mind that Dom wasn't Maria's mother or Marty's wife. The meeting deteriorated into bickering as Jaz realized she'd have to hire an attorney of her own to battle Marty for custody. His leaving her for Dom was becoming a reoccurring nightmare. Jaz clicked Pedro back on the line. "Are you still there?"

"I am. So you understand why I want a baby?" Like Martin, Senior, Pedro hammered his argument home.

Jaz coughed to stall for time. "Have you talked to Steph about this?"

"Not lately, because I'm worried."

Jaz drew in a sharp breath. "About?"

"We've been married for almost a year, and nothing's happened."

Jaz considered faking another call, telling Pedro she couldn't tie up Rosa's line any longer. She could hear her madrina talking. She could hear Maria singing along with *Barney and Friends* in the living room in her funny, high-pitched voice. But mostly what Jaz heard was the beating of her heart as she struggled with what to say.

"Are you still there?" Pedro asked.

"Yes," she cleared her throat. "So you're telling me you haven't been using anything?"

"Not that I'm aware of."

Anger bubbled up. "You think Steph's using birth control and not telling you?"

"I went to the county hospital. They ran all kinds of tests on me."

Jaz rubbed the goose flesh that covered her arms. "And?"

"It's not me."

Her jaw dropped. "You're sure?"

"The doctor said my sperm count was fine."

"And you haven't told Steph?"

"The test results just came back, and after last night and today, I think I know why we're not pregnant. It's because Steph's on birth control, so she can sleep with that Greg--"

"That's ridiculous," Jaz fired back.

"Then why isn't she pregnant?"

"I don't know," Jaz wailed, ready to shut off their conversation, to shut out her own doubts. "Look. I'll drive over tomorrow."

"Are you going to tell Steph what we talked about?"

"I want her to get better, Pedro, not worse."

He heaved a great sigh before he said, "I do, too, because I love her."

"Like you love me? Or you think you love me?"

"¿Qué quieres decir?" He sounded angry.

"I'm saying Steph needs your understanding right now. So please don't jump to any conclusions about Greg or the birth control."

"You talked to her about this, didn't you? Last night. On the phone."

"Yes, and as soon as she's better, you should talk to her about it, too, because if you love her, then you have to accept her the way she is."

"I do."

"Look, Pedro, I'm really sorry, but I have to go."

"Te cuides, ¿eh?"

"Igualmente." Jaz hung up the phone in the kitchen and went to the living room. She turned off the TV, something that normally provoked a fight with Maria. But this time, it didn't. Maria seemed upset that Jaz was flicking tears away. With Esmokey clutched in her thin little arms, she hugged Jaz's legs, only to let go when Rosa ushered a client out of her office.

"Your granddaughter?" the man asked Rosa when Maria ran by.

"I wish," Rosa sounded wistful. "Mark, I'd like you to meet my partner, Jaz Donahue. Maria is her daughter."

"It's been too long. " The man with the lively brown eyes behind bifocals extended his hand. "Do you still work at InfoSys? I haven't seen you there lately."

Jaz squinted at the impish grin framed by a graying goatee. "Mark Hamilton?"

His rosy skin crinkled. Smile lines formed deep crevices beneath his sculpted cheeks. "It was Judith who sent me your way."

"I'll have to thank her for the referral. I'm embarrassed I didn't recognize you."

"This is a new look for me." He stroked his goatee. "It was Judith's suggestion. We've been seeing a lot of each other lately. I was wondering if you ever do personal charts?"

"Occasionally," Jaz interjected before Rosa could get a word in edgewise. "If a client requests it, but it's not our usual focus."

"Would you consider doing one for me? And for Judith?"

"I'm surprised Judith is interested," Jaz answered cautiously. "She knows of my work with Rosa, yet she's never asked me to do her chart."

"The charts would be for me." Mark's grin masked a determination, a single-mindedness Judith characterized as his "self-serving stubborn streak," a description that usually signaled she was about to break things off with him again. Mark's manner bothered Jaz as well. Judith was more than just her former boss. She was a mentor and a friend.

"Mark? May I make a suggestion?"

"By all means."

"It sounds like what you want is a synastry report in which we compare your charts."

"That's exactly what I want. When can you have it ready?"

"Talk to Judith first, then call me back with her information. I need her permission."

"Of course," he acquiesced, though he sounded annoyed.

After jotting down Mark's birth data, Jaz exchanged business cards with him and a few more pleasantries before she showed him to the door.

"You know each other?" Rosa asked once Mark was gone.

"Not exactly. He dates Judith. It's been on again, off again for years, but now . . ." Jaz felt unsure as to whether her hunch was correct. Maybe when she met with Judith today she'd explore her former boss's status with Mark to help her decide how to handle this client.

"You okay, mi hijita? You're wrinkling your forehead."

Rosa's eyes were as dark and dear to Jaz as Mami's. "Marty used to tell me the same thing. He always knew when I was upset. Ay, Madrina, I've made such a mess of things."

"It wasn't your fault."

"If I'd just done things his way, stayed home, had another baby, moved to Orinda . . ."

"If you'd just worked at InfoSys instead of with me . . ."

The expression of love and guilt on Rosa's face cut Jaz as deeply as any blade. She kissed her madrina's cheek. "Don't ever say that. I thank God for the day I met you."

"You know you can stay here as long as you like."

"I know, but I hope you understand Maria and I are only here temporarily because," Jaz hesitated, struck by an oddly important memory, "because you have a daughter of your own."

Rosa startled. Her brows knotted above her pudgy nose.

"You told me about her, remember? That first day we met, when you were trying to convince me you could babysit Maria and run a business at the same time."

Rosa nodded, though she seemed to regret the lapse on her part, as if it were a secret she never intended to reveal. She tightened the sash of her apron and headed to the kitchen.

Jaz followed, feeling as if she were Woofy incarnate, as if she were nipping at her mistress' heels. "So how come there are no pictures of her in the apartment?"

Rosa shrugged. Her stockpot set on the stove, she collected onions from a basket. Green tips sprouted from the scarlet bulbs, like the hyacinths Rosa forced in the vases on the sill.

"If it's no big deal, then why not tell me about her?"

"Now?" Rosa's fingers splayed around the onions, as if she were a juggler who balanced too many balls. "I thought you were going to move the rest of your stuff over here, and then go see Judith about getting your old job back."

"I am," Jaz replied. Rosa looked relieved that the subject of her daughter had been dropped. With Marty threatening to take Maria away, Jaz understood how it must feel to lose a child. She suspected it was why every time she was mistaken for Rosa's daughter, it provoked the same reaction in her madrina, one of great pride followed by even greater grief.

Jaz left Maria in Rosa's care as she made one final trip to the Inner Sunset house. She couldn't fit Maria's tricycle in the Jetta, so she left it out on the sidewalk with a sign on it that said TAKE ME, I'M YOURS! After she unloaded at the Golden Gate Avenue apartment, she set off for the Embarcadero Center where InfoSys kept its offices. Using her cell phone, Jaz called Judith as she rode the Muni. Judith told Jaz she'd meet her in the reception area.

"I'm so glad you're here," Judith greeted Jaz half an hour later. Her eyes were the color of a wet slate roof, and her knit suit was a mossy green. "I've been thinking about you." Judith gave Jaz a hug and the once-over, which produced a frown. "Jazmin? What's wrong?"

"Could we go somewhere and talk?"

"Kate, let Dylan know I'm taking a break, and that I'll be back shortly," Judith told the receptionist who was new. Was she a temp? The young woman's cat-eyed glasses gave her a quizzical look, as if she worked at City Lights Bookstore in North Beach instead of on the tenth floor at Embarcadero Number One. Judith grabbed her trench coat and awning-striped umbrella. Jaz followed her to the elevators. They rode down to street level and walked to a Starbucks where they ordered tall, decaf, nonfat lattes. At a high table, Jaz slouched into her slat-backed chair. "So," Judith stirred Sweet 'n Low into the frothy cap of milk that ran over the sides of her cup, "why do I get the feeling that you and Marty are having problems?"

"Because we are." Jaz had promised herself she wouldn't cry in front of her old boss. She recalled how Judith had made her weep the first day on the job, back when she was fresh out of USF and completely green. Judith should have fired her, should have hired someone with more experience, but she didn't. Instead she gave Jaz a second chance, what Marty refused to give her now. "He's left me." She wiped her eyes with the napkin that came with her coffee.

"Well, then how about coming back to work for me?" Judith had always been a bit of cynic when it came to love, but her take on the situation was so spot-on it surprised even Jaz. "Oh, Judith, thank you. I . . . I don't know what to say."

"Then say yes, because if you remember, I never wanted you to become a contractor in the first place. I only went along with it to help you with Marty. So now that he's gone, you can come back to work, full-time. I assume that's why you called."

"It is."

"Well, then it's settled. So what shall we talk about now? Marty?"

"I'd like to, if you don't mind."

Judith's freckled hand patted Jaz's. "I only hope you won't hate me for what I'm about to say, but I'm guessing he left you for Dom."

"How did you know?"

Judith took a sip of her coffee.

"So everyone knew except me? Carajo, Judith. How could I have been such a fool?" Jaz snapped her stirring stick in two and ran a finger along its rough, splintered edge.

"You know what they say about fools falling in love."

Jaz nodded sadly. "Guess that's why I didn't see it coming."

Judith's manicured nails tapped the table. "The only reason I did was pure coincidence. Mark and I walked into Greens one day, just as Marty and Dom were walking out, and the whole thing seemed very un-businesslike, if you know what I mean."

"So why didn't you tell me?"

"Because I hoped I was wrong."

"How long ago was that?"

"Right after the holidays."

It fit. Since the beginning of the year, she and Marty had functioned as solitary partners who ran along parallel paths. They handed off their beloved daughter as they went about their work and chores, cordial to one another but constrained. By the end of January, lovemaking ceased, which should have been a clue, yet it wasn't. Why hadn't she suspected, Jaz wondered, until she realized she had, last November when she first met Dom, and the day before at Rosa's.

Judith tossed her empty coffee cup in the trash. "I'm sorry."

"Me, too, but enough about Marty. Thank you for sending Mark Hamilton our way. He seemed . . . happy. Does that mean . . . ?"

"We're better than ever." Judith checked her Rolex.

Jaz thought about the watch Marty had given her for her birthday, his attempt to buy her off. Ironic he refused to give her what mattered most, what she craved, which was the gift of time. "Did Mark call you about doing your natal chart? And a synastry report?"

"He did, and you have my permission. I'll have Kate fax you my birth data. The date, time, and place were what he said you needed. So when will it be ready?" Judith asked.

Jaz gulped down the last of her latte. "I'll do it today and fax it back tomorrow. I've got to go home to see a sick friend, to explain to my parents . . ."

"Then come in next Monday, at eight o'clock sharp, and we'll talk about your job then."

"I can't thank you enough, Judith. I need the steady income right now, and the company's medical benefits, because I may have a custody battle on my hands."

"Oh no," Judith looked genuinely shocked.

"Oh yes," Jaz replied. "It seems Dominique Reynolds can't wait to be a stay-at-home mother to my little girl."

Judith smirked. "Until she has one of her own."

Jaz wrapped her arms around her leather jacket, chilled by this thought, determined more than ever to fight Marty for custody, full custody.

"What about child care?" Judith asked as they walked out of the café.

"Rosa Rodriguez, my partner, has always taken care of Maria."

"I had no idea. By the way, Mark loved your web site, Millennial Fears. Catchy name, he thought, and what a great marketing strategy to cash in on this whole Y2K craze. Can you keep a secret?" Judith stopped at the corner to wait for a red light.

Jaz lifted her hand in the Girl Scout salute.

"We're going to Puerto Vallarta for a long weekend. So what should I wear?" Jaz was about to explain she'd never been to that part of Mexico when the light changed, and Judith plowed on. "I think Mark's about to pop the question." That said, Judith reddened. The taskmaster was about to become a fool herself, Jaz decided, because in all the years she had known Judith Tindall, she had never seen her blush.

"I'm so happy for you."

"Neither one of us is getting any younger, and with our children a bit older now, I think a blended family might work." Judith lifted her eyes to the foggy skies and swept back an errant lock of hennaed hair. "The logistics are mind boggling: his children, my children, his ex, my ex."

Jaz blinked hard, her lashes no match against the blustery damp.

"I'm sorry, Jazmin. That was insensitive of me." Judith cast an arm about her shoulder when they reached Embarcadero Number One. "Don't worry. You'll get through this. You'll win custody of Maria, and then, my friend, you'll find the man of your dreams."

Jaz waved good-bye to Judith as she waited for the Muni. She felt almost buoyant. Thanks to her new (old?) boss, she and Maria could leave for Pleasant Valley in the morning.

Back at the apartment, Rosa sat on the couch under the bay window with a photo album splayed open on her lap while Maria played on the floor. "I do have pictures of my daughter, Jazmín. I just don't look at them." Rosa closed the book and set it aside. "Come. Help me with the menudo." As they chopped the onions and added them to the stockpot, Rosa insisted the fumes were what made her eyes water. But Jaz knew better. What Rosa told Jaz clouded her psyche as well. Like the steam that condensed on the kitchen window, tears slid down both their cheeks as Rosa explained she had married a man who became alcoholic and abusive, that she stayed with him only because she was young and scared and pregnant. After her daughter, Angelica, was born, Rosa fled to a women's shelter, afraid for her life and that of her baby. Her cousin, Silvia, convinced Rosa to leave Los Angeles and come to San Francisco to live with Silvia and work at a beauty parlor Silvia ran out of her home in the Mission District.

All was well until Rosa's daughter became a teenager. At eighteen, Angelica ran off with her gang-member boyfriend. Rosa and Silvia both feared Angelica would end up dead, the victim of the drive-by shootings that riddled their neighborhood with bullets. Angelica only saw Rosa or Silvia when she needed money, and they suspected she used it for drugs. It explained the shabby digs Rosa lived in. That she managed on her own was thanks to Eduardo, her client and benefactor. Still, it saddened Jaz that Rosa's daughter had left her with nothing, not even financial security.

Rosa recounted how Angelica turned up at her cousin's apartment one night with a baby. Thrilled that her daughter had left her husband, was clean and sober, and a born-again Christian, Rosa quickly discovered it was a mixed blessing. Upset by the santos, the Tarot cards, and an astrology book Angelica found, she bundled up her daughter and left.

"And you haven't seen her since?" Jaz asked when Rosa fell silent.

She shook her head and stirred the onions that browned in her pot.

"Does Silvia still live in the Mission?" Jaz asked.

Rosa nodded. She sprinkled cilantro on the onions and added pork.

"Then why haven't I met her?"

"We had a falling out. It's why Eduardo suggested I move here."

"Does Silvia know where Angelica is?"

"If she does, she won't tell me."

"So when was the last time you saw Angelica?"

"It was three years ago, the night of my birthday. It was right after I met you."

The memory of their meeting made Jaz feel ashamed. She saw Rosa standing outside her apartment, waving, waiting for a smile, a kind word. Why had she put Rosa off for so long? Her madrina was quiet as she cut up vegetables, only to carry on an animated conversation when Maria came in. Jaz rubbed her arms. "Rosa? What's your granddaughter's name?"

"Maria!" Jaz's daughter smiled.

# Stephanie Bengochea Garcia
## March 17, 1999

*True Friendship is never serene*
*--Marie de Sévigné*

The tapping on the door to her hospital room woke Steph. It squealed open and sounded as agonized as she felt. Jaz came in. "Mom told me you just got in, that you had a terrible drive." Steph's eyelids felt heavy as garage doors.

"When do you go home?" Jaz eyed the IV attached to Steph's arm.

"Tomorrow." Steph pressed the button to bring the bed up. It was a struggle to stay awake. "If everything goes well, not that anything is going well at the moment."

Jaz pulled a chair alongside the bed and sat down. "Everything will be all right."

"No, it won't. I don't want to go back to that rat hole of an apartment we share with Ana Claudia and Carlos. I can't face them. Or him."

Jaz glanced around before she said, "I assume you mean Pedro."

Steph wiped her eyes with her free hand. "He'll want to talk. I'm not ready to."

Jaz took Steph's hand. "He loves you. He told me that on the phone."

"He wouldn't love me if he knew the truth, that I'm attracted to Greg, that I should've had Corey's baby, but I chose to abort, and that I'm considering artificial insemination because we can't get pregnant . . ." Steph stopped, stunned by the look on Jaz's face. "What's wrong?"

Jaz got up, walked to the door, and closed it. The window in the room rattled, a reminder that the storm responsible for the avalanche still raged on, unabated. Jaz sat back down and retook Steph's hand. "When Pedro called me, we talked about a lot of things, including that he'd gone to Madison for fertility testing because he thought he was the one with the problem."

Steph stared at her friend. "He never said a word to me." She gazed out the window at a churlish sky. "What did the doctor say?"

Jaz got up and pulled the curtain around the bed with a metallic *whoosh*, and with that Steph was reminded of her healthy self, the one with long hair that wasn't matted, the perfect complexion that wasn't bruised, the one who wore tight jeans and a chunky sweater, as Jaz did, not the scratchy hospital gown Steph currently endured. "It's okay. Pedro's working."

"I know, it's just that I'm nervous, because he should be the one telling you this, not me." Jaz sat down again, pensive. "The only reason I bring it up is because I'm frightened, because I believe what he told me is true. Pedro's never lied to me before, and I can't imagine why he'd lie to me now, especially about something so important."

"What did he say?"

"That the doctor tested his sperm count, and nothing was wrong."

"Which is exactly what Nancy Adams said, that my eggs are fine. How can that be?"

Jaz closed her eyes and shook her head. "Pedro has this wild theory about it."

"That I'm barren?" Steph stuffed down a caustic laugh. "Did you know that in our church he could leave me for that?" When Jaz looked dubious, Steph said, "I swear, Chica."

"That's beside the point. We both know you're not sterile and neither is he, so . . ." Jaz twisted the hem of her sweater.

"So why aren't we pregnant?" Steph pondered the question as well.

"Being barren wasn't Pedro's theory as to why."

"Oh God . . . He knows about the abortion?"

"No." Jaz pressed her lips together. "He thinks you've been using birth control. Secretly." When Steph's mouth dropped open, Jaz said, "And it gets worse. He thinks you're having an affair with Greg, and that's why you didn't tell him about the birth control."

Tears wet Steph's burning cheeks. "Now I really don't want to see him." When Jaz tried to say something, Steph became agitated. "You don't believe his theory, do you?"

"No, of course not, although this whole thing makes no sense. How could you get pregnant so easily with Corey, then try for almost a year with Pedro, unless," the hair on Jaz's arms stood on end, "unless you didn't try very hard. When was the last time you . . ?"

"He lost interest when we were unable to procreate. So do you understand now why I nearly had a meltdown the other night with Greg?" Beyond the curtain, there was the sound of a door being opened and shut. Jaz started up, only to have Steph motion for her to sit down. When no nurse whipped back the curtain, she said, "I told you, Pedro's at work. So let me finish, because I need you to understand that it was a massage, Jaz, nothing more, though it was wonderful to be touched and not feel guilty, not feel all that pressure to make a baby."

Jaz sighed. "All this time, I thought you and Pedro were happy."

"I love him. That's for sure. But it's like he's my brother, and I'm his sister, or something. I guess that's why you couldn't marry him, either."

"But if you've got eggs, and he's got sperm, and you did make love, at least at the beginning, then why aren't you pregnant?"

"Maybe it's God's way of telling us it's not right."

"You don't believe that, do you?"

"If I were barren, or Pedro sterile, it would almost make things easier. Then our marriage could be annulled, and we could both walk away and start over."

Pedro swept the curtain back. "Is that what you want?"

Jaz closed her eyes. "Ay, Dios mio. How much of that did you hear?"

"Enough to know Steph isn't having an affair with Greg Morris." He frowned at Jaz. "I guess I should've known you'd tell her what we talked about."

"I'm sorry, Pedro, but it was just too important." Jaz looked at Steph. "I love you both so much, and when two healthy people can't make a baby, and they can't even talk about it, well, there's something wrong."

"As soon as I'm better," Steph told Pedro, "I'll make an appointment with a specialist."

Pedro leaned down and kissed her.

Jaz rose. When she got to the door she turned. "Promise me you'll tell each other everything." When Pedro and Steph nodded, Jaz headed out.

# *Jazmín Valdez Donahue*
## *March 17, 1999*

*Donde hay hijos, ni parientes ni amigos*
*(Children's needs come before that of family and friends)*

Jaz let herself into her parent's condominium, surprised to find Papi on the floor beside Maria, helping her with a simple puzzle. He rose brusquely. "Maria went to the bathroom, all by herself." Embarrassed by what he said, he added, "Juana thought that I should tell you."

"Gracias, Papi." Jaz knelt down beside Maria. "Mommy's big girl."

"Ya pues, Hija, so will you come home and live with us?" His gaze was full of longing.

"Ahora no." She gathered her daughter and kissed her father's coppery cheek. "Pero pronto, Papi, muy pronto" she said, feeling her father's sorrow follow her out of the room.

Vexed to find no parking space within a six-block radius of Rosa's apartment, Jaz circled in the Jetta as another Pacific storm unleashed its fury. Like a fire hose cranked to full blast, rain lashed the windshield. The storm would batter San Francisco before blowing east and blanketing the Sierras in snow. The image of Steph buried beneath the collapsed cornice on the northern flank of Pleasant Mountain made Jaz shudder. She banished the image from her brain as she parked, only to step out of the car into an unseen puddle that lurked in the shadows. With one foot wet resorting to an umbrella seemed redundant other than to keep Maria dry. She peeled her daughter from the car seat as the clouds above purged themselves.

The steady downpour plastered her hair down her white turtleneck, the fabric transparent like the nylon bra she wore underneath. She raced down the sidewalk and cuddled her daughter as she planned their arrival. First, it would be off with their wet clothes and into Rosa's claw-footed tub. If that didn't warm them up, there was always the soup that graced her madrina's stove. And once Maria was in bed, Jaz would sit on the couch beneath the bay window and shed her tears with Rosa as the skies over San Francisco shed theirs.

Running blindly up the stairs, she bumped into someone. She slung Maria onto her hip and whipped her hair out of her face. She apologized to the man she recognized as Rosa's landlord and client. "Here," he escorted her into the lobby and knocked on Rosa's door.

"¿Mi hijita?" Rosa looked puzzled. "I thought you were coming back tomorrow."

Jaz set Maria down. "After I run back for our stuff, I'll explain."

"¿Eduardo?" Rosa turned her gaze to the lanky man. "Do you have a minute?"

Bottle-bottom glasses magnified his blue eyes. "Where are you parked?" he asked.

"Way up Turk," Jaz told him.

"Then let me help you, so you don't get soaked."

"I'm afraid it's too late for that." Aware her turtleneck clung to her like a latex glove, Jaz loosened it from her torso, embarrassed by the slurping sound it made.

"I bet you have more than you can carry in one trip."

Jaz felt herself blush. "I do, so if you don't mind, I could use your help." When he nodded, she bustled out the door with Eduardo in tow.

He said nothing as she piled bag after bag on the sidewalk. He held his umbrella over her as she wrestled the car seat from the Jetta. "Let's take the bags first," he suggested.

"If you take the bags, I'll take the car seat. I don't want to risk it being stolen."

"In the pouring rain? You really think someone would steal it on a day like today?"

"You'd be surprised. I had a diaper bag stolen once."

Sharing his umbrella, they hurried back to the Golden Gate Avenue apartment.

"Judith called," Rosa told Jaz as she and Eduardo came in.

"¡Carajo!" Jaz raced to the bedroom. She came out into the hallway and waved the charts at Rosa. "I forgot to fax these." She slapped the pink wall with them.

"I should be going." Eduardo's Mackintosh dripped on the entryway floor.

"Before you leave," Rosa steered the man with the wood-handled umbrella over his arm back to Jaz, "I'd like to introduce you properly to the co-founder of Millennial Fears."

"You're Jazmin Donahue?" Eduardo extended his hand. "Edward Allen."

Her clammy palm clasped his. "If you'll excuse me," Jaz retreated to the bathroom. Ten minutes later she came into the kitchen in a chenille robe, finger-combing her wet hair. Rosa spooned soup into Maria. "Gracias, Madrina. We're both hungry after the drive we just had."

Rosa nodded stiffly. Once Maria was fed, Rosa busied herself at the stove.

Jaz pulled her robe tight. "¡Qué frío! It's colder here than it was in Pleasant Valley." Rosa faced Jaz and pursed her lips. "Not as cold as you were to our landlord. To a client, Jazmín, and a fan. To someone who just helped you lug all your things in out of the rain."

"Por favor, Rosa, I'm not even divorced from Marty, and you want to fix me up?"

"It's never too soon to make a new friend." Rosa ladled soup into a bowl and passed it Jaz's way. "Now, díme. Why are you back a day early?"

Jaz sat down. She studied her wet footprints that marred the kitchen's hexagonal black-and-white tiled floor. She sipped the tortilla soup, avoiding the greasy bubbles that circled in the broth as she savored the soup's flavor. "Mami and Papi are pressuring me to come home when I have to stay here and fight. Once the custody issue is settled, then I'll decide where to live." Rosa patted Jaz's cheek and left the kitchen. She returned with the portable phone and a pad of paper. "You'd better call Judith, before she decides where you'll live."

Jaz flinched when Rosa thrust the phone and pad toward her. She punched in the number, concerned her boss was back a day early as well. "Judith?"

"Everything's fine, Jaz. You're such a worrier. So, where are my charts?"

"They're finished. It's just that I was in such a hurry to leave--"

"No need to explain. By the way, Mark proposed."

"That's wonderful! Congratulations! Do . . . do you still want the charts?"

"With the wedding six weeks away, I figure we should both know if we're about to make a terrible mistake." Judith's laughter tinkled like wind chimes. "I'm teasing, Jazmin. Of course, I want the charts, not that I believe in astrology, mind you."

"Should I bring them with me on Monday?"

"Since we're both back early, why don't you come in tomorrow, and I'll get you up to speed? By the way, did Rosa mention that Edward Allen, her landlord, is a new client of ours?"

Jaz cringed as she envisioned the man she had been less than polite to. "I ran into him, literally, as I was coming in out of the rain."

"I think the two of you might hit it off. He develops software. He's come up with a new forecasting program for small companies. He can tell you all about it at my wedding."

"Judith . . . I'm not sure."

"He's newly single. You're newly single."

"Then we'd bore each other with our problems."

"Since tomorrow is Sunday, I'll see you at ten. Now, let me speak to Rosa."

Jaz handed the phone to her madrina who had listened with great interest to the one-sided conversation. Rosa was all smiles as she reassured Judith that Jaz would attend the wedding with Eduardo, though when she hung up, she looked concerned. "Judith is getting married on a Tuesday?" Rosa clucked. "Es mala suerte, Jazmín. Have you heard the dicho, 'Hoy es martes. No te cases. No te embarques'? Be sure you explain that to her, along with her chart."

Jaz nodded, wondering what Judith would think of superstition as quality control.

# Stephanie Bengochea Garcia
## March 30, 1999

*And the day came when the risk it took to remain tight in the bud was
more painful than the risk it took to blossom*
*--Anaïs Nin*

Steph fidgeted as she sat in the warren of offices beneath the
Madison County Hospital. Pedro pretended to read. His eyes
darted from the trucks that graced the glossy pages of *Car and
Driver* to her. "You all right?" he asked when she rearranged herself
again.

"I can't get comfortable." Her ribs were taped, her arm was
in a sling, and her ankle was in a walking cast. Her face still bore
bruises from her tumble down Pleasant Mountain. The doctors had
left her collarbone alone, saying it would knit itself back together in
time. Even so Steph was ready to climb out of her black-and-blue
skin. She had actually considered submitting to the laying on of
hands, the healing rite the pastor at the Valley Church performed
each week. Perhaps she would be his latest recipient of a miracle
cure. All she knew was she longed to put everything behind her,
what ailed her, body and soul. She shifted, imperceptibly this time,
determined not to attract Pedro's attention, not to wince in pain at
the twinges brought on by a twist in the wrong direction. She had

slept fitfully the night before, awakened by the recurring nightmare of being buried alive, of screaming for Greg in her icy tomb. But after shaking off that dream, she lay awake for hours, fearing this appointment with Dr. Markham even more.

She surveyed the other couples that crowded the waiting room, amazed at how many clients the fertility specialist had. His monthly visits to Madison required appointments up to eight weeks in advance. Nancy Adams had gotten them in, explaining the situation in terms that conveyed the urgency Steph felt. Pedro eyed her before he lost himself behind the windshield of *Car and Driver*. She sensed he longed to get this over with, to get on with his life.

She discerned a pattern in the carpeting. It reminded her of the cinders that dirtied the snow-lined streets of Pleasant Valley as they froze and thawed. What covered the floors of the hospital was similar to what covered the floors of their apartment. It made her think about the night she came home from the hospital. Ana Claudia and Carlos had made chiles rellenos and had hung a banner above the kitchen table in an attempt to create a festive atmosphere. After a dessert of flan, that sickly sweet custard eaten by every Latino family Steph knew, she and Pedro excused themselves, eager to retreat behind the flimsy wooden door of their bedroom and talk.

The agreement was they would tell each other everything, that they would hold nothing back. They would listen to each other and then decide what, if anything, could be done to save their marriage. Pedro plumped the pillows and eased Steph onto them as he prepared for the difficult task ahead. Steph surprised him by asking to go first. She told him about Corey, about the baby and the abortion. She confessed that she had been secretly tested for infertility the day he brought her to the clinic, convinced the problem was hers alone. But when Nancy Adams delivered the news that she was fine, it only burdened Steph more. She dreaded the day Pedro discovered that the problem was his. She knew how much he wanted children.

Steph took a deep breath before she went on, telling Pedro how she had believed that if she became a good Christian wife, God would forgive her and allow her to have another child. But with the news that it wasn't her, and the assumption that it was Pedro, she came to a different conclusion. Perhaps God's plan for her was something other than being a wife and a mother. And now that Pedro had been tested, and nothing was wrong with him either, Steph took it as God's way of letting them know they had made a mistake and shouldn't be together.

In the silence that followed, Steph feared she hadn't made sense. She only knew what she felt, and it had all come gushing out like a flash flood raging down a desert canyon. Pedro looked devastated. She regretted the fever pitch at which she had delivered her confession. None of this was his fault. When she felt brave enough to ask him to share how he was feeling, she was moved by what he said. He spoke of his own confusion when their initial lovemaking hadn't led to pregnancy, his own irrational fear that he was somehow to blame, that it was God's punishment for loving two women at the same time. He didn't know what else to do except pray: to put Jazmín out of his heart and a baby in Steph's womb in the desperate hope a child would bring them closer together, deliver that elusive happiness that money, or better jobs, or even an apartment of their own, wouldn't necessarily do.

He explained what should have been a relief to him--that the infertility wasn't his fault--only planted doubts in his mind. He spoke of his growing jealousy as she spent more and more time with Greg Morris, working for him by day and taking classes from him at night. And then, when she expressed a desire to study therapeutic massage with Greg, Pedro saw it as a move away from a shared vision of raising a family and working at the restaurant, of living a life based on Christian values. By the time rumors of her involvement with Greg reached Pedro's ears, he felt resigned to the failure of their marriage. It just seemed that every time he tightened his hold on her, she slipped away, like sand sieving through his fingers. And while he denied her relationship with her boss publicly, he grappled with his own doubts privately. During the ambulance ride down the mountain, as Pedro fought with Greg, he realized that whether Steph was having an affair with Greg was irrelevant. It was clear that Greg was in love with Steph, and Pedro suspected that Steph was in love with Greg as well.

Pedro ended by asking Steph if she wanted a divorce. In tears, she told him no. They made love, a feat given her injuries, and Steph was encouraged because she had never felt closer to Pedro. It wasn't the blood lust she'd experienced with Corey, or the forbidden desire she still harbored for Greg. It was naked longing that poured forth from her for a man who clearly adored her, bandaged and bruised as she was. That Pedro still loved her, in spite of her inability to make a child, in spite of her anger and fear of his God, in spite of her jealousy over his undying love for Jaz seemed to be the small miracle Steph had prayed for. Afterwards, as they lay in each other's arms, they were just Steph and Pedro, childhood friends, imperfect Christians, a couple like so many others that had stumbled but refused to fall.

A nurse appeared at the door to the waiting room and called them back. After reviewing their inconclusive test results, Dr. Markham asked if they had any questions.

"Why?" Pedro exploded, exasperated. "Why would two people be unable to create a child when that's what their hearts are telling them to do?"

Dr. Markham smiled sadly. "It is a mystery, isn't it?"

"So what do you suggest we do now?" Steph asked.

"There's always adoption. You're both young," he eyed her arm in its sling, "and relatively healthy. You should be able to handle the wait."

"How long?" Pedro asked.

"Anywhere from two to seven years, depending on what you decide to do." He rose and gathered pamphlets off a table. "I'll give you these to look at. Many couples decide it's a better option than what I can offer." He handed the brochures to Pedro.

"And just exactly what do you offer?" Steph asked.

"More testing to see if we can find an answer beyond everything seems normal. There's in-vitro fertilization, which is expensive and not always covered by insurance. There's also artificial insemination, so you do have options, Mrs. Garcia, if you want to bear your own child."

"Could we start with more testing to see if there's a reason that wasn't picked up before, something that could be fixed?" Steph looked at Pedro, relieved when he nodded in agreement.

"Of course," Dr. Markham told them. "I'll have the nurse take the samples today."

"How long until we get the results?" Pedro asked.

"I use a lab in the Central Valley where my main practice is. I should have them in a week. I'll contact you to explain the results in a conference call, if that's okay."

"That's fine," Pedro said before the nurse led him to a separate exam room.

The next morning, Steph rode the shuttle to Pleasant Mountain Ski Area to pick up her final paycheck. At personnel, she filled out a thick wad of forms concerning her worker's compensation claim. Scott Hansen had left a note there, asking her to stop by his office afterwards to rehearse questions and answers for the upcoming OSHA inquiry. She stumped down the hall to Scott's office in her walking cast thankful she didn't have to use crutches the way Mom did after her accident. Steph could get around fairly well, even if her broken arm, collarbone, and ankle prevented her from working ski patrol or waiting tables. To bring in additional income she continued to transcribe the snow survey data for Scott, and she kept the restaurant's books. Steph appreciated Mom's suggestion she do this, the respect Mom afforded her as a fellow wounded warrior. Even so, it was irritating to have everyone else in town asking how long it would be before she returned to work. The question nagged at Steph as well. Fear had led to a deterioration of disposition that was startling, similar to Mom's in the months that followed the rolling of the Blazer. Steph recalled how she hated Mom's martyr's pose, yet she could no longer deny that the same moodiness surfaced in her. Every day she prayed for God's forgiveness in judging Mom, for the grace not to follow in her mother's painful footsteps.

Scott sat at his desk when she rapped on the open door to his office. The director of ski patrol motioned her in and pointed to a chair. "You want something from the cafeteria? I'm having coffee, black."

"Then I'll have tea, herbal," Steph replied, hoping her response would soften his attitude. But it didn't. Scott barked their order into the phone as if he were on his radio, out patrolling the slopes. He raked a hand through his dark blond hair and walked to the window where he paced before an angry sky. "You seem upset," Steph said, though *pissed off* felt more like it.

"If that new storm comes in tonight like the National Weather Service is predicting, we'll have to do another control tomorrow." He faced her. "And nobody wants to, because of what happened to you. I have to tell you that in all the years I've worked here, this has never happened, Garcia. Never." He glowered at the gray clouds beyond the window.

"So what are you saying? That I made a mistake up there? That it's my fault I was nearly killed?" She rose, ready to leave.

"What I'm saying is it was my fault. I trusted Greg's judgment when I knew I shouldn't." Scott returned to his desk and slumped into his chair.

A tap at the door ushered in their beverages. They jittered on a tray carried by an earnest Latino who reminded Steph of Pedro. When the young man set the tray down too hard, it splayed dark liquid across the Pleasant Mountain Ski Area logo on the plastic tray. Scott mopped up the mess with the napkins and dismissed the cafeteria employee with a curt nod, barely acknowledging his accented apology. It upset Steph and made her all the more nervous. "How could this possibly be your fault," she asked, "when it wasn't mine or Greg's, either?"

After a minute of quietly appraising her over the rim of his Styrofoam cup, Scott sighed. "You know I'd love to believe that." He stood, crossed the room, and drank deeply before he turned back to her. "You're amazing, Garcia. Not at all that whiny racer I remember from years ago." He studied the lower slopes of the mountain, through visibility that diminished by the minute. "Even covered in cuts and bruises, you're beautiful. I get why Greg is head over heels for you. But that's precisely the problem. It's why he wanted you up there that day instead of me." Scott approached her, his eyebrows fastened in a frown. "And unlike Greg, I can't use that same excuse. I knew the conditions up top were treacherous, yet I allowed you to do the control, against my better judgment, because Greg is my friend, and I'd trust him with my life, but he," Scott shook his head and tried again, "he wasn't thinking clearly that day. He was . . ."

"Thinking with his dick?" When Scott grimaced, Steph said, "I heard you tell him that as you were bringing me down in the basket."

Scott rubbed his sunburned neck and sank back into his chair.

"Are you blaming me, because there has to be someone to blame?" When Scott said nothing, Steph told him, "It was an accident. Why can't you accept that?"

"Why didn't you accept my offer to go back down? Why were you so goddamned eager to help Greg with the control that day?"

Steph's lower lip quivered.

Scott leaned across his desk. "So what is going on with the two of you anyway?"

"Nothing."

"Bullshit, Garcia." Scott launched himself out of his chair. "If you won't level with me, I'll ask Greg. And if he denies it, I'll have to assume the worst and go with what's been flying around the patrol room ever since Greg hired you at the last minute." Scott braced his hands on the arms of her chair. "Your less than professional relationship with your boss could come out during the inquiry, and like it or not, OSHA will be trying to shove the blame up someone's ass."

She blinked back tears. "It's not an affair."

"Yet." Scott nailed her with what even she thought.

"I don't see what this has to do with the avalanche inquiry."

"If there's fault on anyone's part, there could be sanctions, a firing. My butt's on the line here, and so is Greg's. If you made a mistake up there, you need to admit it now, come clean behind closed doors, so we can all have our stories straight before we talk to OSHA next week."

She nodded.

Scott sat down, swiveled his chair toward her. "What, if anything, do you remember?"

More all the time, she thought. At night dreams about the avalanche deprived her of sleep. By day she experienced what could only be described as panic attacks, brought on by the oddest things, a random smell, an unusual bodily sensation, and *wham*, she was right back there, thudding along, the roar of the ice in her ears. What followed was the reflexive swishing of her hands in front of her face so she could breathe, then the slow painful beating of her heart, timed perfectly to the beep of the transceiver, to her recital of the rosary as she lay, waiting.

But Scott wasn't interested in that. What he wanted to know was how she had ended up in the avalanche's path when she should have been clear, if Greg had accidentally detonated the explosives. "We were both cautious, because we were disoriented by the storm. We could barely see each other. We were in constant radio contact. When I heard the rumble, I called Greg. It was just before the snow hit me."

Scott pushed the Kleenex box across his desk. "Greg didn't toss a hand charge?"

"No! The avalanche was not caused by the detonation of dynamite. That much I'm sure of." Steph bit her lip as she tried to sort it out. "Have you talked to Greg about this?"

"We talked that day off the record, then officially about an hour ago."

"What did he say?"

Scott rose and walked back to the window. "Your stories jive. In fact, they're verbatim." He looked at her, his eyes slits. "Which means you talked to him when I asked you not to."

"No!" Steph defended them against this new accusation. "I haven't seen Greg, and you'll be happy to know I don't plan to, since he's no longer my boss."

Scott sat back down at his desk. "There is one difference in your stories."

Steph glanced up, scared. Was it a trick, or would she learn what had gone wrong?

"Greg says when you radioed he looked up and saw the cornice come down by itself." Scott leaned back in his chair. "If that's the case, it makes it an accident, an act of God." His eyes bored into hers as he waited for her to confirm or deny Greg's version.

"Well, that would be good, wouldn't it?"

"If that's what really happened."

"Scott," Steph said softly, "you were there." He looked away.

"You followed us, didn't you?" He nodded. "I owe you my life. You dug me out along with Greg. It's why you blame yourself, because I could have been killed, and Greg could have been killed, too."

"Not on my watch." Scott's eyes locked on hers. "I assume you heard Greg defend you, tell me it was an accident, that things can go wrong up there, and that's what happened."

"If Greg says it was an accident, then it was." When Scott said nothing, she asked, "So what are you going to tell the insurance people, the worker's comp people, OSHA?"

He studied her. "I'm going to tell them that from my point of view, we conducted ourselves in a professional and safe manner. I'm going to tell them it was a delayed release, and that the cornice triggered sympathetically. It happens, and our training is what averted disaster."

She brushed her wet cheeks and rose, grateful she was free at last to leave. "Steph. There's one more thing." She paused in the doorway. "There's a guy downstairs who thinks he's never going to see you again, because you're a married woman who loves her husband, who in spite of what she feels will do the right thing." Steph looked past Scott at the storm clouds outside. "Talk to him." Scott's tone was kind. "Morris has had a rough morning, just like you."

Steph descended the cement staircase, scarred by the constant clumping up and down of ski boots. When she bottomed out in "the dungeon" as the employees called it since the windows at this level were buried by snow most of the winter, she stumped along on her cast to the end of the hallway. She pushed the heavy door to the patrol room open and peeked in. Greg sat alone, hunched over the logbook. When he saw her he stood.

"I'm fine." She hated the fact she sounded resentful, like Mom when she was on crutches.

Chastened, he backed off. "Was it rough?"

She nodded. Tears welled. "Scott blamed me, then you, then

himself, but," she wiped her eyes, "I convinced him that none of us did anything wrong, because we didn't."

He pulled up a chair as he had so many times that winter, his invitation to talk. "So the question is," Greg said softly, "will anyone buy it?"

Steph gazed at him, alarmed when Greg's eyes iced over. "If there has to be someone to blame," she told him, "let it be me. I don't want you or Scott to lose your jobs."

"It doesn't matter any more, because I lost everything that day."

"You saved me."

"We'll never work together again."

"I'll take your class."

"What about your marriage? Your husband?"

"Pedro and I talked."

Instead of looking defeated, Greg looked shocked. "Did you tell him about that night?"

"I told Pedro I love him because I do and I want our marriage to work."

"Then why do you still want to study with me?"

She hesitated. "Because whether I stay married or not, I want to be a healer. You're a wonderful teacher, so please let me be your student. Don't make me lose that, too."

Greg pushed a pencil and paper in her direction. "Write down your P. O. box, and I'll send you the information." Greg refused to lift his eyes when she pushed everything back.

Her chest tightened. "So this is how it's going to be?"

"This is how it has to be." Steph rose and hobbled to the door. "Wait up, Garcia." She turned, hope rising. "Bet you never thought it would come to this." When she said nothing, Greg continued. "No one talks about the grisly side of ski patrol. If nothing else your accident helped me decide I've had enough. If I'm not fired over this, I plan to resign."

"Greg, please. I'll say it was my fault. You know I'd do that for you."

"I'm sure you would, but that's not the point. Trust me, Steph, this job is anything but glamorous. You've done little more than re-unite lost children with their parents, a bit of triage. Once someone dies on you . . ." he didn't finish. "It's why I'll let you into my class, so you can learn a profession that doesn't involve putting your life on the line, or someone else's. Not that it matters, since everyone thinks you're the teacher's pet."

"See you in class, Morris," she told him before she left.

# Jazmín Valdez Donahue
## April 6, 1999

*Ojos que no ven, corazón que no siente*
*(Eyes unable to see are like a heart that is unable to feel)*

Jaz logged onto the InfoSys server, distracted by the envelope that flickered in the right hand corner of the screen. Steph had finally written, but Jaz's smile faded as she read the e-mail.

CHICA, THOUGHT YOU SHOULD BE THE FIRST TO KNOW THAT IT'S DI-VORCE. SIT DOWN AND GET READY FOR THE REASON. NO, I HAVEN'T RUN OFF WITH GREG. I WILL ONLY SEE HIM AT CLASS, AND WE WILL BOTH WORK HARD TO IGNORE EACH OTHER. AND NOW I'M WON-DERING WHY? PEDRO AND I KEPT OUR PROMISE TO YOU. WE LET IT ALL HANG OUT, SPILLED OUR GUTS THAT FIRST DAY HOME, AND IT WASN'T UGLY. IN FACT IT WAS BEAUTIFUL, THE CLOSEST I'VE FELT TO HIM SINCE OUR WEDDING NIGHT. YES, WE DID IT, AND I THOUGHT I COULD FINALLY BREATHE A SIGH OF RELIEF, THAT WE'D BE OKAY NOW THAT WE WEREN'T SO DESPERATE TO MAKE A BABY.

BUT THEN DR. MARKHAM CALLED WITH THE RESULTS OF THE NEW TESTS, AND IT GOT WEIRD. MY EGGS ARE ALLERGIC TO PEDRO'S SPERM, OR SOME SUCH NONSENSE. ONE OPTION, OTHER THAN ADOPTION, IS

IN-VITRO FERTILIZATION USING EITHER DONOR EGGS OR SPERM, BUT THEN I WON'T BE BEARING PEDRO'S BIOLOGICAL CHILD OR POSSIBLY EVEN MY OWN. DR. MARKHAM SUGGESTED ARTIFICIAL INSEMINATION. WE TOLD HIM WE'D THINK ABOUT IT. AFTER WE HUNG UP, WE WERE BOTH REELING. PEDRO SAID IT WAS A SIGN, GOD TELLING US WE SHOULDN'T BE MARRIED. AND THE HORRIBLE PART IS I'M THE ONE WHO PLANTED THAT IDEA IN HIS HEAD. I BLURTED IT OUT DURING OUR TRUE CONFESSIONS, NEVER DREAMING HE'D USE IT AGAINST ME NOW THAT I KNOW I LOVE HIM, AND I WANT US TO STAY MARRIED.

SO HERE'S THE KICKER. SINCE WE'VE ONLY HAD SEX FOR PROCREATION, OUR CHURCH WILL ANNUL OUR MARRIAGE, AND POSSIBLY THE STATE OF CALIFORNIA AS WELL. IT'S SAD TO THINK WE CAN *#%& OUR BRAINS OUT, AND IT WILL NEVER PRODUCE THE BABY WE WANT, SO WE'RE TOTALLY SCREWED. WE GO TO A LAWYER TOMORROW TO SEE IF HE CAN SORT OUT THIS MESS.

WHAT'S UP AT YOUR END? IS MARTY STILL HASSLING YOU ABOUT CUSTODY? ARE YOU REALLY GOING ON A DATE TO YOUR BOSS'S WEDDING WHEN YOU'RE NOT EVEN DIVORCED YET? AND DO YOU THINK I'VE MADE A MISTAKE BY PUTTING GREG OFF NOW THAT MY MARRIAGE TO PEDRO SEEMS DOOMED? TUNE IN FOR THE NEXT EPISODE OF AS MY WORLD GRINDS TO A FRIGGIN' HALT, JUST IN TIME FOR Y2K. ABRAZOS, STEPH

"Jazmin?"

Startled, Jaz clicked Steph's letter off her screen and plastered on a smile for Judith. "I was just checking to see if Imotors had responded to the bid I sent them."

"I need your opinion on something." Her boss brought the invitation out from behind her back with a flourish. "Tah-dah!" Pressed flowers framed the card's edges. The calligraphy made for a simple yet stunning effect. "Does it meet with your approval?" Judith asked.

"It's lovely." Jaz recalled her own boring, buff-colored invitations with the stilted black script that were oh so formal, oh so Carolyn Donahue.

"I thought that since it's the second time around I'd break all the traditions for good luck. We're not having the ceremony in a church, or on a Saturday. And I'm definitely not wearing white. We want a festive atmosphere, something south-of-the-borderish to remind us of our romantic get-away in Puerto Vallarta. Have you ever been there?"

"No, but I'd love to go sometime."

"Then attend my wedding with Edward."

"Judith--"

"He's very impressed with you."

"He doesn't even know me."

"Which is why he wants to take you, so he can get to know you better. He says Millennial Fears has proven uncannily accurate. He claims it's as good if not better than what his forecasting software does. Not that he believes in astrology, mind you."

"No, of course not," Jaz agreed, though she felt slightly miffed.

"So you'll attend my wedding with him?"

"Anything to please my boss," Jaz replied, trying to sound sincere.

The evening of the wedding, Jaz returned to the Golden Gate Avenue apartment angry that she had given into pressure from Judith to "do something with her hair." Catching a glimpse of herself in the beveled glass in the lobby, she did a double take. It was as if she stared at a vague memory of herself. Why on earth had she allowed her boss to talk her into all this? It was crazy to go on a date to a wedding looking like the high school homecoming queen.

Jaz jiggled her key back and forth until Rosa's door clicked open. Her madrina sat on the couch with Maria beside her. An unknown woman sat in the easy chair before them. She and Rosa both popped up as if they had been expecting Jaz.

"Mi hijita, you look so nice," Rosa gushed. Annoyed, Jaz flicked away a loose curl from her upswept do that tickled her neck. "Te presento Silvia Rodriguez, mi prima."

"Mucho gusto," Silvia replied in a deep, rasping voice.

"Igualmente." Jaz kissed the cheek of a slimmer, sterner version of Rosa.

"Mommy, Mommy! Look!" Maria splayed her painted fingernails.

"They're pretty," Jaz told her daughter. "And they're your favorite color, blue."

Silvia took one of Jaz's hands. "You hair's done, but not your nails?"

"I didn't have time, not that I could afford it." Jaz balled her ragged fingernails into fists.

"How can a professional like you afford not to?" Silvia cocked a penciled eyebrow. It irritated Jaz, her sense that Silvia knew more about her than Jaz knew about Silvia.

"She's right," Rosa agreed. "Let her do your nails, mi hijita."

"¡Sí, Mommy. Sí!" Maria clapped her chubby little hands together.

"We could trade services. I'll have you do a progressed chart for me," Silvia suggested.

"I'd be more comfortable paying you," Jaz replied.

"Then I'll throw in a pedicure and a foot and hand massage." Silvia checked her watch. "You're in luck. My next appointment doesn't arrive at my house until eight."

"¡Perfecto! Eduardo won't be here until seven-thirty," Rosa told her cousin.

"Do you still have all your stuff?" Silvia asked Rosa.

"Claro. Maria, run and get that kit I used on you." Maria disappeared. She returned with a large makeup bag. Rosa clucked at Jaz. "Relax, and wear your silver sandals tonight, because that Eduardo, he's so tall, so guapo." Rosa dug out her dish basin from under the sink.

"You know what?" Jaz leaned against a pink wall and massaged a pounding temple. "This is all just . . . too much."

"Why, Mommy?" Maria ran out of the kitchen and clacked back in. "I think your shoes are pretty, and muy sexy."

"Maria!" Shocked, Jaz couldn't help but laugh at her daughter in stiletto heels.

"You do the manicure, and I'll do the pedicure," Rosa told Silvia. Then she lifted Maria out of Jaz's shoes and set the sandals aside. "It will be fun."

"This is all very nice, Madrina, but I really don't have time," Jaz insisted.

"Sure you do." Rosa scurried about, transforming the kitchen into a makeshift salon. She filled her dishpan with sudsy water. "Silvia works fast, and so do I. We used to do this, until . . ." Rosa glanced at her cousin. Then she carried the tub of water to the chair by the table and motioned to Jaz. "Soak your feet. We'll have you looking gorgeous in no time."

"Me, too, Mommy! Me, too!" Maria jumped up and down.

"Bueno." Jaz slipped out of her shoes and stockings and put her feet in the water. She invited Maria to stick hers in, too. The lavender-scented vapors soothed Jaz's throbbing head.

Silvia arranged the manicure kit, bottles of nail polish, and lotions on the red-and-white checked oilcloth that covered the kitchen table. "What color is your dress?" she asked.

"Mine's purple," Maria told Silvia.

"¡No me digas!" Silvia tapped dagger-like acrylics on the oilcloth.

"Actually, I'm wearing a suit," Jaz replied.

When Silvia grimaced, Rosa said, "Jazmín wears it with a cute little sequined top."

"Not that one," Jaz told Rosa. "That's my old dance club outfit," Jaz explained to Silvia, too embarrassed to admit she had worn it to her high school prom.

Silvia searched her stash of colors and pulled out a sparkly fuchsia.

"¡Eso!" Rosa agreed. "And glue on those cute little charms."

The astrological glyphs Silvia took out of Rosa's kit were plastic and painted silver.

Jaz lifted her feet from the water. "You know, I really don't have time to--"

"They're pretty, Mommy. Can I have some, too, Rosa, on my toes?" asked Maria.

"Por supuesto, mi amor. Bueno, Jazmín. Dámelo." With a towel in her lap Rosa indicated that Jaz should hand over her foot. "Your mommy's going to look so good tonight Eduardo won't know what hit him," Rosa told Maria as she massaged almond scented oil into Jaz's chapped heels. "Now, put your other foot back in there to soak. You, too, Maria."

With a foot in Rosa's possession, and a hand in Silvia's, there was nothing for Jaz to do but surrender to Maria's fantasy that her mommy was Cinderella. All went well until Jaz refused to let Silvia glue on the fake silver charms, which prompted Maria to ask, "Why, Mommy?"

"Because they're too much."

Silvia's mouth settled into a stubborn line. "They're a surefire conversation starter," she rasped, her deep voice as grating as her nail file. "They'll bring you business. Think of it as free advertising." She stuck the first glyph on and prepared another.

"Rosa, will you help me put on my purple dress?" Maria asked.

"Andale pues, nena." Rosa walked Maria down the hallway.

"Alone at last," Silvia murmured.

"Why did you come over here today? Why haven't I met you until now?"

"I guess Rosa was afraid I'd tell you about Angie." Jaz tried to snatch her hand away, but Silvia held on tightly. She eyed Jaz. "I couldn't figure out why my cousin was so protective, but now that I see you, I understand." Silvia sprayed fixative on Jaz's nails. "It's unsettling even for me. The high cheekbones, the wide-set eyes, right down to the Chiclets teeth." Silvia took a box of that gum from a pocket in her colorless floral dress. Popping a white square in her mouth, she waved the box at Jaz who shook her head. "Well, at least in that way, you and Angie aren't alike. Since she stopped smoking she chews gum, non-stop." Silvia snapped hers as she gathered Rosa's tools and polishes and put them back into the makeup bag.

Jaz remembered coming back from her meeting with Judith, how Rosa had snapped the photo album on her lap shut. "Perhaps I do look like Angelica. I wouldn't know, though I think Rosa's been protecting herself as well. She knew if I met you, I'd ask you a lot of questions about Angelica and Maria, like, do you ever see them?"

"Not since Angie left that gang-banger husband of hers. I'm happy she finally wised up and got rid of the guy, but it worries me that she continues to stay away." Silvia zipped Rosa's bag shut and checked her watch.

"You're pressed for time?" Jaz asked.

"Like I said, I have a client at eight." Silvia rose.

Jaz hobbled over to her purse and returned with cash and a business card. "Could you call me if you hear from Angelica?"

"And why should I do that?"

"I need to talk to her." When Silvia said nothing, Jaz added, "I'd do anything to see all of you back together again, especially since I may not be able to stay here much longer."

"Funny." Silvia took the twenties and the card and tucked them in a pocket of her faded floral dress. With a cryptic smile, she said, "I have a feeling you just might get your wish."

Rosa sashayed in with the hanger of the dance club outfit hooked around her neck. Beside her stood Maria in the purple party dress. "You see," Rosa brought her hand out from behind her back and held up the tube top Jaz hadn't worn in years. "Those charms on your nails will pick up the silver in the sequins."

Jaz snatched the spangled spandex top from Rosa. "I'm not wearing that."

"¿Por qué?"

"I'm only doing this to please you and Judith. I should at least be allowed to wear what I want." Jaz removed the hanger from around Rosa's neck and surveyed the skimpy skirt and tight jacket. "I'd scare Edward off in this. It's too . . . "

"What's the matter, Jazmín?" Silvia snapped her gum. "Are you afraid you'll look too Mexican, or too sexy?"

Jaz hurried off to her bedroom. Silvia followed. "¿Qué quieres decir?" Jaz demanded of Rosa's cousin. The doorbell rang. "Oh, God." Jaz tossed the fuchsia spandex suit on her bed. Silvia picked it up and slapped the hanger into Jaz's hands. "¡Póntelo!" Silvia's rasping command set Jaz's teeth on edge. Then she pointed a dagger-like nail the color of freshly drawn blood at Jaz, and added, "And if you don't, I'll make sure you never meet Angie or Maria Rosario." Silvia sauntered to the door. "I'll stall him, and then I'll bring you your sandals."

Jaz stood in the Chevy's restaurant, the site of Judith and Mark's wedding, and thought about her own. She had wanted to be married somewhere other than the University of San Francisco's Saint Ignatius Chapel, which was cold and drafty even on the sunniest day. The solution had been to use the chapel at St. Mary's College in Moraga, a town close to Marty's parents in Orinda. Permission was granted since Martin, Senior was an alumni and generous donor. She recalled her future father-in-law's remarks about the evils of co-education, the pride he took in telling her he had completed his degree at St. Mary's back when it was an all-male school. The decision by Catholic colleges to educate men and women together was a huge mistake in his opinion. Jaz had to admit his son's shotgun wedding to a pregnant Mexican immigrant proved Martin, Senior's point perfectly. Perhaps that's why the change in venue proved futile. Fog poured over the Oakland Hills that day and made everything look drab and dreary, more like winter than summer. A chilly gust nearly tore the veil from her head as she stood outside the chapel's doors. She shook involuntarily at the memory of it, of how the wind-whipped grass looked like it was waving good-bye as she entered the chapel on her father's arm.

Once inside Jaz's spirits rose. Built in the Spanish Colonial style, the chapel was a lovely little jewel box of a church with its stained glass windows, exquisitely carved pews and choir loft. Candles warmly lit the interior, and the scent was that heady mix Jaz associated with a San Francisco floral design shop. The senior Donahues had done the unthinkable and footed the entire bill. Was it guilt Jaz wondered as she watched Judith and Mark's New-Age wedding unfold in a manner so radically different than her own? Or was it to ensure a suitable show, a cover-up for their family and friends? The reason given at the time was Carolyn was the expert, having married off four daughters. Since Marty was her baby, it would be her wedding gift to him. Due to the cost, the distance, and Jaz's parents' reluctance that she marry Martin Donahue, *the third*, Jaz agreed to the arrangement. It still pleased her that Carolyn Donahue had spared no expense when it came to the flowers. Gigantic magnolia arrangements framed the altar. Garlands of gardenias lined the aisles. But it did little good, Jaz recalled, as she stood beside Edward now. Papi had behaved as if he escorted her to the gallows instead of the altar. Maybe that was why the ceremony had been such a somber affair.

*What's the matter, Jazmín? Are you afraid you'll look too Mexican, or too sexy?*

Sylvia's words haunted Jaz as she glanced at Edward. He remained distant from her, like her father. Would he drag her off as Papi had Mami, Juan P., Chuy and Steph, before Jaz had even cut the cake, his excuse being that he had to work the next day? She returned her attention to the ceremony at hand, and while it was touching, there were aspects of it that were over the top. Every time Judith and Mark's children from their previous marriages took part, it was delightful, but every time the female minister took over, it was excruciating. If Judith and Mark wanted this woman to share poetry with the guests, they should tell her to speak up. People were either craning their necks (like Jaz), or had tuned out completely (like Edward).

Perhaps the woman's tunic was Judith's idea of what an Aztec priestess would wear. Unlike the bride, the female minister wore white, and around her neck on a chunky chain there hung an enormous gold medallion. Every time she took a breath and launched into some new platitude about Mark and Judith and the universe, the priestess's medallion slipped into a concealed crack of cleavage. What was even more distracting was the peculiar headband the woman wore. It reminded Jaz of an instrument favored by the doctors of her youth. All that was missing from the perforated disc was the need for the female minister to peer through it.

Because this woman's get-up was beyond ridiculous, Jaz began to laugh, embarrassed when several guests turned toward her with irritated expressions. Concerned Edward might not appreciate her sense of humor, Jaz quieted herself, relieved when the guests turned back to the ceremony as if nothing absurd, let alone comical, was going on. Edward's attention, however, remained elsewhere, his eyes on a woman who stood at the front of the crowd, a tall red-head with stick-straight hair to her waist. Jaz found the woman's hairstyle unusual for someone of her age and apparent sophistication in a city like San Francisco. *Judith is right. I should cut mine.* Jaz tugged at a shellacked curl, ready to shed her girlish image once her divorce from Marty was final.

The attractive woman Edward studied wore a heather brown suit with matching tights and alligator pumps. It made Jaz feel overdressed and underdressed at the same time. Her heels were stiletto, her stockings sheer, and her underwear was white and lacy. A choker of silver balls encircled her throat, and on her fingers were a plethora of silver rings set with fiery opals. Yet all Edward had commented on so far were her nails with their plastic charms, much to Jaz's chagrin.

It annoyed her that Edward couldn't seem to take his eyes off this woman who appeared to attend the wedding alone. She wore tortoise-shell glasses that were oversized on her small oval face. But even those spectacles couldn't hide the perfection of her porcelain skin or her large green eyes. Jaz felt a pang of jealousy, then tremendous irritation at herself. Why had she gotten caught up in her daughter's and Rosa's fantasy? Anglo men were all the same. She might attract them with her dark, exotic looks, but when it came right down to it, they wanted their mothers: light-skinned, light-haired, and light-eyed. It was genetic.

They also wanted their women to be tight-lipped. Jaz's final evening with Carolyn Donahue, just before Marty announced he was in love with Dominique Reynolds, had proven that. Her suegra's hand had been cold as a brass doorknob when she said good-bye. It still bothered Jaz that her mother-in-law knew her marriage was over before she did. How had she missed all the signs? But then she'd never had much luck reading Carolyn's rigid body language. Trying to detect her veiled emotional states at family dinners had been a parlor game, even if it was obvious from the start Jaz would never fit in. She shuddered at the memory of Carolyn's meticulous house. The Donahue home was about as warm and welcoming as a mausoleum.

The strumming of a guitar broke Jaz's train of thought. Relieved the long-winded event was drawing to a close, she experienced what her Latin American Studies professor would have termed cognitive dissonance. The wedding guests swayed to the strains of "Guantanamera." So much for the theme. If it had Spanish lyrics, it had to be Mexican. That was what everyone assumed, even here in San Francisco, a culturally diverse city compared to the rest of the country. That the song was Cuban was a small detail, as unimportant to Judith as the selection of Chevy's as a restaurant that served real Mexican food. But what did it matter? The whole thing was going from bad to worse, if that was possible. The guests were now being encouraged to sing along at Judith and Mark's insistence. The happy couple waved their arms at the audience; Mark in a conductor's stance, Judith beside the high priestess who had just concluded the ceremony. Once the song was over, there was much hugging and kissing as Judith urged everyone to take their seats because dinner was about to be served. Relieved when Edward threaded his arm through hers and walked her to a table, Jaz felt anxious when the mysterious redhead approached. "Fancy meeting you here," she told Edward in a voice that was more smoke than honey. Jaz had trouble placing the accent. Was this woman from the South? She sounded like Jaz's alien roommate from college days, Rosemary Riordan. She and that hothouse flower had never gotten along.

"Kay, this is Jaz Donahue, a business associate of mine."

"Pleased to meet you . . . I'm sorry, your name was?"

"Jaz."

"Well isn't that just . . . jazzy. Donahue, right? Are you related to Marty?"

"Not exactly." Jaz waited for Edward to rescue her, uncomfortable when he didn't. "Other than the fact I'm about to become his ex-wife."

"Well, then, that makes two of us." Jaz turned to Edward, puzzled, until she saw his expression, and it clicked. The attractive southerner was still married to him. "Kay Cameron." She offered her hand. "Used to be Kay Allen before Ed and I split up." Jaz shook the woman's hand, unsure what to say. Nice to meet you seemed disingenuous. The mere presence of this woman in her elegant St. John knit suit had Jaz zipping up the spandex jacket to hers. She felt inadequate, completely unprepared. "May I join you?" Kay asked in a droll voice. Edward stared at his soon-to-be ex-wife stonily, though he did nothing to prevent her from sitting next to Jaz. "Has Ed told you about our arrangement?"

"Kay . . ." Edward warned.

"I just thought she should know before she becomes more than a 'business associate.'"

"Maybe I should leave the two of you to--" Jaz was on her feet.

"That won't be necessary." Edward hauled Kay up by the arm and led her a short distance away. What followed was a heated discussion, the details drowned out by the din of the diners. Edward looked rattled when he returned.

"Should we leave?" Jaz asked. He shook his head. "She's very attractive," Jaz remarked, apropos of nothing, given Edward's disgruntled manner as he watched Kay drift off.

"Not nearly as attractive as my first wife." Edward wore a stoic look on his bearded face. Kay was his second wife? Jaz must have been visibly upset because Edward asked, "What?"

She returned his glassy gaze. "What are we doing?"

"We're on a date. Isn't that how you get to know someone you're attracted to?"

That same warmth rose inside her, as it had when he had helped her in out of the rain.

The serving of dinner gave her something to chew on besides Edward's comment. She smiled at him from time to time, happy the other guests at their table had taken over the conversation. Afterwards, the Best Man orchestrated toasts to the happy couple. When testimonials were given regarding Judith and Mark and the love they shared, Jaz couldn't help but tear up. Her freeze-dried heart thawed as she watched her boss and new husband demonstrate their feelings for each other so freely, Judith fearless now in her public displays of emotion.

With a break in the festivities, Jaz excused herself from a rather tedious conversation about--what else, computers--to repair her hair and makeup. In the restroom she ran into Dom. "Oh." Dom's hand fluttered up to the ruby heart at the base of her neck. "You startled me."

"Sorry." Jaz lowered her eyes, surprised that Dom stood her ground. "I didn't realize you and Marty would be here," she said, as she maneuvered around Ms. Reynolds.

"Mark is one of Marty's top clients." Dom held the door to the stall when Jaz tried to close it. "I'll wait out here, because we need to discuss Maria."

"This isn't the time or the place."

"Marty's miserable, Jaz. He misses his daughter."

"Well, he should have thought of that before he left. I didn't want this. He did."

"When are you going to stop hating him?"

"When he stops hating me." That silenced the indefatigable Ms. Reynolds, no small feat. Jaz shut the door to the stall, her bladder ready to burst. She sat there, worried that if she came out too soon, Dom would ambush her at the sink. Jaz flushed deliberately, relieved to be met only by her reflection in the mirror when she emerged. Her hands rinsed, she dug through her makeup bag for lipstick, a lip liner, and a pick comb. She retraced the outline of her lips in an attempt to downplay their fullness. Then she filled in their color, pressed her lips together, and blotted them with a tissue. Her curls fluffed, she dropped everything back into her purse.

On her way out of the bathroom, she kept an eye out for Marty and Dom. With dinner over, everyone was up, mingling and drinking champagne. "Claire de lune" was being played on a baby grand piano tucked in a corner. Jaz searched for Edward as she walked through the room, unsure if he'd abandoned her due to the awkward confrontation with Kay. Jaz decided she would leave after she congratulated Judith and Mark when she spotted her date seated at the piano surrounded by people who appeared to enjoy his playing.

Edward was musical? Jaz felt her arm hairs prickle. As soon as he noticed her watching, a mischievous grin lit his glass-sheltered eyes. He stood, and to Jaz's amazement "Claire de lune" continued. "I want to show you something." He reseated himself at the baby grand that played without anyone touching it and motioned for her to sit on the bench. Jaz stared at keys pressed by unseen fingers. "It's a player piano run by my company's software." He pushed a button on a drawer above middle C to eject the CD. "I take it you've never seen one before."

Jaz shook her head. "It's hard to believe a disc can produce such beautiful music."

"It's better than a synthesizer, in my opinion, although the idea has yet to catch on, probably due to the cost. The CD isn't particularly expensive, but the piano to play it is."

"Could you put the disc back in? I'd love to hear more." Edward complied. She enjoyed the Chopin etude he used to demonstrate the piano and its software. When the music stopped, the gathered guests wandered over to the wedding cake, which was about to be cut.

"Are you disappointed?" he asked.

"Why would I be disappointed?"

"That I don't play the piano as well as the software does."

"I'm impressed you wrote the program."

"I used to play, years ago, but I never had the patience required to become good."

"Would you play for me sometime?"

"I'd love to, but perhaps we should get over there, so we don't appear rude."

Once the cake was cut, the DJ took over as the master of ceremonies. He exhorted the bride and groom to dance to their song. Jaz had to turn away from Edward to stifle a laugh as Judith and Mark danced to "Guantanamera." She could picture them suddenly, hanging all over each other at some tacky tourist bar during their weekend in Puerto Vallarta. It explained the song's significance. Still, Jaz had to admit that Judith and Mark looked happy, and that the song was lovely and lyrical, popular at a Mexican beach resort she'd never been to.

After the first dance, the DJ continued to spin a succession of ballads. When no one got up, Jaz felt obligated to get the party started. There was no dance floor per se, so she led Edward to an area in front of the DJ, careful not to trip on the uneven tiles in her stiletto heels. After several maudlin numbers, she could stand it no longer. Excusing herself from Edward, she conferred with the DJ. He nodded, delighted to spin a song with a throbbing Latin beat. "Do you know how to salsa?" she asked Edward when she returned. He shook his head, a bashful grin on his lips. "Then just follow me." She positioned his hands on the small of her back and began to undulate in time to the music. It was awkward at first, as Jaz suspected it would be, but Edward caught on quickly, much faster than Marty ever had. His musical inclination must be the key, she decided, as she nestled her body close to his. A crowd gathered to clap them on, casting Jaz in the role of Latina dance instructor to the Anglos. She pulled a woman out of the crowd and paired her with Edward. Watching to see if they had the basic steps down, she took the hand of the woman's husband, judging by the bored expression he wore, prepared to loosen him up. He wasn't the quick study Edward had been, but he warmed to Jaz's sinewy body as it slid against his. She re-paired the married couple and was about to bring out another couple when Marty took her by the hand and snapped her into dance position. "You already know how to salsa." Jaz pushed herself a polite distance away.

"Not according to you." He pulled her back tightly. "How about a refresher course?"

To flee might cause a scene, so she danced with Marty, apprehensive when his body moved suggestively against hers. Worried this might arouse Dom's jealousy, Jaz spun away. When she twirled back she clasped Marty's shoulders, her arms straight, wondering what she would do if he tried to close the gap. But he didn't, so she melded her movements to his and to the music's hypnotic beat. "You're still an amazing dancer," he said. "It's one of the things I loved about you."

She smiled back, only to have Dom cut in and glare at Marty. "Are you going to tell her?"

"Tell me what?" Jaz asked, nervous.

"You'll be getting a call from Father tomorrow, about a new custody arrangement."

"When the judge decided you and Dom can see Maria anytime you want?"

"Only because you misrepresented yourself."

"Carajo, Marty--"

"Is there a problem?" Edward stepped between Jaz, Marty and Dom.

"Not any longer," Marty told Edward. "Come on, Dom. Let's go."

"Good riddance," Edward remarked once Marty had escorted Dom away.

"I think we should leave, too," Jaz said, shaken.

They found Judith and Mark and told them good night. In the parking lot Edward opened the door for her and then he wiped dew from the windshield of his Miata. With the top up the seats were dry but the interior still felt damp and chilly. A convertible probably wasn't the most sensible of vehicles in San Francisco, though it was certainly stylish compared to her old Jetta. "My apartment is close by," he said after he turned over the engine. "Would you like to see it? It's above my office, which I'd love to show you as well."

And although Jaz was tempted, she declined the invitation. Miraculously, there was an empty parking space in front of the Golden Gate Avenue apartment. Up the stairs she skipped to ring the buzzer, alarmed when Rosa failed to answer. Jaz dug her keys from the bottom of her purse to let herself and Edward in. Rosa came out of the bedroom/office Jaz currently slept in with Maria. "Back so soon?" A smile twitched across Rosa's full-moon face.

Jaz tilted her head. "How come you didn't answer?" Maria, bounded out, dressed in a nightgown. "And why aren't you asleep?" Jaz scooped up her daughter.

"Rosa let me watch TV." Maria yawned hugely.

"When I said no hours ago?" Jaz carried her daughter back to the bedroom.

"Maybe I should go," Edward suggested from somewhere down the hallway.

Jaz turned. "No. Please wait. This will only take a minute."

"No fair." Maria thumped her fists on Jaz's chest, unconcerned her mother winced in embarrassment rather than pain. "Make him go away, Mommy, so you can sleep with me."

Jaz plonked Maria down on the bed they shared. "Don't hit me and tell me what to do."

"Daddy called." Jaz stopped tucking Maria in. "He said I could live with him." With that, Maria picked up Esmokey, plopped down from the double bed, and padded away.

"Where are you going?"

Maria faced Jaz, defiant. "I'm going to live with Daddy, because you're mean." Maria slammed the door, which left Jaz staring at the space where her daughter had stood. When the door opened again, it was Rosa.

"I'm so sorry, mi hijita. This is all my fault."

"No, it isn't," Jaz sighed. "It's Marty's and mine."

Rosa frowned. "There's something else I should tell you." Her eyes shifted to the doorway that Edward filled. "In private."

"Then I'll just say good night."

"No. Please don't go. I'll be right there. Won't I?" Jaz turned and widened her eyes at Rosa who nodded and smiled at Edward. As soon as he left, Jaz rose and closed the bedroom door. "I thought you were the one who wanted me to have a nice evening. Well, I did, but now everything's ruined," Jaz whispered.

"I'm sorry about Maria," Rosa had switched to Spanish, knowing the walls of the house were as thin as Japanese shoji screens, and that their conversation might be overheard.

"What happened tonight was inevitable. Marty was at the wedding, and he's upset about the custody arrangement. It's why he called, why he filled Maria's head with promises and lies."

"I feel terrible, but he's her father. I couldn't very well tell him he couldn't speak to his daughter." Jaz kissed Rosa and got up. "Ay, Jazmín, you can't bring Eduardo back here." No longer deflated, Rosa glanced furtively at the door.

Jaz was nonplussed, "Not that I would, but I thought this was what you wanted for me."

"It is, mi hijita. It is. It's just that you can't let him see."

"See what?" Jaz followed Rosa's gaze to the computer. "Ay, no, you didn't."

"I did," Rosa replied, sheepishly. "I thought you said your new laptop was easy to use."

Jaz walked to her Apple Notebook. A natal chart for Edward Allen sat frozen, etched on the screen. Jaz tapped a key, relieved the printer sprang to life and printed out his profile.

"That machine, it's different than mine. I moved the mice--"

"The mouse, Rosa--"

"And everything froze. I didn't think you'd want Eduardo to know that we--"

"That you, Rosa--"

"Okay, that I wanted to check him out, personally."

Jaz ripped the sheets from the printer and stashed them in the top drawer of her desk before she shut down her laptop. "How about we discuss this in the morning?"

Rosa nodded. But when she opened the door and walked Jaz down the hallway to the living room, Edward was gone. With a naughty grin on her face, Rosa turned to Jaz. "So, how about we take a look at his chart?"

"Hasta mañana," Jaz told her madrina, wishing she had taken Edward up on his offer to have a nightcap at his place.

# Stephanie Bengochea Garcia
## May 13, 1999

*It's never too late, in fiction or real life, to revise*
*--Nancy Thayer*

Juana and Steph swept up the rain-flecked steps of the Victorian apartment house. Happily surprised by their early arrival, Rosa showed them in. Once their bags were stashed, they followed Rosa into a kitchen with perspiring pink walls. The room felt dankly warm, like the sweat that clung to Steph's brow. She had trudged for blocks, carrying her luggage, listing like an unevenly loaded ship. And while it had been two months since the avalanche, her neck and shoulders now ached. The scent of cilantro in Rosa's kitchen was as healing as any salve. Steph inhaled, grateful for therapy offered somewhere other than a doctor's office. "I should go call Jazmín." Rosa adjusted the flame beneath a rattling pot and left.

Juana brought a finger to her lips and crept down the hallway, only to return a minute later with Maria in her arms. Her granddaughter rubbed her eyes, sleepily subdued. It wasn't long before Rosa came back into the kitchen. Jazmín was on another line, she announced, and would call back in a few minutes. Then she launched into a tirade, complaining in rapid-fire Spanish that she had just put Maria down for a nap, which Maria now fought. Juana laughed off the scolding and allowed her nieta to burrow into her bosom, saying Maria would survive.

That Juana wasn't offended by Rosa's possessiveness amazed Steph. She couldn't imagine Mom behaving in such a civil manner if she were offered unsolicited child-rearing advice. It was as if Rosa and Juana were sisters, not accidental friends. Steph marveled at the easy way they bantered back and forth, mixing English and Spanish, choosing the language that best captured their mood at any particular moment. Steph prayed what she watched was a preview of the future, that she and Jaz might someday enjoy a relationship like this. Steph had even worn her necklace, the one with the cross, the Pisces symbol, and the Saint Christopher medal, the one Jaz had asked Steph to wear the day she married Pedro.

The ringing telephone sent Rosa off to the bedroom again. Juana seized the opportunity to escape the sultry air in the kitchen and sit on the couch beneath the bay window. Steph followed. Had Rosa tatted all the lace in this room? A valance framed the bay window. Doilies covered the arms of the chairs.

"¿Esteph? How 'bout holdin' Maria for me, ¿eh?"

"I should study for tomorrow." Steph edged away toward the hall.

Rosa bustled in with the phone. "Jazmín says she needs to talk to her mamá."

"Mi vida," Juana began, but her smile quickly faded as she listened to what was being said. "Bueno, but our Reiki class, it start tomorrow. Early. So when we get to see you?"

"Let me talk to her." Steph took the portable phone from Juana. "¿Chica?"

"Oh, Steph, I'm so glad you're here, but I just made plans because I didn't think you'd arrive until later. Would you mind terribly if I wasn't home tonight?"

"No, but hold on," Steph said, as much to Jaz as to the two

women who eavesdropped. She walked down the hall to Jaz's bedroom and shut the door. "It's okay. I'm in your room now, away from las madrinas."

"Good, because I can't remember the last time I felt this excited. You're here! Finally!"

Steph imagined the mischievous smile, the luminous eyes. She knew from Jaz's conspiratorial tone that her gemela del alma was up to something. "So Edward called?"

"He did. Normally I'd cancel, but he wants to show me his latest invention. It's some sort of dance machine that's going to be featured at a club in the Mission."

"I thought he developed software."

"He does, but he also collaborates on the hardware that runs his music programs which are a specialty. Did I tell you about the player piano at the wedding?"

"You did. So what exactly does this dance machine do?"

"I have no idea, but I guess I'll find out, after he makes dinner for me at his apartment. I hate to ask, but could you make my excuses to Mami?"

"Claro." When they were in high school, they covered for each other to their clueless mothers. It felt good to share secrets again, even if Steph wasn't prepared to share all of hers.

"I'd bring Edward by the house, but I already tried that on Tuesday, the night of Judith's wedding, and it was a disaster. I'm afraid I'd scare him off again with my chaotic home life. I don't want to risk it. Besides, I'm not sure I'm ready for him to meet you and Mami, or deal with Rosa and Maria again. So what do you think? Am I being paranoid or selfish?"

"Neither. We've got the whole week ahead of us."

"Unless you go off with Greg."

"Which I won't."

"When does he arrive?"

"Tomorrow night."

"Will you see him, apart from taking that massage class together?"

"I'm here to see you, Jaz. To study Reiki."

"And attend a seminar that Greg just happens to be attending as well. Come on, Steph. It's okay to want to spend time with him."

"Not according to Greg. He thinks I'm looking for a father figure."

"Well, are you?"

"It's more than that."

"Do you love him?"

"I'm trying very hard not to."

"Look, I should probably get off before Judith catches me chatting on company time. But before I go, tell me this: Do you think Greg loves you?"

"We hardly talk. He avoids me at every turn."

"Which must mean he cares or he wouldn't go to all that trouble."

"So what are you saying, that it's junior high all over again?"

"I'm saying you're not the only one afraid of what everyone will think."

"When everyone already thinks the worst? What difference would it make?"

"All the difference in the world if he loves you."

"I've got goose bumps, Chica. So how about you? Are you falling in love with Edward?"

"Oh God, Steph. It would be so easy to do."

"Then go. And dance your ass off."

# *Jazmín Valdez Donahue*
## *May 13, 1999*

*Un buen entendador, pocas palabras*
*(Few words are needed for someone who understands)*

Jaz was supposed to meet Edward at the corner of Florida and Seventeenth at seven o'clock. She felt uncomfortable walking through the Mission after dark. For her this was unfamiliar territory, an odd jumble of commercial and residential properties. Prostitutes plied their trade curbside. Jaz tried not to stare, but she was uncertain as to whether each decked-out woman she passed was, well, a woman. When a car pulled up along side her, she feared the driver was about to make her an offer she would have to refuse. But this was not a problem when a tall, ebony skinned woman shoved Jaz out of the way. She hiked up her skirt and pressed her lips to the car's window, which left a glossy imprint on the glass. Annoyed when the sedan sped off, the woman flipped off the police cruiser that followed in the car's wake. Turning back to Jaz, she rose to her full height, her skin lustrous in the waning light. Waxy circles covered her thighs where her boots left off and her skirt had yet to begin. Had she received those scars from some candle-wielding John? Jaz hurried off to where she was supposed to meet Edward. He'd mentioned in his call that he'd witnessed a sweep from his apartment the night before.

MILLENNIAL FEARS

She was about to abandon the corner where she stood when she saw him coming down the street. With her glasses on she brought him into clearer focus. His beard was neatly trimmed, his raincoat crisply belted. He carried an umbrella as if he were a drum major in search of a parade. He walked past the prostitutes who all seemed to know him. The tap of his umbrella punctuated his cadence. It reminded her of the novels she used to read and transported her back to her undergraduate days at USF, to the fantasy she'd harbored of double majoring in English and Spanish. What a starry-eyed romantic she had been: falling in love with Marty, becoming pregnant, a mother at twenty. Harsh reality had led her from literature to business, to her work in information technology. But perhaps those years of practicality were about to pay off. She would've never paid much attention to Edward if it hadn't been for Judith. And she wouldn't be meeting him now if he hadn't been impressed by Millennial Fears, her decidedly unromantic view of the future she offered the fans of her website, one of whom just happened to be Edward.

Millennial Fears had been born out of a hunch. She felt encouraged as she watched Edward approach and decided not to flee to the comfort and safety of Rosa's apartment. If nothing else, astrology had taught her that everyone feared the future. Ironic it had been on the Ides of March, her birthday last year that she felt inspired to launch her enterprise without the slightest inkling her personal life was about to fall apart. And in spite of it all (or perhaps because of it), she had pursued her vision, creating a web site that was now visited hundreds of times a day. And while many of the visitors were reluctant to log into the guest book, it was always a pleasant surprise to read the comments of those who did. Her cautious investment advice had been gobbled up by the surprisingly superstitious dotcom crowd who suspected the crest of the speculative wave they rode was about to come crashing down.

Reality had set in. The buzz on the street was too many of these start-ups were pipe dreams with no tangible product to sell and little profit to show their impatient investors. It encouraged her that even as the NASDAQ soared, her subscribers believed as she did that it was written in the stars (if not captured by the simple cliché) that what goes up must come down. This was true for any cycle, and what had allowed Jaz to build credibility with the skittish dotcommers was the no-nonsense advice she offered as the end of the raging '90s approached and the new millennium loomed large in everyone's fear-ridden psyche.

"I'm so terribly sorry," Edward apologized upon arrival, "to have left you out here with the rabble." He gestured toward the prostitutes who congregated several blocks away. "The set-up of the machine took longer than I expected. Are you cold?"

"A little." But what chilled her now was the cop that pulled up in a cruiser, to drive off the prostitutes' potential customers. "Does it ever get to you, living in the midst of all this?"

He shrugged and walked her to a building that resembled a warehouse. "Originally, this was just my office, but after the divorce, I converted the second story to an apartment." He unlocked the front door and held it open. "It's very convenient to have no commute."

Once inside, Jaz began to relax. The nondescript building had seemed so dingy she had been careful not to touch it for fear of dirtying her navy blazer and camel-colored trousers. But perhaps that had been calculated on Edward's part, to avoid scrutiny in a neighborhood that housed few residents. The ground floor held the expected maze of cubicles separated by partitions. A fax machine, a copier, and a scanner as well as file cabinets lined the walls of the corridor they walked through. Toward the back there was a room filled with equipment. A piano similar to the one Jaz had seen at Chevy's the night of Judith and Mark's wedding occupied a corner.

Several towers that resembled amplifiers and a large screen occupied the other. In the middle stood a projector hooked to a camera and a computer.

"The prototype for the dance machine is over there." Edward pointed to one of the towers. "The mixing board is connected to that processor you just passed. We play CDs through it. Then we hook the dancer up in front of the screen." He paused. "You know, they used to put on light shows at the Fillmore, and Laserium played at the Palace of Fine Arts for years. I have colleagues who still wax nostalgic about it, the heyday of the San Francisco music scene. It was one of those conversations that led to the design of the dance machine." He cocked an eyebrow above his rimless glasses. "Ever been to a rave?"

"No, but maybe you could take me to one sometime." Jaz removed her glasses, having forgotten she still had them on. "So how do you get up to your apartment?"

"Follow me."

Which Jaz did, to a spiral staircase that led to a loft in sharp contrast to the chopped-up space below. The ceilings were high. A grid of windows covered the far wall. There were rough divisions: a platform bed surrounded on three sides by drawers, a kitchen that featured cherry cabinets, black marble countertops, and industrial-sized appliances. A large Dhurrie rug defined the living area, the splash of color a welcome accent beneath the black leather chairs that surrounded a glass coffee table. It was a striking, eclectic mix, and a far cry from the cozy garage-sale comfort of Rosa's Golden Gate Avenue apartment. "Who did the decorating?" Jaz asked.

"I did." Edward shed his Mackintosh. His shoes were Hush Puppies, those suede lace-ups that had to be a thrift shop find, as were his plaid pants and polyester shirt. And while he looked a bit disheveled, his apartment was anything but. "Besides picking out all the furniture, I installed the cabinets." In the living area he opened the door to what appeared to be a bookcase. "I built this hutch to hold the DVD projection unit and the sound system." A dazzling array of high tech equipment was housed inside.

"It all looks so . . ."

"Complicated?" He was having a hard time maintaining his usual deadpan expression. Jaz regretted her remark, an insult to her intelligence, not his. "I'll show you how it works."

A piano, a classical guitar, and a synthesizer took up the better part of a brick wall. Jaz fingered them lightly. "I'd rather have you play for me."

"Not tonight." His dismissal of her request made Jaz feel like she had the night of the wedding when she cast about endlessly for topics of conversation. But Edward seemed unfazed. He entered the kitchen and searched through the cabinets. "The other equipment will have to wait as well. We only have time for drinks and hors d'oeuvres, I'm afraid." He set out crackers and cheese on the bar that divided the kitchen from the rest of the loft. He motioned for Jaz to sit on one of two stools opposite him. "I know I said I'd cook, but by the time everything was set up at the club, there was no time for shopping." He poured Chardonnay into two glasses and lifted his in a toast. Jaz clinked her flute to his, relieved he wasn't perfect, that his schedule was as hectic as hers. He put his glass down. "Do you like Vietnamese food?"

She adjusted the collar of his shirt. "I have no idea."

His eyes were intensely blue. "There's a restaurant nearby. From there, we'll walk to Samson's." Dinner was delightful, though Jaz was bothered by the spiciness of the food. She ordered lemon shrimp soup, only to gag on her first sip. Edward found this amusing, a Mexican who couldn't handle chili-peppered food. He suggested she trade with him and take his less than sizzling salad. After they had finished their entrees, they roamed Mission, between 17th and 21st streets, popping in and out of bars so Edward could talk to the managers about the dance machine. Jaz admired Edward's self-possessed manner. He seemed at home in places that were foreign to her. He made polyester and Hush Puppies seem cool. With Marty she had visited many a chic restaurant, but bar hopping had never been her ex-husband's thing, even when they were in college. Their sporadic visits to the salsa clubs ended with Maria's arrival. Perhaps live music and dancing would come back into her life if she and Edward continued to date.

They arrived at Samson's at ten, the appointed time to test his invention. The DJ greeted Edward warmly, leaping onto the stage to introduce the creator of the dance machine. Edward smiled broadly at the whistling crowd, and then without further ado, he asked for a volunteer. When no one stepped forward, his eyes cut to Jaz. With the crowd's encouragement, she allowed Edward to pull her up onto the stage, concerned when Edward strapped electrode-studded bands on her wrists and ankles. "What do I do?" she asked.

"Just move. The machine will do the rest."

She stepped in front of the large screen and waited to hear what the DJ would serve up. A Latin beat pulsed forth. She started to dance, and the screen blazed to life behind her. A riot of colors traced off her arms and legs. A camera mounted above the computer processor captured every move and projected it on the screen. Fascinated, Jaz tried different steps, swirling her arms above her head. The colors of the backdrop kept changing, until Edward grabbed the microphone and asked who wanted to be next. As he removed Jaz's wrist and leg bands, the crowd surged around him, the patrons eager now to take their turn before the screen. "It's fantastic," Jaz told Edward when he joined her at the bar. "How long did it take you to come up with it?"

"Years. I was a bit surprised myself when we finally got the prototype to work. There's little profit in it, kind of like the player piano software, but I'd go crazy if all I did was write business programs."

When he glanced at his watch, Jaz snuck a peek at hers, surprised by the lateness of the hour. The hordes still partied on as if there were no tomorrow, or at least none that required their presence at eight in the morning. "Let's get out of here," Edward shouted when the music reached an ear-splitting level. "Clyde knows how to shut the machine down. I'll come back for it tomorrow." Jaz nodded. She planned to take a cab home and was surprised when Edward suggested they walk back to his place.

"Is it safe?" she asked.

"You'll be safe with me," he said, and somehow Jaz knew she would.

As they strolled back to his office/apartment, Edward asked about her consulting. Jaz explained she might have to turn it over to Rosa due to the increasing demands on her at InfoSys. He asked if she liked working with Judith, and Jaz told him she did, but that she preferred consulting. For her it was a creative outlet, like the music software was for him.

"So forecasting business cycles through astrology is your version of artistic expression?" Edward's gaze was warm yet uncompromising.

Jaz attempted to shape her unformed thoughts on the subject. "The art is realized in the interpretation. The advice we give will either speak to you, or not. It's why Rosa and I try to meet with every client. Otherwise the written report can come out sounding like gobbledygook. If you've ever read a report prepared by one of those free Internet sites, you know what I mean. Machines can crunch numbers to produce accurate natal charts, but only a trained professional can interpret them in a way that makes sense."

"Then why aren't you doing that, full-time?"

"I don't know," Jaz admitted. "I was about to say because I need the money, the medical benefits that InfoSys provides me, but if I were to be completely honest, I'd have to say I'm just plain scared to be an astrologer, and an astrologer only."

"So the creator of "millennialfears.com" is as fearful as the masses she advises?" A smile curved Edward's lips. And instead of feeling put down, as she had so often felt with Marty, Jaz felt understood. That Edward would challenge her to face her demons seemed like a good omen.

"So why don't you just do your music and leave the business part to someone else?"

"For the same reason you don't just do your astrology." When she tilted her head, he explained. "I'm a control freak."

"I guess that makes us two of a kind." *Gemelas del alma*. They stood at the threshold of his office/apartment. "I'm wondering if you understand how scared I am to let you get closer."

"Then we can both be scared together." He unlocked the door and led her through the darkened corridor. At the staircase, Jaz pulled back on his hand. "My sixth sense is telling me that if I'm brave, I just might get lucky."

"Ever heard of the seventh sense?" When Jaz shook her head, Edward said, "It's the sense of humor, which we're both going to need to get through this." Then he kissed her with such abandon she couldn't help but kiss him back. They spiraled up the stairs and shed their clothes, and she figured that if she could keep her mouth shut, and Edward could stay away from plaids, they might have a chance.

It was three A.M. when she tiptoed into Rosa's apartment, afraid she'd wake Steph who slept huddled on the far side of Jaz's double bed. "Did you sleep with him?" Steph whispered.

"Claro."

"And?"

"It was so . . . wonderful."

Steph switched on the light. "Then what are you doing back here with me?"

Jaz covered her eyes with her hands. "Ay, Dios mio. I'm not even divorced from Marty, and I'm already in another man's bed."

"I'm just happy you've found someone, that Edward loves you for who you are."

"I think he does. He's totally supportive of me doing astrology. One of his more lucrative pursuits is setting up and maintaining other people's web sites. It got me thinking . . ."

When Jaz didn't finish her thought, Steph asked, "About?"

"That if I wanted to leave San Francisco, after my divorce from Marty is final and the custody mess with Maria is straightened out, I could." Jaz sat up abruptly. "If Edward can maintain web sites remotely, then I could provide my services online from just about anywhere." When Steph didn't seem to understand the implications, Jaz went on. "I don't know why it never occurred to me that I could quit InfoSys and just do Millennial Fears. It would allow me to move back to Pleasant Valley, to live and work and be near you."

"You're kidding." When Jaz shook her head, Steph rolled onto her back. "But even if you quit InfoSys, and everything was cleared up, what about Rosa and Edward? They live here."

"They could come with me." Now it was Steph's turn to close her eyes and shake her head as Jaz pressed on. "I realize I'm leaping way ahead, that it wouldn't be for a while. But I feel like I got my life back tonight, and that I've had a vision of what the future could be."

"That's great, Jaz. Let me know if you have any visions regarding mine."

"Believe it or not it's Rosa I'm worried about, more than Edward. If Maria and I were to leave when she still doesn't know where her own daughter is, or her granddaughter . . ."

"Has Silvia heard from them?" Steph asked.

"She claims she has no idea where Angelica and Maria Rosario are."

Now Steph sat up. "Rosa's granddaughter is named Maria?"

Jaz rubbed her forearms. "I know. It spooked me when I found out as well. And it gets even weirder. The falling out between Angelica and Rosa had to do with astrology."

"But . . . why?"

"Angelica is a born-again Christian."

Steph closed her eyes and flopped down on her back again. "We should get her together with Pedro." When Jaz said nothing, Steph cracked an eye open. "I was being sarcastic."

"But don't you see?" Jaz said. "Then Rosa could leave San Francisco and come with me to Pleasant Valley, if Angelica and Pedro were to hit it off."

"Which is crazy. You don't know where Angelica is, and she doesn't know Pedro."

"Yet."

Steph laughed and rolled away. "We really are las chicas locas, aren't we?"

From beneath her nightgown Jaz pulled out her necklace and shook the cross, the Pisces medal, and Saint Christopher medallion. "We're gemelas del alma, and for some crazy reason I think once we find Angelica, she'll join our ranks."

The following evening, at the Golden Gate Avenue apartment, Jaz was touched by her daughter's unbridled adoration of Steph. After years of avoiding contact with Maria, Steph seemed ready to let herself be loved. Jaz studied them covertly as she folded laundry. Steph seemed healed by her brush with death. There was an inner glow to her that hadn't been there before, which was heartening but a bit disconcerting as well. None of it made any sense until Greg came by unexpectedly. He couldn't take his eyes off Steph anymore than she could take her eyes off him. When he invited Steph to dinner, Jaz practically shoved her friend out the door.

"So did you sleep with him?" Jaz whispered as Steph slipped

beneath the covers of the double bed. Alarmed when Steph said nothing, Jaz switched on the light and saw that Steph was crying. "You've got the whole week ahead of you," Jaz told her. "It's wise not to rush things."

Steph nodded and sniffed. "Are you happy that you let Edward . . . in?"

"Beyond my wildest dreams." Jaz rolled onto her back. "I'll admit we're the odd couple, but he's the one, Steph. I know it. I think I've known it since our awful first date."

"But didn't you feel the same way about Pedro and Marty?" Steph leaned on an elbow.

Jaz didn't answer right away. "Actually, this feels . . . different. I waited a long time before I became intimate with Marty. It was a big deal since we both lost our virginity together."

"You mean, you never slept with Pedro?" The shock on Steph's face was unavoidable.

"No," Jaz told her, quietly. "Ironic, don't you think, if I really was the love of his life, as he so painfully pointed out to you the whole time you were together. We never made love, though it was not for lack of trying on my part." When Steph choked back a sob, Jaz regretted she had never revealed the details of her botched tryst with Pedro at Hidden Lake.

"It explains so much." Steph's voice was constricted by emotion. "Do you realize I would've never married him if I'd known? Oh God, Jaz, no wonder you never come home. No wonder you hate me."

"Is that what you think?" Jaz fought the tears that welled up. "I could never hate you or Pedro. I'm just sorry it didn't work out for any of us." Steph was no longer able to hold Jaz's gaze, so Jaz went on. "I know you love him, just like I do, but what I think we all learned was this: you should never marry your best friend. It's too incestuous. But what matters right now is what happened tonight with Greg. From the way he looked at you, it's obvious he's in love."

Steph shook her head. Her tears flowed freely. "I'm so scared that I'm about to make another terrible mistake, that Greg will end up hating me like Pedro and Corey do."

"They don't hate you, any more than I do. And let's not forget that Greg doesn't exactly have a stellar track record when it comes to relationships. It makes you two of a kind." It was eerie to repeat the words Jaz had said to Edward, even if her analysis did little to comfort Steph. "Be brave," Jaz continued. "You survived the avalanche. You'll survive Greg Morris."

The next morning, after guiding Steph and Juana to the Japan Center where the Reiki classes were being held, Jaz rode the Muni to the Mission to surprise Edward with a visit before she returned to Rosa's apartment. As she approached Capp Street, she realized Silvia's apartment was nearby. She punched up the address and phone number on the screen of her Palm Pilot and considered calling, but it seemed ridiculous since the apartment was only minutes away. Rounding a corner, Jaz felt dismayed by the dilapidated neighborhood she entered. The homeless lolled about on the sidewalk, unlike the area where Edward lived and worked. A chain barred the door Silvia cracked open. "Is Rosa with you?"

"She's at home with Maria. I was on my way to see Edward."

"You should have called first."

"I know, but--"

"But what? I'd ask you in, but," Silvia waved at the newspaper squares spread over the floor, as if she owned a dog, which she didn't.

The hair on the nape of Jaz's neck prickled. "Is Angelica here?" Silvia tried to shut the door, but Jaz blocked it with her high-heeled boot. "I thought we had a deal?"

"She arrived last night, and if she sees you, it'll scare her and the dog and the baby off."

"I understand."

"No, you don't, Jazmín, and neither does Rosa. It's why I let them come and go as they please, without a lot of questions, without making demands on Angie she can't possibly meet."

"What's going on?" Wrapped only in a towel, Rosa's daughter looked as if she had just stepped out of the shower. She stared at Jaz. Then she smirked. "So it's you."

It was as if Jaz stood in front of the full-length mirror on Rosa's closet door. The resemblance was heart stopping, even if Angelica's hair was short and shaggy, and a diamond stud pierced her nose. Silvia sighed and unlatched the door, which allowed Jaz to enter the apartment. Once Jaz found her voice, she asked, "Where's Maria?"

"You mean Rosie?" Angelica corrected. "She's in the bedroom with Bear."

"May I see her?" Jaz asked, expecting Angelica to refuse, surprised when Rosa's daughter motioned to Jaz to follow her.

"Mama?" The little girl seemed frightened when Jaz entered. A big black dog barked.

"It's okay, Bear." Angelica resettled the dog in its corner and dressed her daughter. "Don't be afraid. She's a friend of Grandma's."

"Are we going to see Grandma today?" Rosie asked her mother.

"No." Angelica smoothed her daughter's dark hair. Then she refastened her towel to hide a tattoo. "Why don't you take her out to Silvia?" Jaz offered her hand but the little girl shied away. "It's okay," Angelica said. "Mama will be out soon."

Silvia made coffee as her great niece chattered. Jaz checked her watch and decided to call Rosa. "I'm just going outside to use my cell phone. Tell Angelica I'll be right back." Silvia nodded and resumed her conversation with Maria Rosario as Silvia called the little girl. Jaz felt guilty when she told Rosa she had stopped by to see Edward and would be home soon. She tightened her black wool coat around her and pulled up her high-heeled boots before she walked back into Silvia's apartment. In the kitchen she found Angelica at the table, dressed in jeans and a wife-beater. She sipped coffee and read the *Chronicle*. The silence was stifling until Silvia said she would take her great niece to the Strauss Playground unless Angelica wanted her to stay. Jaz looked at Angelica expectantly. When she shook her head, Silvia led Maria Rosario away.

Angelica folded the newspaper and slung it on the table. "She called you, didn't she?"

"I wish Silvia had. Rosa would love to see you, Angelica. Maria Rosario, too."

"The name's Angie, and my daughter's name is Rosie, got it?"

"Got it." Jaz puffed out her cheeks before going on. "It's strange. I've never visited Silvia at home. It's as if I knew you were here. So why did you decide to come back now?"

"On a whim?" Angie's smile told Jaz she didn't buy her story either.

"Silvia wasn't going to let me in, but I saw the newspaper for the dog, so--"

"You knew. And now you're going to run home and tell my mother that I'm back in town when I don't want her to know." Angie stood and headed for the coffee pot. The tattoo on her right shoulder blade was of a cross, with CRUZ inked inside.

"I won't tell her anything unless you want to see her. It would hurt Rosa too much."

"Not that it's any of your business." Angie returned to the table with her second cup of coffee. "Silvia says you're her partner in crime, that you peddle her lies to the masses."

"We're business consultants, futurists that happen to utilize astrological information."

"In other words, you prey on people's fears, when they should be praying to the Lord."

"How long will you stay this time?" Jaz asked, changing the subject.

"I'm headed back to Tahoe, day after tomorrow, but I won't be there much longe. South Shore's just another big city with the same problems as here." Angie looked as if she patted her pockets for cigarettes, but she took out a pack of Chiclets instead and popped a white square of gum into her mouth. "It's not a good place to raise a child."

"Marty used to tell me that. My ex-husband and I might still be together if I'd just moved to the suburbs. But I love San Francisco, and my daughter loves it here, too."

"How old is she?"

"The same age as Rosie. Did you know my daughter's name is Maria, too?"

Angie rose from the table. She snapped her gum just like Silvia did as she rinsed her mug in the sink. "That's just too weird to be a coincidence." She eyed Jaz suspiciously. "Silvia told me they were both born December 15, 1995. No wonder Mom replaced me with you."

A pit formed in Jaz's stomach. "We may look alike, but other than that . . ."

"Did you know we were born on the same day as well, March 15, 1975? Or did Mom forget to mention that?"

Jaz stared at Angie. She felt terribly betrayed until it all made sense. Of course Rosa hadn't told her. It was why Jaz's madrina had been in no hurry to find her own daughter. Jaz had become Angie's surrogate, as Maria had for Rosie. So what Jaz said was this. "Then we're more alike than you could ever imagine. You see, I love small towns, too. I grew up in one that's located south of Tahoe in the Sierras. It's not like South Shore at all. My whole family still lives there. I could give you their phone number. You might want to go and check it out."

"What's it called?"

"Pleasant Valley."

"Never heard of it."

"Exactly. If you want to raise a child in the mountains, I can't think of a better place."

"You seem so sure that I'll like it, and I'm thinking, how the hell would you know?"

"We're gemelas del alma," Jaz told Angie. *Actually, we're triplets. Triplets!* Jaz knew the timing wasn't right to tell Angie about Steph. "Look, if you won't take my word for it, then maybe you'd be willing to talk to a friend of mine who is involved with an evangelical church up there." When Angie didn't protest, Jaz continued. "How about I give you his e-mail address?"

"What's his name?"

"Pedro Garcia."

"He's Latino?"

"Just like us."

"And his church is Latino?"

"It's a mixture of people, kind of like the town is."

Angie frowned. "I'm not promising anything."

"I didn't expect you to, although it would be nice if you'd promise to call Rosa. She misses you terribly, Angie, and she misses Rosie. I'd feel better knowing you talked to her."

"I bet you would because you're exactly like her. You're very controlling."

"Perhaps, but I'm a lot like you, too. Until recently I've been afraid to go home." When Angie didn't respond, Jaz said, "And now I'm ready to return, and your being here tells me you're ready to return as well." From her purse Jaz took a business card. "Here's my cell phone number." On the opposite side she wrote down Pedro's name and e-mail address. "He's a good friend, a good Christian. Tell him I was the one who suggested you contact him, because you might visit Pleasant Valley." Angie fingered the card. "I've got to go," Jaz said, "so promise me you'll think about it, and I promise I won't tell Rosa that you're here."

"Thanks, Jazmin." Angie read her name off the front of the card.

Jaz slung her purse over her shoulder. "The name's Jaz. Got it?"

# Rosa Rodriguez
## *May 15, 1999*

*I admire two things: the harsh law above me, and the starry sky inside me*
*--Orides Fontela*

As soon as Jazmín comes in I can tell she's mad. "What is it, mi hijita?"

"Don't call me that!" she screams, so loudly Maria turns away from *Barney and Friends* and runs into the hallway, where her mother stands, trembling with rage. "Go to the bedroom, Maria, and stay there until I say you can come out." When Maria just stands and stares, Jazmín stalks over to the TV and switches it off. Once she has whisked her daughter off, she turns and yells, "Rosa, how could you?"

Jazmín never calls me that. I watch tears stream down her face, until I finally understand. "You saw Angelica and Maria Rosario? Where are they, mi hijita? ¡Díme!"

Jazmín shakes her head. "No wonder Angie left. No wonder she doesn't want to see you. It's because . . ." Jazmín sobs so hard she can't finish. "I trusted you, and . . ."

"And now you know," I say quietly. A calm descends on me, a sense of relief. When Jazmín looks up, I motion for her to sit on the couch with me in the living room. "I didn't tell you because I was afraid it would frighten you away. It's why you have to tell me where Angelica is, so I can make it up to her."

"What about me?"

"What I want for you--and for Angelica and Esteph--is for all of you to be happy." Jazmín cries harder. "It's what I've always wanted. But life, unfortunately, is not like that. It's full of unpleasant surprises. It's why I became your madrina, mi hijita, and your mamá became Esteph's, and Silvia became Angelica's. Everyone needs guidance in this world."

"Then why do I feel so betrayed, like all I've been is a substitute?"

"In the beginning, you were. I'll admit that. And while I can't speak for Silvia with Angelica, or your mother with Esteph, for me it has become so much more. I love you, Jazmín. Surely you know that."

"I do. It's why I'm scared you'll abandon me, like Marty did, because you have your own daughter, your own grandchild, and you should be lavishing your attention on them, not me." Jazmín springs up. "It's why Maria and I should leave."

"But your mamá, and Esteph . . ." Jazmín looks as if she's forgotten they are here. She wipes her nose on her coat sleeve. Then she sinks down on the couch, puts her face in her hands, and starts crying all over again. "I know what you're thinking," I tell her, gently, "that you should go home with them, but it's too soon. You have to stay and fight Marty for custody."

"I'm tired of fighting. Marty's not a bad person. I want us to work things out."

"Then why does he want to take your daughter away?"

Jazmín looks up. She wipes her eyes with the heels of her hands. "He just wants his turn. He told me once that he felt left out."

I nod my head slowly. "And we both know how that feels."

2 2 2 2 2 2 2 2 2 2 2 2 2 2 2 2 2

Jazmín's eyes are red and swollen. "At first all I wanted was justice. I felt I deserved that. But now all I want is for Marty and I to get along."

"So you're willing to let Dom act like she's Maria's mother?"

Jazmín sighs. "You act like mine. And like you said, we could all use another mother."

I embrace Jazmín for a long time.

After awhile, she says, "I understand why you did it, Madrina. You were hurt. You were afraid. You'd suffered so much pain, so much fear regarding Angie. You still do. I know, because it's exactly how I feel about Maria. What we both need is hope. And who knows, maybe if we can let go, just a little, we'll become better mamás."

For some reason I laugh. "Which makes absolutely no sense, does it, mi hijita?"

"No. It's why we need astrology. It's what helps us make sense of our lives."

I sniff as I think about what Jazmín has said. Then I shake my head. "No, mi amor. What we need is faith. We're still Christians, and while we see no conflict between the Church and the stars, it's time to let go of our minds and embrace our hearts."

"But what happened with Angie was unreasonable. You didn't deserve that."

"None of us deserve anything in this world, good or bad. Life happens. And while it's helpful to have guidance from astrology--or a madrina--it's the guidance from God that counts. Through prayer He teaches us to have faith and not obsess about the outcome, about protecting ourselves and those we love from what we believe is bad. Otherwise we turn the sacred into magic when what we should do is admit we're not in control, that all we can do is respond. Now, go to Maria. I'm sure she's frightened."

"I will, Madrina. But first, I have to tell you I promised Angie I wouldn't reveal her whereabouts. She isn't ready to see you yet, but she will be. Soon."

I squeeze Jazmín's hand. Then I kiss her cheek. "I'll be back before your mamá and Esteph return. I just want to go up to Saint Ignatius to light some candles and pray. I want to let Him know how grateful I am for . . . everything."

# Stephanie Bengochea Garcia
## May 17, 1999

*Do not fear to be an eccentric in opinion, because every opinion now accepted was once eccentric*
*--Bertrand Russell*

The Monday morning queue for the bathroom at Rosa's reminded Steph of coordinating showers with Pedro, Ana Claudia, and Carlos. It seemed longer than a month ago, the decision she had made to move back in with her parents rather than share a new apartment with strangers. Jaz seemed comfortable living with Rosa, but Steph wondered how temporary the arrangement would be. It bothered her that she still depended on the good graces of others. Would she ever be financially independent, able to afford a place of her own? Sitting on Jaz's double bed, she felt discouraged by what she saw. Her friend's temporary quarters were a disaster. Boxes were piled in every corner. Jaz hadn't had time to unpack them. She'd been working nonstop since Marty left. Photos of Maria were tacked to the pink walls. Steph's chest tightened as she moved closer to the prints. Her "niece" was a study in contrasts. Thick lashes framed azure eyes. Golden hair illuminated mocha skin. Steph traced the heart-shaped face, the ready smile that greeted her whenever she returned from Reiki class. Was it too much to hope for, a child of her own?

"Your turn." Jaz bustled in, her wet hair lank over her shoulders. "I tried to be quick so you'd get some hot water." Jaz whipped off her towel and snapped it at Steph. The last time Steph had seen Jaz naked was years ago at Hidden Lake. It surprised her that Jaz's body appeared unchanged by childbirth. When Steph cinched the tie to her robe, Jaz said, "Your scars will eventually fade." Then she asked, "Is that why you didn't sleep with Greg?"

"No. He's seen me naked, on the night of my birthday when he gave me that massage."

"Our birthday," Jaz corrected. "I'd forgotten."

*I haven't.* Steph took Jaz's wet towel to the bathroom and hung it up to dry. By the time she took a shower and returned to the bedroom to dress, Jaz had left for work, and Rosa had taken Maria to preschool. Steph slipped on footless tights, sandals, and a sweater. Then she stuffed the materials she would need for her second course of the week into her backpack. In the living room her madrina stood on the couch, looking out the bay window. "Juana?"

"Ay, Dios mio, you escare me, Esteph. I just watchin'. You think he's lost?"

"No. Just late." *If he's coming at all.*

"You gonna tell him 'bout last night?" Juana climbed down off the couch.

"I'm not telling anyone what you told me until I know for sure. So please don't say anything, okay?" A horn tooted. Outside Greg's Dodge Ram 4x4 was double-parked.

"You be careful with that Greg Morris, ¿eh?"

Steph kissed Juana on the check. "Ciao, Madrina."

He looked skittish when she got in. "I'm sorry, Steph, about . . . everything."

She nodded, thankful Radiohead played on the tape deck, that he quickly ignored her to negotiate their route. Their class was in Marin County, which meant they had to head north on 101 during rush hour. With a hand to his head, and an elbow out an open window, Greg looked as miserable as Steph felt. As they inched toward the toll plaza to cross the Golden Gate Bridge, white caps and shadows dappled the bay as clear skies replaced the misty ones.

*Did you sleep with him?* Jaz's question had evoked tears, which Jaz had taken as a denial. Why the reluctance to share what had really happened, to share what Juana had said the night before? Perhaps it was because Steph was having a hard time with it all.

Friday night, instead of taking her out to dinner, Greg had driven her to his friends' apartment where he was staying. Buck and Kai Petersen lived near Coit Tower, in a gorgeous penthouse with spectacular views out every window. The Petersens had gone out of their way to make Steph feel at home, yet she hadn't. How could she? Buck was an executive at The North Face. Kai worked at Mountain Sobek Travel, a high-end agency in Berkeley. What Steph did enjoy were the Petersens' stories of how they worked ski patrol with Greg and Scott Hansen when they all took a winter quarter off from Cal. It was their junior year, and Buck and Kai decided they would marry once they were finished with school. It was at their urging that Greg and Scott returned to Berkeley to complete their degrees. After graduation, however, the group went their separate ways: Greg and Scott to Yosemite to climb, then Pleasant Valley to work; the Petersens to Telegraph Hill. And although Buck and Kai claimed to love Steph's hometown what they implied was this: It's a nice place to visit, but not to live.

The Petersens were partners in a Napa Valley winery. They shared tales about this enterprise as they poured samples of their label. Feeling drunk and inadequate, Steph was eager to leave, to have Greg all to herself, but Kai and Buck insisted on cooking for them. After dinner, Steph and Greg offered to clean up, only to have the Petersens disappear and return with luggage in hand, saying they were headed off to St. Helena, to a weekend event at their winery.

Steph's attention was drawn back to the bumper-to-bumper traffic on the bridge when Greg unleashed a sigh. His jaw was tight, and the air was thick with diesel fumes. He obviously hated this aspect of city living. Maybe that was why he decided to live and work in Pleasant Valley, even though he was a college graduate, with a degree in economics no less. Maybe that was why he'd given up a coveted spot at Boalt Hall, and the possibility of a prestigious job at a law firm in the city. What saddened Steph was that Greg seemed to regret his decision now. The Petersens' glittering lifestyle was certainly a world away from his. "We're going to be late, Garcia," he muttered as he downshifted again.

"Why don't you call me Bengochea, since you seem uncomfortable with Steph?"

He shot her a look. Then he rubbed his forehead as if he had a headache. "Maybe we should go over the material in the workbook, just in case."

"I thought you said you knew the teacher."

"That doesn't mean Tuttle will wait, even if he is laid back. He used to live on a commune, smoke dope, but he's straight now, totally legit. He has a booming practice in Fairfax, his own martial arts studio. If it hadn't been for him, I would have never gotten into Tai Chi."

"You do Tai Chi?"

"I've competed in Push Hands tournaments all over the Bay Area."

It was yet another surprise in a week full of them. It bothered her that she still knew so little about him. "Why didn't you stay here, with all your friends?"

His lips settled into an indecipherable line before he said, "I'm considering moving back." Steph's heart pounded. They were barely up to speed on the 101, driving through the oak-studded hills of Marin County when he took the Fairfax exit and followed a surface road through San Rafael. "If Tuttle likes what he sees during the course, he says he'll hire me."

"So Friday night was your way of saying good-bye?"

He threw her a look and shifted gears. "If you had stayed, I would have explained that it's why I'm reluctant to commit to a future."

"Then maybe everything happened the way it was supposed to."

Greg said nothing as they drove past upscale bungalows on Sir Frances Drake Boulevard through San Anselmo. At Fairfax they parked behind the Holistic Health Center. Once inside they walked through a room full of mirrors with a ballet bar and a wooden floor to a second that was filled with massage tables. As soon as "Tuttle" saw them, he gave Greg a bear hug. "I'm Jay." The man with the muscular build and receding hairline shook Steph's hand. "Use that one," he told Greg in a sonorous voice before directing everyone else to their tables.

Jay began by coaching the students through the deep tissue work. At Greg's suggestion, Steph played the client first. She shed her sandals, sweater and footless tights and climbed onto the table. With her eyes closed, she relaxed beneath Greg's touch. *The body never lies, Garcia.* It was what he had told her the night of her birthday, what he had told her Friday once Buck and Kai left, on another night that should have been perfect but wasn't. In the Petersens' granite and maple kitchen she could still hear him saying, "You're trembling," as he wrapped her in his arms.

"I'm cold."

"Really?" He smiled and led her to the master suite.

"Greg . . ."

He didn't allow her to finish, kissing her with a passion that told her he'd planned everything out with the help of his friends. He turned down their bed. Satiny cotton sheets washed over Steph's body as she and Greg made love. Thread count mattered she decided. Whatever price Kai had paid for the silky sheet set, it was worth it. Afterwards, she luxuriated in the Petersens' bed, happy to have Greg take the first shower because it allowed her to take in the understated elegance of the master suite. Grass cloth wallpaper complimented bleached pine floors. Mahogany built-ins were topped by marble. That was the way with the rich, even in Pleasant Valley, the building materials more important than the furnishings. Who would have thought such simplicity could be so chic? Sadly, nothing her mother did could disguise the ramshackle nature of Steph's house, the summer vacation cabin Mom worked so hard to transform into a home. There was only so much Mom could do. Steph thought about the antiques Mom painstakingly acquired and refinished, the quilts she pieced by hand. The floors in the Petersens' penthouse consisted of "distressed" pine, while the oak planks in Steph's childhood home were merely distressed, from all the grit everyone lugged in on their boots. Perhaps that was why Mom insisted that Steph and her sisters shed their shoes in the mudroom, saying it was impossible to knock all the pumice from every nook and cranny of a Vibram sole.

After she took her shower, Greg pleaded with her to stay. He promised he'd have her back to Rosa's in time to meet Juana for their Reiki class in the morning. When he swept her up in his arms and carried her back to the Petersens' bed without waiting for Steph's answer, she said, "Maybe we should use the guest room."

Greg laughed. "It's a little late for that now."

"Because Buck and Kai know what we're doing?" Greg ignored this and lowered her down. His tongue explored her breasts and belly. "Because you've done this before?"

It must have hit a nerve because he let her go. "So what if I have?" Steph rolled away. "Why are you doing this? Why ruin a moment we've both waited so long for?"

"Because I'm not sure you can give me what I want."

He lay beside her and curved his body to hers. "You know I'd give you anything."

"A baby?"

He sat up and ran a hand through his dark blond hair. "I thought you wanted to become a healer, to have your own practice, or work with me."

"I want all of that. I guess that's the problem." When he looked away, she said, "I know you were married before, and that you have no children, but what I didn't realize until now is you don't want any." She followed his gaze out the window to the lights on the Bay Bridge beyond the apartment's wrap-around terrace. "Well, I do."

He took her face in his hands and cradled it in the dim light. "When I look at you, when I hear you talk about it, I think that if I were ever going to have a child, I'd have one with you."

Steph's eyes filled with tears.

Greg kissed them away. "Stay," he whispered.

"Only if you're ready for a baby."

Once again he let her go. "Maybe I should take you back."

"Maybe you should." It was not what she wanted. She wanted a promise of forever. It was why her stomach felt tender now as Greg kneaded it. Was it wishful thinking? She couldn't trust Juana's intuition, even if she did pick up something during their final Reiki session Sunday afternoon. "I have news for you" Juana said, as they rode the Muni back to Rosa's apartment.

"What do you mean, 'news'?"

"Your womb, Esteph. It's full."

So even though she'd kept quiet about it all weekend, Juana had figured it out, that she'd slept with Greg when her marriage to Pedro had yet to be annulled.

"Los angelitos, they watchin' over you," Rosa said. "They give you your heart's desire."

Steph blinked hard. "Greg doesn't want children."

The Muni rattled along. The wires sparked overhead and buzzed until Juana said, "It don't matter what he want, mi hijita. It what you want."

Steph flicked at her eyes before she asked, "So you're saying that I'm . . . ?"

"Eso," Juana answered. "Your heart's desire, ¿eh? With or without Greg."

"But that's . . . impossible."

"What? You don't believe in los angelitos?"

Steph shook her head. In silence she and Juana rode to their stop and walked to the Golden Gate Avenue apartment. Neither of them shared with Jaz or Rosa what was discussed.

*Is Juana right?* Steph had no time to consider this with Jay's suggestion everyone trade places before he demonstrated the next technique. She donned her clothes while Greg doffed his. They had engaged in unprotected sex that night, something she had never imagined doing. Greg had neither asked about birth control nor had he used any. He obviously assumed that she did. Perhaps that's why her gut hurt as she and Greg drove back to the city after their first day of class. "Tuttle offered to take us to dinner tonight," Greg said once they were on the 101. "To some vegan place. I wasn't sure about your plans, so I told him we'd do it later in the week."

"If Jaz will let me use her car, you wouldn't have to pick me up, and you'd be free to--"

"Steph . . . I want us to eat dinner with Jay. Together. If he offers me a job . . ."

"I thought you said you weren't ready for a commitment."

"What I said was I'm not ready for a baby." Steph slid her hands over her stomach, something Greg didn't miss. She buried them in her lap and concentrated on the cars that boxed them in. "Kai and Buck won't be back until tomorrow. I wish you'd stay with me tonight."

"I'm not sure that's a good idea."

"So what are you saying? That this is it, Garcia?"

"Don't call me that."

"Why not? You're still married to him."

"Our marriage is being annulled."

"Because he thought you were unfaithful?" When Steph didn't answer, Greg said, "I told him we hadn't done anything, in the ambulance, on the way to the hospital. There I was, worried about you, and all he cared about was whether you and I were having sex. That's not love."

"It is. It's why our marriage is being annulled, because I can't give him . . ."

"What he wants?" Greg straightened. Then he stared at her as if he finally understood.

"According to the doctor, I can have children, just not with him."

Greg returned his attention to the road. "So that's what Friday night was about?"

"The avalanche taught me that life is short, that none of us know what the future holds."

She watched him closely. He shoved the Radiohead cassette into the tape deck to fill the hollow space inside the cab. When they pulled up in front of Rosa's apartment, Steph said, "I'll take Jaz's car tomorrow." She felt him watching her. When she leveled her gaze to his, his eyes were the color of water. She placed her pointer on his parted lips. "See you in class, Morris."

# Jazmín Valdez Donahue
## May 17, 1999

*Un gran salto, que quebranto*
*(A leap of faith sometimes leads to a headache)*

J az was irritated that Edward was late again. For living and working in the same place, he was constantly elsewhere, at business meetings to pitch proposed web sites or software packages to perspective clients. But then, when she thought about it, she realized she should be thankful he had carved out time to take her to dinner and a salsa club with the schedule he kept.

She never imagined herself falling for someone like him, a man who allowed the scent of Old Spice to permeate everything he wore. He was a walking anachronism from the wood-handled umbrella he carried to the Mackintosh he wore, rain or shine. Yet everything old seemed new on him, as natural as any synthetic blend. In the beginning, Marty had been comfortable, too, though once they married, he insisted Jaz not only iron but starch his shirts and pants, a legacy bequeathed to him by his meticulously dressed mother. And strangely enough, Jaz had been happy to do so, because Marty treated her as if she were exotic, sensual, made of fine silk. Now he acted as if she were the hair shirt he wore every day, like everything she did scratched.

She tugged down on her spandex fuchsia skirt and zipped up the jacket over her sequined top. Edward had asked her to wear this outfit because he found it sexy. He had also asked her to get her nails done. Opals. That's what he'd said her nails looked like at Judith's wedding. Jaz splayed her fingers now. Fiery sparks ignited the blush-toned gels. At least the manicure Rosa had given her was subtle compared to the acrylics Silvia had sculpted on.

The evening was cold and foggy. Jaz wished she had asked Edward for a key. She hadn't because she worried the request might spook him. He had yet to introduce her to his staff. Jaz wondered how they would react to her clacking up the spiral staircase in stiletto heels.

The door to his office opened, and a man walked out. She turned and hoped he wouldn't notice her, but he did. "I don't recall seeing you here before." His nails were well cared for. Was he a metrosexual? He certainly looked young, urban, and hip in his custom-tailored suit.

"I'm waiting for Edward," she told him.

"You and everyone else in this city." The guy had a nice smile. "You're a contractor?" She nodded. "Steven O'Connell." He held out his well cared for hand. "And you're?"

"Jaz Donahue." She took his. "I don't suppose you're Edward's partner, are you?"

The man laughed. "That's a loaded question in a city like this." He had succeeded in making her blush, which meant her face now matched her nails, that fiery sparks burned her cheeks. "I'm having trouble imagining you climbing up to Edward's loft in those shoes."

Flats! Why hadn't she worn flats? Surely Steven O'Connell was teasing, though for some reason his comment made her think about Maria. Her daughter was over in Orinda for the night, at Marty's parent's house across the bay. What if an earthquake flattened the Bay Bridge? Spans of concrete had pancaked on the 480 back in

'89. According to Marty, the state had torn down that freeway, and it was why the view from his new Embarcadero condo was so incredible. "Excuse me," she told Steven O'Connell as she took out her cell phone, annoyed when NO SERVICE flashed back at her.

"Here." He whipped out his, "though I'm sure Edward will be here any minute."

She flipped open Steven's Motorola and punched in Edward's number, only to get his voice mail. Where was he, and why was his phone turned off? Then she remembered he'd said something about meeting Kay Cameron to sign papers concerning the division of assets. Edward was always circumspect in regard to his second ex-wife. Perhaps it had to do with what Kay referred to in her syrupy drawl as "the arrangement" the night of Judith and Mark's wedding. After leaving Edward a brief voice mail, Jaz thanked Steven O'Connell and returned his phone to him. When he left, she dug through her purse for her Nokia and walked down Seventeenth in search of reception. Once found, she took out her Palm Pilot to look up Silvia's number.

"Hello?" A tentative voice answered after eight rings.

"Silvia?"

"No, Jaz. It's me, Angie."

"You're still here?"

"Like it's any of your business." Angie hung up.

Jaz walked faster. She hit REDIAL over and over, only to get a busy signal. She passed several prostitutes along the way, shocked when the tall dark one blocked the sidewalk and snatched the Nokia out of her hand. "Hey, Girlfriend. What's yo' problem?" the woman asked when Jaz tried to grab her phone. "Don't you go touchin' me."

"I won't if you'll give me my phone." Jaz sounded braver than she felt.

The woman rose to her full height. "Why? You tryin' to steal my business?"

"No. So just give me back my phone. Please."

The woman laughed. Then she punched in a number on the Nokia with her thumb. "I will, after I call my pimp and tell him to come down here and teach you yo' manners."

Jaz backed away until she felt something sharp jab her between the ribs. Two other women flanked her now. One held her arms, the other a knife. She was about to shake them off and make a run for it when a siren let out a *whoop* and a police car pulled over.

"All right, ladies. Break it up." An older Latino cop climbed out.

Jaz felt the blade nick her again. A trickle of sequins scattered across the sidewalk.

"IDs everyone," the cop said, as he took a double take of Jaz.

Behind her she heard the knife blade snap shut as all three women produced their driver licenses. When the cop turned back, all Jaz could say was, "I can't seem to find mine." Frantic, she continued to feel around inside her purse for her wallet. A moist warmth spread across the small of her back and stung her with every breath she took. Puzzled, the cop squinted at her before he returned his attention to the other women. Jaz set her bag down on the sidewalk and removed everything, angered because the cop was letting the prostitutes off with a warning. "When they stole my phone?" she cried. "And my wallet?"

"What phone?" The tall one raised empty pink palms.

"What wallet?" The other two flashed white smiles and sauntered off.

The cop scrutinized Jaz, an odd look on his face. "Your ID, ma'm?"

"They cut me," she told him, incensed. "Look." She showed him her back.

"You're new around here, aren't you?" Jaz closed her eyes, sickened by what the world-weary Latino insinuated. "Is that why 'Sister Soul' was giving you such a hard time?"

"Those women took my phone, and my wallet, too." Jaz turned to retrieve her bag, but it had vanished along with the women. "And now they've taken my purse!" When the cop continued to stare at Jaz, as if he knew her, she asked, "Why aren't you chasing them?"

Shaken, the cop snapped out of his trance. "Let's go."

"But--"

He gripped Jaz's arm. "You want me to read you your rights?"

"No, as long as you'll let me make a call when I get there."

Angie arrived at the substation in the Mission quickly. The cop greeted her as if she were his daughter. "You keepin' your nose clean?" he asked, his eyes darting from Angie to Jaz.

"Yeah," Angie smirked. "I'm still up in Tahoe, with Rosie."

"And Cruz?" The cop's wiry eyebrows shot up.

"Nah, I dissed him. I got tired of his shit."

"Smart move." The cop jerked his cleft chin toward Jaz. "You really know her?"

Angie laughed. "She's no ho. She's a friend of Mom's."

"And your Aunt Silvia's? Then what's she doin' hangin' with the girls on Seventeenth?"

"Like I said, she's a friend who was comin' to see me." Angie stared the cop down. "So let her go, Manny. And don't report it, okay? She's already been ripped off tonight, twice."

The Latino cop's forehead crinkled. "I'll do my best," he said before he walked away.

Jaz exhaled and told Angie, "Thank you."

Angie started for the door. "Just don't tell my mother that I'm here, okay?"

"Okay," Jaz agreed, reluctantly. She followed Angie out of the station house. As they walked to Silvia's apartment, she asked, "Why'd you take my call?"

Angie shrugged. "For some reason, I knew you were in trouble."

Jaz nodded. "Why haven't you left yet?"

"Maybe I have," was Angie's cryptic reply.

The apartment was empty when they arrived. "Where's Silvia? And Rosie?"

"At my mother's."

"But I thought you said you didn't want Rosa to know you were here."

"She thinks I left Rosie with Silvia. At least that's what I told Silvia to tell her."

"But . . . why?"

Angie glared at Jaz. "All these questions, when you should be thanking your lucky stars that I saved your sorry ass. If I hadn't taken your call, you might still be down at the station, shootin' the shit with Manny, which gets old really fast, I can tell you from experience." Angie grabbed a pack of Chiclets off the coffee table and shook one out. "That was pretty stupid, taking on those hos over a cell phone. I'm surprised they didn't stick you."

"Oh, but they did." Jaz grimaced as she turned and showed Angie her ruined outfit.

Angie lifted Jaz's ripped-up jacket and sequined tube top. "I'll clean that up for you."

"Thanks, Angie. I'm lucky that cop friend of yours came along when he did, or . . . or I don't even want to think about it." When Angie came back from the bathroom, Jaz noticed two battered suitcases beside the front door. "Are you here to pick up Rosie and leave?"

"What's it to you?" Angie set a bottle of alcohol and cotton balls on the coffee table.

"Are you headed back to Tahoe?"

"Like it's your business." Angie dabbed the cut with a cotton ball soaked in alcohol.

Jaz flinched. The cut was deep. The alcohol stung. Then, it suddenly occurred to her where Angie had been. "You went to Pleasant Valley, didn't you? You saw Pedro."

At first Angie said nothing. She went back to the bathroom for adhesive and gauze. When she returned she taped a pad on Jaz's back. "Silvia told you, didn't she?"

"No, she didn't, but that's not the point. The point is I'm thrilled that you went. So what did you think of my hometown?"

"Actually, I thought it was nice, like that ex-boyfriend of yours. Though why Pedro thinks you walk on water is beyond me. You two seem totally incompatible, like those bumper stickers I saw all over Pleasant Valley while I was there." When this was lost on Jaz, Angie said, "You know, HONK IF YOU LOVE JESUS meets BORN AGAIN PAGAN."

Jaz laughed. Then she felt nervous. "Did Pedro mention anything about my friend, Stephanie Bengochea?"

"Only that their marriage is being annulled, and that she's here in the city this week to visit you." Angie snapped her gum as she studied Jaz. "I don't know. It still strikes me as kind of strange, the way you're all so tight and everything."

"Did you like Pedro?"

"I liked Pleasant Valley, enough to answer an ad in the *Gazette* for Sierra Strippers. You know, the asphalt company? They hired me for the summer, because they liked my suggestion to print up bumper stickers that say LET HER RIP! And put them on their machines."

"Are you leaving Tahoe to get away from Cruz?"

Angie looked away. The diamond stud in her nose caught the light. It frightened Jaz, because Angie's demeanor was usually brash and bold. "It's why I'm leaving tomorrow, before he gets wind that I'm here. I don't want him watching Silvia's apartment, or Mom's."

"He used to do that?"

Angie nodded. Then she went to the kitchen and came back

with the portable phone. "Maybe you should take a cab home rather than the Muni." She handed the receiver to Jaz. "Those hos might still be out there looking for you."

Jaz punched in Edward's number. "Where are you?" He sounded exasperated.

"I'm at 368 Capp. I'll explain when you get here." Edward clicked off. After he arrived, Jaz told him what had happened. Edward called a cab and insisted on riding home with her.

"Be careful," Angie said as they got in. "And tell Mom that when it's safe, I'll be in touch." Silvia and Rosie were gone by the time Jaz and Edward arrived at the apartment. Rosa, Juana and Steph listened to Jaz's tale and exchanged guarded looks when she finished.

"So why do I get the feeling you already know what happened?" Jaz glanced from Mami to Rosa and finally to Steph.

"Because we do. Because Marty called," Steph explained. "He's had a private detective following you. I guess he thought that if he could get something on you before the divorce was final he could go back to the judge with his father about the custody arrangement, and . . ."

"I just gave him what he's been looking for," Jaz completed Steph's thought, stunned.

The day after Maria's fourth birthday, Rosa greeted Jaz as she came into the nearly empty kitchen of the Golden Gate Avenue apartment with a wan smile. "I thought Eduardo went to court with you today." Rosa stacked dishes on a counter.

"He did. He just dropped us off. He has an appointment."

Maria ran in, a drawing clenched in her fist. "I colored a picture for you, Rosa."

"Qué lindo, mi amor." Rosa bent down beside the little girl to admire her artwork.

"This one's for Daddy and Dom, when they come to get me tomorrow."

Rosa glanced up at Jaz, her eyes painful to behold.

"Why don't you put it in one of the boxes in our room?" Jaz told Maria.

"You lost the appeal?" Rosa asked once Maria was gone. She swiped at her cheeks with her fingers. "What about the social worker, the preschool teacher, Judith Tindall?"

Jaz's hand trembled as she filled a paper cup with water. "I guess the judge figured their testimony was prejudiced. At least she granted me unsupervised visitation."

"But you have no criminal record. Manuel assured me of that."

"Which is true, though he wrote in the station's log book that I was brought in for disturbing the peace and associating with known criminals."

"But it was a mistake, mi hijita. He didn't know who you were, or he would have--"

"Manuel was only doing his job. It's not his fault." Jaz took a sip of water. "Not that Marty's father cares. It allowed him to twist the facts, and once the detective showed the judge the photos of me with the prostitutes I knew I didn't have a chance." Jaz drank deeply before going on. "It's why I have to stay, to be near Maria while my lawyer files another appeal."

"Then stay here. With me. Eduardo will extend our lease."

"Edward suggested I move in with him, once Maria has been picked up, and you're on the bus." When Rosa sagged against the kitchen counter, Jaz put her cup down to hug the woman whom she loved as much as her own mother. "I know it's hard, but you have to go without me. Angie and Rosie are waiting for you."

Rosa examined Maria's crumpled drawing. She smoothed it on the counter. Then she went out to the hall and returned with a box. Jaz shook out a page from an old newspaper and handed it to Rosa who resumed wrapping her mismatched dishes. "Bueno. Andale pues."

Jaz squeezed her madrina's shoulder. "There's more." Rosa brought her half glasses up to her pudgy nose. "Marty and Dom fly to Maui on Thursday, the twenty-fourth. They'll stay through the holidays. They're getting married, because Dom is three months pregnant."

Rosa's mouth dropped open. She glanced at the kitchen doorway. "Does Maria know?"

"Not yet. The good news is Maria will be with me for Christmas, and we'll spend it with you and Angie and Rosie and my family in Pleasant Valley."

Rosa shook her head and went back to packing dishes. "I wonder how Maria will feel about having a new half brother or sister in the new year."

"Guess there's only one way to find out." Jaz hugged her madrina and went to find her daughter. In their bedroom, as she packed clothes, Jaz discarded several items Maria had outgrown, something that had elicited a temper tantrum when they moved from their Inner Sunset home nine months before. But today her daughter seemed eerily subdued as Jaz delivered her speech about how wonderful their new lives would be. Gluing herself together with a smile, Jaz sorted through Maria's toys. Her cheeks ached by the time she got to Esmokey. Maria snatched the sad excuse for a teddy bear out of the box. "You take him, Mommy."

"But he's yours," Jaz said gently.

"Auntie Steph says she gave him to you, and that's how you became friends."

So it was true. Steph and her family had given the bear to Jaz her first Christmas in Pleasant Valley. "How about I keep him for you over at Edward's?"

Maria nodded. Then her fingers found her mouth.

"¿Qué te pasa, mi amor?"

"Daddy says I shouldn't speak Spanish to Dom."

"That's because it's the language of our hearts." Jaz held her daughter. "If you're ever unhappy, if you ever need to tell me something that's important, you tell me in Spanish, okay?"

"De acuerdo."

"And now it's time for bed." Maria clung to Jaz. She extracted her daughter's arms from around her neck. "You know better than this." She tucked Maria into the double bed they shared, working hard to remain unmoved by her daughter's tears. "Go to sleep."

"Don't leave. Don't go to Edward's."

Jaz sank back down. "I'll be right here."

"Then why can't I be with you? Daddy says it's because Edward's house is too small."

Jaz took a deep breath. She had overheard Maria fighting with Marty outside the courthouse that afternoon. "The judge decided since you've been here with me and Rosa all this time it's only fair that you live with Daddy for a while."

"Will you miss me?" Maria asked.

"Por supuesto." Jaz stroked her daughter's honey colored hair.

Maria batted Jaz's hand away. "Then why can't I live with you?"

Upset Maria had become a pawn in the chess game Jaz and Marty played, she said, "Daddy will let us see each other as much as we want." She kissed Maria. "Now go to sleep."

Marty and Dom arrived late the next afternoon, after Manuel had taken Rosa's furniture to the Goodwill and her boxes to Silvia's. Once Rosa was on her way to Pleasant Valley by Greyhound, Jaz stood by stoically as Marty swept up and down the steps of the apartment, loading Maria's things in the back of his BMW. When Maria lingered at the top of the stairs, Marty motioned to Dom. "Look what Grandma bought you." Dom whipped out a Gund bear from behind her back. "She has clothes, furniture, everything.

They're in your room at home."

Maria stared at this wisp of a woman who stood before her, wavering like an apparition in her white cashmere coat. "Mommy? Can I take Esmokey with me?"

"Of course. He's in a box in our room," Jaz told her.

Maria dragged Jaz back inside, only to cling to her. "Don't make me go . . ."

Jaz peeled Maria from her waist. "I'll see you soon."

"When?"

"Tomorrow. I'll eat lunch with you at school."

"Esmokey!" Maria cried when Jaz picked her up. Jaz returned for the bear and tucked him into Maria's arms. Outside, she loosened Maria's death grip by whispering, "Be brave. We're fairy princesses. We're magic," before she handed her daughter over to Marty.

The following week Jaz and Maria ate lunch together every day. When Wednesday, the twenty-third, arrived, Jaz picked her daughter up at Marty's condo in a new development near the Embarcadero. The loft looked like a Christmas ad for Pottery Barn. Dom stood by as Jaz stared at wood floors that were so shiny she wondered if they were wet. "Oak has such a luster to it." Dom examined her reflection in the glossy floor, touched her blonde hair absentmindedly, and stroked her still flat stomach.

Maria came in with Marty and immediately hugged Jaz's legs. "Mommy, Mommy! Look what the tooth fairy brought me!" She held up a Kennedy half-dollar.

Shocked, Jaz asked, "Did you lose a tooth?"

When Maria shook her head, Marty looked embarrassed. "It helps her go to sleep."

Jaz nodded. For her the tooth fairy had been El Ratoncito, and instead of tucking lost teeth beneath her pillow, she had given them to Papi who placed each one in a knothole that marred a baseboard in their condo. The rat would find it there, Papi assured her, and would carry it away to her babies to eat. It guaranteed a straight, pearly replacement. Perhaps it had worked. Jaz had never worn braces the way Steph had, not that Papi could have afforded an orthodontist.

"Why can't you and Edward live here with me and Daddy and Dom?"

Marty and his soon-to-be new wife laughed nervously. Jaz just smiled. Her hand found her daughter's head, that Brillo pad of curls that tickled her palm. Up close she could see the gold flecks in Maria's eyes, the dimple that dented her daughter's cheek and broke her heart every time Maria smiled. "We should go," she told her daughter.

Once they'd said good-bye, and Maria's suitcase was loaded in the Jetta, Jaz drove off. On the way to Pleasant Valley, she shared tales of celebrating Christmas in the snow. The following morning, after Mass, Jaz was delighted when Mami suggested they hike to an easily accessible lake to teach Maria how to ice skate. The snows had yet to come, though the cold temperatures had the locals out scouting for lakes frozen solid enough to support their weight. As soon as Papi took Maria to rent skates, Mami said, "I call Esteph and invite her to come."

"How is she?" Jaz asked. "She doesn't write much."

"She say the same thing about you, Hija."

As they waited, Jaz helped Mami pack a picnic lunch. When Steph pulled up in Pedro's black Toyota truck, Jaz turned to Mami. "They're together?"

"Since we come back from visitin' you."

Jaz bounded down the steps. "¡Chica! It's so good to see you. You look . . ."

Steph sat in the cab, wedged between the steering wheel and the driver's seat. The baggy sweater she wore did little to hide her bump. "I'll explain," she said.

Mami stood behind Jaz. "You and Esteph go ahead. I wait here for Papi and Maria."

"Why didn't you tell me?" Jaz demanded once Steph pulled away.

"It's not something I could write about in an e-mail."

"How many months are you?"

"Almost seven and a half."

Which meant conception had occurred in May, right around the time Steph had come to San Francisco. "Please tell me you were artificially inseminated."

"I guess that's one way of looking at it." Steph parked at the trailhead. From the LEER truck cap on the back of Pedro's truck she took out a folding aluminum chair. Heaving it to her shoulder, she began to pick her way over the rocks and ice on the trail.

Jaz climbed behind her. "Does Pedro . . ?" Steph gave Jaz a *Well, duh!* look from high school days and hiked on. "Then we should talk, like we used to, before . . ."

"Before what?" Steph tossed this over her shoulder.

"Before we both fell in love with Pedro, which is when we stopped telling each other everything." Jaz came to a weary halt. Her chest rose and fell. Steph hiked off as if she hadn't heard, or if she had, as if Jaz's plea didn't merit a reply. She headed back down the trail to wait for her parents and daughter below. She stopped when she felt a hand on her shoulder.

"I told you I'd explain, so come on." Steph started up again. "Remember how I went out with Greg that first night he arrived in the city?"

Jaz nodded, winded from the altitude as she tried to keep up. She not only felt estranged from her childhood friend but from her childhood home. She was a flatlander now.

Steph picked up her pace. "I came back to Rosa's apartment that night because when I finally did make love to the man of my dreams, he crushed them." Steph stopped and waited for Jaz to catch up. "He said he was moving to the Bay Area, and that he couldn't make a commitment. Then your mother told me I was pregnant, Sunday night, right after class . . ."

"But . . . how did Mami know?" Jaz panted.

Steph narrowed her eyes at Jaz. "Just how much do you know much about Reiki?"

"Enough to know I won't let Mami near me."

Steph peered down the trail as if she looked for Jaz's mother. "I didn't believe it either until I went to the clinic. I'm not sure who was more surprised, Nancy Adams or me."

Jaz bent over and rested her hands on her knees. "You're sure it's not Pedro's?"

"The baby's definitely Greg's." Steph's face became wistful. "I thought this was what I wanted, but now . . ." she started hiking again. Jaz dragged herself up the trail behind Steph. "After the test came back, confirming the paternity, I told Pedro." Jaz came to an abrupt halt. From her rocky perch, Steph looked down, a beatific expression on her face. "And he was so amazing, said it didn't matter whose baby it was, that he loved me, that we should find an apartment of our own and stop the annulment."

Jaz closed her eyes. "Just don't tell me he offered to stay because He will forgive you."

"My mind's made up, Jaz. Don't try to talk me out of this."

"What about Greg?"

"Greg's gone. He took that job with Jay Tuttle."

"You should tell him."

"He doesn't want children."

"Don't you see? It's Corey Carlsen all over again. You're making decisions that leave Greg out. You should tell him the truth."

"The truth?" Steph scowled. "Don't you dare lecture me about the truth when you've been the queen of deception all these years."

"What? I never lied to you."

"Well, you didn't exactly tell me the truth about being pregnant, or marrying Marty, or how you felt about Pedro, or what happened up at Hidden Lake."

"Carajo, Steph, why does it always come back to that?"

"Because that's when we stopped talking."

They eyed each other silently until Jaz said, "You should tell Greg about the baby."

Steph held her gaze. "Beth will have Pedro. And me. That's all she'll ever need."

"The baby's a girl?"

Steph stalked back down the trail to Pedro's truck, past Mami, Papi and Maria who were on their way up.

Jaz helped make tamales that afternoon. What should have been a joyous holiday tradition was joyless because Steph declined her invitation to help. Jaz asked if she and Pedro could stop by after supper, saddened when Steph told her they had volunteered to work, to close the restaurant for Steph's parents that night. Christmas Day would be spent with Yessenia and Pedro's brothers, after she and Pedro attended services at the Valley Church.

Edward made it in time for midnight Mass. He had to return to San Francisco on the twenty-sixth due to a project he was working on. Jaz was tempted to drive back as well, but she felt obligated to stay, to help Rosa adjust to living in her new mountain home.

It was a relief that Angie behaved like the gemela del alma she was. Jaz enjoyed the time she spent with her, watching their daughters play. In the short time Angie had lived in Pleasant Valley she had changed. Jaz's look-alike no longer chewed gum. She seemed more upbeat, less sarcastic, delighted to have work with Sierra Strippers in the summer, and at the ski area in the winter. She ran a chair lift, which surprised Jaz because Angie didn't seem like the outdoorsy type. But as she opened up and shared her past, Jaz realized the move to Lake Tahoe had begun the transformation. It was there Angie became a Christian and a nature-lover, working at Edgewood Country Club in the summer and at Heavenly Valley in the winter. Her experience as a ski lift operator made her seem like a seasoned pro compared to the young kids who wandered up 395 every November in search of work at Pleasant Mountain.

The morning of New Year's Eve, Angie surprised Jaz by calling her to go snowboarding.

"I'd love to," Jaz told her, "but I can't."

"Why not? I can get you a free pass, cheap rentals in the shop."

"It's not that, it's just, well . . ."

"Well what?" Irritation strained Angie's politeness.

"I . . . I don't know how to snowboard."

"So take your sticks."

"You may find this hard to believe, since I grew up here, but . . ."

"You don't ski? I thought everybody in Pleasant Valley skied."

"You'd be surprised how many people live here and never go near the slopes."

"Then come with me to the party over at Pedro and Steph's tonight." When Jaz remained silent, Angie asked, "They invited you, didn't they?"

"Not exactly."

"Well, then come with me as my guest."

"I don't know."

"Jaz, it's New Year's Eve."

"I know, but Steph and I aren't getting along right now."

"Well, that makes two of us."

Angie picked Jaz up at nine. Pedro greeted them at the door with the same lack of enthusiasm he displayed when Jaz showed up at his wedding unexpectedly. He avoided them all night by walling himself off behind a protective circle of friends. Steph avoided them as well, uncomfortable it seemed any time Jaz or Angie got too close.

No alcohol was served at this church-sponsored event, though songs of praise were offered up as midnight approached. The singing reminded Jaz of Pedro and Steph's wedding. After a countdown and a shout of "Happy New Year!" Pedro kissed Steph. *You wouldn't know the truth if it came up and bit you in the butt . . . You're the queen of deception . . .* Steph's words reverberated in Jaz's head, an echo of their uneasily shared past as she watched her two best friends kiss. Was she deceptive? Not tonight, she decided. The only one besides Pedro who knew the truth about Steph's baby was Jaz. What was harder to see was the ache in Angie's eyes as she watched Steph and Pedro. Jaz understood what it was like to want someone you could never have. Pedro was the man they both had to forget, and it made Jaz empathize with Angie more than she was sure she wanted to.

Tempted to leave, without Angie if necessary, Jaz was pleasantly surprised when the crowd came alive. The guests writhed to Prince's "1999," and REM's "It's The End Of The World As We Know It." Where was Greg Morris Jaz wondered as she danced with Angie. Was he out celebrating with some new young thing? Had he heard that Steph was back together with Pedro, and that she was pregnant? Did he really have no idea the baby was his?

At one A.M., Angie was ready to leave. She had to work in the morning. Pedro and Steph ignored her when she called out goodbye, and while the music was loud, Jaz felt slighted as well. Once Angie had dropped her off, Jaz called Edward.

"I thought you told me Pleasant Valley rolled up its sidewalks at ten P.M."

"So what have you been up to?"

"I've been calling you, repeatedly. When are you coming back?"

"That's what I wanted to talk to you about. Something's come up. I've been invited to speak at Rotary, on Monday, as part of a series called 'Business for the New Millennium.' I guess Mami bragged about Millennial Fears to Bert who's a member. I didn't want to say no, since he awarded me the Rotary Scholarship when I graduated."

"Sounds like the 'local girl makes good' speech."

"It's a way to say thank you, even if I do feel a bit scared to talk about astrology."

"They won't burn you at the stake."

"They just might--figuratively speaking, of course--since many of the members attend the fundamentalist church here. I worry that there could be repercussions for Rosa and Angie."

"Then come back, and put yourself out of your misery, and me out of mine."

Jaz sighed, "If only it were that easy. The problem is if I ever want to live here again I have to do this. I can't deny who I am or what I do any longer."

"Then give your speech, so we can decide where our future will be."

"What do you mean?" Jaz rubbed the goose flesh that covered her arms.

"Your plan, for us to move to Pleasant Valley, once you get custody of Maria. I just don't want you to get your hopes up about an immediate return. This business with Maria could drag on for years, and as far as running Millennial Fears from there, why don't you give your speech and see how it goes?"

"God, I miss you. I'll call you tomorrow."

"Ciao," Edward replied before clicking off.

The morning after New Year's Day, Jaz fretted about what to wear when she gave her speech to the Rotary Club. She went through her bag and discarded one outfit after another. Too casual, too hip, too sporty, too . . . *What's the matter, Jazmín? Are you afraid you'll look too Mexican or too sexy?* Jaz glanced at her ragged manicure. She wondered if she should ask Rosa to do her nails. With her duffel bag empty and no solution in sight, Jaz refolded her clothes and considered a shopping trip to the factory outlet mall, though she doubted a shoe store, a leather specialty shop, or a discount outfitter would provide what she needed.

She suggested to Mami that they take Maria to lunch at Bert's. The restaurant had emptied out by the time they came in. The holiday crowds were already heading back down 395 in order to resume school or work on Monday. Steph ushered them to a table. She was warm with Mami and Maria, though she told Jaz, "So are you pissed the world didn't come to an end?" When Jaz just stared at Steph, she said, "You know, the whole Y2K thing you kept talking about on the Millennial Fears website."

Jaz wanted to explain to Steph that she had misinterpreted what Jaz had written, but she knew there was no point. After Steph took their order, Jaz excused herself from Mami and Maria. She cornered Steph at the beverage station. "I have a favor to ask." Steph pretended she hadn't heard. "Your father asked me to speak at Rotary tomorrow, and I have nothing to wear."

Steph turned toward her, the apron stretched across her belly. "I don't think this is what you're going for." She hustled off to pick up an order. Jaz returned to her table, consoled by Mami and Maria's conversation. Steph brought their order. "I left some clothes at my parents' house when I moved back in with Pedro," she told Jaz. "You're welcome to whatever is there."

"Thanks."

"Just make sure you call Mom to arrange it."

After lunch, Jaz, Maria and Mami went to the kitchen to say good-bye to Papi. It wasn't long before Steph burst through the swinging door. Her apron ripped off, she muttered to Pedro who cooked at the grill that she was taking a break. On a hunch, Jaz crept back to the kitchen door and pushed it open. Greg Morris sat at a table by himself. Mami and Maria were still visiting with Papi, so Jaz grabbed Steph's discarded apron and scooted out to Greg's table.

He folded his menu when she came over. "Where's Steph?"

"She's on a break."

"Tell her to get back out here." Jaz crossed her arms. "Okay, so I heard she's pregnant, but what I'm trying to find out is if she's happy."

"Well, what do you think? You're the one who left."

"Because she told me she wanted to stay with Pedro. What was I suppose to do?"

"Do you love her?"

He nodded. Then he rose. "Tell her I'll take my Bert's burger to go."

In the kitchen, Mami and Maria still talked to Papi. Jaz put in Greg's order and headed to the back steps. Outside, Steph paced back and forth, her hands on the small of her back. "He's in the lobby, waiting for take-out." Steph swung around, her belly slung low, as if the baby had shifted. "When did you say you're seeing the doctor again?"

"God, Jaz. Why can't everyone just leave me alone?"

"He's headed back to the Bay Area, just as soon as he gets his food--"

"Which is where I wish you'd go--"

"And I will, Steph, on Monday, right after I give my speech." Jaz watched her friend, alarmed when Steph winced in pain. "Greg loves you, but he thinks you're happily married, that you're expecting Pedro's child. He says that's why he left."

Steph stumbled forward and doubled over. "Oh God. Oh Jesus."

Jaz ran to her friend. "Breathe!"

"I can't," Steph gasped, her voice barely audible, her features distorted.

"I'll get Pedro." Jaz lowered Steph down onto the back steps and beckoned wildly to him. He came out and pulled Steph up. Her maternity shorts were wet and bloody.

In the lobby, Greg scrambled to his feet when Pedro and Steph rushed past with Jaz behind them. "What's wrong?" Greg grabbed Jaz by the arm and whipped her around.

"Steph's in labor. Her water broke. There's blood."

Greg let her go. His hand went to his forehead. "Are they headed to the clinic?"

"No, to Madison, to County."

"But that's too far. They'll never make it."

Jaz wondered if Greg was right. She ran ahead to the parking lot and slapped her sides with her arms. "They're gone," she told Greg who stood beside her now. When he ran to his truck, she yelled, "Wait!" only to watch the truck's wheels spin on the ice as he pulled out.

# Stephanie Bengochea Garcia
## January 2, 2000

*The only sure thing about luck is it will change*
*--Wilson Mizner*

T he front end of the Toyota shimmied as Pedro sped down the
grade, the needle on the speedometer wavering between 80
and 85. A mere touch of the brakes sent a shudder through the
cab, so Pedro eased off and allowed the truck to glide toward the
distant square of brown that was Madison at the respectable clip of
75 mph. Slumped forward in her seat, Steph tried to breathe calmly,
but the pain was so intense it caused her eyes to tear and her jaw
to ache as she clenched her teeth. Each new contraction felt more
excruciating than the last. Then a sharp pain gripped her uterus,
convincing her they would never make it to the hospital in time.

Pedro slammed on the brakes. The truck skid before it came out
of its fishtail. "¡Qué pendejo!" He shook his fist at the driver's side
window.

Steph sat up, shocked that Greg drove beside them with the
window to his truck down. When Pedro opened his Greg yelled at
him to stop.

"Slow down," Steph pleaded. "You're scaring me." Pedro swore
loudly at Greg in Spanish. There was a burning sensation between

her legs. "Pedro, we have to stop! Now!" A glance from him told her he understood. This was about the baby, not Greg. Steph braced herself for another skid, thanking God it wasn't icy, that Pedro was able to slow down on a roadbed strewn with gravel. When he managed to pull the truck off onto the shoulder, Steph turned to him, "You've got to help me."

The door on the driver's side opened. "Get out of my way," Greg told Pedro, "unless you want to lose your baby or your wife or both." Pedro did as he was told. Greg took Steph's pulse.

"How is she?" Pedro asked. He looked scared.

Greg glanced through the window at the truck cap. "I need to get her back there."

Pedro helped Greg haul Steph up.

"Oh God," she wailed when she saw the mess she had left behind. "There's blood."

"There's supposed to be blood, Steph. You're going to be all right, and so is the baby." Greg helped Steph lie down on a sleeping bag once the door to the LEER cap was opened. Then he pulled off her maternity shorts and underwear and pushed up her Bert's Burgers T-shirt. With a hand on her stomach, his other hand parted her legs. "The head's crowning. It's time to push."

"No," Steph cried "It's too soon."

"The baby's coming," Greg told her. "Push."

Pedro climbed into the back of the truck. When her efforts failed, he held her hand and kissed her sweaty forehead. "Beth's almost here. Try again."

Steph concentrated, grunting and panting until she felt the baby slither out.

Greg immediately cleared her daughter's airway and put Beth on her chest. "I can have you to County in twenty minutes, if Pedro will let me drive," he told her.

"I think you should stay back here," Pedro suggested.

Greg nodded. "If I bang on the window, pull over." Pedro got out. The truck lurched forward and rumbled back onto the road-bed. Greg took the second sleeping bag Pedro always kept in the back of the truck in winter and tried to make Steph comfortable. His hand found her forehead. "Are you all right?" She closed her eyes and shook her head. "I thought this is what you wanted," he said, stroking her hair. "Marriage. A baby."

"She's yours." When Beth began to whimper, Steph held their daughter tightly.

Greg stared at her, then at the window to the cab of the truck. "Does he know?" Steph nodded. "And that's why you didn't tell me?"

"You said you didn't want children."

"I said the only woman I'd want to have children with was you." When Steph began to cry, Greg put his hand on her cheek. "So what do we do now?"

The truck slowed as they entered the Madison City Limits. After several turns the truck stopped and Greg jumped out. He returned with a gurney and the crew from County.

"There are too many people in here," the nurse announced, her head stuck through the doorway. "Visiting hours were over an hour ago."

Mom kissed Steph's forehead. "We should get down to the nursery to see Beth."

"You mean Bronco?"

"Ah, Dad," whined Val, "Beth was born in Pedro's truck, not Mom's Bronco."

Dad clapped a hand on Pedro's shoulder, "I'll pick up some Cuban cigars before we head up the hill, to hand out to the regulars tomorrow."

"We should make a sign, hang it up in the restaurant," Char said.

Val rolled her eyes at her sister, as if this were childish, now that they were both in college. Then she softened and asked, "What do you think, Stephie?"

"Now that we know Beth's going to be all right, it's fine by me, if it's okay with Pedro." When he nodded, Val and Char kissed him and Steph on the cheek. Two dark ponytails followed Steph's parents out the door, the slap of their shoes down the hall counterpoint to their chatter.

"You want anything?" Pedro asked once everyone was gone.

"How about a veggie burger from Bert's, and some fresh lemonade?"

Pedro grinned. "I'll go down to the cafeteria and see what I can find."

Steph held onto his arm. "Don't go. I don't want to be alone."

"You're not."

Steph followed Pedro's gaze to the doorway where Jaz stood watching, much as she had the night of the New Year's Eve party. She waited for Pedro to leave before she set the small gift she held on Steph's lap.

Steph opened the box and marveled at the tiny gold studs.

"When I found out you were pregnant I bought them at Valley Jewelers. It's where Mami bought Maria's before she was born, though I had no idea you'd need them so soon."

"They're beautiful. Thank you."

Jaz glanced about nervously. "Maybe we should cut to the chase. Did you tell Greg?"

"Yeah."

"And?"

"Do you see him here?"

"But he is here. He's been waiting to see you, just like me."

"Where?"

"Last I saw him he was down at the nursery. If you want, I could get him."

"Oh God no. My parents and sisters are headed down there right now.

"Does Pedro know that Greg knows?"

"Not yet." When Jaz looked at Steph askance, she said, "Jesus, Jaz. I just had a premature baby. When have I had time?"

"I know, but Pedro loves you and Beth, which is why you have to tell him, now."

Even with her eyes closed Steph couldn't stop the tears. "I don't want to hurt him."

Jaz sat down and took her hand. "Of course you don't."

"What would you do if you were me?"

Jaz sighed. "I'd follow my heart, and I think your heart belongs to Greg."

"But what about Pedro?" Steph asked.

Jaz grimaced. "I once asked you that very same question, remember?"

Steph glanced at the door. "He'll be back any minute."

"You still love him, don't you?" When Steph nodded, Jaz said, "I still love him, too." Jaz rose, closed the door to the hallway, and leaned against it. "And now there's someone else who loves him as well, whose little girl needs a father. Pedro won't be lonely for long."

A shudder ran up Steph's spine. "That is so weird. You predicted this would happen, that night at Golden Gate Avenue, after I'd been with Greg, and I came back crying. You said if you could just get Angie and Pedro together that you and Rosa would be able to live here."

Jaz nodded. "It's all come true, except for the moving back part."

"Maybe, after you give your speech at Rotary tomorrow, you'll be able to."

"Gemelas del alma. Actually, we're not just twins, Steph. We're triplets."

Steph squinted at Jaz, and then, instantly, she understood. "You mean, Angie . . . ?"

Jaz nodded.

"How long have you known?"

"Not long. Like you said, it's not something I could write about in an e-mail. I planned to tell you while I was here, but when I saw you were pregnant . . ."

"It's okay. In fact, it makes things easier in a way."

"Do you think we should tell Pedro?"

"Not yet. It would freak him out, and he's pretty freaked out already. And who knows. He might just figure it out on his own. So," Steph glanced nervously at the door. Pedro would be back any minute. "Wear my gray flannel pants, the beige wool turtleneck, and the pale blue blazer I hang over it. Tell Mom they're in my closet."

Jaz wiped her eyes. "God, I wish you could be there."

"I will be, in spirit," Steph said as Pedro walked back in with a tray full of food.

# Jazmín Valdez
## January 2, 2000

*Lloraba la casada por su marido y ahora le pesa porque ha venido*
*(The wife cries because her husband is gone,*
*and then because he has returned)*

After kissing Steph and Pedro good-bye, Jaz walked to the nursery. A forlorn figure stood staring a hole through the glass. Greg looked older, less sure of himself. Perhaps it was his hunched up shoulders, the creases in the diamond pattern across the back of his sunburned neck.

Jaz sidled up to him. "She's beautiful, isn't she?"

"Just like her mother. She's mine, you know." Jaz nodded. "So what do I do? Walk away? Let another man raise my daughter?"

"No, because you love her. And I'm not just talking about Beth."

Greg turned back to the window and studied his tiny daughter who slept fitfully in her Isolette. "Why is she in this section, and not over there with the other babies?"

"It's due to her low birth weight, her premature entry into this world."

"But she's okay, right?"

"Yes, although she'll be here for a while."

"And Steph's okay?"

"She is."

Greg hesitated before he asked, "Does she still love me?"

"Of course she still loves you."

"And Pedro?"

"Steph loves you more."

"But what if that's not enough," Greg said. "What if the right thing to do is to let her stay with Pedro and raise Beth without me. He's a good man."

"He is."

Greg glanced around nervously, before he said, "You know, when her parents and sisters came down here to see the baby, I ducked around that corner over there to watch them, and I realized they have no idea that Beth isn't Pedro's child."

"No one does except you and me and Mami, which is a long story. Rightly or wrongly, Steph thought you didn't want children, and she didn't want you to be with her because of Beth." Greg pressed his hands against the glass, as if he were entranced by what lay just beyond. "There's something else you should know." Greg turned to give Jaz his full attention. "Marriage and motherhood are important to Steph." Greg's troubled gaze wandered back to Beth. "I know you love her, but are you willing to offer Steph the security she needs? Because if not, then you should walk away now, and only you and I will ever be the wiser." Greg continued to gaze through the glass, without moving. "Do you need a ride back to your truck?" Jaz asked. "I'm headed up the hill." When he walked away, Jaz smiled to herself and left.

# Stephanie Bengochea Garcia
## January 2, 2000

*When God shuts a door, he opens a window*
*--anonymous*

"You should go," Steph told Pedro after she had finished her hospital meal.

"We should talk."

The dreaded moment had arrived. "I'm sorry about Greg," she began. "I've had no contact with him whatsoever. I was shocked when he walked into the restaurant today."

Pedro smoothed the sheets on her bed. "He's here because he knows."

"I do." Greg's voice turned Steph toward the door.

"Oh God. Just promise me, both of you, that you won't fight."

"I'll be down at the nursery." Pedro rose stiffly. When Steph grabbed his hand, he said, "It's up to you," before he squeezed past Greg who stood half in, half out of the doorway.

Greg pulled up a chair beside Steph's hospital bed. "He's right. I'm not walking away this time." He hung his head. "I had to, after the avalanche, after San Francisco." He gazed up at her. "But I won't leave now unless you tell me to."

"Stay," she said, her eyes filling with tears.

# Jazmín Valdez
## January 3, 2000

*A pregunta necia, disimulada respuesta*
*(To the foolish question a calculated response)*

Jenny ushered Jaz into the mudroom. "Thanks so much," she told Jenny. "I won't be long. I'm sure you're anxious to get back to the hospital."

Jenny placed her hands on Jaz's shoulders and shook her head. "I can't believe you're both mothers now. It seems like only yesterday you were borrowing each other's clothes and spending the night." Jenny let Jaz go and led her through the living room, only to collapse onto the bottom stair. She buried her face in her hands. Her shoulders shook.

In all the years Jaz had known Jenny Bengochea, she had never seen her cry. "Maybe this isn't a good time. I can figure out something with the clothes I have."

"No." Jenny took a deep breath and stood. "I'm sorry. It's just that I've been so worried about Stephie and Beth."

"They're going to be all right," Jaz said, relieved Jenny instinctively believed her.

"You look so much like her. I'd forgotten." Jenny hugged Jaz hard. Then she became her usual, business-like self. "Come on.

Let me help you find that outfit."

"Will you be there today?" Jaz asked as they climbed the stairs.

Jenny nodded. "We're all so proud of you."

And with that, Jaz rewrote the text of her speech again. Her original plan had been to give a brief presentation on the dotcoms and be out of Bert's in twenty minutes flat. It was the safest approach. If she dared to say more, it might embarrass her family and friends. She didn't want to do that, even if it meant she could never live here again.

The outfit Steph had suggested was hanging in the closet of her bedroom, just as she had said it would be. Jenny laid it out on the sleigh bed, over one of her hand-pieced quilts. She refused to let Jaz leave until she was fully accessorized with a belt and pair of Steph's shoes that actually fit. Jaz kissed Jenny good-bye, anxious to get back to her parent's condo and tweak her speech one more time. On the way home she decided to stop by Angie and Rosa's apartment.

Bear greeted her with anguished pants. The Newfoundland's lathery saliva coated the double-paned French door. The radio was tuned to the local country station and blared one of those tunes that told of troubled lives. Had Angie adopted this listening habit to soothe her tortured soul, or was it yet another way to capture Pedro's heart? Jaz's look-alike wore a bemused expression as if she couldn't quite fathom her new lifestyle, either.

"I wish you could stay," Rosa said. "That you didn't have to go back tomorrow."

"We'll talk every day by e-mail. And if you have any problems with the web site, let me know so Edward can provide maintenance."

"I told Steph," Jaz announced. "About . . . us."

Angie glanced at Rosa and asked, "How did she take it?"

"She took it well, I thought, under the circumstances."

"Is she going to tell Pedro?"

"I have a feeling she won't have to."

Angie rubbed her arms as if she had goose bumps. Then she got up and started to pace. "Aren't you nervous about giving a speech?"

"I'm used to it from working at InfoSys," Jaz lied. Her stomach was already turning somersaults. She'd eaten nothing all day.

"That's not what I mean." Angie eyed Rosa before she went on. "Mom seems to think your talk will be about astrology."

"My talk is about forecasting business cycles," Jaz said, worried. Astrology had driven a wedge between Angie and Rosa before.

"It's profitable, isn't it? Pretending to know the future." For some reason, Angie was reverting to her bad-ass self.

"No more so than retirement planning, or trading stocks and bonds," Jaz responded, determined to stay cool. "We help people by suggesting when an infusion of cash or creativity might help their companies. I'll admit I was skeptical at first, but what I've learned is the more you believe in something, the more powerful that belief becomes. And the more power it has, the more it works for you, Angie, no matter what your belief system is."

"So you believe anything goes?"

"I'm a Christian, a Catholic. I believe the greatest bridge between the visible and the invisible is Jesus Christ. In that respect, we're the same. Where we differ is I don't believe astrology is witchcraft. Superstitious nonsense perhaps, but evil, no."

"All right," Angie conceded. "I'll put that aside for now, because I like your concept that 'God among us' is what makes the invisible visible, that Jesus Christ is not just some divinely inspired human being, that he's God in borrowed human form."

"And I believe that, Angie. I really do. So whether I'm casting a chart or fingering my rosary beads, it's about acknowledging God, the invisible force that holds us all together."

"Would you say it's about free will then?"

"Yes, I believe I would."

"Which means you plan to skirt the issue of astrology in your talk today." Angie's expression said *Gotcha!*

"My family lives here, and I want you and Rosa to feel comfortable here as well."

"Well, you don't have to worry about that, because the Valley Church people? They're all about free will. It's los evangelicos you should worry about. Is Yessenia coming?"

"I doubt it."

"What time should we be there?" Rosa asked, eager it seemed to change the subject.

"You're coming?"

"We wouldn't miss it for the world," Angie replied, her tone slightly sarcastic.

"Then I should go," Jaz said, her stomach in a knot as she rewrote her speech yet again.

Yessenia came down the stairs of her condo as soon as Jaz pulled up, as if she'd been waiting. Her face was pale. "I couldn't let you go without telling you that I know."

Jaz's smile faded.

"Pedro told me, last night when he got home." Jaz sighed with relief, though she still felt worried because Yessenia looked heartbroken, as she had years ago when she stood as she did now, telling Mami and Papi that her husband, Raul, was dead.

"Come in," Jaz suggested. "I'll fix us some tea."

"But your speech." Yessenia studied Jaz's leggings and sweatshirt, the outfit on the hanger she held in her hand. "Go. Change. And if you'd like, I'll give you a ride."

"You're coming?"

"Claro. Bert said it would be all right if I stood in the lobby and listened from there."

Jaz's throat constricted. She felt itchy all over, like she was breaking out in hives. *Breathe*, she told herself, as she had instructed Steph at the restaurant when she went into labor.

"Are you all right?" Yessenia asked.

"Just nervous," Jaz said. "So how are you, now that you know?" When Yessenia just shook her head, Jaz squeezed her hand. "I'm sure it was a terrible shock." She led Yessenia to the kitchen and set Mami's old green tea kettle on the stove. Poring over the incredible stash of herbal teas that took up most of the top kitchen drawer, Jaz told Yessenia, "It looks like Mami's got a bit of everything in here. What would you like?"

"For you to sit down and tell me why Estefanía is leaving Pedro."

Jaz honored the request. "Steph's made her decision?"

"Yes, and my son is . . ." Yessenia sobbed. She sounded beyond sad. "He told me the whole story: how happy he was when Steph came back, how he didn't care that the baby was Greg's, how they'd planned to keep it a secret, but now that the secret is out . . ."

"Don't you think it's better this way?" Jaz offered.

Yessenia nodded, only to dissolve into tears again. "All I ever wanted was for him to be happy. At first, I thought he would be happy with you, but then, when God led you down a different road . . ." Yessenia brushed her cheek with her fingers. "It was harder for me to accept Estefanía, but I did, because Pedro loved her. And then, when she became a Christian, I thought this is God's will, but now . . ." The question Jaz feared was in Yessenia's eyes. "You knew, didn't you? That they couldn't have children."

A quick glance at her watch convinced Jaz she would have to be her non-Latina self and get right to the point. "I did, Yessenia, and I'm sorry I kept it from you, but that was what they wanted. It was painful for both of them, not something they could easily talk about."

Yessenia walked over to the open drawer and shut it. "It explains so much, the annulment, why it was over as fast as it began." She looked at Jaz. "And then, they were working hard, going to church, expecting a child. They seemed happy, yet it was all a lie."

"But it wasn't. Pedro and Steph loved each other. They still do."

"Then why would she sleep with another man?" When Jaz had no answer, Yessenia said, "There were rumors all over town, but Pedro always defended her, always denied there was anything between Estefanía and her boss apart from work."

"Which was true, until Pedro and Steph were told by the specialist they couldn't have children, and Pedro decided they should annul the marriage." When Yessenia looked incredulous, Jaz said, "I guess Pedro forgot to tell you that he was the one who wanted out."

"Are you accusing my son of driving Estefanía away?"

"Steph would never blame any of this on Pedro. She loves him, like I do, but I'm sure she agrees with me that neither one of us is right for him." When Yessenia began to shake her head, Jaz said, "Steph's decision will allow him to find someone new, someone who will love him the way he deserves to be loved." Jaz squeezed Yessenia's shoulder. "I've got to go. I've got to get dressed and get over to Bert's. How about I drive us over there?"

When Yessenia nodded, Jaz went up the stairs.

At the head table Jaz sat sipping water, flanked by Bert Bengochea, the president of the Pleasant Valley Rotary Club this year, and Dewey Mitchell, Mami's one-time employer. The wool turtleneck she wore clung to her throat, and the blazer pulled at her shoulders. A hubbub in the lobby announced that Mami, Rosa and Angie had arrived. They waved then disappeared around the corner to sit with Yessenia until Jaz's speech began. Aware the program part of the meeting would start soon, Jaz excused herself. On her way to the bathroom, she stopped by the pick-up counter. Papi smiled and waved her in. Beside him, Pedro flipped burgers on the grill.

"Are you okay?" she asked.

His eyes on the sizzling patties, he nodded, only to look up and startle. "What are you trying to do, Chica? Haunt me?"

"Oh," Jaz clutched her clothes. "Oh God, Pedro. I forgot. I'm sorry."

"Gracias a Dios, Angie has short hair, otherwise . . ." Jaz braced herself, but Pedro merely shrugged. "Buena suerte, ¿eh?" He told her. Then he kissed her on the cheek.

Jaz turned to Papi. "I have to leave right after my speech. We should say good-bye."

"¿Que quieres decir, Hija? You think I would miss your speech?"

"I just thought . . . with you being so busy . . ."

Papi removed his grease-splattered apron and stepped aside. "Pedro offered to take over. I will be out in the lobby with Juana. I want to hear what you have to say." Jaz hugged him. "Be sure to find us afterwards," Papi said when she released him.

Jaz walked back to the head table. "There you are," Bert said, jovially. "Dewey and I were afraid you'd flown the coop." Bert elbowed his old friend.

Dewey didn't smile at Jaz. "Bert tells me you've started one of them dotcoms."

Jaz nodded and sipped her lemonade.

"He says you dispense investment advice. You got some for me?"

"It's all in my speech, Mr. Mitchell," Jaz replied.

"Which you'll be hearing in just a minute, Dewey. So hold your

horses." Bert headed to the microphone. It sounded as if every
Rotarian in the restaurant was clearing their throats. It made Jaz's
seize up. Their eyes were on her. Everyone waited for her to speak.
Bert waited for the coughing to die down before he explained that
because their guest speaker needed to drive back to San Francisco
that afternoon, ahead of a storm, he would conduct the business portion of the meeting after the program. "Which leads me to introduce
a young woman many of you already know. She grew up right here
in Pleasant Valley, spoke no English when she entered kindergarten,
yet she graduated as the salutatorian of her class and was the recipient of the Rotary Scholarship in 1993. She attended the University
of San Francisco, earning a degree in business and computer science.
And while she still works in the city for InfoSys, a well-known company, she is here today to talk about her business cycle forecasting
with Millennial Fears dotcom, a web site she created that received
over 10,000 hits in 1999. She is our first speaker in a series entitled
'Business for the New Millennium.' She is also the daughter of my
head cook, Mr. Antonio Valdez. But most importantly, she is my
daughter Stephie's best friend, and godmother to my first grandchild, Beth. So please join me in welcoming Ms. Jaz Donahue."

Before her in the sea of people Jaz recognized Wally Brown,
the owner of the sporting goods store that had hired her along
with Steph and Pedro to tie flies when they were teenagers. Scott
Hansen sat beside him, Steph's boss at Pleasant Mountain Ski Area.
Nancy Adams, the nurse practitioner, sat with Helen Morgan the
head nurse of the night shift at Pleasant Valley Memorial. And while
these members of Rotary weren't exactly close friends they weren't
strangers. Jaz felt anxious to say her piece and drive Maria back to
San Francisco where they both belonged.

But it was more complicated than that. In the doorway to the
lobby stood the people she cared about most: Mami and Papi, Chuy
and Juan P, Rosa and Angie, Pedro's brothers, Steph's sisters, Jenny

and Yessenia. Jaz's mouth went dry. She sipped her water at the podium and waited for the applause to die down. "Thank you, Bert," she began. "And thank you to the Rotary Club of Pleasant Valley for believing in me, for giving me your scholarship six and a half years ago, which allowed me to pursue my dreams." The crowd responded once again with applause, and Jaz felt the knot in her stomach loosen. "Millennial Fears is a dream come true, though it would be unfair to take all the credit for this idea when the co-creator of the web site is standing at the back of the room today. Please join me in acknowledging my partner, Rosario Rodriguez, who is new to Pleasant Valley, who by bringing a dotcom company to this town proves that alternative businesses can thrive in the Eastern Sierra."

Pushed forward by Angie, Rosa beamed at the crowd that clapped politely. She waved both hands above her head and ducked back into the lobby.

"Much has been written about the dotcoms in the media, how they will be the wave of the future, the new way we do business. And while Millennial Fears may indeed allow me to return . . ." Jaz paused to sip some water. She gripped the podium to stop her shaking. "To return . . . home, I would caution you, particularly as investors, to ask hard questions before putting your hard earned money into any of them.

"Millennial Fears has been successful because it sells a solid product. We provide advice to companies on everything from what to expect regarding the public's reaction to a product, to when profits will surpass capital outlay."

"And just what is the basis of your advice, Ms. Valdez?" Dewey Mitchell asked.

Bert stood. "Ms. Donahue will take questions when she is finished, folks, so if you could please hold your comments until then--"

"Is it true your advice is based on astrology?" Dewey persisted.

"I'd be happy to make this an interactive session," Jaz told Bert, "especially since Millennial Fears is an interactive web site. It's true, Mr. Mitchell. Rosa and I do base our advice on astrology, but it's a different kind of astrology than what people usually think of. It's not what you read in a newspaper or magazine. It's not concerned with whether you were born under the sign of Aries or Taurus. It's based on the belief that all things go through cycles. What we offer our clients is advice concerning where their companies are at any given time."

"Then you admit it's a bunch of hooey," said Dewey, "if I'm being polite, and a dark art, if I'm not."

"That depends on how the information is used. What Millennial Fears dispenses is advice that can be adhered to or discarded. Cycles begin and end. Businesses, like our lives, go through good times and bad. The NASDAQ is approaching record heights, yet I've advised my clients to be cautious, to be wary of dotcoms with no tangible profits to show, no concrete services or products to sell. While my information is based on astrology, it is also logical. What amazes me is how many people ignore all the signs, whether they are posted on my web site or written about in *The Wall Street Journal*. It's about free will, Mr. Mitchell."

"Well, what I learned growing up is there's no such thing as a free lunch," said Bert.

"Except as one of your employee benefits," Jaz replied.

The audience's laughter lightened the mood. "Are there any other questions?" Jaz asked, eager to finish. When no one raised a hand, she said, "Then I'll end on this note. Pleasant Valley is my home, and like so many who have grown up here, I dream of returning to live and work and raise a family in the mountains I love. I've been in San Francisco since I left for college, mostly because the highly paid technical jobs are there. But with the advent of dotcoms and e-commerce, you may see a new type of resident moving in. I envision a day when

I will be able to live and work here, connected by a fiber optic network to my clients, my services available on-line to anywhere in the country, perhaps even the world. But for now, I have to be honest." Jaz looked directly at her parents. "It's still a dream. What I do know is that as we enter the new millennium there is nothing to fear. The future will be full of opportunity for all sorts of entrepreneurs. So as we venture into this new untested territory we must remember what business is about. It's about serving people, and that's what has made Millennial Fears a success. Thank you."

The applause went on for quite a while. Bert gave her a hug before she stepped down from the podium. Even Dewey Mitchell shook her hand, but Jaz didn't need his approval. Her eyes wandered to the lobby, to where her friends and family were. She threaded her way through the tables of seated Rotarians as Bert called the meeting back to order.

"Preciosa," Mami buried her head in Jaz's shoulder.

Her brothers hugged her, then Pedro's brothers, then Steph's sisters, then Rosa and Angie, and finally Jenny and Yessenia. Only Papi stood at a distance, waiting his turn. She was struck by her father's face, how it was soft, like the day when she had surprised him as he played with Maria. He held her, wordlessly at first. Then he whispered, "Hija, I do not pretend to understand what you do, but I know now that you must do it."

Jaz broke from her father, puzzled. "Even if it keeps me in San Francisco?" Papi nodded. "But I want to come home."

"Sí, ya sé." Papi kissed her cheek.

Jaz wiped away a tear "For the first time in six years, I don't want to leave. Everyone I care about is here. But I have to, for Maria."

"And Edward," Papi said. "You should go back for him."

"You like Edward?"

"Claro. I just wonder if he likes us. Why did he leave right after Christmas?"

"Because he's just like you, Papi. He's always working. Though he's willing to live here. So as soon as we get the whole custody thing with Maria straightened out, we will."

"Bueno, Hija. You better get goin'," Mami said. "It already snowin'."

Jaz nodded. "There's someone I should see first."

Mami nodded. "You make it snappy, ¿eh?"

Jaz exited the restaurant and walked through the parking lot to the back steps of Bert's, not wanting to disturb the meeting. Tiny snowflakes already stuck to the windshields of the parked cars. Inside the kitchen, her father was back at work. He nodded at Pedro, his cue to hang up his apron and go outside with Jaz. "I couldn't leave without saying good-bye," she said.

"It's not like we're never going to see each other again."

"I'm so glad to hear you say that, especially after what happened with Steph."

"You're my friends. You always will be. You know that, don't you?"

Jaz teared up. "I do, I mean I did, I mean . . . I don't ever want to lose you."

Pedro held her. "I'll be right here, waiting for you both."

"I don't think you'll be waiting long." When he looked puzzled, she said, "Angie loves you, Pedro. You do know that, don't you?"

He pondered Jaz's words. "Do candles blow out when you walk into a room?"

Jaz laughed. "The next time I come home, let's light some and see."

Judith walked into Jaz's cubicle. "There's somebody here to see you."

"Edward?" Jaz brightened.

"Marty." Judith sat on Jaz's desk.

"Should I be nervous?"

"I think not, though you should be nervous around me. Kate says you haven't gone to the gym with her once since I've been gone." Judith had returned from her Thanksgiving vacation to a spa in Cozumel tanned and toned. For some reason Jaz's lack of exercise bothered her boss, perhaps because it was just another example of her empty promises to change. Still, a personal trainer seemed like a waste of money. Judith's nagging was all it took to make Jaz sweat. "So where's my report?" Judith toyed with the limp tendrils of the spider plant on Jaz's desk.

"Right here." Jaz removed it from her tote. Her decision to continue Millennial Fears had turned procrastination into a performance art. The report had been cranked out in the wee hours of the morning. Sheer terror had kept Jaz going, along with Edward chanting, "You can do it! You can make your deadline! Keep going!"

"How do you like my new pumps?" Judith wiggled her feet. Shoes were important, that was Judith's mantra. You could tell a lot about a woman based on her shoes. *Yeah, like how much she makes.* Jaz's pumps were from Payless Shoe Source. "You know, it's Marty who looks nervous if you ask me." Jaz unscrewed the top to her designer water and poured some onto her thirsty plant. Judith snatched the bottle away. "Don't waste it on that," she said, frowning at the browning leaves, "and don't waste too much of your time on your ex-husband, either." Judith rose. "Tell Kate you're about to take a break, a short one."

Jaz told the receptionist she was leaving. When Marty rose from where he sat, it was all Jaz could do not to gasp. "Is everything okay?"

"No." There were bags under his eyes. He looked pale, rumpled, not his usual GQ self.

"Ay, Dios mio. Did Maria fall off that slide at your new house again?"

"No, no, it's nothing like that. Can I take you to lunch?"

"I only have time for coffee." Jaz swung her purse over her shoulder.

They walked from Embarcadero Number One to Starbucks. Marty did most of the talking. With cash on hand from the stock he'd sold he'd bought a small island off the Panamanian coast where he and the family had just vacationed, where he spent endless hours surfing the Pacific instead of the Internet. The scenario Marty painted was surreal, but then how realistic were her dreams? At times she felt like a fraud, like someone who had grossly overestimated her own abilities. What she knew about start-ups she could fit on a Post-it note, not that she used them. No, it was a measure of her own hubris that she worked at InfoSys and as an e-tailer, simultaneously. Or was it just that with the old millennium dying she clung to the hope that a new and better time was coming.

"Then what is it?" she asked when Marty fell quiet. "Because it sounds like you just got back from an amazing vacation, and yet . . . there's something wrong, isn't there?"

"Yeah," he laughed. "Dom told me Thanksgiving Day that more babies are on the way."

"She's pregnant?"

"With twins."

"Congratulations!" When he gave her a half-hearted smile, she said, "I'm sorry. I thought this was what you wanted: a stay-at-home wife, a house in Orinda, lots of children."

"Yeah, so did I, but when you factor in the commute, and the cost of owning a home on a single salary, as well as Dom's expensive tastes, well . . ."

Jaz took a sip of her latte to hide her smile. Maybe there was justice in this world after all. Still, she felt sorry for Marty. In the end he had married a woman exactly like his mother. "So are you worried about finances?"

"No. I told you. Donahue and Associates is doing better than ever."

"With the new millennium already here?"

"The company still has contracts."

"So was the Y2K just a bunch of hype, like the media's trying to portray it now?"

"No, but it's over." He finished his coffee. "It's time to move on."

"To what?" Jaz felt her neck hairs prickle.

"To day-trading."

"Of tech stocks?"

"What else."

Jaz put her latte down. "Have you even looked at my web site lately?" When Marty shook his head, she said, "Carajo, Marty, why are you always such a burro? Those stocks are overvalued. They'll be headed south soon. This is no time to buy for short-term gain."

"With the NASDAQ approaching 5000? And the strongest bull market in years?" His tone was sarcastic. "You're wrong, which is something you hate to admit." His eyes lingered on her face, "And you're still sexy as hell when you're mad, but we're not here to discuss your assets or my investments. We're here because I need to talk to you about Maria."

Jaz choked on her latte when he veered off in this direction. She dreaded some new tale about what her willful daughter had done. Unable to control her coughing fit, she turned away, comforted when Marty gently slapped her on the back. "Thanks," she croaked.

"Don't mention it. So, are you ready?"

Jaz nodded, though she doubted that she was. Recent wrong doings by Maria had included stepping on the face of her half brother (Martin Donahue, the fourth) while alone with him. Another transgression had occurred at the senior Donahue's house. Maria threw a fit when she was relegated to eating in the kitchen with Dom's au pair because Grandma decided Maria was too young to sit with the adults in the dining room.

Jaz sighed as she rose. "So what did she do?"

Marty walked Jaz out into the December gloom. "It's not what she's done, it's that she misses you," he began as they strolled back toward Jaz's building. "She talks about you constantly. It hurts Dom's feelings. In fact, it's set up a dynamic that's unhealthy for all of us."

"So what are you trying to say?"

"That Dom's detaching from Maria, through no fault of her own." When Jaz stopped, Marty added, "You and I both know Maria can be difficult, that she's . . .

"A lot like me?" Jaz smiled at her ex.

Marty grinned back. "When Dom found out the good news-- and the bad--concerning this pregnancy, we talked, and, well . . ."

"Are you saying you're willing to renegotiate our custody agreement?"

Marty nodded. Elated though she was, Jaz felt unprepared for this. Marty's attitude seemed capricious to her now, completely unpredictable. "I talked to Father about it."

"What did he say?"

"All we have to do is sign new papers. We won't have to go before a judge this time."

It seemed way too easy. "What exactly are you and your father proposing?"

"That you be made Maria's custodial parent, with me and Dom granted visitation."

"How much visitation?"

"With our son, and twin boys on the way, it would be a few times a year."

"You're about to have three children under the age of two, and they'll all be boys?"

"Just don't make any cracks about starting a baseball team. That one's getting old."

"So if I wanted to move back to Pleasant Valley with Maria, you wouldn't fight it?"

"As long as my daughter doesn't forget who I am, it's all right by me."

Jaz threw her arms around her ex-husband and kissed his cheek. "Thank you, thank you, thank you. And please know that Maria loves you, Marty, and she loves Dom, too. She'll never forget you, because I won't let her."

Marty's eyes glistened. He looked more relieved than happy as he straightened up, as if a great weight had been lifted from his shoulders. "You're a good mother. I'm sorry about the detective, what Father talked me into doing. It was wrong." Marty heaved a great sigh. "When you pick Maria up this weekend, I want you to keep her. I'll have the legal part worked out by then." Marty stroked Jaz's cheek. Then he walked off in the direction of the Embarcadero BART station. Staring after him, Jaz felt amazed, but mostly she felt grateful the painful separation from her daughter was ending so amicably.

That evening, once she and Edward had finished dinner, she made her nightly call to Maria and explained what was happening. Afterwards, she spoke to Marty and thanked him again for his change of heart. She promised he could see Maria as often as he wanted. Then she dialed Steph's number in Marin. "Chica, you're not going to believe this."

"You're pregnant?" Steph quipped.

"No," Jaz laughed. "But Dom is."

"Are you serious?"

"With twin boys."

"No way!"

"It's why Marty's decided to give me full custody of Maria."

For a while Steph said nothing. Then she asked, "So when are you moving?"

"Edward says he can wall off a space at the back of the loft--"

"That's not what I mean. When are you moving home?"

"To Pleasant Valley?"

"Where else?"

"Steph . . . why can't you be happy for me? I'm finally getting my daughter back."

Her friend sighed. "I am. It's just that it's taken us all these years to live near each other again. I don't even want to think about you leaving."

"Our friendship isn't based on proximity."

"Yeah, but proximity helps."

"Well, of course it does. But still. Look, are you going home for Christmas?"

"Yeah, but what does that have to do with anything?"

"I was thinking I'd go, too, with Edward and Maria, that it'll be fun."

"Really? Have you forgotten what a nightmare last Christmas was?"

"Come on. We'll actually take Maria ice skating this year, and make those tamales."

"And you'll be giving your family the gift they've wanted for seven and a half years."

"I'm not sure where we'll be living yet. Guess I'll worry about that in the new year."

"Ah yes, the dreaded millennium, the real one, 2001."

"Would you lighten up, please?"

"With the daily doses of financial gloom and doom you've been meting out on millennialfears.com, you're joking, right?"

# Stephanie Bengochea Morris
## December 21, 2000

*Do and you shall be*
*--George Leonard*

*Be and you shall do*
*--Ram Dass*

*Do be do be do*
*--Frank Sinatra*

Steph stood in line at the sporting goods store behind a tourist who paid for gloves and goggles. "Any Hidden Lake Specials, Wally?" she asked, stepping to the front of the line.

In mock seriousness, he told her, "The season doesn't open until April."

"I wanted to surprise my friends, the ones who used to help me tie those flies when we were young. You still sell them, don't you?" Wally nodded. "Who supplies you these days?"

"A couple of skinny minnies that remind me a lot of you and that friend of yours, the one who spoke at Rotary last January, the one who is the astrologer."

"Jaz?"

"Yeah. The one they called your twin. You two still fish up at that secret lake of yours?"

"Not in a long time." None of them had been there since Steph's honeymoon with Pedro. "Do you have any left over from last summer?"

"Two dozen." Wally pulled a Styrofoam case out of a drawer. After purchasing them, Steph returned to Greg's truck. Once she had climbed in, he began to kiss her passionately.

"What?" Greg asked when Steph broke away.

"Habit, I guess." Steph glanced around. "It's our first time back, since--"

"Steph. I should be able to kiss my wife without worrying who's watching, right?"

"Right." She took Greg's hand. "Why don't you drop me off at the Valdez's condo, unless you're prepared to reminisce about old times."

"I told Scott I'd meet him up at the lodge for a drink."

"Say hello to him from me."

"I'll do better than that. I'll bore him to death with these." Greg brandished a fistful of photographs: of Beth; of their wedding at Kai and Buck's apartment Thanksgiving weekend, in which Scott was the best man and Jaz was the maid of honor; of their home in San Anselmo; the Fairfax Holistic Health Center where they both worked. "It'll freak Hansen out, that I'm such a doting husband and father," he pulled Steph to him, "that I'm still crazy in love with you."

When it was Greg who broke away, Steph cried, "What?" to tease him.

"I'd better get you over there fast," he flipped the gear lever up on his truck's steering column, "or we may keep both of our friends waiting."

# Jazmín Valdez
## December 21, 2000

*Lo que aprende en la cuna, siempre dura*
*(What is learned in childhood lasts)*

J az opened the door to Pedro. She flashed him a smile and then
frowned.

"Who were you expecting?" He glanced at his watch. "I'm on
time, aren't I?"

"Yes, but Steph isn't. She should have been here half an hour
ago." Jaz stepped aside so Pedro could come in. His cheeks were
flushed from the biting cold.

"I brought you something." He took two small wrapped packages out of his pocket. "It's something to listen to, when you and
Steph drive back to San Francisco."

"So we won't forget?" Jaz smiled. "I'll never forget. Don't you
know that by now?"

"Do you think I should give Steph the tape, or is it too soon?
Our divorce just became final before Thanksgiving." Pedro glanced
at the door nervously. "Where is she, anyway?"

"She called me on her cell phone, said she needed to stop at
Barker's to buy Pampers."

"Caramba, she should know better than to shop there after five, with all the tourists clogging the check-out lines. Even Angie knows better than that."

"Angie?" Jaz grinned. "Are you seeing each other?"

Pedro blanched. "Did Juana . . ? Or Rosa . . ?"

"No, Pedro. I just . . . knew." A knock at the door sent Jaz to it.

"Sorry." Steph bustled in. Surprised to see Pedro, she said, "I didn't realize . . ."

"Steph, wait." Jaz moved to block her departure. "Pedro has a gift for you."

He smiled shyly at his ex-wife and handed her his present. Steph looked at the small rectangle in her hand. From her coat pocket, she fished out a paper bag. "I bought these, just in case." She handed him the bag. "I didn't have time to wrap them." Steph took an identical bag from her pocket and gave it to Jaz. "Go ahead. Open your gifts."

Jaz and Pedro laughed as they held up the flies.

"How about driving up to the trailhead?" Pedro suggested.

"It's too cold and dark to hike up to Hidden Lake," Jaz replied.

"We could play music and talk." Steph waved Pedro's mixed tape at them.

"Like old times?" Jaz knew she sounded dubious. "I'm not sure."

"Please, Jazmín. Because I have something I need to talk to you about, and Steph."

Steph eyed Pedro, then Jaz. When Jaz smiled, Steph sighed. "All right."

Their winter coats on, they piled out the door of the Valdez condo. Pedro asked Jaz quietly, "Where's your boyfriend?"

"You mean Edward?" Pedro's question made her realize she was unsure how to describe him as well. They had no plans to marry. "He comes the twenty-fourth."

"Like last year?"

"Ay, Dios mio, Pedro, let's hope not." Jaz kept her voice low so Steph wouldn't hear. When Pedro said nothing, Jaz asked, "Is it hard seeing Steph again?"

Before he could answer, Steph stood in front of them and frowned. "Mom's babysitting Beth and the dog. Maybe I should go, let you two drive up there by yourselves."

"No. We want you to come, too," Jaz nudged Pedro. He nodded. "Besides, you haven't listened to his present yet," Jaz reminded Steph.

They squeezed into the front seat of his truck. Jaz straddled the stick shift. A huge moon rose behind the peaks as they drove, the silver disc breathtakingly beautiful, crisply outlined in the thin mountain air. "Did you know it's a special moon tonight?" Pedro asked, "One of the--"

"Brightest in years," Jaz interrupted. She turned to him. "Is that your surprise?"

"That," he told her as he opened the glove compartment, "and these." He handed envelopes to Steph and Jaz. "Open them, please," he said when they both hesitated.

Steph stared at her envelope. "You're getting married to Angie, aren't you?"

Pedro pulled into a parking spot at the picnic area. He gazed at the choppy water of the lake that reflected the moon as if it were a mirror ball. "I should have known you'd guess."

Jaz opened her invitation. "You're getting married on New Year's Eve?"

"Angie thought it'd be a date we'd never forget."

"I'll be there," Steph told him. "So tell me, do Rosa and Yessenia get along?"

Pedro gave Steph a pained look, which made Jaz laugh. She motioned to Steph to put her mixed cassette from Pedro into the tape deck. As the Sting hit "If ever I should lose my faith in you" played, Steph got out and walked around to the driver's side of the truck. "It's your turn to straddle the gear shift," she told her ex, shoving him with her hip across the front seat. Steph took one of Pedro's hand, Jaz the other. They all savored the moment, confident they had found their way back to each other. When the song finished, Pedro punched the fast forward button.

"Don't." Steph reached for his hand.

"You know what I'm looking for, don't you?" He punched on "Fields of Gold."

"Yeah. That song I hate." Steph directed this to Jaz.

"Well, Angie loves it," Pedro replied.

"Of course she does," Steph told him.

There was a moment in which they all looked at one another. Then Pedro burst out laughing. "Feels like old times."

"It does," Steph agreed.

"I never gave you my gifts." Jaz slipped two slim folders out from inside her coat. She watched her friends study the covers, then peek inside and leaf through their reports.

"You said you'd never do our charts, that you couldn't be objective," Steph told her.

"Rosa interpreted them," Jaz replied. "Though the financial outlooks are mine."

Pedro held his as if it would burn him. "I'm not sure I want to know."

"About the future?" Jaz smiled. "Everybody wants to know about the future." When he looked unsure, she added, "It's good news."

"From the mistress of gloom and doom herself?" Steph asked.

"It's over, Steph, the seven years of bad luck." Jaz watched her friend's brow knit. "Don't you remember? The day I left for my college orientation?"

"And you broke the mirror?" Steph grinned as she recalled it. "Maybe that's why you finally got Maria back."

"And you got Beth, and Greg . . ." Jaz's enthusiasm evaporated as she watched Pedro's face fall. "And you're about to marry Angie and live happily ever after, because it really is over, Pedro, for all of us. We're all finally . . . home."

# Rosa Rodriguez
## December 31, 2000

*Colorín, Colorado, este cuento está acabado*
*(It ain't over 'til it's over)*

I apply makeup to my daughter's tattoo. Angelica says she will keep the cross, and when she can afford it, she will have CRUZ professionally removed. She wants to do so many things differently now that she is about to marry Pedro. Silvia does her nails while I style her hair, Maria Rosario's, too. Maria, Jazmín's daughter, will also be a flower girl, and since these gemelas del alma do not resemble each other it is only fitting that they wear the red and green smocked velvet dresses with puffed sleeves and white piqué collars Jenny Bengochea sewed for Estefanía when she was a little girl.

To me it is further proof that God works in mysterious ways. I imagine it will give everyone whiplash when Angelica, Estefanía and Jazmín stand together before the altar at Evanglico. The flower girls have broken the chain as far as physical looks go, but as to their lives? Well, we'll see. I doubt I will follow them as closely as I followed the bride and her bridesmaids. It seems ridiculous to me now, how desperate I was to find Angelica's twin soul, sure that only then I would understand God's plan for my daughter's life. If nothing else I see it as His way of teaching me trust.

"The night of the solstice," Angelica begins, "after Pedro came home from telling Jaz and Steph we were getting married, I remember staring up at the moon, how I told him I could feel its tug on the tide of our lives." Silvia raises a penciled eyebrow and decides to say nothing, to listen as I do. "And the funny thing is he swore he could feel it, too, life's ebb and flow."

"So now he believes in astrology?" Silvia applies topcoat to Angelica's nails and blows on them. "And you do, too?"

"I wouldn't go that far, though you can imagine his surprise when we got our marriage license, and he realized what my birth date was. What we believe is that we're all connected: to God, to nature, to cycles as undeniable as the Earth turning on its axis."

"I can't tell you how happy it makes me to hear you say this," I tell Angelica, "because that is exactly how I feel, Hija. It's as if God has called us all here."

"Even if we're not exactly sure why," Angelica says. She gets up and waves her hands to dry her nails. "Rosie, go get Mama's necklace." Her daughter runs out of the living room I have shared with my daughter and granddaughter that will feel so empty when they are gone. Maria Rosario runs back in. A silver chain dangles from her dimpled hand, and at the end of the chain there is a silver cross, a silver Pisces symbol, and a silver Saint Christopher medal. Angelica takes the necklace from Maria Rosario, fastens it around her neck, and waggles her medallions at me. "To the sisterhood, ¿eh?"

"De acuerdo, Hija, pero . . . where did you get that?" I ask.

"It's my wedding gift from Steph and Jaz." Angelica smiles at Maria Rosario. "We should go."

"Sí," says Silvia. "Andele pues." My cousin and I fuss over Angelica's ivory satin dress, her red rose bouquet, but mostly we touch Angelica to remind ourselves she is the child God returned to us, who emanates His love, and that it is His way of saying, The future will take care of itself if you will simply have faith and believe.

CPSIA information can be obtained at www.ICGtesting.com
231256LV00002B/18/P

9 781432 766665